# Twisted Minds

# Twisted Minds

*Hilary Norman*

All the chara⟨...⟩ ⟨...⟩al persons,

First published in Great Britain in 2002 by
Judy Piatkus (Publishers) Ltd of
5 Windmill Street, London W1T 2JA
email: info@piatkus.co.uk

**The moral right of the author has been asserted**

*A catalogue record for this book is available from the British Library*

ISBN 0 7499 0605 7

Set in Times by
Phoenix Photosetting, Chatham, Kent
Printed and bound in Great Britain by
Mackays of Chatham Ltd, Chatham, Kent

For Henry Norman.
Still with me in so many ways.

My gratitude to the following for their help:

Sarah Abel; Howard Barmad; Jennifer Bloch; agent and friend Sara Fisher; Gillian Green, my excellent editor; PC Steve Gregory for crime scene advice; Rolf Hürzeler; Peter Johnston for police expertise shared with good humour; Jonathan Kern, my husband, for endless support on the home front; Martin Leigh and Jaqueline Nawka of HM Coroner's Court, St Pancras, for invaluable help and patience; Herta Norman, who always knows if it's 'working' or not; Judy Piatkus; Helen Rose for research and advice; Richard Spencer and Sue Moroney; Linda Stern; and Dr Jonathan Tarlow.

\*

As always, all characters, situations – and weather conditions – are entirely fictitious.

Children are completely egoistic;
they feel their needs intensely and
strive ruthlessly to satisfy them.

*Sigmund Freud*

# PART ONE

# 1

Matthew Gardner, an architect from New York based in Berlin and, in the first days of 2000, vacationing in Switzerland, was lying flat on his back in the snow when he saw her.

Just her face. Peering down at him.

Concerned blue eyes, irises finely ringed in black, making the blue more intense. Golden bobbed hair, blowing in the breeze. Flawless azure winter sky overhead, framing the gold.

She was saying something.

'Are you all right?'

Lovely voice. Low. English, with a hint of something more European.

*Perfect*, he thought, still dazed, though tinny music was spoiling the moment.

He craned his head towards the sound. Another face. Boy of about eight, green bobble hat on his head, earphones around his neck. Source of the music and of his fall. Damn kamikaze kid, ears full of noise, hurtling down the mountain at breakneck speed, expecting everyone else to get out of his way.

The boy grinned down at Matthew. A real brat kind of a grin. And then his face disappeared. Music, too.

Thankfully, Matthew turned his head back.

Still there.

'Yours?' he asked.

She smiled. 'No. Mine are over there.'

Matthew turned his head again and the rest of the slope came into view.

A bunch of skiers, some in groups, some solo.

He knew right away which were hers, perhaps because of the colour of their hair. They stood in a huddle, arms around each other, leaning back and laughing, reminding him of a beautiful cluster of lilies, slender and graceful, swaying in the breeze. And then he thought, for some unaccountable reason, of the three daughters of Zeus and Hera.

'The Graces?' he asked.

She smiled, pleased.

'My daughters,' she said.

# 2

'What about the daughters?'

Karl Becker, his colleague and very good friend, asked that question within five minutes of Matthew having told him that he was going to marry Caroline Walters, a Swiss-born widow from London with three children.

He'd returned from St Moritz the previous night and had come into the Berlin offices of Vikram, King, Farrow Inc. with the express purpose of nailing down the verbal agreement he'd previously reached by telephone with Wolf Brautigen, the personnel director – namely, his transfer to the firm's London branch.

Matthew had completed his negotiations, arranged with his landlord to terminate the lease on his apartment, and then, on the dot of noon, had yanked Karl away from his own drawing board, hauled him over to the Bristol Bar in the Kempinski and ordered champagne.

'And they agreed to all this?' Karl was stunned. 'Just like that?'

Matthew knew he was grinning like an idiot. 'There's a vacancy in London, and I qualify, and maybe Wolf's more of a romantic than he looks.'

Karl was a tranquil man, on the whole. Not placid, just calm, the antithesis, he supposed, of what red-haired people like himself were imagined to be. He liked his friends to be content, just as he liked his own world to flow smoothly. He loved his work, adored his wife Amelie, and their son, Heinz, enjoyed the buzz of Berlin, but harboured long-term dreams of moving into the countryside and setting up as a freelance.

He sat in the warm, gently bustling bar, listening to Matthew's plans for packing up and going straight back to St Moritz, and Karl wanted, more than anything, to be joyful for him, but some intuition warned him that Matthew might be on the verge of as much trouble as happiness.

'What do they think of all this?' he asked, carefully, after drinking a toast. 'Caroline's daughters.'

'Hard to be quite sure,' Matthew answered, frankly. 'They seem happy for us.'

'It's pretty important,' Karl said. 'Don't you think?'

'Of course it's important. It was the first thing Caro and I agreed on: that without their blessings, there could be no wedding.'

'So they gave it to you?'

'Not formally, no. Not to me, anyway. Caro says that aside from grieving for their dad, the girls have often missed a male presence in the home. She says they're ready to let someone in. Most of all, she says they want her to be happy.'

'She says.' Karl was wary. 'What have the girls said to you?'

'We haven't had too many one on ones, not yet, but they've been . . .' He hunted for the word. 'Kind.' He tapped the edge of the table with two fingers. 'Knock on wood, so far, so good.'

'What are they like, the girls?' Karl asked.

'Beautiful. Like their mother.'

Karl leaned back, shook his head. 'I never saw you like this before. Crazy in love.' He paused. 'Maybe a little bit crazy, period?'

Matthew smiled. 'Maybe.'

'Marriage after just two weeks is pretty crazy, don't you think?'

'It's going to be a little more than two weeks,' Matthew said. 'We have to get all kinds of paperwork organized, and the Swiss need ten days, minimum, to check them out – there's no problem for Caroline, of course, since she's still a Swiss national.'

'So three weeks,' Karl said. 'Still crazy, Matt.'

'I know what you mean.' Matthew had been prepared for this reaction. 'Believe me, I've said as much to Caro, several times over. Not because I'm not sure about the two of us – I am – but because I have been worried we might be indulging ourselves at the expense of the girls.'

'So this is Caroline's rush.'

Matthew shook his head. 'Mine too, Karl. Though, yes, in a sense, it's Caro who's afraid that if we wait, go on to London and plan our wedding there, someone – immigration, whoever – might just stop us, mess everything up. That's the main reason for the whole whirlwind operation. A *fait accompli*.'

'But you could move in together without being married.'

'We could, but she – neither of us – wants that.'

'You're both romantics then,' Karl said.

'And not ashamed of it.'

'Nor should you be.'

'Practicalities aside, neither of us wants to risk losing the *essence* of what happened to us in St Moritz. Our lives just seeming to fall so perfectly into place.'

'Yours and Caroline's.'

'Exactly,' Matthew said.

'And her daughters,' Karl added.

'Have you gone *nuts*?'

His brother Ethan's reaction on hearing the news by telephone.

Though, just minutes later, being Ethan, he backed off. An accountant in a large practice with a wife, Susan (also an accountant) and young twin sons, Ethan was like their late father in that respect. Edward Gardner had disliked confrontation, had believed in minding his own business. Matthew knew he was more like their mother. Ann Gardner had liked taking chances – especially on people – had liked risks of most kinds. She'd enjoyed taking vacations where she could gamble, ski or scuba dive, and had planned, just before her death, to take hang-gliding lessons. Edward had hated being driven by his wife because of her liking for speed. Yet, ironically, he'd been the one driving the rented Toyota on their Californian vacation when an oil truck on the opposite side of the highway had lost control and killed them both.

So much for not taking chances, Matthew had felt ever since then.

'I want you and Susan – and Teddy and Andy, obviously, all of you – to meet Caro,' he'd told Ethan when he'd made the call from his room at the Carlton Hotel in St Moritz. 'The sooner the better. Before the wedding, if possible.'

'We can't just pick up and cross the ocean, Matt.' Ethan sounded irritable. 'And it doesn't help matters to be asked to drop everything and go rootling through your past for all kinds of papers.' He paused. 'I just don't see what the big rush is. You're

7

almost forty, not some crazy kid. Or maybe if you were both twenty years older, I might understand your not wanting to waste time, but . . .' He'd paused. 'How old did you say Caroline is?'

'Thirty-seven.'

'And a widow.'

'Her husband died three years ago.'

'Not that long ago.'

'But a decent enough interval.'

'For her, maybe,' he said. 'No time at all for their children.'

'We're not talking about little kids, Ethan. Felicity – they call her Flic – is sixteen, Imogen's fourteen and then there's Chloë, who's twelve.'

'Still children, Matthew.'

Matthew spent several minutes telling his brother the same as he'd told Karl.

'Tread carefully,' Ethan said when he'd done, 'whatever Caroline says. Girls who've lost their father that young are bound to be fragile.'

'I know that,' Matthew told him.

'I guess you do,' Ethan had said. 'You've never been an insensitive man.'

'I hope not. God, I *really* hope not.' Matthew paused. 'More than anything, Ethan, I figure what these girls – young women – need, in the long haul, is people to care for them, be on their side. They have their mother, obviously, but I'm really hoping they'll let me be their friend.'

'You've always wanted kids. I just assumed . . .' Ethan trailed off.

'That I'd have little kids. Babies.' Matthew smiled at the thought. 'And maybe we will, who knows? We've talked about it, agreed there's no rush.' He heard the silence, knew his brother was probably thinking of Caroline's age again, moved smartly on. 'But in the meantime, I have a lot of love I can give to her daughters, and I know they may not be ready to let another man love them, but I can be patient.'

'Just so long as you know you may have to be,' Ethan said.

They had talked about the possibility of having children. Matthew had told her late one night – tentatively, not knowing how she might feel about it – how much he would love to have a child with her. 'A baby of our own,' he had said.

8

'I would love that, too,' she had answered, 'more than anything. But we'll have to wait a while, for the girls' sakes. It might be a little too much for them otherwise.'

'Of course,' he'd agreed easily, happy that they both wanted the same thing, felt the same way about the fundamentals. 'Though I guess we can't wait too long.'

'Because I'm old, you mean,' Caroline had said, wistfully.

'Ancient,' he had said, then seen the small furrow on her forehead. 'If it doesn't happen though, if it isn't meant to be, you won't have to worry – not for my sake – because we'll have the girls. Three daughters ready-made by you. What more could a man ask for?'

Caroline had been waiting in her own room while he'd made the call to Ethan.

'He was bound to be shocked,' she said afterwards.

'He was, a little,' Matthew agreed. 'Ethan takes his older brother role pretty seriously.'

'Did he like Jillian?'

Matthew had met his first wife when they were both sixteen, and they had married at twenty-one. Having grown up together, they had, alas, begun growing *apart* almost as soon as the rings were on their fingers. Given a choice, Matthew would have gone on working at it, but Jillian had announced, after just three months, that she wanted a divorce.

'Ethan liked Jillian very much until she filed for divorce,' he answered Caroline's question. 'After that, he couldn't stand her because he felt she'd hurt me.' He shrugged. 'Like I said, he's my big brother.'

'He probably mistrusts me,' Caro said.

'Maybe, until he meets you. Then he'll love you.'

She shook her head. 'There's nothing so special about me.'

'Are you kidding?'

'Not at all.' She paused. 'I'm not bad to look at, but there are thousands of women who look like me.'

'I've never seen any other woman who looks remotely like you.'

'Complete with stretch marks and the start of cellulite.'

'Have you taken a close look at me?'

'You're very handsome.'

9

'Rose-coloured glasses,' Matthew said. 'Or maybe you just *need* glasses?'

'Does it matter so long as I feel that way?'

'Not so long as you still feel it when we get back to London.'

'I still find it amazing,' Caroline said, 'that you really don't mind moving to another country.'

'It's where you live,' Matthew said.

'But most men still expect women to fit in with their own lives.'

'I'm not most men,' he said. 'And I don't have kids. You do.'

'But you've been happy in Berlin.'

'I have been,' he agreed. 'But I'm lucky. I enjoy my work, and my firm has offices all over. I'm a moveable feast.'

As a qualified architect with fifteen years experience under his belt, Matthew had realized long ago that he did not possess the stuff to become a great architect. Yet he was far from bleak. His name would never be intoned with much respect, but he knew he was effective in his own way, and that his contributions to the work he'd been involved with had been significant. He had loved his years in the Manhattan office – finding favour with Laszlo King, the chairman – and Berlin had been good to him, too. Fine projects; pleasant colleagues; the finding of a true friend in Karl Becker; and a splendid apartment near Kurfürstendamm.

Women, too. Attractive, intelligent, sexy women. No shortages there. No lean period to have tipped him over the edge of reason into the arms of the first lovely, clever, kind woman who'd have him.

She was all those things and more. Mathilde Caroline Lehrer Walters (she'd ditched her first name in early childhood back in Switzerland) was beautiful, bright, gentle and sensitive. And sexy. Very. Giving, too. A generous spirit.

And she had fallen for him, just as hard.

That was part of the miracle. For if Caro had said she was 'nothing special', Matthew knew that went double for him. Just under six feet tall, slim, fit, but not spectacular in any respect. His hair was okay, he guessed, plenty of it, brown with a few early silver strands. Eyes grey, nose about straight, mouth average – everything more or less where it was meant to be.

'If I had the talent,' Caroline had said once, while they were making love, 'I'd want to sculpt you.' Richard, her late husband, had been a painter and illustrator, and Caroline had envied his talent, longed for artistic ability of her own. As it was, all her own creativity stretched to, she told Matthew, was needlepoint – her cushions and miniature wall-coverings were much in demand from friends. A very minor gift, she insisted, and one she pursued simply for relaxation.

Matthew had laughed about her wish to sculpt him.

'I'm serious.' She'd shaken her head. 'Not just because of how you look, but because you're so very *real*.' She'd tried to explain. 'The way you are with me. I feel as if *all* of you is here, as if all of you wants to be with me, every part of your body and your mind.'

'That's exactly true,' he'd told her. 'With every part of *you*. Who wouldn't feel that way?'

'You'd be surprised,' Caroline said.

'Anyone who didn't want that would be a fool,' Matthew had said, and they'd held each other tightly and gone to sleep.

So there it was. A reasonably happy man before. Completed by Caroline.

Both Ethan and Karl had cautioned him about their haste, and about rushing into being a stepfather.

Stepfather. A word that conjured up a kaleidoscopic jumble of potential problems. Yet from Matthew's point of view, there was nothing to think about. Caroline's daughters were part of her.

And as she had so accurately perceived, he wanted all of her.

# 3

Caroline's house in Hampstead was a tall, slender, white villa named Aethiopia. Richard Walters had recalled that spelling occurring in a hauntingly lovely poem of Edith Sitwell's, but had failed to discover exactly why the name had been bestowed on the late nineteenth-century house. Caroline didn't care why, when, or by whom. Aethiopia had become her home, and she loved it dearly.

'What do you think?' she had asked, tentatively, as Matthew had looked at it for the first time on the last Friday of January.

He had been too absorbed to answer immediately.

'You don't like it.'

'I do like it,' he had said, slowly. 'It's very . . . female.'

'Is it?' She'd sounded surprised.

'I'd say so.' He'd paused, taking his time. 'Such graceful lines.'

'Yet designed and built by men, for men, I believe.'

'Even so.'

The three-storey house (actually three floors plus an attic) stood about halfway down East Heath Road, with only a small patch of white-walled front garden and driveway separating it from the road, but with a fair-sized rectangle of back garden, possessing a stone terrace, apple trees, flower beds (now winter-barren) and, close to a willow tree near the rear, a concrete, probably privately-built, air-raid shelter, now used by Caroline's gardener and handyman, John Pascoe, for storing tools and passing the time of day. The back of Aethiopia looked down over its own walled garden and other local properties; the front had the tangled wildness of Hampstead Heath to gaze at.

Matthew's previously garnered impressions of the Heath had come from works of art, and he remembered seeing and liking Constable's *The Admiral's House* in Berlin's Nationalgalerie. But neither the wildness nor the sheer open expanse had transmitted itself to him until that first real sighting. Though it was the view from the rear and, in particular, from the little balcony outside the second-floor room Caroline called the Quiet Room, that captivated him most on his first morning at Aethiopia.

'It's amazing,' he said over his shoulder to his new wife, who had remained inside. 'So many rooftops and all different. Come join me.'

'I don't like balconies,' she told him. 'I don't much like heights.'

'But you like skiing.' He laughed back at her. 'You love mountains.'

'I grew up with them,' she said. 'I have faith in their solidness, but I still keep away from precipices.'

'Pity.' Matthew took one more look, then went back into the room and shut the doors behind him. 'It really is wonderful.'

Caroline was sitting in a rocking chair, wearing her pale blue quilted dressing gown. 'I'm glad you like it.' She paused. 'This is probably my favourite room.'

He glanced around. 'It's certainly peaceful.'

If the exterior of the house was female, the Quiet Room, used by Caroline for her sewing, was wholeheartedly feminine, a small sitting room of simple, pleasant comforts. A couch with needle-point-covered cushions, stitched by Caroline herself, the rocking chair carved in white oak, a matching low table, a modest book-case on one wall, and another carved piece of furniture, probably antique, much smaller than a secrétaire, but larger than an apothecary's medicine chest, that held all the tools and materials needed for her art.

'No TV, no telephone,' she pointed out to Matthew.

He glanced towards the radio and CD player on one of the bookshelves.

'Classical CDs.' Caroline smiled. 'And gentle classics only.'

'Are husbands allowed to use the room?'

'Of course. Anyone can use it, so long as they want to be quiet.'

'Do the girls ever come in here?'

She smiled again. 'Not very often.'

\*

13

She'd asked him, soon after their arrival, what he thought about the house from his professional point of view.

'Critically, you mean?' he'd asked her.

'I've married an architect,' she'd said. 'Your opinion's important to me.'

Matthew had looked at her. 'You really love it, don't you?'

'I do, yes.'

'And the girls do, too?'

She had nodded.

'And I love you,' Matthew had said, with simplicity. He saw that she needed more from him, and sought to explain. 'I'm a man first, Caro, an architect second. This is going to be my home, our home. It isn't a project, a piece of work to be appraised.' He paused. 'Home's about atmosphere and comfort and feelings.'

'So how are your feelings?'

'Good,' he said. 'Very good.' He shook his head. 'But I think I'm going to need time to get to know Aethiopia – to get along with her.'

Caroline smiled. 'Her.'

'Definitely her.'

He did still feel that. All Aethiopia's lines had the same purity; even the chimneys were elegant, the balustrades on its balconies delicate. *Intended for women*, he thought abruptly, but refrained from saying. Men tolerated, perhaps even welcomed, but not entirely belonging.

He wondered if Richard had felt that, and if he had, if he had minded it.

*Do I mind it*? he asked himself after they had left the room, then thought about Caroline, sitting in that rocker and, earlier, lying in bed beside him (the bed that had been Richard's, but was now his) naked and so open and easy and content with him. And found that he didn't mind one bit, any more than he thought he minded sleeping in another man's bed. On the contrary, the house seemed all the more fascinating for its womanly attributes.

It was not all that way, of course. The slim entrance hall and sleek kitchen were in keeping with the exterior, but the drawing and dining rooms were more classically handsome – almost dauntingly so, Matthew felt, to a New Yorker accustomed to apartment dwelling and comfortable disorder. In these rooms, the windows were part stained glass, the furniture was antique and

14

gleaming and the rugs Persian, and though thready in parts, they didn't look as if they'd ever been shaken by a puppy or used by kids for fantasy magic carpet rides.

Then there was the study.

'This could be yours,' Caroline had said, showing him around the previous afternoon. 'If you wanted it.'

'Was it Richard's?' He had looked at the bookshelves and mahogany desk.

'It was, at least for the business side of his work. He painted in a studio at the top of the house – an attic conversion.'

'That might be kind of nice for my work too.'

His new wife had winced slightly. 'I'm afraid that Flic has rather earmarked it for herself. She fancies it as a private sitting room for her friends in the future. There's a tiny kitchen up there, too, and a lavatory.' She paused, dismayed. 'I should have thought about your work, realized you'd need somewhere light.'

'I don't really,' he reassured her. 'It's not as if I'm a freelance. I'll be working at the firm's offices.' He shrugged. 'I never had my own studio in Berlin, or in New York.'

'I could speak to Flic.'

'Please don't,' Matthew said swiftly. 'Not if she's set her heart on it. As I said, I've never had my own studio, so I don't need one now. Anyway' – he reached out to stroke her hair – 'the last thing I'm going to want to do after a long day's work is come home and shut myself at the top of the house, away from you.'

'I'm sorry,' Caroline said.

'Why? I'm the newcomer here.' He'd glanced again around the late Richard Walter's study. 'I'll be happy to use this room, though, as a home office, or at least to share it with you and the girls.'

'I do my own paperwork in the Quiet Room.' She paused. 'And you're not a newcomer, Matthew. You're my husband.'

He noticed again how very sensitive she was, especially to other people's feelings.

'Your very new husband,' he said, 'who knows better than to start out with his stepdaughters by disrupting their plans.'

Caroline's daughters had not been present for their homecoming because Sylvie Lehrer, Matthew's new mother-in-law, had suggested to her daughter on the day before the wedding that it

15

might be easier all round if their first night in Aethiopia were uncluttered.

'I'd hate the girls to think I regard them as clutter,' Matthew had told Caroline.

'They won't,' she had answered promptly. 'And Mama's absolutely right about keeping the first night and morning just for ourselves. The girls can stay with her and come home in the afternoon, and then everything can get back to normal.'

'Hardly normal.' He saw anxiety cloud her eyes. 'Things are going to seem – to *be* – different for a while. For us all.'

'My daughters are used to changes,' Caroline said softly. 'Mostly, the unhappy kind. First, when their father was so ill – hospitals and tiptoeing around. Then, when he died . . .'

Matthew waited a moment. 'I've tried a few times to talk to them about Richard, but one of them always changes the subject, so I haven't pushed.'

'Probably right.'

'They've been so great, about me, about the wedding. I couldn't have asked for more understanding.' Matthew hesitated. 'I didn't expect it, you know. Just because you and I had fallen in love didn't mean they were going to approve.'

'I've told you,' Caroline said. 'They've seen how happy you make me. They want that for me.'

'You make it all sound simple,' Matthew said.

'I think it is,' she said.

The wedding had taken place in Bern, organized with exhilarating speed, a close-family-only affair, Ethan and Susan having flown in the previous day. It had, Matthew decided later, been perfect, though he had caught himself wondering, at the odd quiet moment, why Caroline had driven them towards that goal with such urgency. Not that he'd needed much persuasion. He had wanted it, *all* of it, every bit as much as Caro, had not an ounce of regret, had been able to answer his brother clearly on that, at least.

'No regrets,' Matthew had told Ethan firmly, when they were all gathered in the lobby of the Bellevue-Palace, late in the evening after the wedding. 'Not a single one, believe me.'

They were standing by the concierge's desk, having confirmed their various travel arrangements. The women were all standing together some distance away in the lounge, saying their goodnights.

16

'So,' Ethan said. 'Now you honeymoon.'

Three nights at a tiny hotel in Paris, recommended by Karl Becker, while Sylvie took her granddaughters back to London to stay with her.

'And then to your new home.' Ethan paused. 'More of a mystery tour, I have to say, than I'd care to embark on.'

'An adventure, surely,' Matthew said, 'rather than a mystery.'

'I daresay.' Ethan became more upbeat, looked towards the women. 'Susan and I both think Caro's a lovely person, Matt. And Sylvie's a delight.'

'Isn't she just?'

'I wish we'd had more time to get to know them all, especially the girls.' He smiled. 'I guess that's going to be the biggest part of the adventure for you. Instant family's one thing. No such thing as instant fatherhood.'

'I don't expect to be their father,' Matthew said.

'First rule of step-parenting, I guess,' Ethan agreed.

'I'd settle for being their friend,' Matthew said, softly.

Ethan laid a hand on his brother's shoulder. 'You'll do it.'

'Think so?'

'So long as you don't imagine it'll all be easy.'

'I don't,' Matthew said. 'I'm not that much of a fool, Ethan.'

'Never thought you were.' Ethan paused. 'But you are gentle, Matt, and kind-hearted. And gentle, kind people get hurt too much of the time.'

'Caro's gentle, too,' Matthew said, smiling across at the women.

'Yes.' Ethan nodded. 'I think she is.'

He, too, was looking again at the small group.

At his brother's new stepdaughters. Forming a circle, just then, around their mother. Charming, certainly.

Something else about that ring, Ethan thought, that troubled him a little, though he wasn't sure what it was.

Protecting her, probably. Nothing wrong with that.

Except that he thought they might be protecting Caroline against Matthew.

He glanced at his brother, saw that he observed it, too, saw from the slight wrinkle of his brow that it troubled him also.

Just as well, Ethan thought.

# 4

Within an hour of his stepdaughters' homecoming, Matthew knew that what he was feeling was no product of his imagination.

They did not want him here.

Sylvie had driven them over from her flat, less than a mile away, with their cases and a bouquet of brightly welcoming flowers, and the three girls all smiled at him, were polite to him, did as their mother and grandmother bade them, but the smiles were not as they had appeared in Switzerland. They were, Matthew felt, with a thud of deflation, masks.

Except, perhaps, for Chloë's.

'Do you like it?' she had asked him, within minutes of their arrival. 'Do you like our house?'

That '*our*' had excluded him, yet he knew that it had been innocently put. Chloë was still, in some ways, a little girl, showing a new friend her territory. *Friend* being the crucial word. Matthew hoped.

When Imogen came upon him, twenty or so minutes later, as he stood in the back garden looking reflectively up at Aethiopia, allowing himself, briefly, to play architectural games, picturing it as the elevation it had once been on someone's drawing board, she asked him much the same question.

'Well?' she said, quietly. 'What do you think of our house?'

This time, the '*our*' was a very different creature.

He looked into her eyes – brown, unlike her sisters', the same colour as her father's – hoping, he supposed, to find something tentative in them. A touch of suspicion, perhaps. Lord knew he could understand that, could well comprehend the mistrust she might feel because of the tearaway speed of his marriage to her mother.

But it was not just mistrust that he saw, or suspicion.

There was hostility in those eyes, pure and simple, so undiluted that, for an instant, it all but took his breath away.

*Ignore it.*

Easier said than done.

*You're the adult.*

'It's a wonderful house,' he said, answering her question. 'You must love it very much.'

'We do,' Imogen said. 'My father loved it especially.'

He had anticipated that. He hadn't needed Ethan to warn him about the inevitable competition he would face with the late Richard Walters. It was a normal response by a still-bereaved young person, for three years was, in many ways, a mere drop in the ocean when it came to the premature loss of a parent.

'I know he did,' he answered. 'Your mother told me.'

'Has she told you what a great father he was?'

'Yes, she's told me that too.' Matthew paused, about to begin the process of reassurance that he'd expected to have to repeat often in the formative months of these precarious relationships, but Imogen pre-empted him.

'I know,' she said, cuttingly. 'You don't want to replace him.'

'I know I could never do that.'

'No, you couldn't. And don't bother giving me the whole bit again about how much you want to be our friend.'

'Not even if it's the truth?' Matthew asked.

'Speaking of truths,' Imogen said, 'did Mum tell you that she wanted you for companionship?' The eyes sparked with a touch of malice.

'That goes without saying,' he answered calmly. 'It's a great part of what marriage is about.'

'And sex,' Imogen said.

'That, too,' Matthew said, still evenly.

'Mum and Dad's sex life was great,' she said. 'Did Mum tell you that?'

'No, she didn't,' he replied. 'That's private. Her private business, and in the past.' *Mistake*, he thought, and almost winced.

19

'Our father's not in the past,' Imogen said, very coldly.

'Of course not. That's not what I meant.'

They both heard the sound of the glass door to the kitchen opening, and Matthew turned to see Caroline emerging onto the stone terrace, smiling at them.

'Isn't it a bit chilly for standing around?' she called, hugging herself against the wind. 'We're making hot chocolate if anyone wants it.'

'Sounds good,' Matthew called back.

'Very cosy,' Imogen said.

Matthew ignored the sarcasm, started towards the house, then glanced back over his shoulder. 'Coming, Imogen?'

'Wouldn't miss it,' she said.

*Patience*, he reminded himself.

All the Walters girls were bright and strikingly good-looking, though Flic, with her sleek curtain of golden hair and fine cheekbones, was the most obviously beautiful as well as being the highest achiever academically. Imogen disliked school, despite The Grange – the private girls' school in Primrose Hill chosen by Richard Walters because of its special attention to the arts – having a comparatively liberated approach to discipline. Brown eyes notwithstanding, she resembled, at first glance, her mother and sisters, having the same blond hair, hers cut in a swinging bob with fringe, but there seemed a toughness about her that stemmed in part from her long-legged stride and broad shoulders, and in part from her bolshy attitude.

Chloë, the youngest, was also the softest. Blue-eyed, like her mother and oldest sister, her hair was wavier, fluffier, her features sweeter, her nose more upturned, her lips fuller. She claimed, regularly, not to be a baby, but like many youngest siblings had grown accustomed to being led, accommodated, pushed around and protected. However much she protested to the contrary, it had suited her, sixteen months earlier, to have joined Flic and Imogen at The Grange, to have been close to them again on weekdays, back under their more constant protection. It satisfied her, too, to have discovered that, out of the three of them, she was the only one of Richard's daughters to have inherited any of his talent, enjoying painting and drawing and, according to Jennifer Bower, her art teacher, developing quite a gift for calligraphy.

20

Like Caroline, Chloë liked peace and harmony and feared discord. Imogen thrived on and often *instigated* discord. Flic, the calmest and shrewdest sister, had, in the years since her father's death, developed an aptitude for quiet observation and calculation; had also, quite painfully and soberly, come to realize that one could not always have exactly what one wanted, but that one owed it to oneself to contrive, with thought and planning, to come as close as possible to goals of any kind.

The last thing any of the Walters sisters had anticipated, leaving London for their annual skiing holiday in St Moritz, had been that their mother would fall in love, much less come home with a *husband*.

'We have to stop her,' Imogen had exploded in their serene, pale-peachy room at the Carlton.

'I doubt that we can,' Flic had said.

'We *have* to – it's so *sick*!'

Chloë had been off having a skating lesson with her mother and *him*, so Flic hadn't even tried to quieten her sister down.

'I can't *believe* she could be so disloyal to Dad.'

'I know,' Flic said.

'We have to tell her she can't.'

Flic took a moment. 'Remember Lucy Cutler?'

'The anorexic in your class.'

'Lucy's parents were divorced when her mother said she wanted to get married again, so in a way it was almost worse because Lucy's father was alive to see what was happening. At the start, her mother said she wouldn't go ahead if Lucy wasn't a hundred percent for it, and of course Lucy was always going to come first with her. So Lucy told her she was a hundred per-cent *against* it, and her mother went to pieces. And after that, the more Lucy objected, the more her mother dug her own heels in.'

'Get to the point, Flic,' Imogen said impatiently.

Flic shrugged. 'So they got married, and all Lucy had succeeded in doing was becoming her mother's enemy, and her life became horrible. Her stepfather loathed her, her mum sided with him, because now, of course, he was her husband, wasn't he, so now *he* came first with her, whatever she'd said before.'

'So you're saying we just cave in?' Imogen was appalled.

Flic's nod was slow, thoughtful.

21

'I can't,' Imogen said flatly. 'I won't.'

'I think it might be best,' Flic told her. 'Give ourselves time.'

Imogen, a stubborn girl, had not, of course, listened, and had tackled Caroline that evening.

'No one will ever replace your father,' Caroline had told her.

'Not for us,' Imogen had replied, 'but he'll be your husband, so don't tell me he won't be replacing Daddy so far as you're concerned.'

Caroline had told Imogen that more than anything, Matthew would be her friend. Her companion. 'Everyone needs someone,' she'd said.

'You have us.'

A grown-up someone, Caro had said.

'A man, you mean,' Imogen had said. 'For sex.'

Caroline had looked shocked then, and quite satisfyingly – from Imogen's viewpoint – guilty. And Imogen had grabbed that small moment of upper-hand and walked away, knowing that her mother would have a shitty night because of what she'd just said, and maybe the next time Matthew Gardner, the American creep who wanted to step into her father's shoes, not to mention his bed, tried to make love to her, Caroline would think about what Imo had said and tell him to bugger off.

But all that had happened was that the very next day, Caroline and Matthew had announced that they were going to get married right there in Switzerland. And that was when Imogen had realized how right Flic had been about not being able to stop their mother from doing anything she chose to. They were powerless. No one listened to them or gave a stuff about their opinions.

'So what now?' Imogen had asked Flic that morning at their grandmother's flat, while Sylvie was at the hairdresser's. (Sylvie spent more time, Caroline sometimes teased her mother, having her hair done than any woman she'd ever heard of who didn't have at least three public engagements a day, though Sylvie insisted that regular hairdos were the key to the chic appearance she strove to maintain.)

'Now we go home,' Flic had answered simply.

'Do you still say it's going to be okay?' Imogen's scepticism was plain.

'What's going to be okay?' Chloë had asked.

22

'We're not talking to you, squirt,' Imogen had said.

'What's going to be okay?' Chloë had repeated the question to Flic.

'Everything,' Flic had said.

'I know you're talking about Mummy and Matthew.'

'Yes, we are.' Flic was always more patient with Chloë than Imogen. 'That's why I said everything's fine, because it is.'

'So what do we do?' Imogen asked. 'How are we going to handle him?'

'What do you mean?' Chloë turned back to Flic. 'What does she mean?'

'What do you *think* I mean, dumbo?' Imogen had slept badly in one of the bunk beds Sylvie had invested in some years ago so that she could have all her granddaughters to stay at once. 'We're going home to a whole new scene, to a *step*father, for God's sake.'

'I like Matthew,' Chloë said.

'You would,' Imogen said.

'What's wrong with him?' her younger sister asked.

'Nothing,' Flic told her.

'Except he's married our mother,' Imogen said.

'Mummy loves him,' Chloë pointed out.

'*Thinks* she loves him,' Imogen said.

'Imo,' Flic warned her lightly.

'Okay, she loves him.' Imogen yawned. 'But it isn't real love, is it?'

'Why isn't it?' Chloë asked.

'*Real* love was what Mum and Dad had, that's why.'

'Imo,' Flic said again.

'But it's true, isn't it? You know it, and I know it.'

'Mummy told me it isn't the same as with Daddy,' Chloë said, reasonably. 'She says there are different types of love, but she definitely said that she loves Matthew.'

'It's going to be fine,' Flic reassured her. 'It's probably going to be lovely.'

'Matthew says he's not going to pretend to be our father,' Chloë said.

'I should bloody well hope not,' Imogen said.

'Imo, please,' Flic said.

'Oh, for fuck's sake,' Imogen snapped.

'*Imo.*'

*

23

They sat, on that first Saturday of their new life, in the drawing room at Aethiopia, drinking hot chocolate and eating the cake and biscuits that Sylvie had bought that morning at Maison Blanc, all agreed that delicious as they were, nothing could hold a candle to Swiss baking.

'And French,' Matthew said, remembering.

'Was it your first time in Paris?' Flic asked.

'I've been twice before.' He smiled at Caroline. 'Though it might as well have been a completely different city.'

'Did you honeymoon there the first time?' Imogen asked.

'It's cold in here,' Sylvie said quickly.

Flic looked at the fireplace. 'We usually have a fire in here right through to spring. It's a cold room till the sun gets properly warm.'

'We lit a fire last night.' Caroline looked at Matthew and laughed.

'If you can call it that.' He grimaced.

'His first attempt,' Caroline explained to the others.

'Looks a whole lot easier than it is,' Matthew said. 'Took hours to get the smoke out of here.'

'I'll help you, if you like,' Flic offered. 'There's a bit of a knack.'

'Dad had the knack,' Imogen said.

Matthew grinned. 'Maybe I'd be better leaving this to the experts.'

'Good idea,' Imogen said.

'I rather suspect,' Sylvie said quietly but firmly, 'that someone who can design whole buildings is going to be more than up to the job of setting a few logs alight, if he so chooses.'

As far as she could tell, so early in their relationship, Sylvie liked her new son-in-law. She also rather felt for him, in that she was well aware that, however much in love he and Caro unquestionably were, settling down in his wife's house with three at best *tentative* stepdaughters was likely to be fraught with pitfalls.

It was, she thought, perhaps as well that she lived nearby, removed and private but on hand for moral support if need be. Her flat was in Perrin's Lane, a narrow, desirable lane running between Hampstead High Street and Heath Street, an easy stroll from the hairdressers, boutiques, cafés and the abundant and varied restaurants in the village. Born in London, Sylvie had married a Swiss named Erich Lehrer when she was nineteen, had moved with him to Zurich until – after far too many years of putting up with his

24

infidelities for their daughter's sake – she had finally divorced him and brought eleven-year-old Caroline back to London.

'If I can't cope,' Imogen had said to her last night, 'can I come and stay with you, Groosi?'

The pet name was a remnant of Sylvie's Swiss years – not that she had ever mastered the complexities of *Schwyzertütsch*, but she had not cared for the notion of being called 'Grandmother', 'Granny' or 'Gran'. 'Groosi' had appealed to her sense of humour, and had caught on with all three of her granddaughters.

'Of course you'll be able to cope,' she had answered.

'But if I can't . . .'

Sylvie had smiled at her tough, yet vulnerable granddaughter. 'You're always welcome here, darling, you know that.'

'That's about all I do know, Groosi,' Imogen had said.


After tea, Matthew went upstairs to do some unpacking. He was just entering the bedroom when he heard a tread from close behind and turned around.

'Do you like the bedroom?' Flic asked.

'Very much.'

'Is there enough room for your things?' She paused. 'Though I don't suppose all your stuff's arrived yet from Berlin, has it?'

Matthew shook his head. 'Some to come from New York, too.' He started into the room. 'You coming in?'

'So you are making this a full-scale move then?' Flic stayed where she was.

He glanced back at her. 'Of course I am.'

'Only your life seems to have been quite nomadic till now.'

She was, he had already realized, mature and cool for her sixteen years, but she had, till now, been both helpful and agreeable with him. He thought about Imogen's hostility earlier and, looking into Flic's eyes now, their colour so exactly like her mother's, he thought he detected some signs of frost too.

'Not really nomadic,' he answered carefully. 'Just the two places: New York and Berlin.' He paused. 'Until now.' He turned back to face the bedroom. One of his suitcases, still half-full, lay open on the bed, two heavy sweaters and a tie on the spread beside it, a notably male litter in the otherwise feminine room.

Flic came in a little way. 'I expect Mum gave you the full tour yesterday, showed you our rooms. Mine and my sisters.'

25

'No, she didn't,' Matthew said. 'She wouldn't, with you away.' He bent to take a pinstriped shirt from the case. It was clean, but all the packing and repacking had rumpled it. 'Is there a laundry nearby?'

'There are most things near here,' Flic answered. 'Mum says you have your eye on the attic.'

Matthew looked up, surprised. 'Not at all. Your mother told me your dad had used it as a studio, so I just mentioned it might be good for my work, but then she told me that you wanted it and that was that. I wouldn't dream of spoiling your plans.'

'You couldn't,' Flic said. 'I wouldn't let you.'

There it was. Frost into ice. Just like her sister, after all.

Yet half an hour later, back downstairs with the rest of the family, she was as she had been before: friendly and amenable, suggesting they all go together to show him around Hampstead's shops, maybe introduce him to a few locals so that he could feel at home more quickly.

'That was considerate of Flic,' Caroline said as they went up to fetch their coats for the outing. 'You always hope, as a mother, that you're bringing up decent, kind people.' She took a pair of boots from her wardrobe and pulled them on over her slim black slacks. 'I suppose this is a little proof that I can't have done too badly – their making you so welcome.'

Matthew saw how happy she was, had no wish to spoil it, said nothing.

'Imo can be a bit of a brat, of course,' she went on, 'though at least you always know where you are with her because she's so outspoken. But Flic's growing up rather beautifully, I think, and so far, touch wood' – she touched her head – 'Chloë's a sweetheart.'

'She certainly is.' Matthew was glad to be able to agree with that.

'The parka or the cashmere coat?' Caroline moved to the next wardrobe and tugged them both out a little way for him to look at.

'The parka,' he said.

She put it on, then turned to face him.

'I'm very proud of my daughters, you know.'

'I don't blame you,' Matthew said.

'Your stepdaughters now,' she said.

'I know.'

'I hope you'll be as proud of them as I am,' Caroline said.

'I'm sure I will be,' Matthew said.

# 5

The remaining two members of the household arrived on Sunday morning. Isabella Bates, Caroline's Chilean housekeeper, and their five-year-old golden retriever, Kahli – an abbreviation of Kahlil, the name that Richard Walters had insisted upon calling him in homage to Kahlil Gibran, whose writings and paintings he had greatly admired.

'That's Kahli *with* the "h,"' he'd explained to his wife and daughters. 'Kali *without* the "h" – just so you know – was a Hindu goddess of destruction.'

'Rather suitable, I'd have thought,' Caro had remarked, given the then puppy's insatiable appetite for shoes and soft furnishings.

'I hope not,' Richard had said, 'since goddess Kali's cult was characterized by cannibalism.'

Isabella – who always looked after the dog when the family went away – had been with the Walters for longer than Kahli. As Isabella Ríos, she had first come to England as Caroline's au pair, infuriating her middle-class parents a year later by marrying Mick Bates, a waiter and mediocre musician, and moving with him into a garden flat off Kilburn High Road.

'You're going to love Isabella,' Caroline had told Matthew last night.

'I hope she likes me.'

'Why wouldn't she?'

'Not everyone,' he had gently pointed out, 'is going to.'

'Isabella will love you because you love me.' Caroline had kissed him.

'She may not like the disruption.'

'She's very easy-going.'

'She might not trust me,' Matthew had said.

'Don't be silly.' Caroline had looked quite annoyed. 'How could anyone not trust you?'

Their arrival, in the event, brought some relief. Matthew was in the kitchen, Caroline was upstairs in the bath and Chloë was the only one of the sisters downstairs when the front door opened, and for the first several moments, while dog, girl and young woman engaged in ecstatic greetings, he stood a few feet back, watching and feeling uncomfortably like an outsider.

But then Kahli spied him, and his tail stopped wagging as he stared at the stranger halfway between the kitchen and front door.

'Hi there,' Matthew said, softly.

The dog trotted over slowly. Matthew stooped and extended his right hand, carefully, respectfully. Kahli sniffed his fingers, came a little closer, and Matthew stroked the top of his head. The tail began to wag again.

'He likes you,' Chloë said.

She sounded genuinely glad, Matthew noted with pleasure.

'The feeling's mutual.' He fondled the dog's ears gently, enjoying the silkiness and the comforting smell of him, then, remembering his manners, straightened up.

'I'm sorry,' he said to Isabella. 'That was rude of me. I'm Matthew Gardner.'

'Isabella,' she said, simply. She was tall and slim, with pale skin, nut-brown eyes and very dark hair fastened in a long, thick plait. She wore a black and red patterned poncho over a scarlet roll-necked pullover and black straight trousers. She looked, Matthew thought, a very expensive housekeeper.

'I'm glad to meet you,' he said.

'I am too.' Her eyes seemed to assess him. 'Though you are a big surprise for me.' Her accent was attractive, her tone lilting. 'I mean, of course, that Caro's marriage is a big surprise.' She elongated the first syllable of the name, made it sound like the Italian word for darling. *Caa*ro . . .

'Has Kahli been good?' Chloë, cuddling her dog, asked Isabella from the floor.

'Magnificently good,' she answered. 'Where are your sisters?'

'Still asleep,' she said. 'Mummy's in the bath.'

Isabella smiled. 'Caro hates to rise early,' she told Matthew, 'especially on Sundays.'

'So I'm learning.'

She began to walk towards the kitchen. 'Would you like some coffee?'

'I was just thinking of making some,' he said.

'I always take Caro up a cup when I arrive,' Isabella said. 'So now I will just learn to make a little more.'

Matthew wasn't quite certain if she minded that or not.

'From tomorrow,' he told her, 'I'll be at work.'

'So soon?' Isabella asked. 'What a pity.'

She said that, he felt, as if she meant it, hoped that she did *not* mean that leaving his new bride so soon was remiss of him, then told himself, swiftly, that he was being overly defensive.

The London offices of Vikram, King, Farrow were located in a Georgian house, brick-built with wrought-iron balconies and a neat back garden, in Bloomsbury's handsome Bedford Square. Phil Bianco, the New Yorker who headed the London office as managing director, kept the two most beautiful ground floor rooms, complete with exquisite ceilings and fireplaces, for his own use, and his resident 'star' senior architects, Stephen Steerforth and Andrew MacNeice, had the other two most attractive offices. The remainder of the staff, permanent and short-term contract – junior architects, designers, draughtsmen, assistants and secretaries, as well as the tiny PR team and in-house bookkeeper – were closeted off by the kind of partitions that would have made the firm's clients cringe, had they ever been permitted to see them.

'You realize we've bent a whole bunch of rules to accommodate you?' Phil Bianco told Matthew during their first meeting in his office. 'More, I gather, because you're a pet of Laszlo King's than because of your skills.'

'According to Wolf Brautigen,' Matthew said, trying to ignore both the snub and his own instant wave of dislike for the man with snowy-white crew-cut hair and gold-framed designer glasses, 'this post was vacant and I was qualified for it.'

'Along with at least three British residents I could name,' Bianco said coldly.

*

29

'How did it go?' Karl called him that evening, aware this had been Matthew's first day at the London office.

'Not bad.' Matthew had showered and was in the bedroom, changing into a pair of jeans, and Caroline had told him to stay put while she made a couple of dry martinis and brought them upstairs.

'Did Bianco welcome you in person?'

'Oh, yes.'

'Poor Matt.'

'I didn't realize you knew him.'

'I asked around. He's well-known, it seems, for his charm.'

'Why didn't you warn me?'

'Would it have stopped you from moving to London if I had?'

Matthew thought of Caro, on her way up with their drinks.

'Absolutely not,' he said.

# 6

They settled down. The girls, back at school and in their normal routines, seemed better able, probably as a consequence of that, to cope with their new roles as stepdaughters. Flic returned to calm courtesy, and if some or all of that was an act, Matthew was still grateful for the effort; Chloë was as much a sweetheart as she had been on holiday and even Imogen's antagonism became less blatant.

'Let's have a party,' Caroline suggested in bed one night near the end of February. 'All those people wishing us well – maybe we ought to celebrate with them?' She slipped a leather bookmark into her new Ruth Rendell and laid it on her night-table.

'Are we talking big bash or just close friends?' Matthew picked up the TV remote control and turned off CNN. 'I'd certainly love to get Karl and Amelie over here, though I doubt that Ethan and Susan could make it.'

'I hope they can all make it,' Caroline said, 'or it'll be too one-sided.'

'At least I can meet all your friends, and some of the girls'.' He shook his head. 'Chloë's the only one who's ever brought anyone home since I've been here.'

Caro smiled. 'That's not because of you, darling. Imo's always preferred keeping her friends to herself, and Flic's a very independent girl.'

'But they do have good friends?'

'Of course they do.' Caroline hesitated. 'Chloë's best friend's called Beatrice Lang, a sweet, pretty girl. Imo has a wider circle,

31

though I suppose Nicola – from school – and Annie Pereira are the nearest she has to *best* friends.'

'And Flic?'

'Flic's problem, I think,' Caro said thoughtfully, 'is that she really is so mature for her age. Imo says she's very popular at school, and Flic never gripes about her classmates, but I get the feeling she may not really come into her own, socially, until she leaves The Grange and goes to university.' She paused. 'I suppose, too, that maybe because Imo and Flic are so close, they don't need outsiders as much.'

'University might change that,' Matthew said.

'Maybe.' Caroline returned to the subject of the party. 'We'll have to try and get Gabriel up to London.' Richard's father, Gabriel Walters, who lived a rather isolated life these days at his home in Devon, had been more than kind when she'd first broken the news to him. 'And Susanna's coming back next week,' she added, 'and she's dying to meet you.'

'Susanna?'

'Haven't I told you about Susanna?' Caroline looked surprised.

'I don't think so.'

'Susanna Durkin,' Caroline said. 'She's a psychotherapist and a dear friend. I met her years ago, while Richard was still alive. Then, after he died, when Imogen was going through her depression, Susanna counselled her wonderfully.'

'I didn't know Imogen suffered from depression.' Matthew felt a pang of guilt and surprise. 'Are we talking about depressed because of her father? Or clinical depression?'

'Both, I suppose,' Caro answered quietly. 'It was because Richard had died, and so of course we were all unhappy, that I didn't spot that Imo's problems were more serious.'

The guilt magnified. 'How could you not tell me this, Caro?' He was deeply perplexed. 'How could you let us go ahead and do something so guaranteed to upset any teenager *without* that kind of history, without us discussing it?'

Caroline's eyes were startled, wounded. 'It was Imo's private business. I didn't think it was right to tell you about it if she didn't want me to.'

'Okay.' Matthew considered that for a moment. 'But does the fact you're telling me now mean that Imogen's changed her mind or that you're ready to trust me with it?'

The wounded look grew more intense. 'You asked me about Susanna,' she said. 'Telling you about her and Imogen just came naturally.' She paused. 'It shouldn't have, I suppose.'

'So Imogen *doesn't* want me to know?' Matthew reached for her hand. 'Honey, if it sounds as if I'm giving you the third degree—'

'It does rather.' She took her hand away.

'I'm sorry. I just think it might have helped me to know. I'd have realized that I needed to be more patient with her.'

'Haven't you been patient?'

'I guess that isn't the right word. I mean, maybe I might have been more considerate of her feelings.'

'Imo isn't the type of girl who would want special treatment,' Caroline said. 'That's one of the reasons she wouldn't want you knowing.'

'So she *doesn't* want me to know?'

'No.' She paused. 'Now I don't know if I should have told you or not.' The hurt in her expression had gone, but instead there were creases of worry. 'This is all quite hard for me, darling, in some ways. Being a new wife and old mother, if you see what I mean. I didn't really consider that aspect before. These kinds of divided loyalties.'

A new, mild sense of disquiet struck him. What else had Caro not considered before? Or he, for that matter? Had they not, after all, committed an appallingly insensitive and selfish act in marrying so swiftly?

'Matthew?'

He shook his head slowly. 'It is hard for you.' A little of his disquiet drifted away. The deed was done, and wallowing in guilt wasn't going to help now any more than laying guilt trips on his wife. 'I can see that. And there'll be more of it, I'm afraid. It's inevitable.'

'But you're my husband. I should be able to tell you everything.'

'Able to, yes.' Matthew paused. 'I don't think that means you *have* to tell me everything. Especially not when it concerns other people's privacy.'

'But we're talking about our children, not other people,' Caroline said.

'No,' Matthew said, carefully but deliberately. 'Your children,

Caro. My stepdaughters.' He saw the hurt again, felt just a little irritated by it, disliked himself for feeling that way. 'Don't look like that, sweetheart. We're talking about *their* feelings now, not ours. So far as the girls are concerned, they regard themselves as your children, not mine. You know that as well as I do.'

Caroline nodded, pensively.

'Anything you feel you want to share with me, even if it is private,' he told her, 'I'll keep between the two of us. I promise you that.' He reached for her hand again, found it cold, squeezed it, and this time she did not pull away. 'But I'm saying it's okay for you to keep the girls' secrets, even from me.'

'Remarkable, isn't she?'

Matthew was standing watching Caroline three Saturday nights later at their party, when the low female voice spoke from behind him close to his left ear.

Susanna Durkin, to whom Caro had earlier introduced him briefly, was an imposing-looking woman with bold features, dark eyes with heavy brows, a prominent nose and a chin that jutted slightly, giving her a challenging look. She wore minimal make-up, just pale lipstick on her rather narrow mouth, the only weak part of her face – or any other part of her, Matthew decided.

'She certainly is,' he answered, looking back at the object of Susanna's admiration. Caroline was certainly on form, everything about her sparkling this evening, her slim figure and fine legs enhanced by the little black dress and lethally high-heeled shoes she'd bought for the occasion.

Susanna's eyes were still fixed on Caro. 'She looks happy.'

'I hope she is.' Matthew smiled. 'I know I am.'

Susanna inclined her face to look at him. 'Why wouldn't you be?'

He asked himself later if perhaps he'd imagined the sardonic tone, if he was getting into the habit of overreacting to the reactions of people close to Caroline, but he was, on reflection, pretty sure that the remark had been deliberately droll. And why not? he asked himself. Susanna was a close friend of his wife's, probably anxious that Caro had not made a grave mistake, and as a psychotherapist she was bound to peer a little more deeply than most.

'Isn't Susanna terrific?' Caroline asked him moments later as they passed each other, she carrying a tray of sushi, he carrying bottles of red and white wine.

'She certainly thinks you are,' he answered.

'Karl's a sweetheart, by the way.' Her gaze darted around the room, checking that guests were eating, drinking, mingling. 'I can't see him. Is he okay? Not worrying too much about Amelie?'

'He's fine. Probably in the dining room.'

Karl's wife had been planning to come over for the weekend, but she was pregnant again, and Karl had phoned to say that she'd had a touch of bleeding and that the doctor said everything was fine but flying was probably inadvisable. Matthew had told his friend to stay home with her and Heinz, but Karl had known that with Ethan and Susan unable to make the trip, he would be Matthew's only personal friend at the party, and had assured him there was no reason, thankfully, for him not to fly over for one night.

'If I were Amelie,' Caroline said now, 'I'm not sure I'd have been happy about your leaving me.'

'Apparently she pushed him to come.'

'Understanding woman.' Caro brushed his cheek with her own and left him in a soft cloud of Chanel.

Gabriel Walters, her former father-in-law, had decided against coming up from Devon, mostly, Caroline said, because he'd always disliked parties.

'I think you'd like Gabriel,' Sylvie told Matthew after he'd refilled her champagne glass a little later. 'He can be a bit of an old goat, but he's got a lovely sense of humour.'

Matthew smiled at his mother-in-law, had already told her how good she looked in her aquamarine silk suit, her legs almost as perfect as her daughter's.

'What do you think of Susanna?' Sylvie asked.

'I'm not sure. We've only spoken briefly.'

'Caro thinks she's the bee's knees,' she confided, 'but I'm not her greatest fan.' She glanced swiftly around. 'Bit pushy.'

Matthew grinned at her. 'Sylvie, may I ask a personal question?'

'You can try.'

'Why have you never remarried? It can't be for lack of admirers.'

'It hasn't been,' she said candidly, 'though thank you for the observation.'

'So why not?'

35

'Once bitten, as they say.' Sylvie chuckled. 'Or maybe I like men too much to want to ruin things for them and myself.'

'I hope that's not your opinion of marriage in general,' Matthew said.

'Oh, I rather think it is,' Sylvie said.

It seemed to Matthew that the evening spun on around him, that even whilst he was busy talking to guests, getting to know people, ensuring they were having a good time, he was still, inevitably, an outsider and an observer. Aethiopia was playing its part beautifully, he registered, Caroline in her element, the perfect hostess. Isabella and Mick, her husband, were helping, but as guests rather than staff, though Matthew wasn't sure if he liked the musician, and he didn't *think* it was the three rings through his left ear or the stubble on his face – more grubby than designer – but he couldn't help wondering how a man like that had made someone like Isabella fall for him.

But the high point of the evening was the way the girls were behaving towards him. Flic, as predicted by her mother, had invited no one, but was clearly entirely at ease with the older generation of guests. Annie Pereira, one of Imogen's close friends, had been asked to the party but had come down with flu, but Imo had a boyfriend in tow, while Chloë seemed to be having a marvellously giggly time with Beatrice Lang. They were all, unquestionably, thoroughly enjoying themselves, yet all three were still taking the time and trouble, somewhat to his surprise, to check, now and again, that Matthew was okay.

'Having a good time?' Flic, wearing a sleek ice-blue silk trouser suit, asked him as she relieved him of a tray of assorted crostini.

'The best,' he told her.

'Are you all right?' Chloë enquired a little later, with great tact, having introduced him to Beatrice, a very pretty, dark-haired girl with braces on her teeth and slanting eyes.

'I'm just great,' he told her.

'If you need me to introduce you to anyone, just ask,' she whispered.

He smiled. 'I sure will.'

Imogen's approach, upon later reflection, meant the most, especially since Matthew had, early on in the evening, happened upon her and her boyfriend – a nice-looking fair-haired young man of about sixteen – in mid-clinch in the narrow corridor by the study. The boyfriend, to his credit, had stepped away the instant he'd spotted Matthew, wiping his mouth in obvious embarrassment, but Imogen, predictably enough, had looked him squarely in the eye until he had smiled and turned away. And yet a half hour or so after that, she had come into the dining room, tugging the boyfriend by his hand to where Matthew was standing.

'Thought I'd better introduce you properly,' she said, raising her voice to be clearly heard over the din. 'Matthew, this is Tim.' She paused. 'Tim, this is Matthew, my mother's new husband.' She paused and grinned. 'My stepfather, I suppose that makes him.'

Not much, Matthew realized, from most people's perspective, but a public declaration, he felt, of something that just a few weeks ago would probably have made Imogen choke.

'Isn't that the one you've been most worried about?' Karl asked quietly a few moments later.

Matthew nodded.

'The breakthrough you've been hoping for, perhaps?'

'I hope so.'

His hopes seemed further consolidated when Isabella, taking photographs, sought him out in the kitchen where he was opening more bottles of white wine.

'You're needed in the drawing room, Matthew.'

'Be right there,' he said, drawing another cork.

'Now.' Isabella smiled. 'Caro said now.'

Caroline, her mother and the girls were waiting by one of the stained glass windows, Chloë holding Kahli by his collar.

'I found him,' Isabella said from behind him.

'Photo opportunity,' Sylvie told him as he approached. 'Family group.'

'Come on, darling,' Caroline said.

Matthew looked at Flic and Imogen, standing close on either side of their mother, and wondered who would make room for him.

'Come on, Matthew,' Flic said, and cleared a space.

He stepped forward, felt Caroline's hand slip into his and smiled with pleasure as the camera flashed once, then again.

'Isabella,' he said, 'give me the camera so I can take one of you with the rest of the family.'

'In a minute,' Flic said. 'Let's have one of you and us three first.'

It took Matthew a second to be sure.

'Come on, Matt,' Imogen stepped out from her mother's other side.

'Come on, Matty,' Chloë said, and giggled.

Caroline and Sylvie moved away. Behind Isabella, Matthew noticed some of the guests watching, smiling.

'Let's have me and Imo on either side of you,' Flic suggested. 'And Chloë in front, with Kahli – Chloë, you'd better kneel or you'll hide Matthew – you're getting so tall.' She paused. 'How's that, Isabella?'

'Lovely.'

Flic took Matthew's right arm, and then Imogen, on his left side, did the same, and his eyes grew moist, and he felt another rush of happiness.

Karl found him a few minutes later. 'Definitely a breakthrough, I'd say.'

'Looks like it,' Matthew agreed.

'I'm very happy for you, Matt.'

# 7

'You're lucky girls, I'd say,' John Pascoe, the gardener, told Flic two Saturday afternoons after the party, the last weekend of March.

They were sitting near the air-raid shelter at the bottom of the garden. They had always got along particularly well, the svelte Hampstead girl and the old man from Devon who had worked first for Gabriel Walters, and then, after a gap of more than a dozen years, for his son Richard. He had been many things to Richard, driver, handyman, decorator, courier, but Pascoe – old John, as he was most often referred to now by the family – had always derived his greatest pleasure from gardening. These days, with his eyesight, heart and back all starting to betray him, he still liked to potter, had insisted to Caroline that his doctor said there was nothing wrong in his taking a little exercise, especially since it was what his old body was accustomed to, and if she wouldn't let him go on taking care of Aethiopia's undemanding garden, he would just go home and do twice as much on his own allotment out in West Finchley.

Some days Pascoe would come into the house for lunch and tea, but more often he would bring up one of the fold-up chairs he kept down in the shelter and sit beneath his favourite willow tree, usually with Kahli close by, watching the birds at the feeding table he'd set up for Chloë about five years before. Richard's youngest still came out to see the birds when she remembered, but it was generally Flic who liked sitting with him under the willow, drinking the strong, muddy tea he made on his little primus stove down below in the concrete shelter.

'You're lucky,' he told her now, 'to have a decent chap like Matthew come and take care of you all.'

39

'Yes,' Flic agreed. 'We know.'

'Your mother looks well on it, I must say.' Despite all his London years, the West Country lilt still clung to old John's voice.

'Mum's very happy,' Flic said. 'We all are, really.'

'Must have been a bit hard on you, to start with.'

'A bit, perhaps. But we could see how Mum felt, knew how lonely she'd been.'

'So you made him welcome, like the kind girls you are.'

'I suppose so, yes. I hope so.' Flic paused. 'I sometimes get the feeling Matthew's not quite as happy as Mum though.'

'Really?' Pascoe was surprised.

'I don't mean that he doesn't love her, nothing like that. It's just with us.'

'How d'you mean?'

'I don't think I mean anything in particular.' Flic paused again, seeking the right words. 'It's just a feeling. I'm not quite sure he's all that keen on having us around, that's all.'

'Well, I must say, I am surprised by that. He always gives me the idea that you all matter to him a good deal. All you girls.' He shook his shaggy white head. 'Mind, it'll be hard for him too in some ways. Young chap like that. And an American. Not easy. You need to remember that, make allowances.'

'I will,' Flic said. 'We all will.'


Early the following Sunday evening – Mothering Sunday, complete with flowers, cards and an excellent lunch that the girls had put together for Caroline and Sylvie without any help from Isabella, who was home with Mick; a day that had already, from Matthew's perspective, been altogether heartening – Flic came to the study, where he was dealing with overdue correspondence, to ask if he wanted to join her and Kahli for a short walk on the Heath.

'Sure.' He glanced at his watch.

'BST, remember?' Flic said. 'Stays light longer.'

'Who else is coming?'

'No one,' she said from the doorway. 'Mum's snoozing in front of the fire, Imo's holed up in her room and Chloë's doing a still life.' Sylvie had gone home a while ago. 'So it's just us, if you don't mind.'

'Not one bit,' he said.

\*

40

Things really were looking up, he decided with pleasure as he found his boots and the green waxed jacket Caroline had urged him to buy a fortnight ago. He had not much looked forward to their earlier family outing that same day to Hampstead Cemetery. His stepdaughters went regularly – sometimes with their mother or grandmother, sometimes alone – to Richard's grave, but until yesterday, no one had suggested he might like to go along and he hadn't thought it appropriate to suggest it.

'We'll all understand,' Caro had said to him tentatively after dinner, 'if you'd rather not come. But the girls wanted you to know that you would be very welcome, if you did want to.'

'Of course I'd like to come,' he'd told her. 'If they're sure.'

'You know my girls,' Caroline had replied. 'If they weren't, they wouldn't have made a point of asking.'

Standing in the cemetery, observing them by the grave, their sense of love for the man whose mortal remains lay beneath the earth had never felt stronger to Matthew. Richard's women had stood in a tight semi-circle, holding hands, looking silently down at the granite slab engraved '*RICHARD GABRIEL WALTERS* – *Artist, son, husband and father*', and a surge of emotion had seemed to flow back through the air to Matthew, standing a little distance away.

Sylvie had come away first. 'I always like to give them a little time alone,' she'd said quietly. 'Not so much for Caro, but for the girls.'

'Caro misses him, too,' Matthew had said. 'I understand that.'

'Caro's much better than she was. Thanks to you.'

It had been exactly what he'd needed to hear at that moment – and then, soon after, as they'd all walked back to the Range Rover, Chloë had taken his left hand, and just a moment later, Flic had come to his other side and taken his arm. And Matthew had caught Caroline's eye, seen her happiness, and shared it.

It was almost seven o'clock when they crossed East Heath Road, made their way onto the Heath and walked on a little way, getting clear of the road and traffic, before Flic unclipped Kahli's lead to let him run on ahead.

'Did you know,' she said as they walked, 'that hundreds of years ago wolves used to roam around here?'

Matthew did know because Caroline had told him.

41

'No,' he said. 'I didn't know that.'

'And the Vale of Health – which is just west of our house – was a malarial-ridden marsh by the eighteenth century.'

'I read somewhere,' he said, wanting to contribute a level of interest, 'that Hampstead got a mention in the Domesday Book.'

'Called Hamestede,' Flic said.

'I'm impressed,' Matthew said. 'I didn't know you were such a history buff.'

'I'm not especially,' she said. 'But my father taught me all about Hampstead.'

They had been walking and talking and throwing sticks for Kahli, taking time out to observe a family football match and watching the retriever ward off the attentions of a grey standard poodle, when suddenly Flic let out a low cry of dismay.

'What's wrong?'

'My bracelet.' Her distress was evident. 'It's gone – it must have fallen off.' She hunched over, her long hair falling into her face, scanning the grass around her feet. 'I *can't* lose that, I just can't . . .'

'Are you sure you were wearing it?'

'Of course I'm sure.' She roamed around, head still down, searching. 'I always wear it. My father gave it to me, it was his very last gift to me.'

'Okay.' Matthew made his tone positive. 'We'll find it.' He paused. 'Tell me what it's like.'

'It's a *bracelet*,' she flung impatiently, then shook her head, brushed her hair out of her eyes, bit her lip. 'It's gold, little narrow bars of gold. Dad had my initials and birth date engraved on two of the bars.' Her eyes filled with tears. 'Oh, God, I should *never* have worn it on a walk like this.'

'If you always wear it, why would you even think about it.' Matthew had never seen Flic weep. He had an impulse to put his arms around her, but he realized that the best way for him to comfort her would be to find the bracelet. 'We'll have to back-track,' he said. 'Take a few seconds, try and think where it might have happened? Did you catch your sleeve on anything?'

Flic shut her eyes, felt her right wrist, shook her head. 'Not that I remember.'

42

'Never mind. We'll just go back. It'll be okay, we'll find it.'

'I hope so.'

'How about I keep my head down and look, while you navigate?' He grinned. 'I'm not known for my sense of direction.'

'Fine.'

They turned around and the wind, chilly for early April, nipped meanly at their faces.

'I don't suppose Kahli's a good tracker, is he?'

Flic shook her head. 'He can manage the odd stick or ball, but he's never been trained to really search for things.'

'Not much point starting now then.'

'Oh, Matthew, I'm sorry.' A gust whipped her hair in a fan around her face.

'What for? Could happen to anyone.' He took a look back the way they'd come, then bent his head and began walking slowly, scanning every hummock and dip.

'This is very nice of you,' Flic said.

'It was your dad's last gift,' he said. 'It's important.' Something caught his eye, and he squatted momentarily, pushed aside a clump of weeds with his gloved fingers, saw it was just a stone, moisture on it catching the dull light. 'I guess that would have been too easy.'

'It's no good,' Flic said a while later.

'We're not giving up yet.' Matthew was beginning to lose heart too, but he didn't want to admit defeat until they had no choice – though dusk was starting to settle over the Heath, making the search even harder.

'Damn.' She picked up a stick. 'Damn, damn, *damn*.' With the last, she flung the stick hard into the air and Kahli, barking madly, went after it. 'Oh, God,' she said, 'I shouldn't have done that.'

'Why not?' Matthew straightened up. 'He'll just bring it back.'

'Maybe not,' Flic said. 'There are some marshy pools that way.' She peered after the dog, but he'd disappeared, called his name loudly, then winced. 'He got himself stuck once, a couple of years ago. I'll have to go after him.'

'I'll come with you.'

'No,' she said, quickly. 'Please, if you don't mind, please go on looking for the bracelet. I'll go and find him, bring him back.'

43

Matthew looked up at the sky, saw scudding, thickening clouds. 'It's getting dark, Flic, and it's going to rain.'

'I don't mind getting wet if you don't,' she said.

It sounded like a challenge.

'Please, Matthew.' Desperate again. 'I couldn't bear to think we hadn't done all we could to find it.'

'Okay,' he said. 'Just be careful. I know the bracelet's important, but your safety's a whole lot *more* important. We can always come back tomorrow if we don't have any luck today.'

'You'll be at work tomorrow, and I'll have school.'

'Yeah.' He was beaten. 'Okay.'

She started after Kahli, then stopped, turned back. 'You don't really mind, do you, Matthew? I promise to be quick as I can.'

'Just go,' he said. 'I'll keep searching.'

It was a good ten minutes or so later that he realized he no longer knew where he was in relation to East Heath Road.

In fact, he didn't know where he was, period. And there was no sign of Flic or of the dog.

And it was getting darker by the minute.

He looked around, trying to get his bearings.

Hopeless.

From his current perspective, the Heath was a goddamned wilderness. That come nightfall would presumably turn inhospitably dark and spooky.

*Flic and Kahli will be back soon.*

Unless the dog had gone and got himself stuck in one of those marshy pools.

He looked down at his feet, lifted his left boot and put it down again experimentally. Firm enough here.

*Look for the bracelet.*

Time passed. It became darker, began to rain, the wind heightened, the Heath felt increasingly unfriendly. No sign of the bracelet, and by now Matthew had frankly ceased looking for it, being far more concerned with finding Flic and Kahli. He had started calling for them both a while back, had graduated to yelling at the top of his voice, but the strengthening howl of the wind and the trees groaning and creaking and the swishing of grasses and weeds had obliterated any replies that might have come.

Some kind of animal, too. Not a dog. Higher pitched. Maybe a fox?

What was it you called a whole bunch of foxes?

'Flic!' he yelled again, into the rain. '*Felicity!*'

Wolves used to roam around here, she had said.

Hundreds of years ago, he reminded himself.

And then a thought of something a thousand times more alarming than a whole pack of wolves came to him.

What would Caroline say when he told her he'd lost her daughter?

All the lights in the house were ablaze when, at long last, he trudged wearily across the road and up the path to the front door and stuck his Yale key into the lock.

The door opened before he'd even turned it.

'Matthew, thank God!' Flic flung her arms around him.

'You're okay!' He hugged her back out of sheer relief, then stepped back to look at her. Her hair was wrapped in a towel turban and she wore a pale blue bathrobe, and there was Kahli right behind her, not a sign of marsh or even grass on his freshly brushed coat.

'Matty, you're okay!' Chloë ran from the kitchen, threw her arms around him too, while he kicked the front door closed behind him with one muddy boot, shutting out the awful night. 'You're so *filthy* – did you fall in a pond or something?'

'Mum!' Imogen, over at the foot of the staircase, called up. 'He's back!'

'Mum's been going out of her mind worrying about you,' Flic told him. 'We all have, haven't we, Imo?'

A door banged upstairs, and footsteps hurried overhead.

'Mum's been in a hell of a state,' Imogen said. 'She wanted to call the police and get up a search party, but we told her you were probably just lost.'

'He fell in a pond,' Chloë said. 'He could have drowned.'

'I didn't fall in any pond, sweetheart,' Matthew assured her. 'It's just not a great night for traipsing around on the Heath.'

Caroline flew down the staircase and straight into his arms. 'Thank God, oh, thank God.' Her voice was muffled against his wax jacket.

'You're going to get dirty, Caro.' He kissed the top of her head. 'I'm fine.'

She pulled away. 'What *happened*? Where *were* you? Flic and Khali came back ages ago – Flic was sure you'd have been back before them.'

'I got lost,' Matthew said simply. 'I didn't know what had happened to Flic, so I went on looking for her.'

'Anything could have happened to you.' Caroline led him into the drawing room, took his gloves, helped him off with his jacket, propelled him towards the log fire and pushed him down into one of the armchairs. 'You could have fallen, broken your leg, not been found till daylight. You could have got *hypothermia*.'

'But I didn't. I'm okay.' He wanted to stay just like that, collapsed on those soft cushions, shut his eyes and go straight off to sleep, but Caro was still visibly distraught so he made a last effort, reached down and pulled off both his boots, pushing them over onto their sides to spare the Persian carpet, though it was, of course, too late for that. 'I've got dirt all over the rugs, I'm sorry.'

'Who cares about the rugs?' Caroline handed his jacket to Chloë, who carried it back out into the hall. 'All that matters is that you're all right.'

'I am now.' He leaned back again and smiled at her anxious face, saw Flic and Imogen hovering behind her. 'It was just one of those dumb things, a chapter of accidents—'

'Accidents?' Caroline knelt beside his chair.

'Just a manner of speaking.' He put out a hand and stroked her pale cheek. 'First the thing with the bracelet, then Kahli shooting off like that . . .' His gaze fell on Flic's right wrist, on the gleam of a gold bracelet hanging just below the cuff of her robe. 'You found it?'

'Yes, isn't it wonderful?' she said. 'Just after I got Kahli back on his lead. I was so relieved to find him safe and sound, and I wasn't even looking for the bracelet any more, and suddenly there it was, right there by my feet. Incredible.'

'Amazing,' Matthew said. He looked back at the bracelet, wasn't certain if he'd ever seen it before, though then again, he wasn't the kind of man to notice that sort of thing. 'The clasp's okay?'

'Absolutely. It must have just fallen off.' Flic's smile was radiant. 'I wanted to tell you to stop looking, but then I realized I'd run further than I'd meant to, and it was getting dark, so I knew the

46

only sensible thing to do was come home, and I was sure you'd have the sense to do the same.'

'I would have,' Matthew said, quietly, 'if I hadn't been looking for you.'

'I'm sorry,' Flic said.

'Poor darling,' Caroline said.

'And it might have helped if I'd known how to get back,' he added.

Chloë had come back, and Imogen was now standing in the doorway, leaning against the jamb, listening and watching with silent interest, and Matthew was about to say more, but then Caroline stood up and started fussing around, telling Flic to go and make a pot of tea and Chloë to fetch a towel for his hair, asking him if he wanted to go up and get out of his clothes, or have a whisky and some tea first. What he *really* wanted, Matthew thought, was to take a glass of whisky and hot water upstairs, strip off and lie down on their bed, alone, to mull over the truth of what had happened out there on the Heath. But his wife's eyes were still anxious and he didn't have the heart to say he wanted to be by himself.

So it was almost two hours later (after everyone had calmed down and he'd had a long, hot shower and some oxtail soup, and Caro was upstairs getting ready for bed, and Imogen and Chloë were both in their rooms) before Flic came into the kitchen as he was making himself a late-night cup of decaf.

'Not sleepy?' he asked her.

'Not at all,' she answered.

'Want a cup?' he offered.

'No, thanks.' She glanced at Kahli, who was lying on his beanbag bed in the corner. 'Did you let him out for his last pee?'

'I did.' Matthew poured a little skimmed milk into one of the mugs that hung on hooks over the dresser.

'No ill-effects, I hope?' Flic said. 'After the fiasco.'

'All's well,' he said, mildly. 'Though I think I do remember telling you about my sense of direction.'

'So you did,' Flic said, and smiled.

# 8

'You really think she wanted you to get lost?'

'I don't know, but I do think she never lost the bracelet at all.'

'Surely not?'

'There's no doubt in my mind, Karl.'

'It sounds a little far-fetched, Matt.'

'I know.' Matthew paused. 'Don't you think I'd rather tell myself I'm wrong? That I'm reading too much into a genuine accident?'

'You're upset,' Karl said, kindly.

'What I am' – Matthew kept his voice low – 'is pissed off.'

It was after six-thirty on Monday evening, and there was no one else around in the open plan office on the second floor where Matthew and the other junior architects worked in their cubicles, but he could not be certain there was no one else in the building working late and in earshot. Vikram, King, Farrow after hours was the only place where Matthew had felt free to discuss the bracelet incident.

'I'm mostly pissed off because I thought we were over our teething troubles, and I'm pissed off at myself because maybe it's my fault that she still dislikes me enough to play that kind of a game.'

'A nasty kind of game,' Karl commented.

'But just a game.' Matthew was at least clear on that score. 'I'm not suggesting for an instant that Flic wanted to get me hurt. I think she probably meant to shake me up a little. Most of all, she wanted to make me look like a horse's ass.'

'I don't understand why you haven't talked to Caroline about it.'

'Because it's my problem, and because it would upset her.'

'Perhaps you're mistaken,' Karl said. 'Maybe Flic really did lose the bracelet, just as she said she did.'

There it was, Matthew reflected after the call, sitting staring into space. The main reason for his not having talked over his thoughts with his wife. Karl was his best friend, had no reason to take the girls' side over his, and yet even *he* felt Matthew might be seeing problems where none existed. Caro was their mother.

'Working late?'

Matthew swivelled around and saw Phil Bianco in the entrance to his cubicle.

'Just finishing up,' Matthew said.

'And making personal calls?' The frames of the MD's glasses glinted gold.

'I was calling a friend in Berlin,' Matthew told him steadily. 'I used my own AT&T card.'

'Good,' Bianco said. 'Though we do prefer it if personnel use their offices for work purposes only.'

'I'll bear that in mind,' Matthew said.

That wasn't helping much either, he mused as he walked out of Bedford Square into Bayley Street; Bianco's continuing apparent resentment of his presence in London.

*Apparent.*

Matthew analysed his thoughts as he turned into Tottenham Court Road and headed north towards Goodge Street station and the tube journey home. He hoped he wasn't becoming paranoid, either on the work or home fronts. There was, of course, no real reason for the MD to resent him, and even if Bianco did feel he'd been foisted on him because Laszlo King had a soft spot for him, Matthew was sure that the London MD could have vetoed the transfer if he'd chosen to.

Matthew entered the underground station, used his travel card and hurried into one of the lifts that carried passengers to and from the platforms. It was not paranoia, he decided, getting out of the lift and making his way to the trains, that made him feel Bianco didn't like him – not that the guy showed signs of liking *any* of the junior architects. Probably, Matthew concluded, he was just a cold fish who regarded displays of kindness at work as a waste of time and effort.

The Edgware-bound train came into the station and he got on and found a seat. The problem was, none of these things were helping him settle down. Neither Bianco's chilliness, nor being dumped into the mopping-up stage of an uninspired shopping complex in Clapham (his penance, presumably, for the flakiness of his move), nor finding most of his colleagues less friendly and motivating than those he'd worked with in Berlin and New York. Though perhaps, he decided as the train thundered through the dark tunnel, the stand-offishness was just a 'last-man-in' thing, in which case time would take care of it, might even soften Bianco's opinion of him.

He wished he could feel as confident about his stepdaughters.

He arrived at Aethiopia to find Susanna Durkin sitting at the kitchen table with Caroline, three-quarters of the way through a pizza and drinking red wine.

'Did I forget an arrangement?' He shook Susanna's hand and bent to kiss his wife's cheek. 'If I did, I apologize for being late.'

'No arrangement,' Susanna answered. 'Just a spur-of-the-moment impulse of mine to show up with pizza and Chianti.' She smiled up at him. 'I hope you don't mind too much.'

'Susanna actually brought two pizzas,' Caroline said, 'but the girls pinched the second one and took it up to the attic with a video.'

'Poor Matthew,' Susanna said.

'I'll make you something as soon as you're ready,' Caroline said.

'You relax,' he told her. 'I'll make myself something after I've taken a shower.'

'Don't rush,' Susanna told him. 'Caro and I are never short of conversation.'

At the door, Matthew paused. 'I didn't know Flic had installed a TV up there.'

'Oh, yes,' Caroline told him. 'She's made it quite cosy now. TV and VCR – even one of those DVP things.'

Matthew smiled. 'DVD.'

'Caro's a dreadful technophobe,' Susanna said. 'We both are.'

Matthew waited for his wife to set her straight, but she said nothing. 'I wouldn't say that's true of Caro. She knows her way around our PC better than I do.'

'Your husband thinks you need flattery,' Susanna said to Caroline.

'No,' Matthew said coolly. 'I just respect Caro's abilities.'

'I'm glad to hear it,' Susanna said.

The evening progressed irritatingly from his perspective. In addition to dinner, Susanna had also brought Caroline the offer of a commission for cushion covers and wall-coverings from a shop on Muswell Hill Broadway, close to where she lived and worked.

'Sounds terrific,' Matthew remarked, making himself an omelette.

'It's important to Caro, you know,' Susanna told him, 'to be *doing*.' She made it sound as if he might not be able to comprehend that. 'Something independent.'

'As I said, I think it's terrific.' He looked directly at Caroline. 'Will these be similar to your previous work, or is it a new concept?'

'They'll be in my usual style, I suppose,' Caroline answered, 'but all the designs are to be linked with local history.'

'There was a well in Muswell Hill, I gather,' Susanna reasserted herself, 'back in the twelfth century, that was supposed to have healing properties. Do you know the area, Matthew?'

'Not yet.' He flipped his omelette, poured himself a glass of white wine from the fridge, brought the bottle across to offer to the women.

'I think we've had enough,' Susanna said.

He ignored her. 'Caro?'

'Not for me either, darling.'

'No hangovers for you,' Susanna said, 'with all that work to do.'

'They want a dozen cushion covers,' Caroline explained to him, 'and three of the wall-coverings to begin with.'

'So she'll be working flat out for quite a while,' Susanna said.

'Why do you let her do that?' Matthew asked Caroline later in bed.

'Do what?'

'Answer questions for you.'

'She doesn't.' Caroline seemed surprised. 'Does she?'

51

'She did this evening.'

She had been studying one of her old patterns, a pair of glasses perched on the end of her nose. Now she took off the glasses and put down the pattern. 'I had a feeling you didn't like her.'

'I'm not sure I like the way she tries to take over all the time,' he admitted. 'It's unusual for a shrink. The ones I've met seem to say as little as possible.'

'They prefer you to talk.' Caroline glanced sideways at him. 'You've seen shrinks? Though by the way, Susanna hates being called that.'

'I did see one, a couple of times, after Jillian filed for divorce.'

'Her idea?'

'Actually mine,' Matthew said. 'I was sad and confused, and a friend suggested I see someone.'

'Did it help?'

Matthew grinned. 'Not really.'

'Maybe that's why you dislike Susanna.'

'I think dislike's too strong a word,' he said.

'Good,' she said. 'Because she's been a very good friend to me.'

'I know.' He felt a touch of remorse. 'Good friends are hard to come by.'

'You miss Karl, don't you?' Caroline said.

'We speak regularly.'

'I know, but it's not quite the same, is it?'

'No, it isn't,' he agreed.

She snuggled up, kissed his left shoulder. 'I hope I'm your best friend now. I feel that you're mine.'

'I'd like to think so.' He kissed her on the mouth.

They began to make love a moment or two later, and afterwards Caroline went straight to sleep and, drifting off himself, Matthew remembered his talk with Karl at the office, and wondered why he hadn't mentioned it to Caro.

He knew why, of course. Because of the subject matter.

The bracelet.

*Forget the bracelet.*

He went to sleep.

# 9

Over the next month, Matthew became keenly aware of a shift in the atmosphere between himself and the girls. Like sound being edged up to a higher pitch that was painful to him, but that others could not hear. He and Ethan had had a great-aunt named Alice who had, during their boyhood, often complained about noises in her head. Years later he had realized that it had almost certainly been tinnitus, her suffering probably acute and very real. But back then no one had seemed to believe her, perhaps simply because no one else had been able to hear the misery-inducing sounds.

He'd found himself thinking of Great-Aunt Alice quite often lately.

Not that his problems had anything to do with sounds. Just nastiness. A particular kind of nastiness that he could, had he chosen to, have ended or at least diluted simply by talking to Caroline about it. And yet, as April gave way to May, Matthew still hoped not to have to do that.

Caroline was a more vulnerable person than he had realized at the beginning of their relationship. Had anyone suggested to him at the time that she might have a streak of weakness, Matthew would have slammed the notion immediately, for the very dynamism of their love affair and wedding had, he thought, shown both determination and forcefulness. Lord knew he had no regrets about the marriage – he loved Caro more than ever – but accompanying the sensitivity which he cherished, *was* a certain weakness. Her threshold of psychological pain seemed quite low, her hopes, in certain respects, unrealistic, in that she wanted everyone she cared about to get along, was dismayed if they so much as argued. She coped well enough with her daughters' internal spats, seemed to accept them as a natural part of the growing-up process. But anything more serious than that upset her badly. And because Matthew loved Caroline and was himself soft-hearted, he hated seeing her upset.

Though the time was coming, he realized, when he might have no choice but to tell her what was going on under her own roof.

Flic was the instigator, of that he had no real doubt. Imogen's dislike of him was more overt, more obviously passionate, her older sister's contempt less outwardly vehement. Yet Flic was the brains behind their campaign against him.

The tricks played on him since the bracelet incident had been *just* small enough to have made him appear petty had he complained about them. Telephone messages were not passed on to him; insignificant for the most part, except that in two cases his lack of response had brought fresh aggravation at VKF. Several letters left by Matthew on the hall table for posting – a general family arrangement – had never reached their destination. The first, a note to his former bank in Berlin, he had assumed simply lost; but then a clutch of late-payment requests had arrived, and finally Ethan had called to chide him for forgetting to send the twins birthday cards (which Matthew had most decidedly *not* forgotten, and which cards had also contained instructions for Andy and Teddy to go to FAO Schwarz to collect gifts ordered for them).

A rat, he had decided.

Possibly two.

Remembering precisely which day he'd left the kids' envelopes for posting, he had checked with Isabella, who usually took care of such tasks for the whole family.

'I posted everything on the table,' she'd told him, 'but there was nothing for the United States.'

'There should have been two envelopes, medium-sized and blue, I think.'

'Nothing like that,' Isabella had said firmly. 'I would remember, I'm sure.'

'I'm sure you would,' Matthew had agreed. 'I must be mistaken.'

He had known he was not mistaken, had found himself briefly wondering if perhaps it might be Isabella who had deliberately failed to post his letters or pass on the messages. But even allowing for the possibility that the generally charming housekeeper *might* not be entirely happy about the altered balance of Caro's household, might be harbouring private resentments against him, Matthew doubted that she would stoop to such a juvenile level. Whereas these were probably just the kind of stunts petulant teenagers might pull.

Still, it had seemed absurd to interrogate the household for the sake of a few items of mail, so he had simply bought belated birthday cards, called the twins to explain, paid the interest on his credit card payments as requested, and kept silent.

And then he'd become aware that items of mail sent *to* him had begun going astray. On weekdays, Matthew was gone before the postman called at the house, but one Saturday morning he picked the mail up from the mat and opened a letter from his embassy, asking why he had not replied to their previous enquiry appertaining to his immigration status, and then another from David Munro – Caroline's accountant – gently chastising him for ignoring his last *two* letters.

Still, Matthew elected not to exaggerate the issue, simply posed a couple of casual questions over dinner one weekend, enquiring if someone might have accidentally picked up items of his mail with their own.

'Hardly,' Caroline had replied. 'If we had, we'd have given them to you.'

'It's not a mistake we're likely to make,' Flic had pointed out, 'since we don't have the same surname.'

'Mummy does,' Chloë had said.

'We know,' Imogen had said.

One evening in mid-May, Susanna, back from Tuscany, telephoned Caroline to say that she hoped that her postcard had arrived. Caroline told her it had not.

'That's odd,' Susanna said, 'because I made a point of putting their equivalent of a first-class stamp on it, since it was a photo I particularly wanted you to have. A *trecento* Madonna who – so they say – was finished by an angel after the artist fainted while painting her face. She so reminded me of you, Caro, I could hardly believe it. I do hope she arrives.'

She phoned every day for a week after that, asking if it had come, until finally, at the Sunday lunch table, Matthew suggested that if the wretched card failed to materialize, Caro should put Susanna out of her misery by telling her she'd found a photograph of the painting in a book.

'Actually,' Flic said suddenly, 'I think I've seen it.'

'The painting, you mean?' Sylvie asked.

'The postcard,' she said.

'So it did arrive,' Caroline said, bemused. 'Where did you put it, Flic?'

'Nowhere,' Flic answered. 'I just remember seeing it.' She turned to look at Matthew, who was spooning roast potatoes onto his plate. 'Didn't you have it?'

'No.' He put down the spoon and accepted the gravy boat from Chloë.

'Yes, I'm sure you did,' Flic insisted. 'Now I come to think of it, I think I saw you carrying it into Dad's study.' She winced apologetically. 'Sorry, I keep doing that. I mean *your* study.'

'Don't worry about it,' Matthew said easily. 'But I didn't see any postcard.'

'Maybe you didn't actually notice it,' Flic persisted, 'but you were carrying a bunch of papers at the time, and the postcard – this picture of the Madonna – was right at the front, I'm sure of it.'

'Perhaps you should go and have a look,' Imogen suggested.

'I think it can probably wait till we've finished lunch,' Caroline said.

'Of course it can wait,' Sylvie said. 'Such a fuss about a post-card.'

'You said it,' Matthew agreed, 'not me.'

'Don't you like Susanna?' Imogen picked up on his tone.

'I don't know her very well,' Matthew answered.

'I don't like her very much,' Chloë said.

'Really?' Caroline was surprised and disappointed. 'You've never said so before, darling.'

Chloë shrugged and popped a piece of roast lamb into her mouth, and Sylvie grinned at Matthew, who figured the time had come to change the subject, and asked Caroline how her work had gone that morning.

'Very well,' she answered. 'I'm loving it.' Her eyes still rested on her youngest child. 'Thanks to Susanna,' she added.

Matthew had almost forgotten about the postcard by the time they'd finished the *tarte tatin* that Sylvie had picked up for them on her way. Caroline was asking Imogen to help with the washing up, and Imo was, as usual, making excuses, and Matthew told Caro he was in the mood for dishes, and Sylvie said that she could not recall *ever* being in the mood for washing up, and Chloë asked her grandmother if she'd come out for a walk with Kahli, but Sylvie said that it was raining, and she wasn't having her hair done again till Tuesday, so a walk was out of the question.

'Found it.'

They all turned to look. Flic stood in the doorway, holding up a postcard and smiling. 'Told you I'd seen you with it,' she said to Matthew.

'Where was it?' he asked as she handed it to her mother.

'On the desk in the study,' she said. 'Under a pile of stuff in a tray.'

'You shouldn't have looked through Matthew's things without asking him,' Caroline rebuked her mildly.

'Sorry,' Flic said.

Matthew regarded her, coolly and briefly, then deliberately transferred his gaze to his wife. 'Seems I'm more absent-minded than I thought.'

'It doesn't matter.' She brought over the card to show him. 'It is a lovely painting,' she said, 'but really not worth all that fuss, and it certainly doesn't look anything like me.'

'Why are you showing it to him?' Imogen asked. 'He's obviously seen it.'

'Imogen.' Sylvie gave her a sharp look. 'You're being rude.'

'I found something else too,' Flic said, 'while I was looking.'

'Did you now?' Matthew said, proceeding with the washing up.

'Two envelopes addressed to your nephews.'

Anger was rising inside him slowly, steadily, like water heating in a kettle, but he suppressed it, picked up a sponge and squeezed Fairy Liquid onto it.

'Your birthday cards, darling.' Caroline sounded as if he ought to have been pleased to find them.

'The ones you were asking Isabella about,' Flic said.

'Just leave them on the table, please,' Matthew told her.

'Didn't you say some other letters had gone missing too?' Flic asked him.

'Maybe Flic should go on looking?' Imogen suggested.

'Maybe Flic should mind her own business,' Sylvie remarked.

'That's a bit harsh, Mama,' Caroline said.

'How about giving me a hand here, Chloë?' Matthew said.

'I wanted to take Kahli out.'

'Fine,' he said. 'Then how about the rest of you go do whatever you want, and I'll finish up here in peace and quiet.'

'The girls should help you,' Caroline said. 'I really need to go up to the Quiet Room and carry on working.'

'You do that.' Matthew glanced at her, saw that his crispness had surprised her, pricked her over-sensitive skin, decided that for once that was just too bad.

He washed and dried every piece of crockery and cutlery by hand and polished the glasses till they sparkled. They had a dishwasher, but on this occasion, so far as he was concerned, he needed the therapy.

And then he left the kitchen, passed the drawing room, saw Sylvie and Imogen watching television, and went upstairs to Flic's room.

He knocked.

'Come in.'

She was sitting on the end of her bed. The bedspread was patterned in white and lilac, the colour theme for the whole room. It was a charming bedroom, the embodiment of innocent femininity.

Matthew felt slightly nauseated.

'I have just one thing to say to you, Flic.'

'What's that, Matthew?' She looked utterly calm.

'You may not be aware, but it is an offence – actually a crime – to tamper with other people's mail.'

'Yes.' Still unruffled.

'Keep out of my things in future, please, Flic,' he told her, quietly. 'Do not touch my mail or any of my property, and kindly stay out of my study.' He paused. 'I repeat, *my* study.'

That got through. He saw it in her eyes and in the slight flush on her cheeks.

'Do we understand each other?' he asked.

'I certainly understand you,' she said.

58

# 10

They went too far.

Caroline had a food allergy. She had mentioned it to him in Switzerland after cautiously checking the ingredients of a fruit salad. Mangoes, she had told him, made her sick.

'Badly sick,' she had said. 'With a rash.'

'Is that common?' he'd asked her. 'I never heard of it before.'

'I don't know.' She'd shrugged. 'I used to love them, too.'

So, no mangoes. Matthew knew it, as did Caro's daughters, and Sylvie, and, of course, Isabella, who did so much of the family's shopping and cooking.

Not, therefore, a mistake that could easily be made.

It was Thursday, the twenty-fifth of May, just a few days after the unpleasantness with the letters. Matthew and Flic had been coolly polite to each other since, but feeling that he had now made his stand clearly to her, he was hoping they might start to move on. Isabella was off supporting Mick, who had a gig in south London that evening, and Caroline was becoming anxious about her commission. The sewing, which had till recently been a relaxation for her, had been giving her bad headaches over the last few weeks, and now her stress was being exacerbated because the shop in Muswell Hill was agitating for early delivery.

'I just can't think about cooking,' she had said to Matthew that morning, while he and the girls were finishing up their breakfasts. She never ate at that time, had a cup of coffee at most. Flic had muesli most mornings, Imogen had toast and Chloë had Sugar

59

Puffs and fresh grapefruit. They were usually quiet first thing, focused on the small TV that stood on the island unit in the middle of the kitchen.

'No problem,' he had told Caroline. 'I'll cook.'

'Are you sure, darling? I'd suggest take-away, but the girls have been having too much junk lately.'

'I like cooking,' Matthew had said.

'Nothing special, just something simple.'

'Leave it with me.'

'How about Chinese?' Flic suggested.

'I said no take-away, darling,' Caroline said.

'I meant home-made Chinese.'

'Don't be silly,' Caroline said. 'That's much too complicated.'

'Actually,' Matthew said, 'I know a rather good Chinese recipe, and it's not at all hard to pull together.'

'We don't have a wok,' Imogen said.

'My recipe doesn't need a work,' Matthew told her. 'It's a kind of a hotpot.' He stood and carried his plate, cup and saucer to the sink. 'I'll shop on the way home.'

'You're making me feel very guilty,' Caroline said. 'If you have a bad day . . .'

'If I have a bad day, then I'll change my mind and make pasta.'

'Yuck,' Chloë said.

Matthew grinned at her. 'It's okay, honey. It'll be my Special-Sweet'n Sour-Almost-Chinese-Hotpot.' He glanced at the other two. 'Anyone who doesn't like sweet and sour speak now.'

The shopping was a pleasure. Between Cullens and two of the small multi-ethnic grocery shops near Goodge Street, he found all he needed and ended up with two big plastic carriers jammed between his feet on the tube home.

'Let me help,' Caroline said, watching him unpack and organize himself in the kitchen, Kahli intensely interested in the smells. 'Or let the girls help.'

'They have homework, and I like cooking solo, especially when I'm being creative. So you get on back upstairs to your cushions and leave me to it.'

'I'm hungry already.' Chloë came in as her mother was leaving.

'Tough.' Matthew hefted their biggest casserole out of a cupboard and shooed her out of the kitchen. 'Man at work, sweetheart.'

He set to, chopping, rinsing, cleaning up after himself as he went. He was always tidy at the start of a cooking spree, lining items up in rough order of use: skinned and boned chicken thighs and breasts, bamboo shoots, ginger, spring onions, garlic, fresh apricots, lemons, honey, coriander, rock salt and chilli peppers.

'Looks promising.' Flic stuck her head round the door. 'Need some help?'

'No, thanks.' It was still an effort not to be chilly with her, but he tried. 'Go finish up your own work and I'll yell if I need anything.'

He'd forgotten flour for thickening, could find none in the larder, but then he remembered that plain yoghurt would do the job pretty well, and after that, it was plain sailing. He switched on the radio to Jazz FM, poured himself a glass of Chablis, waited until the casserole was safely simmering, then poured a second glass and went up to the Quiet Room.

'How's it going?'

Caroline was frowning as she stitched, stooped forward over her work, glasses on the end of her nose. 'Not too badly.' She took off her glasses and looked up at him. 'How are things in the kitchen? Still self-sufficient?'

'Entirely,' he said. 'Flic came in to offer help a while back, but I said she should study instead.'

'Good.' Caro leaned back in the rocker. 'They all need to work hard from now on – exams aren't far off.'

'They're all smart girls.'

'I know, but Imo can be lazy, and Chloë daydreams.'

'They'll do okay.' He paused. 'I'm going to take a shower.'

'Is it safe to leave the dinner?'

'All under control.'

'Where's Kahli?'

He grinned. The retriever was shameless when left alone with food.

'Shut out of the kitchen,' he said.

It was a fine dinner. They sat in the kitchen, even Imogen finding it impossible to disguise her enjoyment.

'I think I'll leave all the cooking to you from now on.' Caroline spooned more into her bowl. 'I'm sorry Mama isn't here. She'd love this.'

'Can I give some to Kahli?' Chloë looked down at the dog beside her.

'Much too spicy for him,' Caroline said.

'Poor Kahli,' Chloë said.

'Better not leave the left-overs near him,' Imogen said.

'What left-overs?' Flic asked, helping herself to more.

Caroline's sickness began less than an hour later.

Matthew was appalled. 'Is it food poisoning? The girls are fine so far, touch wood, and I feel okay.'

'Oh, God,' she said wretchedly, and staggered back into the bathroom.

'Who's your doctor?'

'Howard Lucas,' Caroline called weakly. 'Number's in the book.'

'Where's the book?'

'Kitchen,' she said, and groaned.

The whole household was wide awake, all three daughters hovering anxiously in the bedroom doorway while they waited for the doctor.

'I don't remember her ever being as sick as this.' Flic was pale.

'Except for that time after the mangoes,' Imogen said.

Flic nodded, and put her arm around Chloë's shoulders.

'There weren't any mangoes in the hotpot, were there?' Imogen asked Matthew.

'Of course not,' he answered. 'I know about her allergy.'

Howard Lucas arrived about three-quarters of an hour after the worst of the sickness had passed. He spent several minutes alone with Caroline before emerging.

'I've given her an injection, which should settle her.'

'What do you think it is, doctor?' Matthew asked.

'Looks like a reaction to something she's eaten,' Lucas said. 'She has a rash.'

'Told you,' Imogen said to Flic.

Lucas looked sympathetically at Matthew. 'I gather you cooked some kind of Chinese dish this evening.'

Matthew nodded. 'But strictly no mangoes.'

'Could be something else,' the doctor said.

'Can I go in?' Matthew asked.

'For a minute or two, then I think she'll go off to sleep.' Lucas smiled at the girls. 'Why don't I go down with my favourite patients and you can join us when you've tucked her in?'

Caroline was already dozing. Matthew stroked her hair, kissed her cheek, then quietly left the room and walked downstairs. They were all in the drawing room, Kahli included. Matthew offered the doctor a drink, but Lucas declined.

'I used apricots.' Matthew's mind was ticking over. 'In the hotpot, I mean. Could they have done it?'

'Doubtful,' Dr Lucas said.

'Mum eats apricots quite often,' Imogen said.

'So you do think this is another allergy thing?' Flic asked.

'It's possible.' Lucas returned his attention to Matthew. 'It might be as well to try to ascertain what caused it this time. These reactions sometimes increase in intensity the more often they occur, and we don't want poor Caro to have to go through anything like that again unnecessarily.'

'God, no,' Matthew said.

'What else was in your recipe, besides apricots and chicken, do you recall?'

'I'll make a list.' Matthew looked around distractedly.

'I'll get you a pen and paper,' Flic volunteered.

'I think Kahli needs to go out,' Imogen said.

Flic and the retriever left the room.

'Are you sure you wouldn't like a drink, doctor?' Matthew asked.

'I'm driving,' Lucas said, 'and I want to be able to sleep when I get home, so I won't have coffee or tea either.' He smiled. 'You could probably use a brandy.'

Matthew shook his head. 'I just can't stand to think I might have done that to Caro.'

'Not your fault,' Lucas said. 'It's almost inevitable, from time to time, with sensitive people.'

The door opened and Flic came in carrying a white plastic bin bag, a curious expression on her face. Kahli, beside her, was sniffing eagerly at the bag.

'What's that?' Imogen asked.

'Tonight's rubbish,' Flic answered.

Matthew thought he understood, started towards her, smiling. 'I don't need that to help me remember what went into the hotpot,

Flic.' He put out his right hand to take the bag from her. 'Let me get that back in the trash.'

She pulled away from him, held it closer. 'Keen to get rid of it?'

'Flic?' He was bemused.

She undid the knot at the top of the bag, and pungent smells wafted out.

'Flic, that's disgusting,' Imogen protested.

'What are you *doing*?' Chloë wanted to know.

'Can we please get that into the kitchen.' Matthew was becoming annoyed.

'Good idea,' Howard Lucas said.

'Fine.' Flic walked quickly ahead of them, dumped the bag on the table, then turned to face her stepfather. 'I thought you said you knew about the mangoes.'

'I do.' The beginnings of real understanding came to him then, too unpleasant to contemplate, and he tried to push the thought out of his mind.

Flic inserted a hand into the bag.

'Oh, yuck, Flic,' Chloë said.

Flic withdrew something, held it out to Matthew.

Mango skins. No doubt about it.

No doubt in his mind, either, about how they'd got there.

Except that if he was right, it meant that Flic had actually gone so far as to put mangoes into the dinner, knowing what they would do to her mother.

He felt suddenly chilled to the bone.

The doctor and Imogen were looking at him curiously.

'I didn't use mangoes in the hotpot,' he said, quietly and precisely, too shell-shocked to properly feel the anger that he knew would come soon enough. 'I used apricots, as I told you. I bought them from a store near my office after work.' He looked straight at Flic. 'I know the difference between an apricot and a mango. It is not a mistake that is possible to make.'

'Quite,' Flic said.

'You put so much spice in it,' Imogen said. 'That's probably why we couldn't tell.'

Lucas shifted uncomfortably. 'At least this does seem to tell us what's caused the problem,' he said. 'That's the main thing.'

'Surely the main thing,' Imogen said, 'is that Mum was given mangoes to eat?'

64

'Accidents happen,' the doctor said.

'Yes, they do,' Matthew agreed, sounding infinitely more calm than he felt. 'Except that if mangoes did get into the dinner I served this evening, I didn't put them there.' He looked at Flic again. 'Perhaps it was someone else's accident?'

'Like who's?' Imogen demanded. 'We all know about Mum's allergy.'

'Dr Lucas is right,' Flic said, abruptly. 'It's obviously an accident.'

'And Caroline's going to be fine, which is all that counts,' the doctor said.

'Of course it is,' Flic said.

And after that, as truth, in all its ugliness, continued to pierce Matthew's outward bubble of calmness, he found it was as much as he could manage to ask the doctor if he wanted to be paid now, or if he would send his bill, and then to see him to the front door and thank him for coming.

When he turned from the door, he saw that all three sisters were standing between him and the kitchen, watching him.

'You'd better go to bed, Chloë,' he said.

'Okay.' She looked miserable.

'Your mummy's going to be fine,' he told her.

Chloë nodded and started up the staircase.

'We'll talk about this tomorrow,' he said to the other two.

'Damn right we will,' Imogen said.

He walked across to the staircase, placed one hand on the banister rail to steady himself. 'I'm going to sit with your mother now. Please turn out the lights when you're ready.'

'Don't you want us to look in and say goodnight?' Flic enquired.

The blood was pumping in his ears and he felt intensely sick as he started up the stairs.

'No,' he said.

# 11

He woke very early on Friday morning, turned off his alarm clock, saw that Caroline was sleeping soundly, and eased himself quietly out of bed.

The corridor was silent and still dark. He went downstairs, was greeted enthusiastically by Kahli, emerging from the kitchen, and went directly into the study. Richard's study. He doubted, this morning, if it would ever really become his room, thought it might now always remain a place with a desk and bookshelves borrowed from a dead man.

It was too early to call the office, but he typed and sent a fax to Gary Higgins, the secretary shared by all the junior architects, to be there on his arrival:

*Due to family illness, I may not be able to get there till afternoon. Clapham files all updated and on computer. Apologies.*

He went into the kitchen, let Kahli into the back garden, put water in the coffee maker, spooned Costa Rican blend into a paper filter, and switched on the machine.

He looked at the cupboard under the sink that concealed the rubbish bin, then went over and opened it. The lid, pulled by a string attached to the inside of the cupboard door, opened automatically. There was a clean plastic bag inside the bin, top edges neatly folded over the rim. The bag containing the 'evidence' had obviously been taken outside.

Not that he would have known what to do with it had it still been there.

Demand that his wife's daughters be fingerprinted, for comparison with prints on the skins of a couple of mangoes?

Absurd was not the word.

He let the dog back inside, drank some coffee, sat with his thoughts for a while, until about the time he knew the girls would be getting up, then went quietly back upstairs into the bedroom.

Caroline was still sleeping, knocked out, he supposed, by whatever had been in the shot the doctor had given her. And, of course, by the attack of illness itself.

Too restless to go back to sleep, loth to disturb her, he sat down in the armchair over by the window. The curtains were not completely drawn, and through the opening he could see dawn rising behind the rooftops and chimney pots. He thought, looking at the purity of the light, that it was probably going to be a lovely day, weather-wise.

Every-other-wise, it was going to be unlovely in the extreme.

He wished, more than anything, that he did not have to tell Caro. That he could just go on letting things ride, allowing her to believe that everything in the Walters-Gardner household was peachy. But last night had rendered that impossible.

He looked back at the bed, saw how peaceful she looked.

She was peaceful mostly because he had been lying to her. He knew now that keeping the troubles from her had been cowardly on his part. He had meant it kindly, of course, but she would regard it as a lack of trust, perhaps even disrespect. He had assumed, perhaps incorrectly, that she was not strong enough to face the truth. He should have had more faith in her.

*Didn't want to hurt her.*

He was damned well going to hurt her now.

He sat in the chair as the day lightened. Beyond the room, the house came to life. Downstairs, the front door opened and closed softly as Isabella let herself in. He pictured her bending to pick up *The Times* and *Daily Mail*, then greeting Kahli before letting him out into the garden again.

Sure enough. There was the back door, opening, closing.

And a while later, the sound of letters thumping onto the mat.

He dozed, woke again as the girls got up, went about their morning routines. Twice, he heard them right outside the door, listening, probably debating whether or not to come in and see their mother. But no one did come in, so he supposed they had decided not to disturb her.

*Fine to poison her, though*, he thought about Flic.

He was uncertain if Imogen had been in on it. He thought not, imagined Flic not being able to trust her more transparent, more obviously emotional sister to sit calmly through that dinner, knowing it would physically harm their mother. But he also thought that once Imo saw the point of what Flic had done, saw it had been done to make *him* look guilty of causing Caro's illness, she would back Flic to the hilt.

Once or twice, as the household shifted and creaked, sounds of breakfast television and conversation reaching his ears, Matthew noticed Caro stirring, and steeled himself for her awakening. But she did not waken, not then, nor when the girls left the house to walk to the tube.

At last, he stood up, stiff-legged, walked quietly to the door, reached for the handle to open it.

'Hello.'

'Hi there.' He turned, saw she was sitting up, smiled at her. 'How're you doing?' He walked back, round to her side of the bed, sat on the edge, reached for her hand. 'Feeling better?'

'Much.' She smiled back at him. 'Tired, but so much better.'

'Thank God,' he said.

He told her to stay put, told her the girls had gone to school and that he was home for as long as he was needed and that, if she could face it, he was going to make her a slice of toast and bring her some tea.

'Just the tea, I think,' she said.

'Sure?' he asked her.

She nodded. 'I'll try and eat something a little later.'

He went to the door.

'Did Isabella come?' she asked.

'Got the girls their breakfast, saw them out, right on time.' He smiled again, almost brightly. 'So no problems there.'

*Coward.*

\*

Isabella's response to him was no different from usual. She was concerned about Caroline but as friendly as always, which presumably meant that none of the sisters had treated her to their version of events.

'Caro's much better.' He filled the kettle with fresh water. 'Though all she wants for now is tea.'

'So no work for her today.' Isabella knew, as they all did, about the cushion deadlines.

Matthew shook his head, took a tea bag from the white jar.

'Not that rubbish,' Isabella said. 'I will make her real tea, but very weak.'

He thanked her, said he'd decided against going to his office at all, wanted to stay home with Caro and make sure she took things easy, and Isabella said that was a good idea.

Leaving her in charge of the tea, he wandered out into the garden where old John was just arriving, and told him about Caroline's bout of illness.

'I knew something must be up with you home on a weekday morning,' the old man said. 'Give her my love, won't you?'

Matthew assured him he would, threw a ball for Kahli, who'd followed him outside, then went back inside.

If Caroline kept her tea down and then, perhaps, graduated to toast, he would have to tell her the truth. At the most, he could wait another hour or two, give her a chance to recoup a little, maybe take a soothing bath.

But Flic might phone, or even come back from school early.

Or Dr Lucas might call, or drop by.

No choice.

# 12

'I don't believe you.'

He had known it was what she would say, or at least what she would feel, yet still it hurt to hear it. He looked into her face, hoping to see something reassuring, for those words could be said in different ways. People said 'I don't believe it' sometimes, meaning that they *did* believe whatever it was but found it astonishing or incomprehensible or too awful to *want* to believe.

But Caroline had said them flatly, a bald no-frills statement, and her expression did nothing to soften the words.

'I don't believe you.'

*You.* Not *it*. There was the difference, of course.

He'd tried to keep it as light as possible, but there was no longer anything light about it.

'It must have been a mistake,' she said about one episode.

And then: 'You must have been wrong about that.'

And later: 'They won't have meant anything by that.'

All different ways of trying to dismiss what Matthew was telling her, of telling him that he'd been overreacting to situations that were perfectly normal, or at least explicable, in a household with three teenagers. But he continued doggedly nonetheless, watching her expression changing as he talked.

Dismay first, then distress. Then a falsely blithe desire to dismiss. Palpable shock after that, followed by a clear, fierce resolve to disbelieve. And finally, most dispiritingly from Matthew's point-of-view, what seemed like detachment. Both from what he had been telling her, and worse, from him. So that was what it came down to, he realized. She could *not* cope, after all, could not face it. He had been right about that.

'Why didn't you tell me these things when they happened?'

'I hoped I could work it out without your having to know.'

'But if you'd told me, at the beginning, it would never have come to this.'

'Possibly not.'

'No possibly about it,' Caroline said.

'The girls kept it from you too,' Matthew pointed out.

'They're *girls*,' she said. 'You're an adult. My husband.'

Only blame in her eyes now, all for him.

'The girls wouldn't have wanted me hurt,' she said. 'They knew how much I wanted this marriage to work, knew how lonely I'd been. Of course they thought it best to keep their unhappiness from me.'

He was silent. Rendered speechless by the sheer injustice of her reaction. After what he'd just told her. 'Can't you see that they were deceiving you,' he asked after a moment, 'not protecting you?'

'No,' Caroline said. 'I can't see that at all.'

They were still in the bedroom, but she had got out of bed some time before, unable to lie there any longer, had put on her robe and slippers and paced for a while as he talked, then gone into the bathroom to splash her face with cold water, before returning to sit in the armchair by the window. Matthew had begun to pace, too, then moved to the end of the bed, then stood again, and now he was perched on the window ledge near her, trying to stay close, hating the distance growing between them.

It was there, nonetheless.

She saw his distress. 'If you couldn't cope with being a step-father, you should have told me right away. I could have under-stood that. I knew it might be hard for you.' She shook her head. 'But you led me to believe everything was all right between you and my daughters.' She paused. 'You were the deceiver, Matthew.'

'I don't see it that way.'

'No. I don't suppose you do.'

'Neither should you.' He saw now that he had a whole new fight on his hands. 'Haven't you heard what I've been telling you? The

71

things they've done? Mostly Flic doing them, working them out, but with Imo backing her all the way.'

'How can you *do* that?' Caroline stood up, ran a hand through her dishevelled hair. 'How can you sit there calling them by their pet names, while you're accusing them of such terrible things?'

'It's what we call them.' Matthew felt bewildered and frustrated.

'So now it's "we", is it?' she asked him coldly.

'Of course it is.'

'Not until now, clearly.'

She sat down again in the armchair, her hands trembling.

'Maybe you're not well enough for this,' Matthew said. 'Maybe we should take a break, let you rest for a while.'

'*Rest*? You think I could rest now?'

'I guess not.'

'It's quite ironic, you know,' she said grimly. 'Your not telling me. Not trusting me to cope, when it's perfectly clear that *you've* been the one not coping, that if I had known, from the beginning, what was going on, I could have taken control, dealt with it.'

'That may be true,' he admitted. 'But I kept hoping you wouldn't need to.'

'So you've said.' She paused. 'You must at least accept that you were wrong not to tell me.'

'With hindsight, of course.'

'I *could* have dealt with it all, you know. I could have smoothed things over, stopped them getting so out of control.'

'Maybe.'

'No maybe about it. I'm their mother.'

'And apparently,' Matthew said, quietly, painfully, 'I'm just the proverbial wicked stepfather.' He paused. 'Though frankly I'm not sure I've even graduated to that status in their eyes.'

'What do you mean?' Caroline asked.

'I get the feeling, sometimes, that neither Flic nor Imogen accepts that our marriage really took place. That they still think I'm a kind of holiday romance, brought home for a while on their mother's whim.' The idea took hold, rang horribly true. 'A temporary problem.'

\*

72

Isabella came up to ask them about lunch then, and they both grasped the break with relief, unpleasantly aware that that too was temporary. Caroline asked Isabella if she'd mind bringing her something very light up on a tray, and when Matthew said that there was no need, that he'd bring it to her, Caro cast him a glance of something so close to dislike it sickened him.

Howard Lucas telephoned a little later to enquire after her. Matthew, downstairs in the study – having just checked in with the office – answered and told the doctor that Caroline was feeling a lot better, though still very tired.

'Would you like to speak to her yourself?'

'In a moment.' Lucas paused. 'That must have been difficult for you last night.'

'Yes, it was,' Matthew said.

'Problems between teenagers and stepfathers,' Lucas said, 'come in many varieties, you know. Please don't imagine you're alone.'

'I don't suppose I am.' Matthew hesitated, then went on quickly, knowing it had to be broached. 'The thing with the mangoes—'

'I can assure you,' the doctor cut in gently, 'that not for a single moment did I think you did such a thing deliberately.'

The words sounded benign, but they might as well have been a slap.

'The point, doctor,' Matthew said, very clearly, 'is that I didn't do it at all.'

There was another short pause. 'Well, whatever the case, I don't think your wife needs to be troubled with it, do you?'

*Too late.*

'Best to keep undue stress away from Caro, don't you agree?' Lucas added.

There was something cautionary in his tone.

'Until she's over the attack, you mean?' Matthew asked.

'That, of course,' Lucas answered. 'But I meant in general.'

In other circumstances, Matthew might have tried to find out exactly what the doctor meant, but that would have meant telling Lucas that she already knew about the mangoes and much more, and he wasn't sure he was up to that.

'I know you'll take good care of her,' Lucas said.

'I'll do my best,' Matthew said.

*

73

He stayed downstairs, waited until Isabella had gone up to fetch her lunch tray and returned with it to the kitchen.

'She's hardly touched anything.' Isabella tipped the plain one-egg omelette she'd cooked into the waste disposal.

'Is she sleeping now?'

'No, but she seems very tired.' Isabella paused. 'And depressed, I think.'

Whether or not she had heard any of what they'd talked about, Matthew knew that Isabella had to have been aware of the long conversation in the bedroom that morning. He was tempted, briefly, to confide in her, then decided that if Caro had chosen not to tell her what had gone on, then it certainly was not his place to share a private family matter.

'She's certainly very down,' he said.

He glanced at the oven clock. 13:58. If the girls stayed at The Grange all day, they would be home at around five, but there was always a chance that one of them might find an excuse to leave early, and there was a whole lot more ground that he and Caroline needed to cover before that.


'I don't want to talk any more,' she said.

She was back in bed. The coldness had gone, but her eyes were dull, as washed out as her face.

'We have to talk, Caro.'

'I think we've talked quite enough.'

'No,' Matthew told her, gently, 'we haven't. We have some major issues to deal with, whether we like them or not.'

'I don't want to deal with anything more right now.'

'You can't just ignore the things they've said and done.'

'The things you've accused them of doing, you mean.' Cold again.

'All true, though Christ knows I wish they weren't.'

'So you say.'

He hadn't realized how stubborn she could be. He turned away, gritting his teeth, walked over to the window. John Pascoe was still down in the garden doing a spot of weeding, and Isabella was talking to him, with Kahli a few feet away, sniffing out something in a flowerbed. He envied them the normality of the scene, then took a breath and turned back.

'What about the mangoes, Caro?'

74

She looked at him steadily. 'You were the cook last night.'

Anger rose in him, and it took an effort to quash it. 'I left the dinner simmering for a while, remember? I brought you up a glass of wine to the Quiet Room, and then I went to take a shower.'

'So you're suggesting that Flic, my own daughter, crept into the kitchen while you were showering, and popped a few mangoes into your hotpot. Knowing that they would make me ill.'

'I think,' he said carefully, 'that making you ill was a necessary by-product so far as Flic was concerned. I think that the object of the exercise was to make it look as if I had done it.' He thought. 'Or perhaps the real object was to create this very situation.'

'Meaning?'

'A situation in which I would accuse them, and you would not believe me, after which we would be at loggerheads.'

Caroline said nothing.

'So what's your take on this?' he asked. 'What's your alternative scenario? That I did it myself?'

'Not deliberately,' she said.

Howard Lucas had said much the same thing, Matthew remembered, except that the doctor was a stranger, and this was his wife.

*And the girls' mother. Don't forget that.*

As if he could.

He tried again to stay on track, fight fire with fire. 'But since I knew about your allergy, if I had added the mangoes, it couldn't possibly have been anything *but* deliberate, could it?'

Again she said nothing.

'Caro, for God's sake!' He was anguished. 'You cannot possibly, for one second, imagine that I could do that to you!' His chest felt tight. 'Even if I didn't love you – even if I didn't *like* you. Caro, I wouldn't do such a thing to my worst *enemy*.'

She hardly seemed to be listening, appeared deep in thought.

'What?' he asked. '*What?*'

'Why couldn't it,' she said finally, 'be the other way round? Given that you've been failing to get along with them.'

'I don't understand.'

'You said that the object of the exercise might have been to get us at . . .' She tried to remember the word. 'At loggerheads.'

'I did.'

'You might just as well have been trying to set me against my children.'

'That's insane,' he said.

'Why is it?' she asked.

His blood was pumping too hard in his head. 'I'm supposed to have virtually poisoned you because I want to turn you against your daughters.'

'Is it more insane than what you've just suggested?' Suddenly there were tears in Caroline's eyes and two hot splashes of colour on her otherwise pale cheeks. 'Is it surprising that I should come up with something like that after the things you've been telling me?' She bit her bottom lip to stop herself from crying. 'Things you've chosen to tell me when I feel so *rotten*?'

Matthew slumped down into the armchair. 'No,' he said. 'It's not surprising at all. Though the time of telling really wasn't chosen by me.'

She looked down at her hands on the duvet cover. 'Not according to you, no.'

He sighed. A long, slow, sad sigh.

'I'm sorry,' she said, softly. 'I'm sorry not to be able to simply believe you.'

'Me, too,' he said.

'But you have to understand,' she said. 'They're my daughters.'

'Yes,' he said.

# 13

Little more was said on the subject for the rest of that day.
Matthew told Caro that he had said all he could for the moment,
and that it was now in her hands. Caroline said that she thought
that was true and that, if he had no objections, she would deal with
it her way. He said that of course he had no objections, so long as
she *did* deal with it.

The girls came home from school at the usual time, spent a little
while with their mother, went to their rooms to change and do
their homework, then went back downstairs to have their dinner,
cooked for them by Isabella, who was staying late.

Chloë, happy to have found Caroline on the mend, was as
sweet-natured as ever to Matthew, and in Isabella's presence – and
in Chloë's, too, he noted – both Flic and Imogen were cordial
enough to him.

Until later, after Isabella had gone home and Chloë had gone to
bed.

They came to the study to find him.

No pretence now. Not even the courtesy of a tap at the door.
They came straight in, Flic first, then Imogen, closed the door
behind them and came and stood together, shoulder to shoulder, in
front of the desk.

'From what Mum says,' Flic said, 'you've had a pretty bad
day.'

'As you would expect,' Matthew answered.

'We thought you would,' Imogen said. 'We got together in the
lunch break and tried to picture you trying to persuade our mother

77

what evil children she has.' Her face was full of malice. 'We knew she wouldn't believe you.'

'I wouldn't say that,' he said.

'We would,' Flic said. 'More to the point, so would Mum.'

'She doesn't know you're in here now, does she?' Matthew said.

'I suppose,' Flic said thoughtfully, 'you could start carrying a tape recorder, switch it on for the next time we tell you how we really feel about you.'

Imogen nodded. 'Good idea, Flic. Don't you think, Matthew?'

He didn't answer.

'But just imagine what a prat you'd look when you tried playing it back to Mum or anyone else,' Flic said. 'And all we'd have to do would be to tell them what you'd done to make us so horrible.'

Matthew still said nothing, just sat there shaking his head.

'Why don't you just go?' Imogen asked him.

'Not yet, Imo,' Flic said. 'He won't give up as easily as that. Will you, Matthew?'

For one more moment, he neither moved nor spoke. And then he stood up, slowly and calmly.

'Get out,' he said softly.

'And if we don't?' Imogen asked.

'I'm asking you – telling you – to leave this room now.'

'Our father's room,' Flic said.

He shook his head again. 'Whatever.'

'Will you hit us if we don't?' Imogen asked.

'Not the type,' Flic said.

Matthew walked around the desk, passed close enough to Imogen to smell perfume and cigarette smoke on her. He opened the door, stood back, gripping the handle, like a doorman at a hotel. 'You're right about that,' he said. 'I never have been the type.' He paused. 'Though there's always a first time.'

They did not move.

He looked into their faces, said nothing more.

'Enough,' Flic said, to her sister. 'For tonight, anyway.'

'Sure?' Imogen asked.

Flic smiled, not even glancing at Matthew.

'We've made a decent start,' she said.

And they left the room.

*

Chloë, unable to sleep, came into Flic's room an hour later, found Imogen there, too, lying on her side in Flic's bed beside her sister, looking at a photograph of their father on the bedside table.

'Why are you both still being so awful to Matthew?'

It was unlike Chloë to approach anything ugly in such a head-on fashion. An open girl in general, the twelve-year-old had nevertheless inherited her mother's dislike of tension, often choosing, if possible, to ignore unpleasantness.

'We're not,' Flic told her. 'Not really.'

'No more than he deserves,' Imogen added, sitting up.

'Why?' Chloë asked. 'Why does he deserve it?'

'You know why,' Imogen said and shivered.

She was wearing one of the old T-shirts that their father's publishers had printed as part of a promotion the year before his first stroke. After he had agreed (against his personal taste) to illustrate a children's story about a cow named Astrid, Richard Walters had made more money than in all the years in which he'd striven to produce what he termed 'worthwhile' work. The book had become a series, and in the same year in which they had printed the T-shirts, sweatshirts and mugs and brought out Astrid milk jugs and butter dishes and trays, the publishers had also repackaged the whole Astrid backlist behind the latest book. When it became clear that Richard's affected right side was never going to recover sufficiently for him to continue working profes-sionally, they had struck a deal with him, commissioning a new illustrator to work alongside him, using his ideas and copying his style. The second, fatal stroke had come less than a year later. But for a few T-shirts and sweatshirts in pristine condition stowed safely away in one of Imogen's wardrobes, the garments were by now frayed and faded from repeated wearing and washing, since Richard's middle daughter slept in them night after night, what-ever the season.

Aethiopia tended to be a cool house at night, even in summer. In winter it could be icy even with the heating on full blast, espe-cially when the wind blew off the East Heath. Flic, whose bedroom, like Imogen's, faced the Heath, regularly wore flannel pyjamas to bed. Her mother bought her pretty nightdresses now and then, but for all that Flic was aware of her good looks, she reasoned that so long as she was sleeping alone at home, she might as well be comfortable. Not that she had any great desire to sleep anywhere else, or *with* anyone else, for that matter. Flic knew that Imogen, who thought about sex a great deal, found her own lack of interest in boys odd, but the fact was, Flic didn't seem to care one way or another about men or sex.

She had other, more important, things to think about.

'I thought you liked Matthew now,' Chloë said, sitting on the end of the bed.

'We've tried,' Flic said. 'But he doesn't deserve it.'

'I don't see why not.' Chloë paused. 'I've heard you both sometimes saying awful things about him. I just don't understand *why.*'

In one swift, smooth movement, Imogen pushed the covers away and slid down to the bottom of the bed. 'Children who listen at keyholes sometimes get their ears cut off.'

'Imo, don't,' Flic said. 'No need for that.'

'There's every need,' Imogen said, 'if the little brat's going to snitch on us.'

'She isn't.' Flic wriggled down the bed to sit beside Chloë. 'Are you?'

'I wouldn't know what to snitch about,' Chloë said warily.

'And if you did know?' Imogen asked.

'She still wouldn't snitch,' Flic said.

Imogen was unconvinced. 'It's time you realized that blood's thicker than water,' she said. '*We're* your blood, squirt, not *him.*' She said the *him* with distaste. 'It doesn't matter what you think, you still side with us, okay?'

'Okay.' Chloë stood up.

'I mean it.' Imogen got off the bed too.

'Imo, stop bullying her,' Flic said.

'She's always bullying me,' Chloë complained.

'But she is right,' Flic told her. 'You do have to realize that.'

'Okay,' Chloë said again.

Flic lowered her voice. 'When it comes to Matthew and Mum, it doesn't matter whether you think you understand why we're doing something or not—'

'Or whether you agree with us or not,' Imogen added.

Chloë kept her eyes on Flic. 'But I *don't* understand.'

'Because it's complicated,' Flic said. 'But you will understand eventually.'

'All you have to understand right now,' Imogen said, 'is that Matthew is scum.'

'But he isn't,' Chloë said, then quickly back-slid a little. 'I don't think he is.'

'Because you don't know much,' Imo said.

'I know you're vile to me,' Chloë said defiantly, 'and I hate you sometimes, and I don't hate Matthew at all, because he's always nice to me.'

'He's bad news,' Flic told her, still quietly. 'For Mum, sweetheart. It's a fact, an absolute fact.' She read the muddle in her sister's big blue eyes. 'Mum's very vulnerable.'

'She probably doesn't know what vulnerable means,' Imogen said.

'Of course I know,' Chloë said.

'You remember how poorly Mum was after Daddy died,' Flic said. 'And she was really just starting to get back to normal, wasn't she, before Christmas? Before Switzerland.'

'Before he got his claws into her,' Imogen said.

'But he fell in love with her,' Chloë said.

'Spare me,' Imo groaned.

'But he *did*,' Chloë insisted. 'And Mummy loves him.'

'But Mum doesn't always know what's best for her,' Flic told her, softly, confidentially. 'We're her children, we're the closest people to her in the whole world. It's our job to protect her.'

'Matthew's going to end up hurting her.' Imogen was more reasonable now. 'It may not look like that to you now, Chloë, but it's true.'

'That's why we have to stick together,' Flic said. 'You do see that, don't you, darling? We're sisters, and aside from the three of us, there's Mummy and Groosi, and that's *all* there is, okay?'

Chloë nodded. She was suddenly very tired and drained, wanted to go back to her room and go to sleep.

'So if anyone asks you about tonight, or about *anything* to do with us and Matthew, you just tell them you don't know about it,' Flic said. 'All right?'

Chloë nodded again. 'All right.'

'Let us down,' Imogen said, 'and there'll be big trouble.'

'It's okay,' Flic said soothingly. 'She's with us, aren't you, Chloë?'

'Yes,' Chloë said.

'Better be,' Imogen said.

# 14

Matthew was almost grateful to return to work.

The weekend had been dismal, the distance between himself and Caroline remaining unbridgeable. They had slept together, but that had been the only concession. Several times, when they were alone, Matthew had tried closing the gap, reminding her of their love, but Caro had been unyielding.

'Please let's stop this,' he'd said, finally, on Monday morning.

'How?'

'We need to talk, fix things.'

'We tried talking.'

'Not really,' he'd said. 'We've hardly spoken all weekend.'

But she had only sighed, and more minutes had ticked by and Matthew had remembered his already less-than-perfect status at VKF, and had gone to work.

'Family illness?'

Phil Bianco walked into the second floor office at eleven minutes past nine, walked directly into Matthew's cubicle and asked the question.

'My wife,' Matthew said.

'Serious?' Bianco's tone indicated that in his book nothing short of myocardial infarct was grounds for taking a day.

'Food poisoning,' Matthew said.

Bianco's left eyebrow lifted clear of his spectacle rims. 'Any more family crises,' he said, 'you take as vacation. Clear?'

'I already logged it as vacation,' Matthew said coolly.

'Good.' Bianco turned on his heel, walked back to the outer door, then turned back again to take in the rest of the team. 'Same goes for all of you. VKF doesn't run holiday camps.'

Matthew waited for thirty seconds after he'd gone. 'Sorry, guys.'

'No problem.' Katrina Dunn smiled from behind her drawing board. A red-haired Scot in her mid-twenties known as Kat, she'd arrived in the firm less than a month before, a breath of fresh air from Matthew's viewpoint, with her refusal to pay any heed to the closed-rank atmosphere he had encountered. 'Bit of a Nazi.'

'I take exception to that,' Nick Brice said in his Etonian voice.

'You take exception to most things, Nick,' Kat told him.

'Bianco's just a stickler,' Robert Fairbairn, an earnest young man, said.

'Just doesn't like wankers,' Mark Loftus, a gifted but unpleasant south Londoner with a haircut one step away from skinhead, said.

Matthew suppressed the urge to punch Loftus and tried to return his focus to the Clapham project.

'If you had food poisoning, Loftus,' Kat remarked, 'I bet you'd like your wife to stay home and look after you.'

'Loftus's wife has left him,' Nick Brice said.

'Oh,' Kat said. 'I'm sorry to hear that.'

'Don't be,' Loftus told her, and grinned. 'She'll be back.'

'She leaves him twice a year,' Brice said.

Several unkind ripostes came to Matthew's mind, but he maintained his silence, his spirits sinking deeper by the minute. He longed, not for the first time, for the warmth of the Berlin office or the intensely creative buzz of the New York parent ship.

He looked dismally at his board. He was growing to hate Clapham and its interminable loose ends, had been hoping for some involvement in a new office project at Tower Hill being spearheaded by Stephen Steerforth, but had missed a key breakfast meeting in April after *someone* at home had failed to pass on a phone message from Gary Higgins. Work, therefore, was not likely to prove his saviour, at least not in the near future.

He glanced at his watch. Not even nine-twenty.

Purgatory came to mind.

*Life is shit and then you die*. A cheery aphorism he'd learned at school.

Eight more hours of this.

And then he got to go home.

Sylvie was waiting for him when he emerged, winding down the window of her bright red Peugeot and waving. 'I've come to give you a lift,' she called out. 'Unless you have other plans.'

'None.' He walked around to the other side, opened the passenger door and got in. 'Not just passing, I assume?'

'Not exactly,' she admitted, starting the engine. 'Bit of an ambush, I'm afraid. Hope you don't mind too much.'

'Not at all.' He thought, as a matter of fact, that Sylvie was the only family member – Chloë possibly excepted – he didn't mind being ambushed by this evening.

She nosed into the rush hour traffic. 'Want to go straight home, or do you think we might stop somewhere for a drink?'

'A drink sounds pretty good,' Matthew said. 'Though if we're going to be a while, I should call Caro.' He paused. 'Or does she know about this?'

'I told her I was going to speak to you.' Sylvie shook her head. 'No need to call. Isabella's staying late, and Caro's feeling quite herself again.'

He waited until they were in Tottenham Court Road, edging towards the traffic lights. 'So how do we do this?'

'I think we should start by you giving me your side of the story,' Sylvie said.

'Hasn't Caro told you all the gory details?'

'In her words. I'd like to hear yours.'

Matthew felt a flash of gratitude. 'It goes back some way,' he said.

'Can't be that long.' Sylvie smiled. 'We've only known each other a few months.'

Matthew returned the smile, wryly. 'Forgive me if I say that, just occasionally, it seems a hell of a lot longer.'

Sylvie concentrated on manoeuvring the car out of one lane and into another, then glanced at him. 'So,' she said, 'from the beginning might be best, don't you think?'

The journey, along Hampstead Road, through Camden Town, up to Highgate, took more than forty minutes, and Matthew talked

84

for the entire duration. Sylvie wanted to go to a pub called The Flask, which she said was one of her favourites, which surprised Matthew somewhat.

'I never picture you in pubs,' he told her.

'Where do you picture me?'

'Cafés and restaurants. In Kensington or Paris or Zurich, or Hampstead, of course. Just not pubs.'

'Most of them not worth going into these days,' she agreed. 'Places with revolting names and machines with flashing lights.'

'And music,' he added.

'Loosely speaking,' she said.

There was nowhere legal to park, but Sylvie persevered, finally leaving the car on a yellow line, nearside wheels up on a grass verge. Matthew pointed out that they might get a ticket or worse, but Sylvie no longer cared.

'If we get clamped,' she said, 'we'll take a taxi home and worry about the car tomorrow.' She locked the doors and looked up at him. 'I don't know about you, but I need a rather stiff drink.'

'Whisky?' he said as they walked towards the pub.

'Double,' she said, taking his arm.

'Don't forget you're driving,' he said.

'Not if we're clamped.'

The attractive, low-ceilinged pub was crowded, but while Matthew bought their drinks, Sylvie pounced on two seats in a corner.

She wasted no more time. 'This is not the sort of thing Caro needs, you know.'

'Of course I know,' he said. 'Believe me, it isn't doing much for me either.'

'But you're stronger,' she said.

'I'm sure I should be, but I'm not feeling it right now.'

'Whatever you're feeling,' Sylvie said, 'you are much stronger than Caroline.' She paused. 'Emotionally. Psychologically.'

Matthew said nothing, but recalled what Howard Lucas had said about protecting Caro from stress.

'She's suffered from depression, you know,' Sylvie told him quietly.

Matthew frowned. 'I didn't know. Caro told me that Imogen went through a bout after Richard's death.'

'Yes.' She paused again. 'An inherited tendency, perhaps. Unproven.'

'But the same thing, in Caro's case? Bereavement depression, I mean?'

'Mm.' Sylvie took a lingering sip of her whisky.

'Caro said that Susanna treated Imo when she was depressed,' Matthew said.

'And Caro too,' Sylvie said.

'She didn't tell me.'

'I think I can understand that, can't you?'

'No.' He paused, thought about it. 'Not really.'

'She may be ashamed of it.'

'Of what? Being a sensitive person?'

'Perhaps ashamed isn't the right word. Embarrassed may be more like it.'

'But I'm her husband.'

'With whom she fell madly in love very quickly,' Sylvie said. 'With whom she had no time to build up the deep trust that ought – ideally – to come before marriage.'

'It's the trust thing that's troubling me,' Matthew said. 'I told Caro that for Imogen's sake, if for no other reason, she ought to have told me about her depression.'

'And you feel that was when she ought to have told you about herself too?'

'Yes,' Matthew said. 'I do.' He paused. 'If it were the other way around, I know I'd have told her.'

'You can't be sure about that.'

'I think I can be.' He paused again. 'I love her, Sylvie,' he said simply. 'I'm completely committed to her. Sickness and health. I believe in that.'

'I'm glad to hear it,' Sylvie said.

Matthew looked straight at her. 'Do you believe what I've told you?'

'Why shouldn't I? You're not a liar, are you?'

'No, I'm not,' he said. 'But I thought you might feel the way Caro does. Preferring to believe that your granddaughters wouldn't do the things I've said they have.'

'I would very much prefer to believe that.'

'But?' Matthew said. 'I feel there was a "but" in there, or at least an "although".'

'Yes, there was.' Sylvie sighed. 'Shades of grey, I suppose.'

'Meaning my version's too black and white?'

'Exactly.' She looked at him appreciatively. 'I'm glad my daughter chose a clever man. I'm not very good with stupid people.'

'Richard seems to have been a very clever man.'

'In some ways.' She paused. 'You're sensitive, too, Matthew.'

'Maybe too much so?'

'I'm not sure there *is* such a thing as being too sensitive, so long as a person can be rational at the same time. You and Caro, for example, wouldn't last a year if you were a cold fish.'

'Do you think we will last?' It was a painful question, and quickly he swallowed down the last of his whisky.

'I hope so,' Sylvie said. 'Provided you both remember that nothing is black and white.' She leaned closer, her voice soft but clear. 'Caroline needs to accept that her daughters have been damaged, to a degree, by pain and loss, and by the amazingly insensitive actions of two such supposedly sensitive people.'

Matthew flinched.

'It was wonderfully romantic, Matthew,' she went on. 'But frankly, from the girls' perspective, it must have been quite shattering.' She saw his dismay, reached across the table and gave his hand a generous squeeze. 'I'm not really blaming either of you, just pointing out what I feel must lie behind the girls' actions. Flic is hugely protective of Imo, you know.'

'And they both adored their father.'

'All the girls did.' Sylvie paused again. 'Accepting that is your part of the deal.' She shrugged. 'Caro, I'm afraid, has to come to terms with their imperfections. And you have to come to terms with what's driven them.' She smiled wryly. 'If you choose to, that is. You might decide it's all too much.'

'And then what?' Matthew asked. 'Walk out on them?'

'If that's what you choose,' Sylvie said.

'I'm not a quitter,' he told her.

'No,' she said. 'I didn't think that was your style.'

'Anyway,' he added, 'I couldn't walk out on Caro even if I wanted to.'

'Love,' Sylvie said, understanding.

'Yes,' he agreed.

'It can be a bit of a curse, can't it, sometimes?'

Matthew thought of his wife's sweetness and fragility. 'I could never think of anything to do with Caro as a curse.'

'No,' Sylvie said. 'Of course not.' Another wry smile. 'Though I think you'd have some difficulty considering the girls a blessing right now.'

'You could be right there,' Matthew said.

The red car was where they had left it, neither clamped nor even ticketed, and the flow of traffic was freer now, the rush hour past. They drove around the Heath along Hampstead Lane, through the bottleneck between the Spaniards Inn and the little eighteenth-century tollhouse opposite, along Spaniards Road back past the old horse pond and down East Heath Road.

They had hardly spoken during the journey, both tired now, both immersed in their own thoughts.

'So,' Matthew roused himself as they neared the house, 'do I tell Caro I know about her depression? Or might she feel you'd betrayed her confidence?'

'As you see fit.' Sylvie brought the Peugeot to a halt. 'If it were my marriage, I think I'd place an embargo on secrets from now on. You certainly don't need to worry on my account.'

She declined, when he invited her, to come in.

'I daresay you'd like me there as a buffer,' she mocked gently, 'between you and your troublesome women, but I think not.'

'And I thought you liked me.' Matthew grinned.

'Oh, I do,' Sylvie said, 'very much. But I think you'll find that things have calmed down now. Don't forget I saw Caro this morning.'

'Right.' He turned to kiss her cheek warmly. 'How can I thank you, Sylvie?'

'I haven't done much,' she said.

'You wanted to hear my side,' he said. 'And you said that you believed me.'

'Just remember,' she said. 'Shades of grey.'

'On all sides,' Matthew said, opening his door.

Sylvie smiled. 'You'll do,' she said, and pushed him gently out of the car.

# 15

Sylvie was right about things being calmer.

No teenage lynch mob lay in wait.

Not even an especially angry or unhappy wife.

She waited until the girls had gone to bed and they were sitting in the drawing room with two glasses of brandy.

'I've talked to Flic and Imo,' she said. 'About everything.'

'And?'

'And I can see now how a series of random, accidental situations may have built up in your mind into something far more deliberate and unpleasant.'

Matthew's heart sank.

'The girls are genuinely sorry for their part in the whole misunderstanding, but I have to say I think they'd find it very difficult to apologize to you directly, because you have, of course – at least in their eyes – accused them unjustly.'

'Unjustly,' he repeated flatly.

'Though I can see now,' she said hastily, 'why you did that, I truly can. And I can't tell you how sorry I am for seeming not to believe you. It must have hurt you badly, and that's the last thing I wanted to do, and I know it's the last thing you wanted for me too.'

Matthew sat beside her, mildly shell-shocked, a part of him wondering how it was possible for a woman as logical as Sylvie to have a daughter as blind to truth as Caroline. But then he looked at her, saw the artlessness in her face, remembered what Sylvie had said about depression, and he thought about all she must have gone through in the past several years, with Richard's first stroke and then his death, and with having to guide their children through that misery. And then having to deal with Imogen's depression while feeling just as dark and lost herself . . .

*Leave it*, he told himself.

Another, wiser, part of him knew that it was not the right way to go, that they would almost certainly live to regret it. *No more secrets*, Sylvie had advised him. Yet she had also talked about sensitivity. If he challenged what Caro had just told him, he suspected he might be doing that to satisfy his own pride, his own sense of injustice. And if his personal grievance was the only secret he was keeping, surely that was in a just cause? The cause of not wishing to hurt Caroline any further.

'So can we do that, do you think?' she asked him. 'Put all this behind us, get past it? Move on, as they say?'

*Not without dealing with it*, a voice in Matthew's head told him. But his wife's eyes were bluer and more imploring than ever.

'I think so,' he said.

'I know so,' Caro said.

The problem was, she didn't just want to get past it. She wanted to forget that it had ever happened. To obliterate it. The girls were her willing assistants to that end, and she, as time passed, was their unwitting accomplice. In her presence and in their grandmother's, and in the company of all others, just as before, Flic and Imogen reverted to behaving with charm and compliance towards Matthew. Alone with him, however, they were unfailingly hostile.

There were no more ugly tricks. There was no need for them. They were still at war with their stepfather, but the nature of the war was, he became steadily more certain, developing into a war of attrition by two smooth-faced, clear-eyed young women utterly focused upon wearing him down. Their weapons were in some ways appallingly adult, in that they were conceived with blatant cunning, yet in other ways they resembled the weapons of very young children. Like a one-year-old who will eat happily for one person but spit out food with another, Flic and Imogen would sit beside Matthew at dinner and converse like happy, well-bred young ladies; but if Caro was working or absent and had asked Matthew and the girls to fend for themselves, either Flic or Imo would refuse to touch anything he had made for them, or if they were the ones cooking, they would make only enough for themselves.

It was outrageous behaviour, yet they got away with that and similar acts of flagrant rudeness over and over again. Sometimes, Matthew ignored them; at other times he either challenged them or tried to find ways to punish them appropriately, but there was nothing he could deprive them of that mattered to them more than their war with him.

The difference now was that he no longer kept the incidents from Caroline. And she no longer claimed not to believe him, but chose instead, all too often, to shrug off his reports of her daughters' atrocious behaviour.

'They're young women,' Matthew pointed out more than once. 'You're acting as if they were notorious two-year-olds.'

'I'll speak to them again,' she said, also more than once, usually on a sigh, and when she did so, Imogen and Flic were all wide-eyed innocence, increasingly concerned about what might be causing their stepfather to invent such curious stories.

'They really care about you now, darling,' Caroline told him.

'They're lying to you,' he said, unequivocal now, no room left for gentle ambiguities as the battle with her daughters raged on.

'My children don't lie,' she said.

'If only,' he said.

One Sunday evening in mid-June, he took Kahli for a stroll and, having posted some letters on the way back, he passed a black Ford Escort parked on the corner of Heath Side and East Heath Road, and saw that inside the car, wrapped in the arms of Tim, the young man who'd come to their party in March, was Imogen. In her left hand, weaving a languid smoke trail, she held a cigarette, her mouth otherwise occupied in deeply kissing Tim, while her right hand appeared to be tackling the zip in his jeans.

Matthew took a breath and rapped on the passenger window.

Tim's head jolted back and his right hand, which had been exploring inside Imogen's bright pink, skimpy, midriff-exposing top, shot out and plunged downwards, dragging her fingers off his zip. Imogen, however, seeing who had knocked on the window, merely stared at Matthew, an elated, defiant stare, before placing her cigarette between her lips and taking a long drag.

Matthew tried opening the door, but it was locked.

'Imogen,' he said.

She turned her back. He walked around to the driver's door, and the young man, looking desperately caught out, opened his window.

'Tim, isn't it?'

He nodded.

'Do you have a driver's licence, Tim?' Matthew enquired.

The teenager didn't answer, but his cheeks grew warm and his eyes took on a distinctly hunted look.

'I'll assume that's a no,' Matthew said.

'Not exactly,' Tim said.

Matthew wanted to haul the young man out of the car, but had an idea that the law might regard that as assault and decided not to risk it, knew, too, that there was no possibility of his persuading his stepdaughter to come with him.

'I'm not going to tell you what to do, Tim,' he said quietly, 'except that what I trust you're going to do is walk Imogen home within the next ten minutes – and I mean *walk*, not drive. If she doesn't show up within fifteen minutes, I'll call the police.'

Tim's cheeks were now scarlet.

'I'll have her home,' he said. 'Walking.'

Matthew made a point of checking his watch. 'Ten minutes,' he repeated.

'Yes,' Tim said. 'Definitely.'

Imogen came through the front door three minutes after the deadline Matthew had set, saw him standing, waiting, in the entrance hall, glanced swiftly around to make sure there was no one else to see, then clicked her fashionably heavy heels, threw him a sharp Nazi-style salute, and walked, quite unhurriedly, upstairs.

Matthew found Caroline in the Quiet Room, stitching a cushion cover. She looked up, saw his face, gave one of her sighs.

'More problems?'

He described the incident and waited.

'Are you sure?' Caroline asked. 'That it was Tim, I mean?'

'I spoke to him. Of course I'm sure.'

'But he's far too young to drive.'

'Obviously.'

Caroline set aside her sewing and stood up. 'I'll go and speak to her.' She looked flustered and upset. 'I didn't even know she was still seeing Tim, much less going out with him today. She said she was seeing Annie Pereira.'

'Better go talk to her.' Matthew paused. 'And Caro?'

She was already at the door. 'What?'

'Don't let her bamboozle you.'

He supposed, afterwards, that given their recent record, the outcome had probably been predictable. Yet still it took his breath away.

Imogen had told Caroline that none of what he had described was true. Not a single *word* of it. She said that she had not been with Tim, that as her mother knew, they'd broken up, that she had been with her friend Annie, who would certainly vouch for her if Caro felt she needed to check up on her.

'And have you?' Matthew asked, after Caroline had come to their bedroom to report what Imogen had said. 'Not that it would mean much, since clearly Imo will have told Annie to cover for her.'

'Imogen wouldn't do that,' Caroline said.

'Imogen would do *exactly* that,' Matthew said. 'Imogen is a calculating little liar, and I really, *really* cannot believe you're falling for it – especially when we're dealing with something so dangerous.'

'But even if Imo had been out with Tim instead of Annie,' she said, 'Tim's only sixteen and a really nice boy. He doesn't seem the type to break the law by driving underage.'

'Do you happen to know what car his mother or father drives?'

'I've never met his parents,' Caroline said.

'Perhaps it's time you did.'

'Oh, God.' She sank down on the end of their bed. 'I wish I knew what . . .'

'What, Caro?' Matthew asked.

'Nothing.' She shook her head. 'I'm just so tired of these battles.'

'You were going to say you wished you knew what to believe, weren't you?'

'No.' She looked up at him. 'No, Matthew, I wasn't. I was going to say I wished I knew what to *do*.'

'So you're not suggesting I'd make up a thing like that?'

'No, of course not.' She said it wearily.

93

'So you accept that Imogen's lying to you?' He needed to persist this time, knew it was vital he force her to face the truth for once.

'Most teenagers do that, I suppose, trying to get out of trouble.'

'She's fourteen, Caro.'

'Almost fifteen.' She put up both hands, in a kind of surrender. 'I know,' she said. 'She's far too young, and the driving business is terrifying.'

Matthew thanked God, silently, for small mercies.

A new thought struck him. 'Is she on the pill?'

'*No.*' Caroline looked appalled. 'Of course not.'

'Maybe she should be,' he said.

'She most certainly should *not* be.'

He held down his irritation, decided that pregnancy and STDs were still down the list when compared with the potential for car crashes. 'You are going to speak to Tim's parents, aren't you? Ask about the car, if they know he's driving.'

'It could be very difficult,' she said.

'Get their number, and I'll gladly call them.'

'I don't think that would do your relationship with Imogen much good.'

'I don't think it would make the slightest difference,' Matthew said.

'So did Caro speak to the boy's parents?' Karl asked a few days later on the phone.

'No,' Matthew replied. 'She still claims she's going to, but I'm pretty sure she's too nervous of how Imogen might react. She swears she's going to watch Imo like a hawk from now on.'

'Nothing much you can do about that then,' Karl said.

'This whole thing with both girls is driving me nuts,' Matthew said frustratedly. 'And no one seems to see what they're like but me. They're such damned good actors. Even Sylvie's falling for them, and Isabella, of course.'

'Chloë must know the truth,' Karl said. 'You said they behave badly in front of her these days.'

'Her mother won't question Chloë,' Matthew said. 'And if she did, I'm sure she'd deny it out of loyalty.'

'But Chloë's still quite sweet when she's alone with you.'

'That's true.' Matthew paused. 'I wouldn't put it past them to threaten her.'

94

The line went silent for a moment.

'Sounds a little extreme, Matt.'

Matthew's mouth pulled into a tight, strained smile. 'You don't believe me either then?'

'I didn't say that,' Karl said. 'I think you're very upset again.'

'Understatement,' Matthew said.

'What can I do for you?' Karl asked.

'Not much.' Matthew shook his head. 'Not a damn thing, I guess, except let me blow off steam.' He paused. 'And believe what I'm telling you.'

'Of course I believe you, Matt.'

Talking to Ethan was no better. Matthew had tried for a long while to avoid having to let his brother know that things were not going well. Not that Ethan was the kind of man to say he'd told him so, but until quite recently Matthew had still been hoping to find some path through this wholeheartedly unpleasant step-parenting minefield.

No longer.

Most of all, Ethan seemed sad for him. Though sad *about* him was perhaps nearer the mark. Beneath every word spoken by his older brother as Matthew unburdened himself, lay disappointment. Ethan Gardner was clearly disheartened by his kid brother's failure to cope with his wife's daughters. He didn't say as much, but it was there all the same. He had warned Matthew about taking on another man's children. He had warned him about marrying in such great haste. He didn't exactly say anything about repenting at leisure, but it was there nevertheless.

Worst of all, like Karl, Ethan did not, Matthew felt, entirely believe him.

'They can't be quite as bad as you paint them, Matt,' he said at one point, light-heartedly. 'You're making them sound like a cross between the Mob and kids in one of those awful spawn-of-Satan movies.'

'Not quite as bad as that.' Matthew tried to keep it light too.

'They just sound to me like two unhappy young women who'd barely learned to cope with losing their dad when you breezed in.' Ethan paused. 'Wrong word, I know, Matt.'

*Wrong everything*, Matthew thought.

So much for big brother.

# 16

'He's imagining things, Mum,' Flic said to Caroline on the last Saturday afternoon in July as they were coming out of Waterstone's in the High Street, having bought four paperbacks, including one of Cate Merrill's *Blair Witch* series chosen by Flic (against Caro's better judgment) for Imogen, who would be fifteen tomorrow.

'I don't think so.' Caroline lingered outside the shop, trying to remember what it was she'd forgotten to buy and wishing for at least the hundredth time that this wretched situation would finally – please, God, *happily* – resolve itself. 'I know he's miserable about you girls, and that's certainly not my imagination.'

'But he is imagining us not liking him,' Flic insisted.

'Candles,' Caro remembered abruptly. Isabella had baked a cake, and even though Imo would probably yawn and say she was far too old for birthday cake, even Flic agreed that her sister would be inclined to sulk if there wasn't one.

The day was warm, so they walked slowly down the broad but crowded pavement into Rosslyn Hill towards the party shop, pausing briefly to gaze into Ronit Zilkha and Hobb's, then going into The Body Shop so that Caroline could buy some pot pourri for the downstairs loo. The shop was busy, the fragrances relaxing, though once back outside the illusion of calm was instantly gone.

'Maybe that used to be true.' Having let her mother drift away from the subject, Flic relentlessly brought her back. 'Us not being sure about Matthew, I mean. But it really isn't true any more, and we've tried so hard to convince him, but he just won't seem to accept it.' She paused. 'I'm not quite sure that he wants to.'

Caroline sighed, stopped again outside Gap. 'Want to go in?'

'No,' Flic said. 'You can't keep on pretending this isn't happening, Mum.'

'I'm not,' Caroline said. 'Though I often wish I could.'

They continued down the hill, leaving the trendier boutiques and bustle behind, passing Snappy Snaps, the newsagents and a series of service outlets, and Caroline paused again outside the delicatessen that Sylvie had renamed 'Pure Heaven'.

'They only delivered yesterday, Mum.'

'So they did.' Caroline sighed, another escape hatch blocked off by her persistent daughter. 'Oh, Flic, this is all making me so unhappy. And poor Matthew's really getting fed up.'

'I'm sorry.' Flic's long fringe, in need of trimming, brushed against her eyelashes, and she flicked it back. 'Really sorry for Matthew, too, but I'm much sorrier for you.' She tucked her arm through Caroline's and walked them on past the Victorian Gothic unitarian chapel. 'You're my mother.' She squeezed Caro's arm more tightly. 'I can't help caring more about you than him – surely that's natural, isn't it?'

'Of course it is,' Caroline said. 'And Matthew's the first to understand that.'

'Then how come, however much we try to get along with him, he keeps on seeing problems that really don't exist?' At last they'd reached the party shop. 'That's what I'm trying to tell you, Mum. I'm beginning to wonder if he actually *wants* things to be better between us.'

Caro drew away, the frown between her brows deepening. 'What do you mean, Flic?' She was growing exasperated. 'Why on earth should Matthew not want things to get better? It's a ridiculous thing to say.'

Flic shrugged, and opened the door of the shop. 'If you say so.'

Matthew had not been looking forward to Imogen's birthday, the first family birthday he had participated in. He had privately been hoping that Imo might want to celebrate with friends, perhaps even with Tim, but Caroline had told him – in strictest confidence – that they really had broken up, and that Imogen was now officially 'off boys' and apparently looking forward to a family-only barbecue at home.

'I expect Richard was a dab hand with the charcoal,' Matthew had said lightly.

'As a matter of fact,' Caro had smiled, 'he was useless at it. He never got the coals hot enough, and he used to get very impatient and throw fuel all over it, and I was always afraid he'd set himself alight.'

'Probably what Imo's hoping I'll do,' Matthew remarked.

And his wife had sighed.

He'd been especially careful as the birthday had approached, had asked Caroline what kind of present she thought he should buy Imogen.

'We'll buy something together,' she had said. 'Surely?'

'Fine,' he'd said. 'Though maybe I should still get her a little personal something, show her I made the effort.'

'That's a lovely thought,' Caroline had said with pleasure.

And it might have been, had his true motive not been to give his stepdaughter one less opportunity to snipe at him.

'So,' he'd said, 'any ideas?'

Caroline had said she'd have a ponder, and then later that same day, Flic had come to tell him that Imogen would adore anything from Lush, especially the bath bombs, and Matthew had instantly decided to go anywhere *but* there, and had taken up Caro's suggestion of a Jean Paul Gaultier perfume instead.

He almost laughed at his own wariness as he lit the barbecue, at the absurd sabotage scenarios passing through his mind. He was reasonably sure, he decided – making a kind of private game of it – that the food would not have been tampered with, firstly because risking poisoning the entire family – even if they *could* find a way to pin it on him – might be too extreme, and secondly because he guessed it would be beneath Flic and Imogen to use the same kind of trick twice.

Nothing went wrong. No disasters, not even a hiccup. His charcoal caught beautifully and turned white-hot, his timing of all meats, poultry and vegetables was spot-on. No poison. No hidden mangoes. No uncontrolled blaze. Not even so much as a case of indigestion. The food was fine, the beer, wine and Cokes all ice-cool and delicious. Everyone except Chloë got a little merry, but no one got drunk. Halfway through the afternoon, Isabella arrived with Mick and gave Imogen a CD by someone called White Stripes and a twisted snake ring from Camden Market, and the birthday girl was relaxed and happy, and Matthew thought how lovely she looked when her face wasn't taut with dislike or disdain, and found himself wishing yet again that things could be different between them . . .

Isabella and Mick had left again by the time the family gave Imogen her gifts. They were in the drawing room now, the garden doors still open, the air of gentle relaxation continuing. Sylvie had bought Imogen the new mobile phone she'd wished for – the best one, according to Imo, for texting – and a handsomely-boxed collection of dramatic make-up from Harvey Nichols. Chloë had bought her a Robbie Williams CD, and Flic had taken her own recommendation (knowing that Matthew had not) and wrapped a whole armful of products from Lush – and *there* was one of those moments, with a subtly arched eyebrow from Flic to emphasize that she'd known he wouldn't trust her advice. It *was* only a moment, though, and Imogen was still opening parcels and the mood was still fine, and she'd come to the brilliant emerald-green and vivid pink silk wrap that Caroline had chosen as their main gift; and Imogen loved it and tied it around her bare midriff, and it blew in the breeze from the garden, its knotted silk fringes narrowly escaping being set alight by the birthday candles on the cake that Chloë brought in.

When it came to Matthew's perfume, she thanked him with enthusiasm, even kissed his cheek, and for a moment he almost fell for the act, but then he caught the glint in her eyes and was reminded of the way things really were.

'See?' Caro leaned across the sofa to murmur softly. 'She was really pleased, you could see that, couldn't you, darling?'

'I'm glad,' Matthew said, and left it there.

But an hour and a half later, festivities over and the evening growing cooler, he left Caroline, Sylvie, Chloë and the dog sitting in the drawing room, and went upstairs to fetch a sweater for Caro. As the bedroom door shut behind him and he walked across to the chest of drawers, he heard footsteps out in the corridor. He dug out the cream cotton V neck his wife had asked for and left the room again.

To reach the staircase, he had to pass the bathroom next to Chloë's bedroom. The door was open and Imogen was inside, standing beside the lavatory, holding something in her right hand.

The perfume bottle he'd given her.

Her eyes were on him.

Matthew knew he should turn away, knew it would have been the smartest move, the one that would have infuriated her most. But he couldn't help staring as she tilted the bottle and poured every last drop of its contents into the bowl. And then flushed it. And smiled at him.

He handled it as best he could. He nodded, gave the smallest of bows, a touch of courtliness about it that vaguely satisfied him, then went on his way back downstairs.

'Caro.' He called her quietly from the drawing room door. 'I need a word.'

He saw the little frown wrinkle her forehead as she got up, knew that she realized it was going to be something upsetting connected with her daughters, and he was sorry about that, of course, but there were times, he decided, when keeping the peace because his wife had once been depressed just wasn't on.

He drew her into the kitchen and told her, quietly and calmly.

'It's not the perfume, Caro – that's just an idiotic piece of waste by an arrogant, spoiled, immature girl.' His anger was rising, despite his best intentions. 'It's the fact that Imogen – and I daresay Flic had a hand in it – the fact that they clearly feel they can be as obnoxious to me as they like without their mother raising even the smallest objection.'

Caroline was upset, bewildered. 'I can't take this in.' She leaned against the refrigerator door. 'You're telling me that Imo actually took your lovely perfume and flushed it down the loo?'

'After she'd made certain I was watching, yes.' Matthew shook his head. 'I'm only telling you this now because I want you to realize that I'm not prepared to spend any more time being nice to Imogen today, birthday or no birthday.'

'No, of course not.' She shook her head. 'What would you like me to do?'

'That's your decision,' he said. 'I'm not telling you to do anything, just making sure you know that small as this is, it's one piece of shitty behaviour too many.'

'Yes,' Caroline said. 'Yes, of course it is.'

'Okay.' Matthew leaned forward, stroked a couple of strands of her hair off her face. 'Now I'm going back in to sit with your mother and Chloë. I won't tell them about this, obviously.' He turned towards the door. 'Coming?'

'In a minute,' she said.

He stopped, looked back at her. 'You know,' he said, very quietly, 'I'm really beginning to wonder if maybe Imo shouldn't be seeing someone again.'

'What sort of someone?' Caroline asked, though she knew what he meant.

'A shrink,' Matthew said.

Caroline waited until he was back in the drawing room, then she poured herself a glass of Evian from the fridge, drank half of it, saw that her hand was shaking, lowered the glass into the sink and left the kitchen. Matthew and Sylvie were talking, in calm, gentle voices, two civilized grown-ups getting along beautifully at the end of a lovely day, and Chloë was fondling the retriever's ears.

Her eyes filled with tears, and angrily she brushed them away and went upstairs.

Imogen's door was closed. Caroline knocked on it, received no answer and opened it tentatively. The room was empty. She paused, listened, heard voices coming from Flic's room next door, and went inside, softly shutting the door behind her.

She was not in the habit of entering any of her daughters' rooms without their knowledge, other than to collect dirty washing and either to tidy up or resolve to tell them to do so. And going into Imogen's room without actual permission, ignoring the PRIVATE sign that her middle child had hung on her door at the age of twelve, was often the equivalent to lighting blue touch paper on a firework and forgetting to withdraw.

But Imo's birthday gifts were all just lying there, openly, on her bedspread, wrapping paper strewn around, and cards. And there, beside Sylvie's phone and Isabella's and Mick's CD, was the distinctive silvery tin containing Matthew's perfume.

Caroline went over and picked it up. It was still sealed and from its weight in her hand there was no question that every ounce of perfume was still inside the bottle.

The door opened behind her. She turned, steeling herself for an eruption.

Imogen and Flic both stood in the doorway.

'What's going on, Mum?' Imogen asked.

'I'm sorry, darling.'

'Why are you looking at that?' Imogen asked, unexpectedly calmly.

Flic said nothing, just stood, watching.

Caroline couldn't think of a viable fib. 'Oh, dear,' she said, weakly.

Flic came further into the room. 'What's the matter, Mum?'

'You look upset.' Imogen closed the door behind them. 'Who's upset you on my birthday?'

'Bet I can guess,' Flic said, grimly.

Caroline looked at the tin in her hand and put it back down on the bedspread.

'What are we supposed to have done now, Mum?' Imo asked.

Caro looked at both her daughters, into the faces she had loved with utterly faithful passion from the days they were born, and knew, with a dull, heavy thump of emotional pain, that if push came to shove, her allegiance had to lie with them.

She told them what Matthew had said.

'You see?' Imogen stalked over to the window and stared out over the Heath. 'See what we have to put up with?'

'So what did he see you pouring into the loo?' Caroline asked.

'Nothing.' Imogen turned back to face her mother. 'I haven't poured anything into any loo. From any bottle.' She paused. 'I mean, why *would* I?'

'Exactly, Mum,' Flic said, gently.

'But why would Matthew invent something like that?' Caro said helplessly. 'It would be so—'

'Petty?' Flic supplied.

'Stupid,' Imogen added.

'Stop it, Imo,' Caroline said. 'Both of you. Please.'

'We're sorry, Mum,' Flic said, 'but we've both had just about enough of his horrid, pathetic inventions.'

'A gutful,' Imogen added.

'We're tried hard,' Flic said. 'We honestly have.'

'So has Matthew,' Caroline said defensively.

Imogen gave a small derisive snort.

'I hate to say it, Mum,' Flic said, 'but I really think you need to deal with this.' She paused. 'I think Matthew's got some problems.'

'Big time,' Imo said.

When Caroline emerged from Imogen's room, Matthew was standing at the top of the staircase, waiting for her.

'I thought you were talking to Mama,' she said.

'She's taking a nap.' He paused. 'So?'

She took a breath. She had hoped to postpone this till later or next day or, if she was perfectly honest, forever. No chance of that now.

'Can we go into our room, please?' she said.

Later on, looking back, they both found it frightening how rapidly they had slid downhill, like sledders out of control on ice, to somewhere far below simply *worse*.

'You said,' Caro began, 'you thought Imo had problems.'

'Has,' Matthew said.

They were standing in the middle of the room facing each other tensely, body language confrontational, like warriors rather than lovers.

'You said you thought she should see a shrink.'

'Shrink. Psychologist. Counsellor.'

'Susanna, perhaps, or someone like her.'

'That's not for me to say,' Matthew said.

Caroline hadn't realized until then how angry she was with him for that suggestion alone – the suggestion that her daughter was mentally ill. Excluding the real possibility that he might have invented the tale that had led to that suggestion.

'The perfume you gave Imo is still in its bottle,' she said quietly. 'I've seen it.'

'Maybe you saw another bottle,' he said.

'No,' she told him. 'I went into her room when she wasn't there, and I saw the tin with all her other presents, still sealed.'

Matthew stood very still, thinking. 'Then clearly she took another Gaultier bottle and poured that away. Maybe an old, empty one that she filled with water and poured down the pan. So *what*? It's still the same piece of nastiness, the same level of contempt for me.' He paused. 'Can't you see that, Caro?'

'Imogen just told me that she poured nothing out of *any* bottle.'

'Then I'm sorry to say so again, but Imogen is a liar.'

103

'She's my daughter.' Caroline's jaw was clenched.

'Believe me,' Matthew said tightly, 'I'm all too aware of that. If she and Flic were not your children, I'd have stopped giving them the time of day long ago.'

Caroline shut her eyes for just a second. 'Flic says she thinks you're the one with problems.'

'Does she? And what do you think?'

'I think she may have a point.' She paused. 'In fact, I've been wondering – I was thinking about it even before today – if maybe you might like to talk to Susanna about things.'

He was speechless.

'It wouldn't have to be Susanna, of course,' Caro said.

'It wouldn't,' Matthew said, very quietly.

'No, of course not. Whoever you think.'

'A shrink of my choice, in other words,' he said.

She realized, suddenly, that she had gone too far, that a great invisible barrier had just slammed down between them. Awful fear and sadness swept over her, yet she could not see a way back, just stumbled on. 'Not really a shrink at all,' she said. 'Just some kind of counsellor, to help with—'

'Stop it, Caro,' he cut her off.

'Matthew, I'm sorry, but you don't appreciate how awful this is for me.'

'For you?' he said. 'Not for me?'

'Yes, of course for you, too,' she said. 'But they aren't your children.'

'Thank God,' he said fervently.

'Matthew,' she reproached.

He laughed, once, harshly. 'Are you *kidding* me?' For once, the hurt in her beautiful eyes scarcely touched him. 'Can you possibly imagine I would want to lay claim to those two unfeeling snakes?'

'That's nice.' Caroline was scrambling up onto higher ground, not knowing where else to run for cover. 'You've already called them arrogant and spoiled.'

'Because that's what they *are*, though most of all they're screwed up, and you know they are, and I can almost understand your wanting to try to deny that to yourself, but—'

'How do I know *you're* not the one who's screwed up?'

He didn't answer.

'How do I decide who to believe, Matthew?'

'Maybe we should postpone this. Wait till your mother's gone home, wait till later.'

'I can't postpone it,' Caroline said. 'I couldn't bear to go back downstairs now and pretend that things are fine, normal.'

'No,' Matthew agreed. 'Nor could I.'

'So why suggest it?'

'Because I'm afraid that any minute now I'm going to tell you how I really feel, and maybe I won't be able to keep on talking quietly and reasonably, as if I were speaking to some stranger instead of my wife.'

'You want to shout at me,' she said.

'I don't want to shout at anyone, least of all you,' he said. 'I've never much enjoyed losing my temper.'

'Susanna thinks it might be better if you could,' Caroline said.

He stared at her. 'You've talked about this to her?'

'Yes,' she said. 'I had to talk to someone. Haven't you?'

'Yes.' He nodded slowly. 'Yes, I have. I've talked to Karl and to Ethan.' He shrugged. 'Of course you had to talk to someone. I just wish it weren't—'

'Susanna?' She paused. 'You see?'

'See what?'

'She's another one you've never liked.'

'Not especially, no.'

'You see?' she said again. 'You do have these fixed ideas about people. The people I'm closest to.'

'Oh, no.' He saw where she was heading. 'Oh, no, you don't, Caro. Don't you even *think* about trying to label me that way.'

'Which way?'

He went over to the bed, sat down heavily on the edge. 'I can almost hear her.'

'Who?'

'Susanna.' He shook his head. 'What does she tell you? Let me guess. That I'm jealous, of the girls and of her? Because I feel you're closer to them than me?'

'Maybe it's true,' Caroline said.

'Jesus,' he said. 'Jesus.'

'What?' She came and sat down beside him. 'I'm just trying to get a sensible perspective on all this awfulness, darling.'

105

He looked into her face. 'You really don't see it, do you?'

'See what, Matthew?' she asked, patient now.

'The truth,' he said. 'About Flic and Imo.'

'But aren't we going beyond that now? Isn't that the point of what I've just been saying?'

'What?' he asked. 'That it isn't anything to do with them? That I've invented their whole campaign?'

'Not exactly *invented*,' Caroline said.

'Jesus,' Matthew said again. 'Jesus *Christ*, Caro!' He was back up on his feet, and his frustration was intolerable now, hot and burning in his chest.

'Matthew, please,' she said from the bed. 'Please let's try to be reasonable, let's try to find the right way to deal with this.' She stood up. 'If you don't want to see Susanna, then at least—'

'Will you stop? Will you just *stop*?' Finally, he was yelling.

'Matthew, please—'

'Not one more word,' he said, 'not one more *word* about Susanna, not in relation to me, okay? If you and your fucked-up daughters want to consult a woman who doesn't seem to know there's supposed to be a line between being a shrink and a friend, then go ahead.' He was still shouting, and he didn't like that or the things he was saying to her, yet at the same time it felt good, it felt *fine* right now. 'If you want to kid yourself that Flic and Imo are good, decent, blameless girls, and this is all my fault, I can't stop you.'

'I think Susanna must be right,' Caroline said.

He stopped yelling.

Instead, he went to the door, opened it, went out into the corridor and straight down the staircase, not even glancing towards the girls' bedrooms.

'Matthew?' Sylvie stood outside the drawing room door. 'Are you all right?'

'No,' he said. 'I'm afraid I'm far from all right.'

And he went to the front door, opened it, walked through it, shut it behind him, quite normally, not slamming it.

And walked away.

# 17

He went back, of course. In the first place, he'd taken nothing with him, not even his wallet. In the second, he *wanted* to go back. He'd told Sylvie that evening in the pub in Highgate that he was no quitter, and it was still, he hoped, true. He might have married in haste, but he had been one hundred per cent conscious of what he was doing, and why. Love. And liking. And the tremendous, overwhelming desire to be with Caroline above all else.

He had questioned that desire quite aggressively as he'd walked off his anger and frustration that summer's evening. Had too much of his need to marry her stemmed from the loveliness of the whole package that was Caro? He had counted off, yet again, stomping down East Heath Road, all the reasons he'd fallen so hard, comparing her to his first wife. Jillian had been beautiful, too, and sexy, and clever and sophisticated, and they had been good friends forever before they'd married, and yet their marriage had been disastrous. In Caroline, the lovely widowed mother of three, the heart of her charming, tight-knit European family, maybe it had been the things he *hadn't* been able to see that had drawn him so forcefully to her side? Had he perhaps been so foolish as to believe that because, with Jillian, familiarity had proven so little help, the excitement of the voyage of discovery would have the opposite effect?

In many ways, it had. Life with Caro, the woman, the individual, was pure pleasure. Left alone together, given space and time, they got along famously, and Caroline's vulnerability had, if anything, made Matthew love her more, not less. Even her shying away from discord, her genuine, if unrealistic, yearning for harmony, made him wish, if possible, to shield her from pain.

*Ought to work both ways*, he thought as he walked through South End Road, past the neighbourhood restaurants and grocery stores, gradually shedding the worst of his vexation.

That was the heart of the problem. Caro was too intent on shielding her daughters, at his expense. She had put him first by marrying him, and the guilt of that act seemed to make it impossible for her to take his side now, even when she knew he was in the right. And maybe that was normal; maybe most mothers, in her position, would choose their children over their new husband?

Karl and Ethan had both warned him about Caro's daughters, and he hadn't listened. How, he still remembered thinking at the time, could three beautiful young girls represent anything other than additional joy?

*Live and learn, Matthew Gardner.*

He had learned. Was still learning. Still hoping, though increasingly more against the odds, that he wasn't going to screw up a second marriage, and with it this time the lives of more than just two people. Still hoping that time, patience and love might yet see them all through.

So he went back.


'I have a compromise to suggest, if you're willing.'

He had waited until late, until he was as sure as he could be that his stepdaughters were all sleeping or, at least, out of earshot.

'What kind of compromise?' Caro asked warily, lowering the novel she had been pretending to read.

'I think that perhaps, on reflection, we might all benefit from some kind of family therapy.'

'Not with Susanna, I take it?'

'I don't think that's her area of expertise, is it?' Matthew ignored her irony. 'But even if it is, no, definitely not with Susanna.' He paused. 'But someone else. Someone detached, someone used to dealing with step-family problems.'

She thought for a moment. 'Yes,' she said. 'I think family therapy might be a very good idea.'

'If the girls agree,' Matthew said.

'I think they will,' Caroline said.

'I hope so,' he said.

'Thank you, Matthew,' she said.
'You're welcome.'

'You *are* joking,' Imogen said.
'Hardly,' Caroline said.
'No way,' Imogen said. 'Absolutely no *way*.'
'I agree,' Flic said.
They were in Caroline's Range Rover, driving home from school along Primrose Hill Road. Chloë had gone to the cinema with Beatrice's family, so their mother had felt it a good opportunity for a private moment with her two older girls.
'But darlings, why not?' Caro was upset, though not entirely surprised.
'Because we don't need therapy,' Flic told her simply. 'Because the only person round here who does is Matthew.'
'But you've both told me you want to try to make things better.'
'We did want to,' Flic said. 'We've been trying for more than six months and all he's done is throw it back in our faces.'
'And now he's trying to compromise by suggesting some family therapy, because a *family* is what he wants us to be – and I'm beginning to think that it may be our last chance.'
'We already are a family, Mum,' Flic said.
'We were before he came along,' Imogen said.
Caroline felt her spirits slump deeper.
'It's not our fault,' Flic said as they drove round the back roads of Belsize Park.
'We're not talking about fault,' Caroline said.
'*He* is,' Imogen said.
'Or he would,' Flic added, 'if we went to his *therapist*.' She stressed the word with distaste.
'Anyway,' Imogen said, 'I wouldn't go to some stranger.'
'It wouldn't be so bad,' Caroline coaxed. 'We'd all be together.'
'I don't want to be together with Matthew and a strange shrink,' Imo said.
'Nor do I, Mum,' Flic backed her up.
'So what do I tell him?' Caro was becoming annoyed. 'That you refuse point-blank? That you won't even consider the one thing that may help our marriage?'
'Tell him,' Flic said, thoughtfully, 'that there's only one way I'd

consider any kind of family therapy, and that's if we all go to Susanna.'

'Matthew doesn't want to go to Susanna,' Caroline said.

'See?' Imogen said.

'He thinks we'd be better off with someone detached.'

'Someone he'll probably want to tell his side of things to before we even get there,' Flic said.

'He wouldn't do that,' Caroline said.

'I won't go to a stranger,' Imogen said again. 'No way, Mum. No bloody way. You can't make me.'

'I can't make them go,' Caroline told Matthew that evening in the Quiet Room.

'I guess not,' he said.

She read the irritation in his face. 'They're not little girls, Matthew. We can hardly drag them there kicking and screaming.'

'Nor would I want to,' he said, fighting to stay patient.

'So what do we do now?' she asked.

For a moment he said nothing. Then he shook his head and gave a soft sigh. He had pretty much assumed this would be the outcome. A pair of up-and-coming control freaks like Flic and Imogen were not likely to willingly enter into a situation in which they would be so patently *out* of control.

'Okay,' he said. 'We'll try Susanna.'

'Really?' She was startled.

'But no one talks to her before our meeting,' Matthew said emphatically. 'I mean, I'm sure she already knows all about our problems, but—'

'She knows a little,' Caroline said, 'but not much. Truly.'

'Not from you, maybe, but don't you think the girls have talked to her?' He gave a wry smile. 'What am I saying? Chances are one of them's in their room right now on the phone to her, paving the way.'

'You mustn't be so cynical,' Caroline protested.

He smiled again, tiredly. 'I never used to be.'

'No,' she said. 'I realize that.'

If he had ever doubted it, one session was more than enough to convince Matthew that it was a pointless exercise.

110

They gathered, on the first Saturday of August in Susanna's sitting-cum-consulting room in her semi-detached house in Muswell Hill. It was a spacious, pretty room with large bay windows, several vases of blue and violet flowers and a number of small, neatly framed comical drawings of cats on the walls. It was a room that might, at another time and in other circumstances, have felt pleasingly cool and calm, but today it felt muggy and warm.

'Would you mind switching that on, Matthew?' Susanna indicated a large pedestal fan just behind his chair.

'I'd be delighted.' He stood up.

'I'd rather you didn't,' Flic said, sitting beside him. 'I'm going to a party this evening and if my hair gets blown around it'll be impossible.'

'Your hair always looks lovely,' Caroline said.

'Not when it gets blown about,' Flic insisted. 'And there won't be time now for me to wash it again, will there?'

'You could change seats,' Matthew suggested.

'I'd much rather you didn't,' Susanna said, having seated them all with deliberation in a small, only slightly spread-out semi-circle which, she'd explained, she thought might be beneficial to the session.

The semi-circle began from the left with Chloë sitting next to Imogen, and from the right with Caroline, sitting beside Flic, with Matthew in the middle.

'Why doesn't Flic swap with Imo?' Matthew suggested.

'If I sit close to fans,' Imogen said, 'I get a neck-ache.'

'I really *would* prefer it,' Susanna said, 'if you all remain where you are.'

Meaning, Matthew decided, grimly, in a position of maximum discomfort from his point-of-view. Kept apart from Caro and Chloë, the two people who might have lent him a degree of support; sandwiched between his two young Nemeses; and right in the middle, which, he felt, was probably designed to make him feel like the focus of an inquiry. Like a defendant.

'I've tucked you in the middle, Matthew,' Susanna said, 'to place you right at the core of the family.' She smiled at him, then looked at Flic. 'So you'd be more comfortable with the fan off, would you?'

'Please.'

Which seemed, from Matthew's perspective, to set the tone for the rest of the afternoon. Susanna said that she hoped they would all speak in turn, saying exactly how they felt about the state of the family, after which, she said, they would have more of a to-and-fro exchange.

'Caro, would you like to go first?'

'Not really,' Caroline said.

Susanna said nothing, just smiled, very gently, and waited.

'Oh, dear,' Caro said.

'Take your time,' Susanna said.

'There's no need,' Caroline said. 'My feelings are actually very simple. Very straightforward. I love my children and my husband.' She looked at Matthew. 'And I only said "children" first, darling, because it seemed natural, because, I suppose, they came into my life long before you.'

'It's okay,' Matthew told her.

'Let's allow Caro time to have her say, shall we?' Susanna chided him.

Matthew gritted his teeth.

'Go on, Mum,' Flic said.

'We won't interrupt,' Imogen said.


'A total waste of time and energy,' Matthew told Karl on the phone on Monday. 'Caro and I made an attempt, and we, at least, were both sincere about it.'

'But not the girls?' Karl asked.

'Chloë excepted, of course. Poor kid hated it.'

'What did she say when it was her turn?'

'Not much,' Matthew said. 'That she loved us all, and she didn't understand why we couldn't all just be happy together. She's pretty young for her age, and her sisters like keeping her that way.'

'Probably they like having a baby sister.'

'I think it suits them, makes her easier to manipulate.'

'You need to be careful, Matt,' Karl said.

'Tell me about it.'

'No, I mean you should be careful not to see everything Felicity and Imogen do as part of a plot against you.'

Matthew felt his jaw clench with disappointment but tried to stay light. 'Still think I'm paranoid then, Karl?'

'A little, I suppose,' Karl admitted, 'though I don't really blame you.'

Matthew said nothing.

'Perhaps you should try again,' Karl said, 'with another thera-pist, as you first suggested. Be straight with Caro, tell her you'll go on with the counselling, but only if it's on really neutral terri-tory.'

'Waste of time,' Matthew said grimly.

'Bad attitude, Matt,' Karl said.

And so it went on. His first August in London. One minute high summer, the next cool and damp. His marriage limping on. The girls off school – little difference from his point of view, since he was at work. They grumbled to Caroline about the lack of holiday plans, but she and Matthew agreed that a family trip would almost certainly be disastrous at present.

'Why can't we go without him?' Matthew had heard Imogen asking her mother one day in the kitchen, well aware that he was in earshot.

'I wouldn't want to go on holiday without him,' Caro had answered, and he had been filled with so much love and gratitude that he'd almost gone out to a travel agency to book tickets for her and the three girls. Except that – he'd realized just in time – his gift of love would probably have been turned against him, too. 'Glad to get rid of us,' he could almost hear Flic or Imo saying, making their mother wonder if it were true.

There had been no more pushes towards therapy, either with Susanna or anyone else. Caroline seemed resigned that such sessions would be pointless, that unless all participants came with open hearts and minds, no amount of counselling could do much good. Her defeatism, though he shared it, made Matthew sad.

Everything this summer was making him sad.

Except for work, which had taken an upward turn soon after Imogen's birthday. All Stephen Steerforth's Tower Hill jobs had gone, but Bianco's other golden boy, Andrew MacNeice, had suggested to Matthew that he compete for a share in his next project, a new church near Canterbury. The successful applicants would ultimately work to MacNeice's own designs, but the brief for their submission was liberatingly non-specific; the aspiring architects could offer designs for either the whole building or for a single element within the whole.

In the early weeks of his marriage, Matthew might have been

reluctant to work overtime. Now, work became his luxury, his submission to MacNeice his greatest pleasure.

'Still at it?' Katrina Dunn came back into the office just before eight one evening in the middle of the month, having left her cheque book in her desk drawer, and found him hunched over his board. 'Any chance of a peek?'

Matthew sat up and stretched. 'It's for Canterbury.'

'I assumed.' She smiled. 'I won't breathe a word to anyone else, you know.'

'I don't think people are lining up to hear about my work, Kat.'

'And I'm not in the running myself.' Her soft Scots lilt was persuasive.

'Even if you were,' Matthew said, 'I'd be glad of your opinion.'

He leaned right back so she could take a good long look over his shoulder. She was small and trim, and had recently had her red hair cut short, its natural bouncing curls suiting her personality.

'Wow,' she said.

He felt a kick of pleasure, followed instantly by doubt. 'Is that "wow" as in "this is okay", or as in "this is so shitty I can't think of anything kind to say"?'

Kat looked away from the drawings and at him. 'Don't you know?'

Matthew shook his head. 'I might have,' he said, 'in the past.'

'Why not now?'

He shrugged.

'I'm sorry,' she said. 'I'm being nosy.'

'No, you're not,' he said. 'Just interested.'

Kat looked back at the board. 'This is more than okay. It's wonderful.'

'You think?' Matthew looked at his drawing of a church in the round, a glass-walled, silvery steel-and-glass-spired building surrounded by wooded gardens and gentle pathways and two pools with benches all around.

'Definitely,' Kat said. 'Airy in summer, sheltered in winter.' 'And you're inviting nature into church instead of sealing it out.'

'Obviously it's never going to see the light of day.'

'Never know,' Kat said. 'MacNeice might love it so much he might dump his own plans.'

*

114

Increasingly, as he saw how hard Caro found it to do constant battle with Flic and Imogen, Matthew decamped to Bedford Square to bury himself in work. Clapham was finally mercifully finished, and with his Canterbury entry now submitted, he was working on the new wing of a psychiatric hospital in Surrey with Kat and Robert Fairbairn, and that project was proving stimulating.

'I'm glad the work is better for you,' Karl said in early September.

Matthew heard dubiousness in his friend's voice. 'But?'

'Only that it sounds now as if you're using it in order to escape from home, and that's not so good.'

'Nothing a million or so other guys haven't done through the years.'

'Not when they're newly-weds.'

'Newly-weds don't usually have three teenage kids, two of whom really *wouldn't* cross the road to spit on them if they were on fire.'

'I guess not,' Karl agreed.

# 18

'You said we'd be rid of him by summer,' Imogen reminded her older sister during one of their late night counsels of war in Flic's room. 'You said we could imagine summer here at Aethiopia, and picture it without him. And now it's almost autumn, and he's still here, and he's *happier* than he was instead of more miserable.'

'He does have more staying power than I expected.'

'He's like clinging ivy.' Imogen shuddered. 'I can almost feel him putting his suckers all over our house. I feel as if we'll never get them off if we wait much longer. It's making Aethiopia feel dirty, it makes *me* feel dirty, imagining him pawing Mum every night in Dad's bed.'

'Take it easy, Imo.' Flic looked at her sister, hunched over on the duvet at the end of her bed. She always worried when Imogen got too intense; it made her remember how ill she'd been after their father's death – how ill she and their mother had both been.

'I can't help it.'

'Of course you can.'

'I can't. You have to do something, Flic. You *have* to, before it's too late.'

'Shush,' Flic said. 'I'm thinking.' Something Imogen had said just a moment ago had sparked an idea.

'You're always thinking,' Imogen complained.

'Shut *up*, Imo, I think I've got a new plan.'

'Better be a bloody fantastic one.'

116

It was so simple Flic couldn't imagine why she hadn't thought of it before. But then, as she'd come to realize, the simple ones were always the best, the most foolproof.

'Actually,' she said slowly, 'I think it is.'

'Tell me,' Imogen said.

'Only thing is, though, it's going to be mostly down to you. A real acting job.'

'At least that's something we know I'm quite good at.' Imogen had been landing plum roles in school drama productions long before they'd gone to The Grange. Chloë was the artist, but Imo, it had been said, had real potential as an actor.

'You'll need to be,' Flic said.

Three evenings later, on a Wednesday, Imogen turned up without warning at the flat in Perrin's Lane.

'Isn't this the evening you have extra maths?' Sylvie asked.

'Yes.'

'Then why are you here instead of there?'

'Because I need to speak to you, Groosi.'

Sylvie looked at her often troubled, often troublesome grand-daughter, and suppressed a sigh. 'Do we need tea?'

'You probably will,' Imogen said.

She waited while her grandmother busied herself in her tiny modern kitchen, then carried the tray for her into the living room, a calm room decorated in pale rose, with burr walnut furniture including a longcase clock, a Chinese carpet and a group of abstract paintings by a young Swiss artist. There were photographs everywhere and four vases of roses, but no plants, for Sylvie claimed that even the hardiest of houseplants died within an hour or so of crossing her threshold.

They were seated on the sofa and the tea had been poured before Imogen came to the point. 'I don't know how much more I can take, Groosi.' She paused. 'And I don't want to upset Mum any more than she already is.'

Sylvie's apprehension grew. She took a sip of tea, and waited.

'He's still doing it,' Imogen said. 'Still whingeing on to Mum about us.'

Sylvie put down her cup. 'Matthew doesn't strike me as a whinger.'

'He's complained to you about us, hasn't he?'

'He's told me his side of the story, yes.'

'I know you're on his side, just like Chloë and Mum,' Imogen said disgustedly.

'I'm not interested in taking sides, Imo, when it comes to my own family.'

'But *we're* your family, not him.'

'Matthew's married to your mother now. He is your stepfather, like it or not.'

'He makes me sick,' Imogen said.

'I know he wishes—'

'I mean *really* sick,' Imogen cut in. 'All the time lately.'

Sylvie frowned. 'Your mother hasn't said anything.'

'She doesn't know.'

'That isn't clever, darling. If you're ill—'

'I'm not ill,' Imogen said, 'not like that.' She shook her head. 'But my stomach's in knots, and I can't concentrate on anything, and I never sleep properly at night in case . . .' She stopped.

'In case what?'

'You won't believe me.'

'What won't I believe?' Sylvie was getting a bad feeling.

Imogen shook her head again. 'It isn't as simple as that.' She stood up. 'This isn't as clear-cut as Matthew accusing us of things. This is different, Groosi.' She paused. 'And it's just possible that it *might* be my imagination.'

Sylvie watched her granddaughter walk over to the windows and gaze down into the courtyard below. 'Imogen, you've come here because you have something to tell me, so please just tell me.'

Imogen turned around. 'It's the way he looks at me.'

'Looks?'

'You know,' Imogen said, meaningfully.

Sylvie stared at her.

'I knew it,' Imo said. 'You don't believe me.'

Sylvie shook her head, aghast. 'Imo, you can't mean . . .' She took a deep breath. 'Tell me exactly what you do mean.'

'I mean that he *looks* at me, when we're alone. At my breasts. And my legs, sometimes. He looks at me like some men do, you know, in the street. Like a pervert.' Her bottom lip trembled. 'That's why I feel sick all the time, and why I can't sleep, because I'm always afraid he's going to come into my room.'

'But he hasn't. Has he?' Sylvie's heart was pounding. 'Imogen, does he ever come into your room?'

'No,' Imogen answered. 'At least . . .'

'Imogen, *tell* me.' Sylvie was quite sharp.

'I was just going to say not that I know of.' Imogen shrugged. 'I can't tell you what happens when I do fall asleep, and I have to sleep sometimes, don't I?'

It was the shrug that had signalled the seed of doubt in Sylvie's mind. Though it hadn't quite registered at the time. She had been too shocked, too appalled, to register anything but Imogen's words and their connotations.

Her first impulse had been to accompany her granddaughter home, to go straight to Caroline and report what Imo had told her, to insist that if there was even the *smallest* possibility that it was true then Matthew must be asked to leave right away.

'No,' Imogen had said. 'You can't tell Mum.'

'Of course we can. We have to.'

'She'll *lose* it. She's been depressed enough lately.'

'I don't think so,' Sylvie had said. 'She may have been a bit low for a little while, but—'

'Groosi, I know what it's like to be depressed.'

'But darling, if this is true, it has to be dealt with.'

'I thought you believed me,' Imogen said defensively.

'Yes, I do,' Sylvie said. 'Of course I believe you.'

'Then why say "if it's true"?' Imogen had become tearful for the first time. 'I *said* you wouldn't believe me.'

Sylvie had tried to calm her, had pointed out that Imogen had herself said that she might have been imagining things.

'I wish I was. But I still don't want you to tell Mum.'

'Then why,' Sylvie had asked, 'did you choose to tell me, Imo?'

'Because I thought someone should know. A grown-up in the family.' Imogen had paused. 'Just in case.'

'*Just in case.*'

Those words had echoed in Sylvie's mind all that night, long after she had sent Imogen home in a taxi. She had checked first to make sure that Caroline was there, and she had told her daughter some half-truths, saying that Imo had skipped her extra maths class and come to visit her instead, and that she was concerned because she seemed rather down and had admitted to feeling generally unwell for a while, so perhaps Caro ought to keep an eye on her.

'She's seemed fine to me.' Caroline had sounded surprised.

'She doesn't want a fuss,' Sylvie had said. 'Just keep a check on her, darling.'

'Of course,' Caroline had said. 'I always do.'

Which was perfectly true, Sylvie realized afterwards. Which made it somewhat unlikely that Caro would not have noticed if Imogen was being sick or not doing her homework or suffering badly from insomnia.

Of if her own husband was taking an unhealthy interest in one of her daughters.

All that night, Sylvie lay in bed poring over what Imogen had said that evening, and over things she herself had heard and witnessed, to a lesser degree, over the past several months. All the unpleasantness. All the accusations, flying back and forth like tennis balls.

She remembered her drink at The Flask with Matthew in the spring, recalled how dreadfully upset he had been over the mango business and over the girls' attitude towards him in general. He had been perplexed that Caro hadn't trusted him with her history of depression, but had, at all times, talked about her lovingly and caringly. And she, finally, had told him that she had believed his side of the story.

She had believed him then.

And now?

She liked Matthew. Still. Very much.

But then, of course, *someone* probably liked most child molesters.

*Stop that.*

It was a dreadful, appalling thought.

But then, it had been an appalling accusation.

One that had to be dealt with.

She got up very early on Thursday morning – no great hardship, for once, given her inability to rest, let alone sleep – and beat the rush hour to be outside Matthew's office as he arrived.

She spied him turning into Bedford Square before he noticed her, and got out of the Peugeot to greet him.

120

'Sylvie?' He was startled, then, instantly, anxious. 'What's happened?'

'Nothing,' she said. 'At least, not in the sense of an accident or illness.'

Matthew glanced at his watch, saw it was not yet eight-fifteen. 'How long have you been here?'

'A while.'

They found a parking space, walked round to Tottenham Court Road and went into a small café where half a dozen people were tucking into bacon sandwiches and fry-ups, or just smoking over cups of tea and coffee.

'Just black coffee for me, please,' Sylvie told Matthew, and sat down at a corner table to wait while he ordered at the bar. 'I hope I'm not interfering with some important meeting,' she said when he joined her.

Matthew shook his head. 'Breakfast meetings are mostly for the bigger guns.'

'Uncivilized inventions,' she said.

He had never seen her so tense. 'Sylvie, please. What's this about?'

'All right,' she said.

She found it quite shocking to see the change in his face as she told him. He looked, for a few moments, as she imagined he might in twenty or even thirty years from now and perhaps ill into the bargain. Grey and sick. Too dazed to speak.

'I haven't gone to Caro yet,' she said quietly.

He shook his head.

'Are you all right?' she asked.

'What do you think?'

'I'm sorry,' Sylvie said. 'I thought it best to tell you right away. And I wanted, I suppose, to gauge your reaction.'

'How have I scored?'

She ignored the bitter irony, just sat and waited, trying to keep her eyes averted from the man at the next table who was stuffing chips and baked beans into his mouth.

Another shake of his head. 'I don't think I know what to say any more. Or what to do.' He paused. 'I'm going to have to do some long, hard thinking.'

'Yes,' she said. 'I can understand that.'

121

Matthew looked into her face quite abruptly, like a man just waking up. 'Are you waiting for a denial, Sylvie?' he asked. 'Because if you are, you're in for a long wait. This isn't the kind of accusation I'm going to dignify with denial. I hope you see that.'

'Yes,' she said. 'I think I can see that.' She paused. 'You haven't asked me if I believed Imogen.'

'No, I haven't,' he said.

'If you *were* to ask me that,' Sylvie said slowly and painfully, 'I would tell you that on reflection, having done what I said I wanted to – gauged your reaction – I don't think I do believe that what she told me was true. Though I shouldn't like to hazard a guess as to what that may signify for her. She may, for example, believe it.'

'I doubt that very much,' Matthew said.

'I don't know,' Sylvie said, 'if I would rather you were right or wrong about that.' She paused again. 'So far as you're concerned though, Matthew, I've always regarded myself a fairly good judge of character.'

He nodded. 'I won't thank you for that. Maybe I should, but I can't. It's just too . . .' He stopped, glanced around, saw that most of the people in the café had gone, glanced at his watch. 'I have to go.'

'Of course.'

Matthew reached into his jacket pocket, withdrew some cash and put it down on the table for their untouched coffees. He began to rise, then sat back down again. 'So what's next?'

'From my standpoint, you mean?'

He nodded.

'I'm not sure that I want to tell Caro about this,' she said. 'Unless you want me to.' She paused. 'Do you think we should tell her?'

A little of his colour was returning. 'In a normal family situation,' he said slowly, 'in a normal, healthy marriage, I'm sure the answer would be yes, of course she has to be told.' He took a breath. 'But this family is far from normal, I realize that now. It's certainly not healthy.'

Sylvie nodded. She was feeling sick, as she had for most of the night. Lack of sleep and early mornings often disagreed with her. But this was entirely and horribly different. 'I shall not tell her,' she said after another moment, decisively. 'The rest, for the moment, at least, is up to you.'

*

He passed through the day still too shocked to fully confront the enormity of what Sylvie had told him, found, later on, that he could remember little of what had gone on in the office; some work with Kat and Fairbairn on the hospital project, his own input minimal. He considered, at around six, not going home, thought, as he had a number of times before, that Aethiopia was still not, probably never would be, *his* home.

He wondered what he would do about Imogen's latest ploy when he did get there. Nothing, probably. What, after all, could he do that would be effective or useful, let alone helpful?

*You have to tell Caro*, a small, sane voice in his head said.

To what end? he asked it back. To treble her unhappiness? To place hideous suspicions of him in her mind? Suspicions that, once there, might never be completely eradicated? To create more friction between them? Which was, surely, precisely what Imogen and Felicity, that gruesome twosome, were hoping for.

The sane voice castigated him for cowardice, said it was irresponsible of him not to tell his wife. *She'll find out anyway, and then it will all be ten times worse*. True enough. But he also knew that when he did tell Caroline, he would have an immense and ugly fight on his hands. Very likely, if he was to maintain any dignity or personal integrity, a fight to the finish.

*Them or me.*

And if it came to that, Matthew realized that he needed to be prepared to lose. Because in a matter of this nature, when it came to a mother and her children versus their stepfather, the man was bound to lose.

*Better safe than sorry*, Caro would feel, even if a part of her knew that Imogen might be lying.

*No smoke without fire.* That old chestnut would be in there too.

She might feel that she could no longer risk leaving him alone with any of her daughters, not even Chloë. *Especially* Chloë, of course.

Just in case.

He knew he would not tell her yet.

# 19

'You know the golf weekend the firm wanted me to go on,' Matthew said to Caroline that evening.

'Mm.' She was lying on their bed, eyes closed because she'd had one of her headaches for much of the day, and though the pain was the result of too many hours spent sewing over the past several days, she was already fretting over losing valuable time on the latest cushion-cover commission Susanna had wangled for her from the Muswell Hill shop. That, and other, far more important, things.

'The one at the hotel in Surrey,' he said.

'Selsdon Park,' she said, eyes still shut. 'Nice place. Or it used to be.'

'You told me,' Matthew said. She had said, when he'd first mentioned the invitation, that Richard had once taken her and the girls and Sylvie there. It had been a handsome neo-Jacobean style hotel with a beautiful golf course set among ancient trees, though Caroline hadn't played golf, and Richard had despised the sport and the dogged passion it seemed to inspire in those who did play.

'You said you didn't want to go,' she said now.

'I know,' he said. 'But I think I've changed my mind.' He paused, then pushed on. 'I thought it might be good for us.'

'Us?' At last, she opened her eyes. 'But it's this weekend, isn't it?'

'Tomorrow till Sunday evening.'

'I can't.'

'Why not?'

124

'My commission, for one thing. I'm getting very behind.'

'Bring it with you,' Matthew suggested. 'No reason why you couldn't sit in a nice hotel room or down in the lounge and sew, if you really felt you had to.'

Caroline thought about that. She remembered the splendid view she and Richard had had from their bedroom that time. The thought of indulging herself with room service breakfasts and walks with Matthew and, perhaps, some more private, intimate time with him, was suddenly desperately appealing.

'The girls,' she said.

'Your mother would probably come here,' he said. 'Or they could go to her.'

'They hate those beds,' Caroline said. 'And there's Kahli.'

'I'm sure they could all manage very well here, with Isabella's help.' Matthew paused. 'Why not call Sylvie, ask if she'll come to stay?' He sat on the side of the bed, put out his hand and stroked her hair. 'We could use some more time together, don't you think?' He felt treacherous, trying to lure her away, keeping the truth from her.

'I would love more time with you, Matthew. I hope you know that.'

'I do,' he said.

She sat up. 'I'll call Mama now.'

Sylvie said it was fine with her, so long as she could keep her usual Saturday hair appointment because her hair was particularly dreadful this week.

'Your hair's never dreadful,' Caroline said.

'It's either my hair or my face,' Sylvie said. 'I'd rather blame it on the hair.'

'Are you sure you don't mind coming? It's very short notice.'

'I'm delighted for you and Matthew,' her mother told her. 'You should have all the breaks you can manage while you're young.'

'I don't feel very young these days,' Caroline said.

'Stop that, Caro,' Sylvie told her. 'It's all in the mind, as well you know.'

Caroline only remembered then, abruptly and with shame, what her mother had told her about Imogen not feeling well. Maybe, she said, in view of that, she ought to stay at home after all.

'I can keep an eye on her just as well as you,' Sylvie said.

'I don't know, Mama.'

'I do,' Sylvie said, with great firmness.

Once she knew they were going, Caroline buzzed around the house with new energy, organizing food and choosing clothes. She had asked all three girls if they minded, and Imogen had made a bit of a fuss, said she didn't want her to go, but Flic had told Imo not to be so selfish, and then Chloë had asked if she could come to Selsdon Park, and Flic had told her not to be silly; of course she couldn't go on a romantic weekend.

'If you're not sure,' Caro had said to them all, 'I won't go.'

'We're perfectly sure,' Flic had answered for her sisters.

'I'm not,' Imogen had said sulkily.

'Knock it off, Imo,' Flic had told her.

'It's really a business thing, you know,' Caroline had pointed out. 'Matthew's firm's golf weekend – not really romantic at all, probably dinners at long tables and everyone being sporty and dull at lunchtimes.'

'I'm sure you'll find some time alone,' Flic told her.

And Imogen had looked quite sick, and Caroline had felt another wave of guilt and had asked her if she wasn't feeling well, but once again Flic had intervened and said that Imo was perfectly fine and that Caro should stop worrying and get on with her packing and the last-minute shopping she'd said she needed to do.

'What the hell are you playing at?' Imogen said furiously as soon as Caroline and Chloë were out of the way. 'The *last* thing we want her to do is go off with him.'

'Of course it is,' Flic said.

'So why did you tell her to *go*? She would have stayed – all I had to do was ask her, and all *you* had to do was shut up.'

'Which would have made us the selfish step-brats,' Flic pointed out. 'Whereas doing it this way, my way . . .'

'What way? You've as good as shoved her through the door with him!'

Flic smiled. 'Wait and see. Watch and learn.'

It was Chloë who knocked on her mother's and Matthew's door in the early hours of Friday. A tap first time, then a louder knock, before she opened the door.

'Mummy?' It was too dark for her to see. 'Mummy, are you awake?'

'Chloë, what's the matter?' Caroline sat up, instantly awake.

The light came on as Matthew switched on his bedside lamp. 'What's up, honey?' he asked.

'Flic's ill.'

'I'm coming.' Caroline got out of bed, found her dressing gown.

'Shall I come too?' Matthew asked.

'Better wait,' his wife said, already at the door.

'Tell me if you need me,' he said, and lay back again, disliking himself for the barb of mistrust that had pricked at him the instant he'd heard Chloë's words.

But Caro had told him earlier how forceful Flic had been about her coming with him to Selsdon Park; how, when Imogen had not wanted her to go, Flic had really told her. And Chloë had asked if she could come along, Caro had reported, but apparently Flic had dealt with her too.

Matthew had wondered, right away, what that might mean, what new scheme they were planning that might benefit from he and their mother both being away. Probably, he'd guessed, they'd be using the time alone with their grandmother to further taint her opinion of him, though Sylvie was no one's fool, and the weekend with Caro could only strengthen their partnership . . .

He knew now, sure as eggs were eggs, there would be no weekend.

'She's really poorly,' Caroline told him a little later. 'She has a temperature and her head's banging, poor thing, and she says her whole body's aching.'

'It's come on very suddenly.' Matthew was out of bed now, pulling on his bathrobe. 'She seemed fine earlier.'

'She says she wasn't all that fine, apparently,' Caroline said, 'but she didn't want to worry me because she thought I might not want to go away.'

'And do you?'

'Of course I *want* to,' she said, 'but obviously I can't now.'

'Obviously,' he said. 'Are you calling the doctor?'

'In the morning, probably, depending on how she is. Flic hates a fuss.'

127

'How high's her fever?'

'A hundred and one,' Caroline said.

Matthew wanted to ask if she had been there when it was taken, but knew Caro would not appreciate the implications of his asking.

It occurred to him, briefly, guiltily, that maybe she really was sick.

'Are you sure about not calling the doc?' He paused. 'Is her neck stiff?'

'No, thank God,' Caroline said promptly, knowing he was thinking about meningitis. 'I asked her that, of course. And there's no rash, I checked that too.'

'So probably the flu,' Matthew said.

'Or one of those odd viruses.'

He walked over to the door. 'How about I make us some tea?'

'I'm going to sit in Flic's room for a while, darling.'

'Sure,' he said. 'I could bring you both some up.'

'That would be lovely,' she said. 'I'm really sorry. About the weekend.'

'Me, too,' he said. 'I'll tell them about Flic. They won't miss me.'

'You can still go,' Caroline said.

'I don't want to, without you.' He opened the door. 'How about we wait and see how she is in the morning? Maybe she'll be better.'

She was not, of course. As he had expected. She was, according to her mother – who had come back to their bed a little after four, getting up again when Matthew's alarm went off at six – still feverish and aching badly.

'She keeps saying I should still go with you,' she said at the door of their bathroom while he dried himself after his shower.

'Maybe she's right.' Matthew sprayed himself with anti-perspirant. 'Your mother's going to be here, after all. I'm sure there's nothing Sylvie can't deal with.'

'Except that I don't want Mama catching anything horrid.' The edge to her voice suggested that he ought to have thought of that himself. 'Last time she had flu, Mama got pneumonia afterwards.'

'I didn't know that. Your mother always seems so strong.'

128

'Touch wood.' Caroline tapped her forehead. 'It was a long time ago, but I still like to be careful.'

'Sure.' He squeezed toothpaste onto his brush. 'Oh, well, can't be helped.' He knew his brightness sounded forced. 'I'll tell Bianco I can't come.'

'No,' she said. 'Don't do that.'

'I told you last night, I don't want to go without you.' He brushed his teeth vigorously, then rinsed and spat. 'I wasn't really planning on going, after all.'

'Sounds like the kind of thing you ought to be doing though, doesn't it?'

'Politically, you mean?' Matthew brushed shaving foam over his face.

'Since Bianco invited you—'

'Along with almost everyone else in Bedford Square.' He began shaving.

'But still, since you've always thought he didn't like you, and since he is your boss, like *him* or not . . .' She left the rest unsaid, came in and bent to pick up his bath towel from the floor.

'I can do that.' He went on shaving.

Caroline folded the towel neatly and hung it over the warm rail. 'I really think you should go, darling. It'll do you good. And it is a lovely place.'

Matthew glanced at her sideways. 'Trying to get rid of me?'

'Don't be ridiculous,' she said, rather sharply.

'I was kidding,' he said.

'I know.' She leaned against the tiled wall. 'I'm tired from being up in the night, and I'm upset at not being able to go with you – and I'm always on edge when one of the children is ill.'

He managed not to remind her that Flic was almost seventeen. 'That's why I want to stay with you.' He splashed on some cologne, kissed her cheek, and pushed her gently ahead of him back into the bedroom. 'It's getting late.' He went across to his wardrobe, took out a shirt.

'I definitely want you to go,' Caroline said, decisively. 'Have a nice time, maybe get onto a better footing with Bianco, and get to know your colleagues better.' She paused. 'I don't want Flic spoiling it for you, even if she can't help being ill.'

He stopped buttoning the shirt. 'Is that what's worrying you? That I might blame her for this?'

'Mightn't you?' Caroline said steadily.

'Not if she's really sick,' he said, just as steadily, 'which I expect she is.'

'Of course she is,' she said.

'There you are then,' Matthew said.

Imogen had just looked in on Flic, who was lying in bed, eyes closed.

'Flic?'

Flic opened one eye, saw her sister was alone, opened the other and sat up.

'Is this real or are you faking?' Imogen whispered.

'What do you think? Told you I'd handle it, didn't I?'

Imogen regarded her with admiration. 'You're an even better actor than me.'

'Mum won't go now,' Flic said, quietly but confidently. 'No way.'

'You'll have to keep it up till tomorrow,' Imogen said.

Flic lay back against her pillows. 'You're not talking to a beginner.'

'And then what?' Imo asked. 'Are we going to use the weekend to keep up the pressure?' She glanced around at the door, lowered her voice. 'Groosi obviously hasn't told Mum what I said about him.'

'You begged her not to.'

'Yeah, but we both thought she would, didn't we?' Imogen paused. 'Maybe I should do it myself? Break down or something, make her drag it out of me.'

Flic shook her head. 'I keep hoping you'll learn about subtlety one day, but you never do.'

'No, I don't,' Imogen agreed, 'because your bloody subtlety's got us nowhere, has it? He's still *here*, isn't he?'

They heard footsteps. Flic closed her eyes, rumpled her hair a little more.

'Get out, Imo,' she said.

'Think about it,' Imogen whispered fiercely. 'If Mum does stay with us this weekend, we have *got* to make use of it.'

'Out,' Flic said.

*

Those last few remarks about Flic's illness and the mutual reproach couched within them, lingered between Matthew and Caroline as he left the house, having agreed to take his travel bag. He would go to Selsdon Park, he told Caro, provided Flic grew no more sick – in which case, he wanted her to tell him so that he could come home.

'For moral support, if nothing else,' he said on the doorstep.

'All right,' she said.

'Of if you just change your mind about my going and want me with you.'

'I won't,' she said, wrapping her blue cotton dressing gown more tightly around herself, though it was warm and there was no one but him to see her.

'In which case,' he said, 'I'll play the company game, play golf as badly as I always do and try not to alienate Bianco even more.' He managed a smile. 'Maybe even get to dislike Loftus and Brice a little less.'

'Have a good time anyway,' Caroline said, absently.

Matthew leaned in to plant a gentle kiss on her mouth. 'Don't overdo things, will you? Your head was pretty bad yesterday.' He paused. 'You don't think you might be coming down with the same thing as Flic?'

'So you do believe it *is* a real illness, do you?' she asked.

'I never said I didn't,' Matthew said.

'Anyway,' she said, 'my headache was just the usual, so you don't need to let that worry you, do you?' She took a step further back into the house. 'Go on,' she said, 'or you'll be late.'

He turned towards the path, then paused again.

'I'll call you when I get to the office,' he said. 'See how she is.'

But the door was already closing.

He called home three times during the day, aware that he was doing it out of duty, a feeling that sat badly with him. He would have liked to care very much about how his oldest stepdaughter was feeling, the way one usually felt when people one loved were ill. Not that even any small part of him wished Flic anything other than good health. Yet he could not pretend to care in that way.

'She's about the same,' Caroline told him each time he called.

'Maybe I should cancel,' Matthew said at the end of the second call.

'We've been through that,' she said, irritably, and he didn't suggest it again.

He tried a new tack that evening after he'd checked in at the hotel and was comfortably ensconced in his room. 'Maybe,' he suggested, 'if Flic's better tomorrow, you could make it for Sunday lunch. It's not far, just a little way from Croydon.'

'I know where it is,' she reminded him. 'But even if Flic is better, I'll have to catch up on my sewing.'

'I guess so,' he said.

'Anyway,' she added, 'I've told Mama not to come.'

The room was a single, overlooking the golf course, with all the amenities he needed. Mostly, he realized, it had a very welcome sense of peace and quiet.

It came to him then that if Caroline had decided to leave Flic to Sylvie and accompany him, she would either have been phoning home every couple of hours or worrying about her daughters, and that it would, therefore, have been little better than having them here.

Matthew sighed, opened his window, took a breath of air, then looked back at the bed, thought of the night ahead and found, to his shame, that he was rather looking forward to it.

# 20

He telephoned on Saturday morning, before his first round of golf.

'I was sleeping,' she said, a note of complaint in her voice.

'Bad night?' he asked.

'Not great,' she said.

'How's the patient?'

'Still poorly yesterday evening, but she was fast asleep when I looked in this morning at about five.' Caroline yawned.

'Go back to sleep, sweetheart,' Matthew said. 'Sorry I disturbed you.'

'It's all right,' she told him. 'Isabella's coming by later for a while, so I should get a break then.'

The morning, to his surprise, was pure pleasure. The course was beautiful, the weather fine, the landscape lovely, and Matthew's game started out just well enough for him to avoid humiliation. Nick Brice turned out to be better company away from the office; Robert Fairbairn, a tormented golfer, tore at his hair on every hole; Mark Loftus had not shown up – no one appearing to miss him; and Bianco seemed to be playing some kind of exhibition match with an earnest Stephen Steerforth hard on his heels.

Kat Dunn, on the other hand – looking terrific in tartan slacks and a white short-sleeved shirt – appeared to Matthew to be more intent on venting some kind of fury on her golf balls than on aiming them towards the holes.

'Something up?' he asked her on the fifth.

'Could say that,' she said shortly.

133

'Can I help?'

'No,' she said, striding on.

'How are you feeling now?' Caroline asked Flic at around eleven o'clock.

'Lousy.'

'Poor darling. What can I do for you?'

'Nothing.' Flic turned over on her side. 'I'll be all right, Mum, so long as I get plenty of sleep.'

'Best thing for you,' Caroline said. 'And plenty of fluids. I'll keep bringing you water and soup.'

'Just sleep, Mum,' Flic said. 'I'll call if I want anything else.'

Caroline crept out of the room and, finding Imogen outside, lifted a finger to her lips to keep her quiet and motioned to her to move along the corridor.

'I'm going out to Nicola's,' Imogen said.

'I thought you were seeing Annie.'

'I told you Nic.' Imogen looked impatient. 'What's the difference?'

'No difference, I suppose.' Caroline looked at her searchingly. 'Are you all right, darling?'

'I'm fine.' Imogen looked towards Flic's door. 'How is she?'

'Wanting to sleep.'

'Chloë wants to go out too.'

'Where?'

'I don't know. I heard her asking Isabella if she'd take her out.'

'Oh,' Caroline said, feeling irritated.

'Shall I go and tell them no?' Imogen asked.

'No, thank you,' Caroline said. 'I'll deal with it myself.'

But on the way downstairs, irritation faded and the notion of having the house to herself except for Flic – who would probably sleep most of the time – seemed seriously tempting. Time to work. And to think, about certain immensely important things that, till now, she'd had all too little private time to contemplate.

'By all means' – she found Isabella and Chloë in the kitchen – 'go out for the afternoon, so long as you take Kahli with you.'

'But I wanted to go to the cinema,' Chloë said.

'Well, you can't,' Caroline said, 'not with a dog.'

'But why do we have to take Kahli?'

'I thought you loved him?'

'I do, but—'

'Then either you take him, or he gets shut out into the garden for the whole day till you get back, because I can't take care of your sister and do my work *and* worry about whether Kahli needs to go out every five minutes.'

The retriever had, of late, taken to doing almost that, though Mr Peterson, their vet, had given him a clean bill of health.

'Of course we'll take him.' Isabella, seeing Caro's unusual resolve, stepped in. 'We can see how many places will allow him to come inside.'

'They won't let him stay long,' Chloë pointed out, 'if he starts peeing.'

'He won't,' Caroline said, then hesitated. 'Are you sure about this, Isabella?'

'Completely,' she said.

By the eleventh hole, Matthew was feeling tired and fed up. For one thing, he hadn't taken out a trolley and his bag of clubs was starting to feel like a sack of lead. For another, his game had deteriorated to the point where he felt he might as well be hitting the balls backwards. But most of all, he had suddenly begun feeling guilty about Caroline.

'Off with the fairies, aren't you?' Brice breezed past with his trolley.

Matthew took a morose swing, missed his ball and tee, sent a divot of earth flying into the air, and swore.

'Leave something for the rest, Gardner,' Bianco remarked loudly, from the passenger seat of the buggy being driven by Steerforth.

Matthew waited till they'd gone, then tried his shot again.

'God*damn* it.'

'You look almost as fed up as I was earlier.'

He heard the Scottish accent and looked around to see Kat, still fresh-looking and far happier than before. 'Is it my imagination,' he enquired, 'or does the whole of VKF just happen by every time I screw up another shot?'

'Paranoia,' Kat said.

'That again,' he said.

'Sorry?'

He shook his head. 'Nothing you'd want to hear about.'

'I don't know,' she said. 'Sounds interesting.'

135

'What happened to your troubles? A while back you looked like you were assaulting your balls with a deadly weapon.'

'Therapy,' Kat said.

'At least you were hitting more than chunks of the course.'

'So what happened to your good mood?' she asked. 'Is it just the game or did someone piss you off?' She paused. 'Or should I mind my own business?'

'Not really.' He glanced back, saw players approaching. 'Isn't this where I'm supposed to play or let them through?'

'I don't read rule books,' Kat said.

'If I let them go ahead,' Matthew said, 'it'll just take me longer to finish.'

'You could finish right now,' she said.

'Wimp out, you mean? Bianco would just love that.'

'I'll wimp out with you if you like. I could use a drink.'


Caroline asked herself, after they'd all gone out, why having the house almost to herself today should feel so different from being alone during the week. Probably, she decided, it was because she usually felt under pressure to complete mundane tasks for the sake of the family.

Still, today was an odd day to be feeling free, given Flic's illness. In fact, it was appalling for her to be feeling that way partly because her daughter was probably going to be feeling too ill to make demands, which meant that she could sew and focus on herself rather than worry about taking care of her. But then again, Caroline excused herself, so far as work was concerned, she did have to consider Susanna's position. Her friend was always so good to her, had hardly said a word about their not continuing with the family therapy, or grumbled about her being late with her commission.

Today, though, was presenting her with a golden opportunity to catch up, a chance to sit in her beloved Quiet Room and get on with things; and if Flic did need her, she'd be available, and if not, by the time Matthew got back on Sunday, she might possibly be finished . . .

Just two things to take care of first. Check on Flic, see if she wanted anything. And then the other thing. The thing that had, she really was beginning to suspect, been giving her the headaches and making her far rattier than necessary with Matthew.

136

Maybe. Perhaps.
*Oh, God.*

Matthew and Kat got back to the hotel – aware that they'd been seen skulking off by Steerforth, which meant that they would probably both go down another notch in Bianco's books – and went to their respective rooms to freshen up before meeting again in the bar.

Matthew arrived in his room and went straight to the phone. The number at Aethiopia rang more than ten times before Caroline picked up.

'What's wrong?' he said right away.

'Nothing's wrong.'

'You took so long to answer,' he said, 'and you're breathless.'

'I was in the Quiet Room,' she said, 'trying to get some work done.'

She sounded, yet again, more irritated than glad to hear from him.

'No one else around to answer?' he asked lightly, wanting to avoid a row.

'They've all gone out, and Flic's sleeping – or she *was* – so I thought I'd use the time to try and finish the order.'

'Good idea,' he said. 'Sorry I got you out of there.'

'You weren't to know,' she said. 'How's your morning been?' It was an afterthought, which made her feel guilty. 'Did you play?'

'Badly,' Matthew answered. 'Or actually, quite well to begin with, and then it all went to pot.'

'Isn't that the nature of the beast?' Caroline said. 'Richard always said that golfers claim to love it, then suffer like mad all the way round.'

'I didn't even make it all the way round,' he told her. 'A colleague who'd had enough too came back with me. We're going to have a drink before the others get back for lunch.'

'Good idea.' Caroline's mind had already tuned out. 'Actually, darling, I think I might put the machine on while I'm working, so if you phone again, just leave a message and I'll call you back.'

'Sure.' The banality of their conversation was frustrating him. He'd been thinking about her, had hated the way they'd parted yesterday, and now she sounded so distant and he hadn't told her how he felt. 'Wish Flic better for me, won't you?'

'I will,' she said. 'Goodbye, darling.'

'Don't work too hard,' he said.

But she had already hung up.

# 21

It was after one before Caroline settled herself back into the Quiet Room.

She had looked in on Flic after the phone call to see if she wanted a bowl of soup, and while she'd been heating that up in the kitchen, John Pascoe had arrived to do the mowing, and Caro had asked if he'd mind leaving it for another day.

'Have a sandwich before you go,' she had suggested.

'Wouldn't say no,' old John had said.

So she had taken Flic up her soup, then come back down to make a thick-cut cheese and pickle sandwich, just the way Pascoe liked it, and she'd nibbled, somewhat absently, at a more thinly-cut one with him and made him two cups of tea before he'd left. After which she had gone up to check on Flic, who'd finished her soup and was ready to snooze again, before finally going back up to the second floor.

Where she had switched on the radio to Classic FM, just in time for the start of Relaxing Classics at Two, poured herself a glass of Evian, opened one of the balcony doors, and sat back down in her favourite rocker.

And closed her eyes. Thinking. About what she now knew to be true. Wondering exactly how she felt about it.

And then she opened her eyes again.

And took up her sewing.

# 22

When Isabella and Chloë came home with Kahli just before six, the house was quiet.

'I'm going to *die*' – Chloë headed for the kitchen, the dog following – 'if I don't have a Coke.'

'Have water instead,' Isabella suggested. 'Better for your teeth.'

'Yeah, yeah,' Chloë said, which was how she knew Imogen would answer that kind of nagging. Just lately, she had begun to realize that she might have more to learn from Imo than she'd previously thought. And from Flic, of course, who was older and far cleverer. But maybe if she began trying to be just a bit more *like* Imo, she might stop treating her with such contempt.

Kahli went to the back door and looked at her expectantly.

'You've just been,' Chloë told him, and opened the fridge door. He whined.

Chloë took out a Coke, sank down onto one of the chairs, snapped open the can and tipped it straight into her mouth the way Imogen did and their mother hated.

Kahli whined again and began scraping at the base of the door.

'In a *minute*,' Chloë said, and picked up that morning's *Weekend* magazine.

Isabella tapped softly on Flic's door and, hearing no answer, opened the door and looked in to see that she was lying on her side, her back to the door.

'Are you awake?' Isabella asked very quietly.

'Mm?' Flic turned towards her. 'Hi,' she said.

Isabella came into the room. 'How are you feeling?'

'Bit less achey.'

'Good.' Isabella thought that, if anything, she looked worse than before. 'Is your mother upstairs?'

'Think so. She said she was going to work.'

'Okay,' Isabella said. 'Would you like something?'

'A cold drink, maybe. In a while. No hurry.'

Isabella looked at the rumpled bedclothes. 'I'll come back before I leave, make your bed if you like.'

'Lovely,' Flic said. 'Thank you.'

And she turned away again, face back to the window.

Down in the kitchen, Kahli's scratching and whining were getting too distracting to ignore.

'Honestly.' Chloë sighed, put down the magazine and got up. 'You really are a pest sometimes, Kahli.' She went over to the door and opened it, and the big dog barrelled past her and out into the garden.

'No manners,' Chloë said.

Isabella went up the stairs to the second floor.

The door to the Quiet Room was closed.

She knocked.

Music was playing inside the room, but Caroline did not answer.

'Caro?' Isabella turned the door handle.

The door would not open, appeared to be locked.

Caroline never locked the door.

'Caro?' Isabella called more loudly.

The music was soft, gentle, very sweet.

From a distance – from out in the garden, she thought – she heard Kahli barking, loudly, urgently. Not his usual bark.

Isabella knocked sharply on the door, tried the handle again.

'Caro, are you all right?'

And then she heard the scream.

She almost flew down the stairs, heard Flic emerging from her room as she ran.

Chloë was still screaming. A terrible, shrill, blood-curdling sound.

'I'm coming!'

Isabella ran into the kitchen, saw the garden door open. Kahli came running in to meet her, still barking, clearly agitated, then rushed out again ahead of her. The screaming seemed to rise through the air and surround her, like the screech of a flock of startled gulls lifting off the ocean.

'Chloë, I'm *coming!*'

She ran out into the garden.

Chloë stopped screaming.

Isabella's own mouth opened, but nothing came out.

Behind her, in the doorway, Flic, in her T-shirt, feet bare, stood, frozen, rigid. Staring at Chloë's back and at the sight beyond her.

Caroline lay face down on the flagstone terrace.

Still dumb, Isabella put out her right hand, fingers splayed as if to stop someone, something. No one moved. Chloë just stood there, looking down at her mother's body, not screaming any more, not saying anything, just standing there. Flic was still in the doorway.

Only Kahli was moving, running back and forth, panting, his claws scraping against the stone, no longer barking, perhaps because there was no longer any need for him to do so.

No need for anyone to do anything.

It was so utterly clear that Caroline was beyond help. It was clear from the position of her body, from its unnaturalness, from the ugly angle of her head and neck. From the blood that had seeped, a while ago, Isabella could see, from beneath her face over the stone.

Two flies crawled in the blood puddle.

Isabella dragged her gaze from them to Chloë, saw that the girl was shaking violently from head to foot, and forced her legs into action. She went up behind Chloë, put both arms around her and turned her, slowly but firmly, away from her mother, back towards the house.

Flic, ashen-faced, stepped aside to let them through.

'She's dead, isn't she?' Her eyes were disbelieving, yet it was a statement, not a question.

Isabella nodded, went on steering Chloë through the kitchen and on into the drawing room, pushing her down, very gently, into an armchair.

141

'Flic,' she called, her voice trembling.

Flic did not answer. Isabella left Chloë, went back into the kitchen, saw, through the window, that the older girl was now outside, looking down at her mother.

Isabella went to the door. 'Flic, come and take care of Chloë.'

Flic didn't move.

'Felicity, your sister needs you.' For a moment, Isabella felt dizzy, and then she dragged herself together, strengthened her voice. 'I have to telephone.'

Flic turned around. 'Who?'

'The ambulance.'

'What for?' Flic asked dully.

'I have to call them,' Isabella told her gently. 'And Sylvie.'

Flic nodded.

'Come into the house, please,' Isabella said. 'Chloë's in the drawing room.'

'I want to cover her,' Flic said.

'I'll fetch something,' Isabella said, 'in a moment.'

Flic nodded again, started towards her, then stopped.

'Don't call him,' she said.

'Who?' Isabella asked.

'Matthew,' Flic said. 'Don't call Matthew.'

'Of course I must call Matthew.'

'Why?'

'He's her husband,' Isabella answered simply.

She could barely hear the sound Flic made in reply as she came through the doorway and passed her, on the way to her sister in the other room.

It sounded almost like a kind of soft, choking, human growl.

142

# 23

The call from Isabella came while Matthew was shaving before dinner.

Afterwards, he walked back into the bathroom and stared into the mirror for a few minutes at his part-shaven face and expressionless, suddenly unfamiliar eyes, and then he returned to the bedroom, packed his bag, pulled on a pair of jeans and a T-shirt and went downstairs to pay his bill.

'Just extras, Mr Gardner,' they told him, and he put down some cash, oblivious of either what they had asked for or how much he had laid on the counter, and they handed him his change in a kindly fashion, as they might have taken care of some very elderly or infirm visitor who understood neither their language nor currency.

He walked out into the early evening air and stood quite still outside the entrance for several moments, staring past parked cars and tennis courts and flowering bushes and trees, seeing neither those things nor the guests who strolled along the pathways or in the grounds.

'Do you need some help, sir?'

A uniformed hotel employee was peering at him.

It was only then that Matthew remembered that he did not, of course, have a car; that he had come from London, in fact, in Nick Brice's old Alfa Romeo.

'A taxi,' he said, then added: 'Please.'

143

There were three cars parked outside Aethiopia when his taxi pulled up in East Heath Road; the Range Rover and a police car in the driveway, and Sylvie's outside, parked crookedly, one wheel up on the pavement – and as Matthew recognized the little red Peugeot, a great wave of pity for her buffeted him.

'Need some help, mate?' the driver asked, by way of a nudge.

Matthew looked at the meter and knew he didn't have enough cash on him. 'I'll have to go inside,' he said. 'Get some money.'

The man told him it was okay, and Matthew opened the door and stepped down onto the pavement. It felt strange beneath his feet. Everything felt strange.

He looked at the house. He had never, in his entire life, less wanted to enter any building.

'Well, go on then, mate,' the driver said.

Matthew turned around and stooped a little, so he could see the man's face. 'I'm sorry to be slow,' he said. 'My wife just died.'

'Oh,' the driver said, at a loss. 'Take your time then, mate.'

Matthew turned back to face the house and saw that the door had been opened. Isabella stood in the doorway, a policeman beside her on the step.

He began to walk towards her.

The house, the constable had explained, after he had written down Matthew's name and the time of his arrival in a log, was being treated, for the time being, as a crime scene. That did not, the young man said, mean that any crime had been committed, but a case of this kind required certain precautions.

'What does "this kind" mean?' Matthew asked him.

Which was when Isabella, having paid the taxi driver, came and took hold of his arm and drew him inside.

Sylvie, she said, was in the drawing room with Imogen and Chloë. Flic was in bed, having been sedated by Dr Lucas, who had left, but would be returning later.

'How are they?' Matthew angrily shook his head. 'Idiotic question.'

'Bad.' Isabella's eyes were raw from crying. 'Very bad.'

Matthew took a step towards the drawing room door, then stopped. 'I'm sorry about the money. I'll give it back to you later.' He tried to think. 'Or tomorrow. I don't know how much I have in the house. I'm sorry.'

144

'Please,' Isabella said. 'I don't care about the money.'

'No, but still.' He saw the pain in her face and left it alone. 'Thank you,' he said. 'For calling me, too.'

He knew that he was prevaricating, knew that he had to enter the room, but his legs felt like pieces of wood, numb, like the rest of him.

They were all on the sofa, huddled together. Imogen's head leaned against Sylvie's left shoulder, her face hidden, and Chloë half-sat, half-lay, her head buried in her grandmother's lap.

She saw him first.

'Matthew!' She scrambled jerkily off the sofa, ran to him, let him put his arms around her. 'Mummy's dead, Matthew.' Her voice was full of tears and her body heaved with sobs against him. 'She's really, really dead.'

'I know, honey,' he said, softly, and went on holding her.

'Matthew,' Sylvie said from the sofa.

'Yes,' he said, and extricated himself gently from Chloë's arms.

He walked around the sofa and looked down at Caro's mother. She didn't move, because Imogen's head was still resting on her shoulder. Her eyes were haunted and red, the mascara she had presumably applied that morning, in another life, was smudged, panda-like, and her always-immaculate hair was dishevelled.

'I'm so sorry,' Matthew said.

Sylvie began to ease herself away from Imogen.

'Don't move her,' Matthew said. 'It's okay.'

'No,' Sylvie said, faintly. 'It isn't.'

He stood still for a long moment, uncertain how to proceed. There were two questions he wanted to ask, but neither seemed appropriate with Imogen and Chloë there. Yet with Sylvie not really able to move away from them, he had no choice.

'Where is she?' he asked, softly.

'They took her away.' She had to swallow before she could tell him. 'They've taken her to somewhere in St Pancras. There's a policeman outside who can tell you.'

The numbness seemed to hold him there, almost like anaesthetic.

He asked his second question. 'What happened?' He paused. 'Isabella said she fell.'

'Yes,' Sylvie said. 'From the balcony.'

145

'Balcony?' He heard his own voice, heard how stupidly it echoed the word, heard the incredulity in his tone. And suddenly it came to him that maybe there had been a terrible, wonderful mistake, maybe it hadn't been Caro who had fallen, because she never set foot on balconies, did she?

'The one outside the Quiet Room,' Sylvie said.

Imogen didn't speak or look at him. Her eyes were open but not, apparently, fixed upon anything, seeming to gaze into the silken left sleeve of her grandmother's blouse. Had Isabella not already said that Howard Lucas had been here and was returning, Matthew would have gone directly to call him, but clearly that side of things was under control.

'Why is the policeman here?' he asked.

'The ambulance people called them,' Sylvie said. 'Routine, apparently, in situations like this.'

*A case of this kind*, the constable had said.

Sylvie was looking up at him. 'Because she fell.'

'I see.' Matthew looked over at Chloë, who was sitting on the floor now, cuddling up to Kahli who had not, he realized, come to greet him as usual.

He looked back down at Sylvie.

'I need to go and see her,' he said, very quietly.

She nodded. 'Of course you do,' she said. 'Forgive me for not moving.'

'Don't be silly,' he said. 'Imo needs you.' He paused. 'Isabella said the doctor gave Flic something?'

'He gave her an injection,' Chloë said from the other side of the room. 'Because she started screaming, and wouldn't stop.' She paused. 'I screamed, when I found Mummy.'

Matthew glanced down at Sylvie, horrified, and she nodded wordlessly.

'Should I stay and help?' he asked her. 'I want to go and see Caro, but . . .'

'Go now,' Sylvie told him. 'You need to.'

'Yes,' he said, and then, because he had to ask, because that foolish fragment of hope was still lurking at the back of his mind: 'Did you see her, Sylvie?'

'Yes,' she said, and her eyes were full of pity and under-standing. 'I did.'

*

146

The viewing room at the mortuary was attached to the local Coroner's Court, beside an old cemetery and park. The young woman who escorted him to the room had already attempted, with sensitivity and kindness, to persuade him to wait until private arrangements had been made with the funeral directors.

'But you said that would mean waiting till after the post mortem?'

'I'm afraid so.'

Matthew looked at the closed door. There was nothing to indicate what lay behind it, no sign, no weightiness. Just a door.

'I don't want to wait,' he said.

She told him to take as much time as he needed.

And left him with her.

With her. And yet utterly removed from her.

Caroline lay beyond a window, her body draped in gold-braided purple velvet, only her face visible, her head resting on a small pillow. There was a dressing on her forehead, and, had it not been for the heavy gown, she might have looked almost like a patient unconscious after surgery.

Only almost.

She was there. And yet she was not.

It had been different after his parents' deaths. The accident had happened in California, and so it had taken longer for him and Ethan to get to see them afterwards. And that had been so great a horror in itself, the viewing of their bodies, because their injuries had been so grievous, and the warnings from the mortuary staff had not helped the brothers at all, and so far as Matthew had been concerned, the battle to eradicate those final images of Edward and Ann Gardner had been even more painful than coping with their deaths.

This was entirely different.

The covered wound aside, Caroline looked perfect. The way she often looked while sleeping. *Had* looked.

No more.

'I can't take this in, Caro,' he said, softly, standing there in the small plain white-walled room.

He put up his right hand, laid his palm flat against the glass. He felt a savage urge to smash the window, pick her up, *hold* her.

No one but Chloë had held him back at the house. Isabella had taken his arm, but other than the anguished embrace of his youngest stepdaughter, no one else had so much as touched him. He'd fully accepted that Imogen's needs had taken precedence with her grandmother – of course they'd had to – of *course*. But right now, in this terrible, barren, end-of-hope place, Matthew realized that he had desperately needed to have some small physical comfort; and in a more normal family, he would surely have been able to sit with them, among them, so that they might have tried to grieve together, perhaps to howl out their futile outrage. Have shared their pain.

He'd known, all the way to London in the back of the taxi, how it would be. That knowledge, he realized now, had been one of the things that had prevented him from feeling too much of anything on the journey. The hideous sense of being, for a time, emotionally paralysed – not quite *human* – had been more frightening, he thought in retrospect, than it had been protective. Preferable, he was sure – if anything about this could *be* preferable – if he had been able to sit in the taxi and sob out his agony, to feel like a man rather than a lump of wood.

'I'm so sorry, Caro,' he whispered. 'About everything.'

He shut his eyes, trying suddenly, desperately, to retrieve the memory of how she had felt, of her softness and warmth, of the smell of her, but he couldn't *remember*.

Unbearable.

He opened his eyes, felt tears on his face, found it made no difference, that weeping was not, after all, the help he'd thought it might be. No help at all. It only served to caution him against letting go, in this place, because once he began, he might not be able to stop.

'*How*, Caro?' He pressed his face against the window, his breath misting the glass. 'How did this happen? I don't understand. You hated that balcony.'

From outside the door, he heard the sounds of voices.

'I don't *understand*,' he said again.

And then he stepped away from the glass and looked down at his wife of less than eight months.

Months.

No time at all. Scarcely more than a beginning.

Suddenly, he wanted to scream.

*

The constable was still outside, standing in the dark, when he got back, nodded as he made another note in his log, remembering Matthew from earlier, and as before, Isabella was waiting for him, telling him quietly that there was a detective waiting for him.

'There was something . . .' She stopped as the drawing room door opened and a man in a dark suit came out.

'Mr Gardner?'

'Yes.'

'Detective-Sergeant Ross, Hampstead CID.' The man shook his hand. He was around Matthew's age but balding, what hair he had gingery, and fine freckles dusted his head and face. 'My condolences, sir.'

His eyes were hazel and searching. New dread gripped Matthew. He had not, till this instant, imagined there could be anything more *to* dread.

'Thank you,' he said.

'Shall we?' The detective indicated the drawing room door.

They were all there now, Flic too, sitting in an armchair wearing a big blue cotton sweater over her dressing gown and white socks on her feet. Her legs were drawn up beneath her, and she was alarmingly pale. Matthew bent and kissed her cheek, found it cold. Flic neither moved nor spoke. Matthew straightened up and looked at the other three on the sofa. Sylvie sat where he had left her, though Imogen now sat on her right and Chloë on her left. The awful, disturbing sense of unreality came back, submerging him, detaching him.

'Are you all right, Matthew?'

Sylvie was looking at him, concerned. He shook his head, fumbled his way to the armchair on the far side of the sofa and sat down heavily. His mother-in-law rose, walked over to the drinks cabinet, found a bottle and poured something into a glass, brought it swiftly to him, bent and put it into his hand.

'Come on,' she said, gently. 'Take a sip.'

She kept her own hand wrapped around his, as if she thought he might drop the glass otherwise. A kind, sensible gesture, typically Sylvie, enough to bring hot tears rushing painfully into his eyes.

The brandy burned on its way down, brought him back.

'Thank you.'

Sylvie let go of his hand but remained beside him.

'I'm sorry,' he said.

149

'Please don't be,' she said. 'Taking care of my family's the only thing keeping me halfway sane today.'

He put up his left hand to cover his eyes.

'Take your time, Mr Gardner.'

Matthew removed his hand and saw the policeman waiting patiently near the sofa. He looked at his stepdaughters, then at Isabella standing in the doorway, Mick behind her in the hallway. Only the dog was missing from the family group.

And Caro.

'Where's Kahli?' he asked no one in particular.

'In the garden,' Isabella answered.

Matthew nodded. 'I'm okay,' he said to the detective.

'Did you see Mummy?' Chloë asked, softly.

Matthew nodded, found himself unable to answer.

'Was she all right?' Chloë asked.

Imogen made a strange sound, like a choked-off moan.

'When you're ready then, sir,' Detective-Sergeant Ross said.

'For what?' Matthew asked.

'To go upstairs,' Ross answered.

'Upstairs?'

'To the Quiet Room,' Sylvie said. 'It was locked when . . .' She faltered.

Isabella came a little way into the room. 'When we found Caro,' she said. 'I tried to open the door, but she had locked it.'

'And then I found her,' Chloë said. 'In the garden.'

Matthew remembered her saying something like that when he'd first come home, before he'd gone to St Pancras. She said it again now almost as if finding her mother had been an achievement, a feat. She had said earlier, in that same way, that she had screamed when she'd found Caroline. He shut his eyes in an attempt to blot out the image of how it must have been, and Susanna, abruptly and irrelevantly, came into his mind. He wondered if anyone had told her.

He opened his eyes.

'Why would Caro have locked the door?' he asked belatedly. 'She never locked it.' He looked around, as if seeking to be corrected. 'Did she?'

'Not that I know of,' Sylvie said.

'The key was in your wife's pocket,' Ross told him. 'It was found by one of the paramedics.' He paused. 'When you're ready, sir?'

150

Matthew got up slowly, feeling sick. 'I'm ready now.'

'I'm coming too,' Sylvie said.

Chloë, too, began to rise from the sofa.

'No, darling,' her grandmother told her. 'You stay here with Flic and Imo.'

'I want to see,' Chloe said.

'Best do as your grandmother says,' Detective-Sergeant Ross said.

Chloë sat down again, looked uneasily at both her sisters, neither of whom had spoken since their stepfather had arrived back.

'Shouldn't Flic be in bed?' Matthew asked Sylvie quietly as they left the room with the detective. 'I thought the doctor gave her something.'

'Clearly not a match for Flic's will,' Sylvie said. 'Once she was awake, she said she couldn't bear to stay in her room alone.'

'I don't blame her,' Matthew said.

He thought, as they walked up the staircase, that for the first time in a long while, if ever, he probably did understand – or might, at least, be coming close to understanding – all his step-daughters' feelings. Though he doubted it would be reciprocated.

He understood that, too.

*At what a price?*

Ross broke the seal across the door of the Quiet Room so that they could enter, then switched on the overhead light. At first glance everything looked as it might have if Caroline had just left her work for some ordinary reason – and seeing it all so normal, the rocker, the sewing, the whole room, Matthew experienced another of those senseless rushes of hope. They were wrong, after all, it *was* all a terrible mistake, Caro *had* gone out, perhaps to do some shopping, and any minute now she would come through the front door and call out to them . . .

*You saw her.*

In that place.

Detective-Sergeant Ross remained just inside the door. 'Sir?' He looked at Matthew. 'Does anything here strike you as out of the ordinary?'

Matthew looked over the room.

Normal. *Normal.* Caroline's feminine, peaceful refuge. A

151

Joanna Trollope novel, closed, on the couch. The cushion cover on which she had apparently been working on the low carved table. One tiny drawer of the antique chest open, revealing small reels of cotton and silk threads. A bottle of Evian also on the table, a half-filled glass with lemon slice still floating. The only minute sign of disorder a small pair of scissors on the carpet between the rocker and the glass doors.

One of them open.

'Nothing,' he answered, and felt that the detective was gauging his reaction, though why he couldn't imagine.

*Because fatal falls off balconies had to be explained.*

'Sure?' Ross asked.

Beside Matthew, Sylvie made a small sound, like a tiny, soft moan, and he glanced at her, saw how ashen she was. 'Want to go down?' he asked gently.

She shook her head. 'I'm all right.'

He reached for her right hand and she let him take it, grip it, as glad of the support, he thought, as he was.

'Nothing at all out of place?' Ross pressed.

'Only the scissors, I guess.'

'Nothing else?'

'No.'

Any last vestiges of the delusion of normality were gone. Matthew looked at the rocking chair and wanted, urgently, to sit down in it, to sit where she had sat, feel her warmth again, though he knew that was, of course, long gone.

Ross walked slowly across the room towards the balcony. 'Sir? Would you mind?'

Matthew's stomach clenched in dread, but he squeezed Sylvie's hand, then let go. 'Why don't you sit down?' he said to her softly.

In silence, she bypassed the rocker and sat down on the small couch.

The policeman had already stepped out through the open door, and stood on the narrow balcony, waiting. Matthew took a tight, shallow breath and joined him. The world beyond was semi-dark, lit by street lamps and other occupied homes.

Ross peered over the railing at the garden below. 'Is there a floodlight that could be switched on, Mr Gardner?'

'Yes,' Matthew said. 'The switch is in the kitchen.'

He steeled himself to move to the edge and gripped the handrail.

'The railing,' Ross remarked, 'is quite high.'

'Yes,' Matthew said.

He remembered his first visit to the Quiet Room after his arrival at Aethiopia, when Caro had refused to come out onto the balcony with him to look at the view, remembered laughing at her gently because she loved mountains yet feared heights.

'She hated heights,' he said now, the significance of the statement seeming to clamour in his own ears.

'Did she?'

'She said she did.'

'You seem unconvinced.'

'Not at all,' Matthew said. 'It's just that she was a good skier.' He paused. 'She said she felt differently about mountains, because she'd grown up with them.' He glanced back at Sylvie. 'She used to live in Switzerland.'

'How did Mrs Gardner feel about this balcony?' Ross leaned over the rail. 'Quite a drop.'

Matthew felt sick again. 'Yes.'

'All right, sir?' Ross asked.

'No,' Matthew said.

'Just another minute, if you don't mind.'

Matthew gritted his teeth.

'How did your wife feel about this balcony, in terms of her fear of heights?'

'She . . .' Matthew hesitated. 'She wasn't keen on it.'

'But she used it?'

'No, not really. It's not really big enough to sit out on.'

'But to stand out on,' Ross persisted, 'to admire the view or to look down into the garden?'

'Yes. Big enough for that.'

'So did she? Stand out here?'

'I don't know,' Matthew said, then realized he sounded as if he were prevaricating. 'I know she didn't like it, but I was seldom in here with her. This was her place, for working and just being peaceful. That's why it's called the Quiet Room.'

'You said downstairs that she never locked the door?'

'Not to my knowledge.' Matthew thought about it. 'Though she might have, sometimes, I guess. I wouldn't have known.' He clarified again. 'When I did come in here, it was only to see her, so naturally the door was open.'

'But not today,' the detective-sergeant said. 'Apparently she was working in here today, yet the door was locked.'

'Yes,' Matthew said. 'Apparently.'

He thought he could see where this was going, and found it unbearable to contemplate. Yet it *was* going there, no doubt about it. The next line of questioning, he realized now, would be as to Caro's state of mind, and from there, the horror would go on spiralling down into emotional depths from which none of them would ever fully recover.

'You must be exhausted, Mr Gardner,' Ross said.

'Amongst other things,' Matthew said quietly.

The other man patted his arm in a gesture of kindness, then stepped back into the room, ahead of him. 'I'll be leaving now, Mrs Lehrer,' he told Sylvie. 'Let you all get some rest.' He saw her begin to rise. 'Please stay where you are.'

She rose despite him. 'I'll come down with you.'

She went ahead of them to the door.

'If it isn't too inconvenient, Mr Gardner,' Ross said, 'I'd like to keep this room locked and sealed for the time being.'

'Sure.' Matthew wondered how the detective might have reacted if he'd said he wanted it kept open. Though that was, for the moment, the last thing he wanted. He could not imagine ever wanting to set foot in the Quiet Room again.

'Just in case we need another look,' Ross said. He walked back over to the balcony, closed the door and locked it. Then, extracting another key from his jacket pocket, he returned to Matthew's side, motioned him out of the room, then switched off the light, came out into the hall, closed and locked that door too, and pocketed the key.

And resealed the door.

Sylvie and Matthew regarded one another.

Both in agony.

# 24

Over the next several days the questioning seemed to go on for ever, sparing no one entirely, although Ross and the female colleagues who accompanied him on every subsequent visit to the house were very gentle with all the girls, especially Chloë. They were not, in fact, unkind to anyone in the shattered household, and the detective sergeant made it clear, as soon as he felt able, that there was no suspicion of foul play in Caroline's death. Not that anyone in the family had even contemplated such a thing – though it *had* occurred to Matthew by then that had he not been out of town, Flic's and Imo's imaginations might possibly have leapt to all kinds of conclusions.

Both he and Sylvie knew, however, what *was* being mooted.

But neither of them talked about it.

Talk – anything more than the briefest, most trivial of conversations – seemed beyond them all. Sylvie had slept at Aethiopia from that first night, had brought over some belongings from Perrin's Lane next day, and was living in the guest room two doors from the Quiet Room. It was a comfort for them all to have her there, but from Matthew's point-of-view it was especially easing. Caroline's mother formed a human barricade between the older sisters and himself. In her presence, Flic and Imogen seemed to feel compelled to be civil to him, and somehow, almost miraculously, Sylvie organized things so that she was always present.

They were all civil to each other, all too closed off inside themselves to be otherwise. Matthew felt, truly and desperately, sorry for the others, but knew only how *he* felt, unable to cope at that early stage with more. The house seemed to him permanently dark and cold, even when outside it was warm and sunny. His bleakness felt etched through to his bones, his unhappiness vast, his guilt – *almost* irrational, but not sufficiently so as to allow him to deny it – all-consuming. Certain dominant, reproachful thoughts trod like invisible armies of hobnailed boots back and forth across his raw psyche. He ought to have been *with* her. He ought not to have gone away without her. Had he been at home, it would not have happened.

He went out for walks, on the Heath mostly, slogging through the roughest parts he could find, *wanting* mud and brambles and stinging nettles and uprooted trees, avoiding easy beauty or comfort wherever possible. He took Kahli with him only once, for though, frankly, the dog consoled him more than any of the humans in the household, he was met on their return on that occasion by Chloë, standing just inside the front door.

Angry-eyed, she snatched Kahli by the collar, startling both man and animal. 'He's not your dog,' she said and turned away, yanking the retriever with uncharacteristic roughness into the kitchen.

The *'ifs'* in his thought processes piled up in a mental dung heap, though this dung was useless, fertilizing only hopelessness. If he had been a better stepfather, had fought harder to make better friends with Caro's daughters. If he had been stronger, tougher. If he had taken the troubles more in his stride, kept his complaints to himself, not saddled his wife with them. If he had been less selfish, had forced himself and Caroline to consider the girls' feelings more at the outset, instead of marrying in such crazy haste.

If he had left when Flic and Imogen had first made it so abundantly plain that they wanted him to go; if he had been less determined not to be a quitter; if he had given way to what had, truthfully, sometimes seemed almost tempting. If he had just *gone*.

The desire to leave now was, at times, so intense that he could taste it. His thoughts would sink into the pitifully few months of his marriage and the vicious hostility of those two young women and he would become filled with bitterness and resentment – but then he would happen upon one of Caro's family huddled in such naked despair, filled with such bewilderment and grief because of

156

*their* loss, their pain, and he knew he could not possibly go now. For Caro's sake, if not theirs or his own.

How would she have reacted to his thoughts, his selfishness?

*All your fault? Your doing.*

No, not Caro. That would never have been her way, she would never have wanted him so deeply, savagely hurt, any more than she would have wanted it for any of those she loved.

Then *why* was she gone?

That was the one question Matthew found he had to shrink from each time it presented itself, which it did over and over again, like a loud, painful echo. And all the other questions related to that one would continue to be asked, by the police and by the Coroner when the inquest was held. Why had Caroline fallen? How had she fallen? What exactly had *happened* that afternoon on that balcony?

Unanswerable.

Too painful to *try* to answer.

Besides, there was plenty of time for both questions and answers.

Endless time. All of it, forever, without Caro.

# 25

The results of the post mortem examination held only one surprise.

Most of the findings had, according to Howard Lucas, been more or less as might have been anticipated. Caroline had died as a result of multiple injuries. Toxicological analysis carried out on specimens of blood and urine had shown that she had neither consumed alcohol nor taken drugs that might have affected her actions or responses. The rest, Lucas said, seemed commensurate with the nature and circumstances of the fall.

Matthew tried neither to listen nor read.

He knew what the pathologist and GP were saying. That Caro's wonderful body had smashed when it had collided with the paving stones three floors down. That she had probably flailed frantically and vainly during that final descent, scraping and cutting and bruising her poor hands and breaking her fingernails.

He had already known all he needed to and more.

Except, of course, for this one wholly unexpected thing.

Almost more shattering, more *shredding*, than all the rest.

In the circumstances.

At the time of her death, Caroline had been two months' pregnant.

He told Sylvie, for the news had come to him first, as next-of-kin. She had known no more about it than he had. They both knew that Caro's periods had been irregular since their marriage. Though not before that, he remembered her telling him. Stress, he had supposed, and felt sad about at the time.

'Do you think she knew?' he asked her mother.

'Perhaps not,' she said. 'Probably not, since she said nothing to either of us, or even to Howard Lucas.'

They wept together for a while, held each other.

'What do we do about the girls?' he asked her.

'You mean, do we tell them?'

Neither of them spoke for a few moments.

'I think not,' Sylvie said at last. 'What do you think?'

'I think,' Matthew said, 'that it would only cause them more pain.'

'And nothing to be gained by it,' Sylvie said.

Except, he thought, but did not say, that they might, in their irrational and now grief-stricken fashion, hate him even more than they already did.

'Nothing at all,' he said.

She thought of something else. 'We'll have to tell them before the inquest.'

*The inquest.*

More horror.

He looked at his mother-in-law's poor, white face.

'Yes,' he said.


He wept alone at night. Before hearing the news that the post mortem had brought, he had wept for the loss of Caro, for the warmth and joy and comfort of her physical presence, for the spiritual companionship of her soul. Now he wept for the child she had been carrying.

For their child.

His own child.


He had returned to work after nine days, encouraged to do so by Sylvie. She, who had always disliked early mornings but could no longer sleep for more than a few hours, was up for breakfast and there with the girls when Matthew came home from the office. Always there for him, for them, *between* them.

'I don't know how I'd cope without you,' he told her late one night.

'You don't have to,' Sylvie answered.

Kind and generous as she was, Matthew knew he could not be entirely certain that one reason for her constant presence might not be her wish to stand guard over her granddaughters. Imogen's monstrous accusation against him seemed to have happened light years ago, yet it had only been levelled on the Wednesday before Caro's death. Sylvie had said she had not believed Imo, but she had *also* said it was possible that Imo believed her own story. Sylvie had said that it was his decision whether or not he told Caro about it. He had not, of course, told her, and for that, at least, he was now profoundly grateful, for imagining Caro in possession of those kinds of nightmarish doubts in the last days of her life would have been unbearable – especially so, if she had known about her pregnancy.

Unless Sylvie had . . .

He refused to contemplate that. *Refused* to. Yet the ugly nugget of a thought returned to haunt him and to spawn more like it.

What if Sylvie had changed her mind? What if she had, after all, told Caro?

Even more intolerable, what if Imogen had told her on that last day?

What if . . .?

*Don't go there, Matthew.*

The inquest had been swiftly, routinely opened and adjourned for reports for a month, but the Coroner had released Caroline's body directly after the post mortem. In fresh torment as to how best and most sensitively to deal with her funeral, Matthew had decided finally to raise the matter at a family meeting.

'All I want,' he had said after supper one evening, 'is to do the best for Caroline and for you. If you want to take care of the arrangements yourselves, then I'll respect that – though I think it might be tough on you all.'

'I can't speak for the girls on this,' Sylvie said, 'but I for one would be grateful to have you arrange things. With our input, of course, when it comes to things such as hymns or readings.'

'I wouldn't organize a thing,' Matthew said, 'without consulting you all.'

No one else spoke for a few moments.

'Flic?' he said, finally. 'What do you think?'

'I don't know much about arranging funerals,' she said quietly. 'Mum and our grandfather took care of things when Dad died.' She had lost weight since Caroline's death, and her fine cheekbones, so like her mother's, were more accentuated than ever, too much so.

'There's no question of your having to deal with things alone, obviously,' Matthew assured her. 'I just didn't want you to feel I was taking over.'

'I don't really mind,' she said.

Matthew looked at Imogen, who was sitting very still. She, too, had lost weight, and her eyes were darkly ringed.

'Me neither,' she said.

Matthew turned to Chloë. 'How do you feel about it?'

'Okay,' she said. 'I suppose.'

Out of the three, the change in Chloë had been the most disturbing. Before Caroline's death, she had still possessed a slight chubbiness, but now that last relic of childhood had all but disappeared, and though she had neither Flic's near gauntness nor Imogen's deeply shadowed eyes, she looked far too thin and, more worryingly, she had become very withdrawn.

'After Richard,' Sylvie had told Matthew, 'Chloë had Caro to cling to, of course, so it was easier for her to go on being a child. But now her Mummy's gone too, and I'm afraid it may represent the end of childhood for her.'

Matthew thought Sylvie was right. The loss of her mother did represent far more than grief and shock, for Chloë, he felt, was more multi-layered and complicated. She felt, he sensed, suddenly grievously disappointed with life, almost offended by it. She had grown up in such a protected environment, had presumably thought her father's stroke and subsequent death the very worst that life could throw at her.

'Did Mum ask for anything?' Flic asked suddenly. 'Funeral-wise, I mean.'

'Not that I know of,' Matthew answered.

'Nor I,' Sylvie said.

'What about in her will?' Flic asked.

'I don't know,' Matthew said. 'I haven't seen it.'

'Haven't you?' Imogen sounded surprised.

He shook his head. 'I haven't really thought about it.'

'Haven't you looked for it?' Flic asked.

'No.' Matthew paused. 'I presume it's with her solicitor.'

'Bill Standish,' Sylvie confirmed. 'The will is lodged with him. He phoned me a few days ago.' She looked at Matthew. 'I'm the executor, and Bill's an old friend. He'll be in touch with you soon, I expect.'

'Fine.' Her executorship was no surprise to Matthew, since Caro had mentioned it some months back. She'd been contemplating amending her will to include him, and he had asked her, quite emphatically, to put that idea on hold at least until they'd been married for several years.

'Can we have "Silent Night" at the funeral?' Chloë asked abruptly.

'That's a carol,' Flic said, 'not a hymn.'

'She'll be asking for Robbie Williams next,' Imogen said.

'Shut up,' Chloë shouted suddenly, violently. 'We're talking about Mummy's funeral, and all you can do is be horrible.'

'They're just talking about music,' Sylvie told her gently.

'They're not,' Chloë said. 'They're making fun of me, as usual, and I hate it!' She jumped to her feet and ran out of the kitchen.

'Shit.' Imogen looked dismayed.

'I'll go and talk to her.' Flic got up.

'In a minute,' Sylvie said.

'Surely we're finished here, aren't we?' Flic looked at Matthew. 'We've said we don't mind you making the arrangements so long as you talk to us about them, okay?'

'Okay,' he said.

'So can I go now, Groosi?'

'Of course,' Sylvie said, and looked at Imogen. 'You can go too if you like.'

Imogen got up. 'Aren't you going to have a go at me for swearing, Groosi?'

'Not really,' Sylvie said. 'I felt like swearing too.'

Matthew smiled, but said nothing. He was conscious that the questions about Caroline's will had represented a test which he thought he had probably passed. One thing less for Flic and Imo to accuse him of.

And they had agreed to his involvement in their mother's funeral.

That had surprised him, he had to admit.

162

Of all the ways to effect a breakthrough, of sorts, it was assuredly the saddest.

The funeral took place on the eleventh of October, a Wednesday.

A few people came just for him, which helped Matthew a little. Ethan came with Susan, having left Teddy and Andy at home with their maternal grandmother, and Karl came, too, again without Amelie, who was now too heavily pregnant to travel. Robert Fairbairn came from VKF, and Kat, and, to Matthew's surprise and gratitude, Nick Brice. Phil Bianco had written a nice enough note, and a couple more letters had come through from the Berlin office, with one deeply touching phone call from Laszlo King in New York.

'If you need anything,' he'd told Matthew, 'either in London or back home, let us know and we'll do our best.'

The chairman's way, Matthew thought, of telling him that if he wanted to go back, there would probably be a place for him back in the Manhattan office.

It felt, he was forced to admit to himself, like glimpsing, through thick dark fog, the far-off glimmer of a candle in a familiar window.

It was, he supposed, that single word. Home.

He went through the funeral on a kind of remote. He had done his best with the arrangements, for Sylvie and the girls, and for Caro herself, and all the effort had helped prevent him from dwelling constantly upon his personal loss. As a consequence, however, the events themselves seemed like extensions of the planning; things happening around him for other people, little to do with him. Or with Caro and himself as a pair. Matthew and Caroline Gardner, married couple, had begun to cease to exist, he thought, not at the time of her death, but at around the time that the family and the vicar had started discussing eulogies, all dwelling lengthily on Caroline's loss of Richard. In that same way it ended, it seemed to Matthew, as her coffin was lowered into the grave beside her late husband's.

Borrowed and now returned.

'I think,' he heard Flic say to Imogen later, back at the house, while guests milled around the drawing room drinking sherry and whisky and tea, 'maybe we should take down Dad's stone and have a new one made for them both.'

'Maybe,' Imogen said.

Preferably, Matthew thought wryly, with no mention at all of his name, as if his marriage to their mother had never existed.

'It'll depend on what *he* wants, I suppose,' Flic said.

Matthew looked across the room at her, past people he didn't even recognize, to see how much hostility there was in her expression, for he had been conscious, over the past couple of weeks, of waiting for the other shoe to drop.

'I suppose,' Imogen agreed.

They both saw him looking at them. Flic gave a small, sad little smile, and Imogen gave him a nod.

'Cease-fire still holding, I see,' Karl commented softly from just behind him.

'At least,' Matthew said, 'so long as there's an audience.'

'Don't you think it might be more than that?' Karl asked. 'A truce, maybe?'

'I don't know,' Matthew said tiredly. 'I doubt it.'

'So negative,' Karl said sadly.

'You think I wouldn't prefer it to be different?'

'I think' – his friend laid a gentle hand on his arm – 'you've been through too much to know exactly what you want or need right now.'

'A little peace,' Matthew said, softly but forcefully, 'is what I need. To allow me to grieve for my wife.'

'I hope,' Karl said, 'that you get it.'

# 26

The ordeal of the funeral past, now they all dreaded the inquest, scheduled two weeks later. They hardly spoke of it, but the feeling seemed to spread right through the house, a kind of mud in the atmosphere that choked off any possibility of normal, forward-looking thought process, that destroyed appetite and natural sleep. Two family birthdays came and went; Sylvie's fifty-eighth, ignored at her explicit request, and Chloë's thirteenth, no less bleak for all their attempts at marking it with cake and presents.

As the day drew closer, Sylvie, always the family rock, showed the most strain, became snappy, noticeably thinner, worrying them all deeply, but she rejected suggestions of seeing the doctor, pointed out sharply that she needed no diagnosis and still had the same small bottle of sleeping pills that Dr Lucas had prescribed for her immediately after Caroline's death.

'I don't want that kind of sleep,' she said.

'You need to rest,' Matthew said.

'I need my daughter back,' Sylvie said. 'But since I can't have that, I need to have the horrors over so that I can at least pretend to go on with living.'

'I know,' Matthew said.

'I know you do.' She paused. 'What about the baby?'

He had been dreading this moment almost as much as the inquest itself.

'Which of us should tell them?' he asked.

'It's your decision,' Sylvie said. 'Though I think, perhaps, it might be better for them if it comes from me.'

'Can you bear it?' he asked her.

'As well as I can bear any of it,' she said.

He waited, during the next twenty-four hours, for something to happen, for some response from them, ugly, painful or simply sorrowful, but there was nothing.

'Have you told them?' he asked Sylvie the following evening.

'Yes,' she said. 'They were very quiet about it.'

'None of them has said anything to me.'

'I wondered if they might.' Sylvie paused. 'Too hard for them, perhaps?'

'I expect so.'

'Chloë wept a little, then asked me if it would have been a boy or girl. Another sister, she said, or a brother. I told her that I didn't know. She said she would have liked to have a baby brother.'

Matthew felt a swift jab of grief. 'And the others?'

'Flic was composed – you know how she is. She thanked me for telling her, then put her arms around Chloë. Imogen didn't say anything, just went to her room.' Sylvie looked at him. 'I'm sorry they haven't come to you.'

'I don't think I expected them to.' He paused. 'Do you think I should speak to them about it now?'

'I don't know,' Sylvie said.

'If things were different,' he began, then stopped.

'Yes,' Sylvie said.

He knew he would say nothing.

The day loomed with painful slowness, then, like a jet on final approach, it seemed to roar upon them with frightening speed.

The evening before, Chloë began her first period. All Matthew knew about it, till Isabella enlightened him, was that one by one after dinner, the other members of the household disappeared into her bedroom and stayed there.

'Is Chloë ill?' he asked Isabella when she emerged.

'No.' The Chilean woman smiled. 'She's menstruating.'

'First time?'

Isabella nodded.

'How's she doing?' Matthew asked.

'She's sad,' Isabella said, 'because Caro prepared her for this day.'

Matthew kept his distance, knowing he was not wanted, but later, passing the room when the door was open, he glanced in and saw them all, clustered together in a kind of knot of femininity, and for a moment he was reminded of the evening of his wedding day in Bern, when he'd seen Caroline's daughters forming an exclusive circle around her. He remembered, too, coming home to Aethiopia for the first time and telling Caro that he felt the house was female, a woman's house.

He felt that again now, as keenly as if the house were speaking to him. Telling him that he did not belong here, never had.

He shook the thought away.

Karl had talked about a possible truce, and in fact, the seedlings did seem at times to be bearing fruit. Small things, like Flic offering to make him cups of coffee or asking how his day had been.

'I fell for that before, though,' Matthew had told Karl on the phone, 'for quite a while, and all the time they were just playing games with me.'

'They hadn't lost their mother then,' Karl had said.

'No, they hadn't,' Matthew had granted.

He had almost given up trying to make Karl or Ethan see the truth about his stepdaughters. He still wished for them to be right, but saw no real logic in the notion that Caro's death should make Flic or Imo loathe him any less. On the contrary, it seemed to him.

That was one of many reasons for his growing dread of the inquest, of course. That they might be planning some kind of testimony to make the Coroner feel that he had made Caro's life unbearable.

Which was not, of course, altogether a lie, God help him.

The fact that the girls gave no such testimony was the only bright spot when the inquest into Caroline's death was resumed.

The entrance to the Coroner's Court was just yards from the mortuary, but Matthew kept his eyes averted, determined at least to try to hold it together, for the girls and for Sylvie, who was very pale but composed.

The courtroom was old, rather austere but dignified, a little like church, Matthew thought, but with more plush red and well-polished dark wood. The Coroner presided, like a judge, a coat of arms on the wall behind him, the Coroner's Officer positioned to his left; but the jury pews were empty, and with only the family, Susanna and Detective-Sergeant Ross present, the atmosphere seemed to possess, despite the strain, an air of privacy, almost of intimacy. There was plenty of space, but they sat close together: Flic beside Imogen, then their grandmother, holding Chloë's hand, Matthew beside her. Susanna, erect and resolutely calm, sat on the pew immediately behind them.

Sylvie was the first to be called into the witness box and sworn in. She held the Bible and read the words on the card, speaking into a slender microphone, and was then asked to confirm her daughter's personal particulars for the court.

And the questioning began.

They were kindly, carefully posed; the same questions, for the most part, that they had all asked time and again and found no answers to. Could Sylvie think of any reason why Caroline should have locked herself into that room, when no one in the household was aware of her having previously done so? Especially at a time when one of her daughters was ill in bed on another floor of the house? Sylvie could think of no reason. She could not recall Caroline ever locking herself into any room.

'To the best of your knowledge, Mrs Lehrer,' the Coroner asked, 'was Mrs Gardner in the habit of leaning over the balcony railing outside that room?'

'Not that I'm aware. Caroline disliked heights. She seldom went out onto balconies, even in hotels.'

Asked about the state of Caro's marriage and the fact that she had been two months' pregnant, Sylvie testified that aside from a few inevitable teething troubles, her daughter had been very happily married, had been very much in love with her husband, that the love had been reciprocated and that, of course, her pregnancy would have brought great joy to her and to Matthew.

She was the first witness to be asked the question they had all dreaded most.

'I have to ask you this, Mrs Lehrer,' the Coroner preceded it with great gentleness, 'though I realize it will cause you more distress.'

Sylvie nodded, but said nothing. Watching her, Matthew noticed, in addition to the loss of weight, a host of small lines

168

around her eyes and mouth that had not, he thought, been there a month before.

'Do you know of any reason why your daughter might have taken her own life?'

Sylvie's answer was immediate and clear. 'None.'

'I gather that Mrs Gardner had previously suffered from depression?'

'Yes. Following the death of her first husband.'

'And this was a short-lived depression?'

'Comparatively,' Sylvie answered. 'The acute stage was quite short-lived, though of course there was a great deal to cope with in general.'

'Of course.' The Coroner paused. 'You referred a few minutes ago to "teething troubles" in your daughter's new marriage. Nothing there, Mrs Lehrer, that you feel might have revived Mrs Gardner's depression?'

This time, Sylvie did not respond immediately. She appeared to be thinking, considering. Matthew watched and waited, scarcely breathing.

'Mrs Lehrer?'

Sylvie shook her head. 'Nothing.'

'Forgive me, but you seemed to be pondering something,' the Coroner said, still with that extreme gentleness. 'If there is anything at all that might help shed some light on this tragedy, this is the time for you to speak of it.'

'I do realize that,' Sylvie said, 'but there is nothing to speak of.' She took a breath. 'I was thinking back, over our last conversations, over private family events in general. But no,' she said, with finality, 'there was nothing.'

'You're quite certain, Mrs Lehrer?'

'Quite certain,' Sylvie said. 'As I've already told you, the last time I spoke to my daughter, she was quite content. She had encouraged Matthew to go on his firm's golfing weekend without her, despite Flic's – Felicity's – illness. She was planning to use the time to catch up with her work. And if she knew about the baby ...' She hesitated. 'I'm sorry, I've told you all this already.'

'Yes, Mrs Lehrer, you have,' the Coroner said. 'Thank you.'

\*

In an effort to spare them, the Coroner asked Imogen and Chloë informally if they had anything they wished to contribute. Both answered that they did not, after which Flic – the the only person at home at the time in question – was sworn in.

She held the Bible and the card given to her.

'I swear by Almighty God that the evidence I shall give shall be the truth, the whole truth, and nothing but the truth.'

Matthew braced himself.

The Coroner began by extending his sympathy, then asked her to go over, from her perspective, the events of the day leading up to her mother's death.

'There weren't any events, really,' Flic said. 'That was the thing. My being ill, I mean.' She paused. 'I didn't know anything was happening. I was asleep most of the time.' Her eyes filled, and she had to swallow her tears.

'Take your time, Miss Walters.' The Coroner paused. 'Would you like a glass of water?'

'No, thank you. I'm all right.'

The questions went on for a little while, but led nowhere other than, perhaps, to an increasing of Flic's already great misery at having been in the house, yet utterly unaware of the tragedy. The Coroner told her, then reiterated for emphasis, that she had nothing whatever to blame herself for.

'I trust you believe that, Miss Walters,' he said. 'It is extremely important that you understand and accept your blamelessness.'

She thanked him, left the box, returned to her seat. The Coroner asked Imogen and Chloë again if they had anything to add or wished to comment upon, and as they had the first time, they both replied, with frozen faces and unsteady voices, that there was nothing they needed to say.

'Nothing,' Imogen added, 'that would make any difference.'

'Are you quite certain?'

'Yes,' Imo said.

Matthew was called to the witness box. His heart pounded uncomfortably as he took the oath, and his body ached with tension.

'In the knowledge,' the Coroner said, 'that at the time of Mrs Gardner's death, you were out of London, I can only offer you my very sincere condolences, and ask you the same question that I

170

have asked a number of other witnesses.' He paused. 'Do you know of any reason why your wife might have contemplated taking her own life?'

'No,' Matthew said, his voice husky with stress. He shook his head and cleared his throat. 'No,' he repeated. 'If I had thought for a single second that there was even the smallest chance of Caro feeling that way – of being that *unhappy* – I would never have left her, never have gone away . . .'

He broke off, shut his eyes for a moment, then opened them again and stared down at his right arm. A tiny loose thread in the fabric of his sleeve became a focal point for a second or two, allowed him to detach a little, calm down, then raise his eyes again and face the Coroner.

'Are you all right, Mr Gardner?'

'Yes. Thank you.' He swallowed. 'I'm sorry.'

'Please don't apologize,' the Coroner told him. 'This is a great ordeal for all concerned.' He paused. 'If I may continue, I have just a very few more questions.'

'Of course,' Matthew said.

He glanced across the court, saw that Sylvie's eyes were full of sympathy, and shame swept over him for his weakness in the face of her remarkable strength.

'Casting your mind back, Mr Gardner, over the last few days spent with your wife, can you remember anything occurring that caused her particular distress?'

Matthew's mind flew directly back again to his breakfast meeting with Sylvie and to Imogen's allegations. He looked again at his mother-in-law, seeking the slightest hint in her expression that might suggest that she felt he ought to raise the point, even if doing so might harm Imogen as much as his own reputation.

Did he imagine the tiny, almost imperceptible shake of her head?

Whether or not, his decision was made.

'Nothing,' he answered. 'Nothing that I knew of at least.'

'Did you find her distracted, perhaps by something you didn't understand?'

'By the pregnancy, you mean?'

'Perhaps.'

'I've thought about that, obviously,' Matthew said, 'over and

171

over again. I wonder if she might have been planning to tell me about the baby that weekend, think that if I hadn't gone . . .'

'You were not to know,' the Coroner said.

Matthew shook his head, swallowed, made himself go on. 'She was very happy, full of energy, once we'd decided to go on the weekend trip together, before Flic – Felicity – got sick. Caro always liked to throw herself into things body and soul, though of course, once she knew her daughter had the flu, there was no question she was going to stay behind.'

'Didn't that upset you both?'

'A little.' Matthew thought back yet again to the edginess that had crept between them towards the end, tried to push the memories away. 'I told her I didn't want to go without her. She more or less insisted I should, said it was the right thing for me business-wise. And she talked about getting on with her own work.'

'With which she had fallen behind.'

'Yes.'

'Did you argue about whether or not you should go?'

'No,' Matthew said. 'We talked it back and forth for a while.' He recalled the moment when he'd implied that Flic's flu might not be real, glanced at his stepdaughter now, saw her pallor and her entirely real suffering, and pushed that memory away too. 'Caro was insistent I go without her.' He paused. 'So I did.'

'Is there anything else you wish to say, Mr Gardner?'

'No,' Matthew said. 'I don't think so.'

The Coroner thanked him, reiterated his sympathies and let him go.

Susanna gave her evidence clearly and calmly, for the most part, making it plain from the outset that her viewpoint as Caro's psychotherapist might possibly be somewhat coloured by the fact that the deceased had become a close and cherished friend.

'To clarify, Miss Durkin, you felt that Mrs Gardner was unhappy about the fact that her husband was not getting along with her children as well as she had hoped?'

'Undoubtedly,' Susanna said. 'Though I do believe that Matthew – Mr Gardner – felt equally unhappy, in his own way, about that fact.'

'In his own way?' the Coroner queried.

'The girls are not his own children,' Susanna said simply.

'However sincere his desire to get on well with his stepdaughters, however much he wanted it for Caroline's sake, he could never have felt as deeply as she did.'

'Do you think that Mrs Gardner's pregnancy might have caused more friction?'

'It might,' Susanna said, 'if the girls had known about it.'

'But they did not.'

'I don't think anyone did – except maybe, of course, Caro – Mrs Gardner.'

The question came again. Did Susanna feel that Caroline's unhappiness over her husband's relationship with her daughters might have led her to take her own life?

'Absolutely not,' Susanna answered categorically. 'All other considerations aside, she would never have done that to her children.' She paused to look at Sylvie. 'Caro would never have done that to anyone she loved. And if she did know about the baby, she would never have done it to her unborn child.'

Her testimony continued a while longer. Even during the time of Caroline's acute depression three years earlier, she had never, so far as Susanna knew, been suicidal. The Coroner asked about the work that Caro had been engaged in at the time of her death, aware that the commission had come her way through Susanna. Caroline, Susanna said, had taken pride in her needlework. It had troubled her that she had fallen behind with her latest commission, hence her pleasure, as reported by Sylvie, in having some time to herself that last weekend to catch up with it.

'Is there any possibility,' the Coroner asked, 'that falling behind might have distressed her severely?'

'Enough to make her suicidal?' Susanna shook her head firmly. 'Certainly not. Caro was a practical person with sound priorities. Work was work, nothing more.'

Detective-Sergeant Ross was summoned to give evidence. Asked, towards the end of his testimony, about the height of the railing around the balcony outside the Quiet Room, he described it as sufficiently high for Mrs Gardner to have had to either climb up, or to pull herself up, in order to put herself in a position of real danger. Ross stated that he had found it somewhat improbable that she could have simply fallen from the balcony, but following their enquiries and investigation, the police had felt satisfied that there was no reason to suspect foul play.

The Coroner then read out both the pathologist's report, and a second report previously submitted by Howard Lucas, in which he testified to the generally sound state of Caroline's health, and said that, to the best of his knowledge as her GP, there had been no recent diagnosis or underlying problems that might have been preying on her mind, and that Caroline had not consulted him about her pregnancy.

The Coroner's Officer declared the evidence concluded.

There was a heavy pause. Chloë shifted for a moment, but the others were all completely still. Matthew, whose heartbeat had returned to normal, felt it accelerate again. From outside, he became aware of the sounds of children playing.

Normality, he thought, and envied them.

In his summing up, the Coroner referred again to the testimonies of each witness, and to both the doctor's and the pathologist's reports. No defence injuries had been found, the lacerations to Mrs Gardner's fingers and palms had been commensurate with those of a person desperately struggling to grab hold of something as she fell; and the toxicological analysis had determined no presence of either alcohol or drugs in her blood. The police investigation had ruled out foul play.

He came to the question of suicide.

Though Caroline had suffered from a short period of depression in the past, the Coroner felt that this had been directly connected with her first husband's death, that she was apparently very happy in her new marriage, and that her new pregnancy would only – as Mrs Lehrer had said – have brought more happiness.

The locking of the door did not in itself prove anything sinister; there could have been any number of reasons for Caroline to have wished to shut herself in, perhaps for a short while. And from all the testimony he had heard, the coroner did not feel that such a loving woman, perhaps aware that she was expecting another child, and well-known for her concern for her family's welfare, would have taken her own life while one of her beloved children was lying ill in bed one floor below.

There was no evidence in this case, the Coroner continued, of Caroline stating either verbally or in writing that she intended to commit suicide, or that she was unduly depressed, or that she had previously harmed herself.

'With the evidence I have heard, I am therefore not satisfied that Mrs Gardner had the intention of taking her own life.'

Matthew experienced a slender, tenuous wisp of relief.

The Coroner turned his attention to the possible verdict of Accidental Death, and pointed to Detective-Sergeant Ross's statement that it would have been improbable for Caroline to have simply fallen from the balcony.

The relief was already gone.

'Mrs Gardner's state of mind at the time of her death, however,' the Coroner went on, 'is not, of course, known. Nor, probably, will we ever know what drew her to the edge of that balcony on that afternoon.'

Matthew knew he was holding his breath, glanced at the girls, saw that they and their grandmother were all utterly immobilized with tension.

And then the Coroner did the one thing that none of them had anticipated.

He recorded an Open verdict.

Matthew realized afterwards, when he was finally alone, sitting in Richard's study, sipping a whisky and staring into space, that he had spent much of the inquest feeling a little like a murderer terrified that his crime was about to be laid bare.

He had heard it said that innocent people accused often enough of sins, sometimes began to doubt themselves.

Not that anyone, at any time – at least after Detective-Sergeant Ross's first visit to Aethiopia – had raised even the slightest suspicion of foul play. It had been the spectre of the possibility that Caro might have *wanted* to die that had haunted him – that had, he was sure, haunted them all.

Suicide, at least, had, thank God, been ruled out. By the Coroner himself.

Yet the 'accidental' verdict he had hoped for – expected in the absence of suicide – had not been granted to them.

'Open.'

Not clearly enough an accident. No blame attached to anyone, but no real finality to ease their burden.

'*Open.*'

At least there had been no more accusations against him by Flic or Imogen. Christ knew he had waited, in a state of suspense, for one of them, or Sylvie, or perhaps even Susanna, to use the wreck of his relationship with his stepdaughters to load the evidence towards suicide. But no one had done that.

He kept a photograph of Caro, one of those he'd taken of her in St Moritz, on his desk, Richard's desk, and he picked it up now, looked into her laughing eyes.

Whatever the verdict, she was still dead. Still gone for ever, leaving behind her a trail of misery and doubts and 'what ifs' and unanswered questions.

The Coroner had said that they would probably never know what had drawn Caro to the balcony's edge.

*'Nor, probably, will we ever know . . .'*

Words intended to bring closure, Matthew supposed, to help alleviate pain.

And infinitely less agonizing than a suggestion of suicide.

And yet. And yet.

*'Open.'*

Matthew set down the photograph again, his hand trembling.

# PART TWO

# 27

'At least,' Flic said to Imogen on the fourth of November, two Saturday afternoons after the inquest, 'he will go now. Eventually.'

They were sitting at a table in The Place to Eat at John Lewis in Brent Cross, waiting while Chloë queued up at one of the counters for coffee, since they were only here because she had whinged to Isabella and Matthew about all the stuff she was running out of that she could only afford to buy – on her pocket money – in the bigger shopping chains.

Flic disliked the centre, avoided all such places whenever possible, infinitely preferring small shops or what she considered *real* stand-alone department stores like Harrods and Harvey Nichols and Selfridges. Imogen's shopping tastes were more erratic, like her moods; complacent about living in Hampstead, she would, if she'd had her own credit card, probably have spent every Saturday in South Ken or Covent Garden, but as things were she contented herself on the whole with sprees in FCUK and Gap.

Not that anything could be said to be contenting her these days.

Nicola had wanted to come with them today, and Annie had been nagging at her to get together too, but Imogen didn't want to see either of them. Flic and her family – her *real* family – were all she needed or could cope with right now. Flic more than anyone, since no one else could even begin to understand.

She'd 'expressed' herself (Susanna's explanation to Sylvie after the event) in the middle of that week by walking out of school at

179

eleven o'clock, going to a hairdressers at Camden Lock and having her hair dyed black and cut spikily short.

'Expressing her anger,' Susanna had said when she'd come to the house for a glass of wine that evening. 'Has she had anything pierced, do you know?'

'She said not.' Sylvie had been doubtful. 'I hope not.'

'Maybe she's done it to look a bit more like her father.'

'Do you think so? Richard would have had a fit.'

'So would Caro,' Susanna had said.

And they'd both smiled, and then they'd both wept.

The new hair had made Imogen feel better for an hour or two, but that was all.

'You don't know that he'll go,' she said now, morosely, reaching into her bag to finger the pack of Marlboro she'd talked Flic into buying for her earlier. 'He hasn't said, has he?'

'Not yet,' Flic said, calmly. 'But he will.'

'I suppose.' Imogen looked around for Chloë, saw she was only fourth in the queue. 'I won't even want the bloody coffee by the time she gets it.'

'Not her fault,' Flic said. 'Try and calm down, Imo.'

'How can I?' The brown eyes were despairing. 'I can't take much more.'

'You have to.'

'I *can't*.' Imo managed to keep her voice down, yet it still sounded like a small, anguished yelp. 'I mean it, Flic.'

'What's the alternative?'

'I could die.'

'No, you couldn't.' Flic had heard the threat umpteen times before, was able to cope with it, but her own calm was spurious, her sister's nosedives into bleakness and panic deeply worrying to her. 'You couldn't leave me or Chloë, and you couldn't do it to Groosi.' She glanced at the coffee queue, saw that Chloë was now third in line. 'You just have to stay focused, like me.'

'On *what*?' Imogen almost spat the words. 'Everything's ruined forever now. We wanted him gone and Mum back to ourselves, and instead . . .' She stopped, shook her head, unable to go on.

'All the more reason to focus on him leaving.'

Imogen took a deep breath, shut her eyes for a moment and leaned back against the bench-seat. 'It won't be right now, even if

180

he does go.' She opened her eyes. 'He won't be punished. He'll get to run back home or wherever he fancies next and start a new life with some new woman, and we're just bloody orphans.'

'But at least he'll be out of our lives,' Flic said, 'and it'll be just us and Groosi, and Isabella and Mick can move in, and Aethiopia will feel like ours again.'

'Will it?' Imogen asked quietly.

'Definitely.'

Chloë moved into second place.

'And do we deserve that?' Imo asked even more softly.

'Absolutely,' Flic said.

'I'm not so sure.' It was a whisper.

Flic saw the self-torture and felt almost helpless. She wasn't used to feeling that way, hated it. Much as she hated everything these days.

'She's being served,' Imogen said.

'Good.' Flic managed a smile. 'Focus, Imo, okay? One step at a time. Coffee first, a bit more shopping, then home. And keep thinking of how much better it *will* be once he's gone.'

Imogen gave her back a pale, cracked version of a smile. 'Can I have a ciggie on the way back?'

'If you must.'

'I must.' The smile was gone again. 'If I don't have a cigarette, I'll lose it.'

'No, you won't,' Flic said.

Imogen's eyes were intense. 'I will.'

'So you'll have a cigarette,' Flic said.

181

# 28

'I think,' Sylvie said to Matthew that same afternoon, while the girls were out shopping, 'it's time we talked about your plans.'

'What kind of plans?'

They were in the drawing room, where Matthew had earlier lit the first fire of the year because Sylvie had complained of feeling cold.

'I've been assuming,' Sylvie went on, 'that you will, ultimately, be thinking about leaving us.'

Matthew didn't respond. His mother-in-law had taken him by surprise, and he found that he needed time to let her words percolate.

'Perhaps,' she said, forging on, 'I'm entirely wrong, but I thought you might be feeling the need to escape, go back to Berlin, perhaps, or maybe New York.'

The word 'escape' hung in the air.

'I don't know,' he said. 'I haven't really thought about it yet.'

'Haven't you?' Sylvie sounded surprised. 'I'm sure I would have, if I were you.' There was no hint of censure in her tone, just honesty. 'After all you've endured here, even before we lost Caro.'

'I'm not sure I believe that,' he said. 'That you'd be contemplating running out on everything, I mean.' He smiled at her. 'You're tougher than that, Sylvie.'

'Is that how you would see it? As running out on us?'

He nodded. 'I think so.'

'Why?'

The baldness of the question threw him for another moment. 'Because when Caro and I got married, I don't recall adding a rider to the vows: "But if you die, I get to dump all marital responsibilities and walk out on your kids".' He grimaced slightly. 'Not that they wouldn't cheer the instant I started packing.'

'Maybe,' Sylvie said. 'Maybe not.' She smiled. 'Or maybe not as loudly as you might expect.'

Matthew glanced swiftly at her. 'Have they said something?'

'About your leaving? Not exactly.'

'What then?'

'Chloë has begun asking questions about how things are going to be from now on. I think that probably means she's afraid of whatever next big change is going to rock her life.'

'Poor kid,' Matthew said.

'Imogen hasn't said anything,' Sylvie continued, 'but Flic did say, out of the blue the other day, that she can't seem to see ahead any more. She says she's always had a knack for being able to picture almost any given situation in the future, even *tailor* it – that was the word she used – to how she wanted it to be.'

'Then make it happen,' Matthew said.

'You think that's what she tried to do about you, don't you?' Sylvie asked. 'A spot of deft tailoring of your marriage to her mother? Cut you out of her picture?'

'Don't you think that?'

Sylvie sighed. 'If that was what she wanted, she's had a devastatingly different result, hasn't she?'

'Poor Flic. It must feel like the worst possible nightmare.'

'You really are a very kind man,' she said.

'I haven't always felt very kindly over the past several months.'

'I know,' Sylvie said. 'But you stayed the course.'

'I loved Caro,' he said simply.

'Didn't we all?' Sylvie said.

It was true to say that Matthew's feelings towards his two older stepdaughters had softened somewhat. Mostly, he supposed, that could be put down to compassion, his awareness of the totality of their loss. But it was also true to say that since the inquest and the Coroner's ruling against suicide, life inside Aethiopia had become a little easier from his point-of-view, because Flic and Imogen had all but ceased riding him. Shock, still, he told himself, and the powerful grasp of grief on their emotions, creating an unnatural, and almost certainly temporary, time-out.

'Kindness aside,' Sylvie said now, 'and as much as you loved my daughter, you should know that I will fully understand if you do decide to leave us.'

Matthew looked at her. 'Would you like me to go?'

'Not at all,' she answered promptly. 'But it has to be your own decision. For one thing, as Caro's husband you have certain rights. You know she wanted you to feel you could go on living here.'

He shook his head. 'She didn't know anything was going to happen to her this soon, and I don't feel we were married long enough for my rights to play much of a part.' He took a breath. 'You have rights, as do the girls, obviously. Including their right to want to be left alone with you now.'

Sylvie was silent for a moment. 'There are other factors to consider. Stability, for one.'

'You represent stability,' he said. 'The grandmother they've known and loved all their lives.'

'The girls have begun to grow used to you.'

'Grown used to hating my guts.'

'Maybe,' Sylvie admitted. 'But despite the antagonism, it's still you they've been living with for over three-quarters of a year.' She paused. 'The last year of their mother's life.'

Matthew said nothing, for what his mother-in-law was saying did not, for once, ring true, which puzzled him a little.

'And then there's Chloë,' Sylvie went on. 'Still very much a child, and extremely fond of you.'

'Even now? I haven't been sure of that lately.'

'Especially now, Matthew.'

They were interrupted then by the girls' return, but later that night, after they had all gone upstairs to bed, Matthew realized that Sylvie had been waiting to resume their conversation.

'I think I'd like a drink,' she said.

He stood up. 'Tea?' She often drank tea with lemon at night.

'Cognac, I think, please.'

He poured two drinks, returned to the sofa.

Sylvie took her cognac, had a sip. 'Have you had any more thoughts about what we were discussing this afternoon?'

He was surprised. 'I didn't realize there was such a rush.'

'There isn't,' she said.

'Are you certain about that?'

She didn't answer.

'Okay,' he said, not wanting to challenge her too vigorously. 'You said earlier that stability was one of the factors to be considered. What were the others?'

'I think,' Sylvie said, 'that there would be advantages for the girls to go on having a male role model.'

Matthew's laugh was ironic. 'Me?'

'Certainly.'

'They had that with their father.'

'Their father's dead.' Sylvie sounded matter-of-fact.

'But he lived long enough, clearly, to be all the role model they needed.' He paused. 'The kind, loving, talented daddy they adored.'

She said nothing.

'That is all true, isn't it?' He was thrown by her lack of response.

'That they adored him, of course.' She hesitated, appearing to listen for a moment, then stood up, walked across to the half-open door and closed it fully before returning to her chair.

'Richard,' she said, quietly, 'was not the paragon you seem to think he was.'

Matthew felt a curious sensation, an almost physical sense of foundations shifting. 'What was he then?' he asked.

Sylvie took her time. 'He was, I believe,' she said slowly, 'the kind of man who did not very much like women.' She saw Matthew's face, shook her head. 'I'm not speaking about sexuality. I mean something far more fundamental.' She gave a small smile. 'You like women, Matthew, as a generalization. You like and respect us.'

'Unquestionably.'

'Richard did not.'

Matthew felt stunned. 'But I was under the impression—'

'That's an appropriate word,' Sylvie cut in. 'Richard gave a tremendous *impression* of being the opposite of what I've just said. Especially with his daughters. I think he put on his finest

185

performances with them – but then, they were his biggest admirers, weren't they, his sample audience?'

'I assumed he had an ego,' Matthew said, 'but then again, he did have a special talent, and the two often go hand in hand.'

'Do you like his work?' Sylvie enquired.

Matthew considered. 'Some of it.' He paused. 'The lightweight work, perhaps, more than the less commercial.'

'Astrid the cow, you mean, as opposed to his would-be Blake attempts?'

Her acerbic tone startled Matthew. 'I thought you loved his work.'

'Did you ever hear me say that?' Sylvie asked, more mildly.

He thought about it. 'Maybe not. But it's the feeling I've always had, from the whole family. Richard Walters, minor genius.'

Sylvie shrugged. 'Maybe I did tend to follow the party line, particularly after his death. The girls were – are – so very sensitive about their father.' She paused. 'As was Caro.' She kept her voice carefully low. 'The fact is, I found most of his work rather mediocre and pretentious.'

'You sound scornful.'

'All Richard's real success – though his financial underpinning stemmed from his father – came from Astrid, a very charming little cartoon of a cow. Astrid was fine, I liked her very much, and I also liked my daughter having security, *and* I knew how important it can be to some men to make their own pile.' Sylvie paused. 'I would have had greater respect for Richard if it hadn't been for his pretentiousness.'

'You were talking about his relationship with the girls.'

'He turned them into his entourage,' she said with some distaste. 'Took them to book launches and gallery openings to show them off, made a big thing of telling everyone that his daughters were his inspiration and his greatest fans.'

Matthew waited for her to go on. 'You said he didn't respect women. Did that include Caro?'

'In some ways, I'd say so.'

He paused. 'She did love Richard, didn't she?'

'Caro adored Richard. They all did.' Sylvie gave him one of her gentle smiles. 'All I'm trying to say is that, for my money, you're at least as good a role model for the girls as he was.'

'They certainly don't feel that way.'

'They're still young. And they don't see their father as I did. Nor should they, I suppose.' She held out her empty glass. 'Would you mind?'

'Not at all.' He refilled it, brought it back, sat down again. 'How did we get into all this?'

She took a quick sip, fortifying herself. 'I'm very sorry to have to do this to you, Matthew.'

He felt a prickle of foreboding. 'What's happened?'

'Nothing too awful.' She put down her glass. 'Hopefully, not much more than a damned nuisance.' She took a breath. 'I had a lump removed last week, from my breast. They did a biopsy, and it was malignant.'

'Oh, God.' Matthew's mind swung back to an evening during the week when Isabella had stayed late and he hadn't seen Sylvie till next day. 'Last Wednesday?'

'Yes.' Sylvie went on briskly. 'Anyway. No big drama, thankfully. No more surgery, at least for now. But there will have to be treatment, and all that entails.' She grimaced slightly.

Matthew left his chair and came to her, crouched down, took her hand. 'Sylvie, I'm so sorry. What can I do?'

'I suppose that's what I've been building up to in a rather lame fashion. If I do have the treatment, radiation, whatever, then—'

'If?' He jumped on the word.

'If,' she repeated, calmly. 'If I agree to it, I may not be up to much for a while. Not up to taking care of three girls.'

'There's no *if* about it.' Matthew still held her hand. 'You have to have the treatment. Whatever they say is best.'

'No,' she said. 'I don't. Not yet, anyway.'

'You do,' he said, forcefully. 'And of course I'm going to stay. You can't imagine I'd walk out on you now?'

'No,' she said again. 'That's just the thing.'

'I don't understand.'

'I don't want you staying because of this, because of *me*.' She pulled her hand out of his.

'I'm staying,' he said flatly. 'Do the girls know?'

'Not yet.' Sylvie paused. 'Go and sit down, Matthew. Please.' She waited as he returned to his chair. 'What the girls need now, more than anything, is a period of stability. We agree on that, I think?'

187

'Of course.'

'Ideally, I'd like to try to maintain what's left of the status quo. A man in the house. A gentle, decent person who cares for their welfare. The man who loved their mother.'

'No problem there from my perspective.'

'But it's only fine,' Sylvie said, 'if you really care. It isn't fine if you'd rather escape, be somewhere else. If that is the case, we'll manage – we do have Isabella, after all. We would cope perfectly well.'

'You won't have to cope.'

'You mustn't answer just like that.' She paused. 'I promise you that if you do choose to leave, I'll never hold it against you.'

'But you might not have the treatment, so as not to rock the boat for the girls?'

'I might delay it a little.'

'No way.' He was emphatic. 'You're going to let them zap this thing now.'

'And feel I've trapped you into staying?'

'Not trapped at all,' he told her. 'I answered that before you told me, didn't I? When I married Caro, I took on her children, for better or worse.'

'You're a dreadful liar, Matthew.'

'Not a liar.' He forced another smile. 'Maybe just an optimist.'

'And what exactly are you finding to feel optimistic about?' Sylvie asked. 'Lord knows I could some optimism myself.'

'Just the old law of averages,' he replied. 'I figure we've all had the "worse". Now it's just a matter of sitting tight and waiting for the "better".'

'Amen to that,' she said.

188

# 29

They decided that Sylvie would wait until Friday evening to tell the girls. She let them eat dinner first, managing to eat a little herself and to chat about their day.

Flic broke through the sham first.

'So what's up, Groosi?' she asked, midway through the pecan pie that Matthew had brought home for dessert. 'And please don't say "nothing", because you've been weird for days and you're a rotten actress.'

Sylvie smiled at Matthew. 'No Oscars for me then.'

'Apparently not.'

Imogen hunched forward in her seat. 'So he's in on whatever this is?'

'What?' Chloë's hackles were up too. 'And don't tell me to go to bed, because I won't go.'

'Easy,' Matthew said gently, seeing the strain on Sylvie's face. 'Why not give your grandmother a chance to answer?' He met her eyes, saw her slight nod, then laid down his napkin and rose to his feet. 'I'm going to take Kahli for a walk.'

'It's raining,' Sylvie said.

'We won't melt.' He clicked his tongue at the retriever, who got up, shook himself and trotted over to him. 'Unless,' he said to her, 'you want me to stay.'

'No,' she said. 'We'll be fine.'

He walked up to the top of the road, strolled slowly in the wet autumnal darkness around Whitestone Pond before tramping rather disconsolately down Heath Street, passing a restaurant in which he and Caroline had enjoyed a romantic dinner.

'Matthew?'

He looked up from wet paving stones to see Kat Dunn from the office. 'What are you doing here?' he asked, as if Hampstead was an outlandish place for her to be on a Friday evening.

'I've just had dinner with some friends.'

Matthew looked around.

'They're still at it,' Kat said. 'I said I was tired.'

She was casually dressed in jeans, with a cream heavy cotton roll-neck sweater and a hooded rain jacket. She looked fresh as a daisy.

'You don't look tired,' he told her.

'You do,' she said, and looked down. 'Gorgeous dog. May I?'

'Be my guest,' Matthew said. 'Kahli loves women.'

'Kahli?' Kat crouched down and gently stroked the retriever's head, then graduated to scratching between his ears, prompting tail-wagging and sniffing. 'Wasn't she some kind of goddess?'

'So I'm told,' he said, 'though this is short for Kahlil, as in Gibran.' He saw her glance up, mystified. 'Don't ask.'

She straightened up, looked at him more closely. 'How're you doing, Matthew? Or is that a stupid question?'

'I'm getting by,' he said.

'I don't suppose' – a gust of wind blew back her hood, exposing her fiery cropped hair – 'you have time for a drink?'

Matthew checked his watch, saw that he'd been out for about twenty minutes. He didn't want to leave Sylvie unsupported for too long, but neither did he want to break in on an intimate family discussion too soon.

'I thought you were headed home,' he said.

'One for the tube won't hurt.'

They crossed over the narrow street and went into the Coach and Horses. It was crowded and noisy. Kat launched herself right into the mob towards the bar, but Matthew, unexpectedly unsteady, kept a grip on Kahli's lead and held back. Too many people, too much laughter, he told himself, but he knew it was more than that: a strong, if irrational, sense of guilt about walking into a pub with an attractive young woman, even if she *was* just a colleague who knew that he was newly widowed and had loved his wife deeply.

190

*Too soon.*

Kat came back to his side. 'Are you okay?'

'Not really.' He felt the retriever press against his leg. 'And I think it's a bit much for Kahli.'

'I think it's a bit much for us all,' Kat said. 'Let's get out.'

'I'm sorry,' he said.

'Don't be daft.' She pushed past him, opened the door, turned back to yank at his sleeve. 'Come on, let's get outside.'

The cool damp air was a relief.

'Better?' Kat asked.

'Much. Sorry,' he said again.

'What for? It was much too crowded.'

Sylvie came back into his mind. 'I guess I ought to be getting back,' he said. 'I'll walk with you to the station.'

'There's no need.'

'I'm going back that way anyhow.'

They walked down the hill in silence, crossed the road again.

'Things must be very bad for you at home right now,' Kat said at the entrance, green eyes gentle. 'Your wife's family must be wrecked.'

'They are,' Matthew said. 'And no, it isn't easy.'

'I know there's nothing I can to do to help,' she said. 'Except maybe listen, if you ever feel like talking.'

'That might be good,' he said.

'I'm told I'm not a bad listener,' she said. 'And I'd like to return the favour.'

He looked blank.

'That time in the bar, at the hotel,' she said, 'when I told you about the fight I'd had with my boyfriend.'

The day Caro had died.

The pang of guilt hit him again.


The atmosphere in the house was thick enough to slice as he walked back in.

Silence.

He unclipped Kahli's lead and watched him head for the kitchen, waited for greeting voices, heard none. He went to the drawing room door, glanced in, saw it was empty, turned back towards the staircase and was about to start up when he heard a sound from the study.

191

Flic was sitting behind the desk. Her legs were drawn up so that her feet rested on the edge of the chair, and her arms were wrapped around her legs, hands clasped just below her knees. She had been weeping.

'Hi,' Matthew said, gently.

She began unfolding herself, slowly, as if to get up.

'Stay there,' Matthew told her. 'If you'd like.'

She nodded. 'Thanks.'

'Anything I can do?'

She shook her head.

He started to leave, then changed his mind. 'I know I'm probably the last person you want to talk to about this. But if you do feel like it, any time, I'm here.'

'Okay,' she said.

'Where are the others?'

'Upstairs.' She paused. 'I'd leave Imo to herself, if I were you, but Chloë might be glad to see you.'

'Where's your grandmother?'

'She went upstairs too.'

He went in search of Sylvie first, up to the second floor, knocked gently on her bedroom door, got no answer, and then, hearing Mozart, faintly, from along the corridor, he walked slowly towards the Quiet Room.

He waited another moment before knocking, playing a foolish mind game, allowing himself to imagine that when he opened that door he would find Caro inside, sitting in her rocker . . .

He knocked.

'Come in.'

He opened the door. Sylvie was sitting on the couch.

'Nice walk?' she asked.

'Damp,' he answered. 'You ready for company, or would you rather be alone?'

'Alone, I think,' she said. 'In a minute or two.' She patted the couch. 'Have a seat, and I'll tell you how it went.' Her mouth tugged wryly. 'Which won't take more than a minute.'

Matthew sat down beside her. He still found it hard being in this room, seemed to take no comfort – not yet, at least – from being surrounded by Caro's favourite things.

'I suppose the appropriate expression,' Sylvie said, 'is "as well

192

as can be expected".' Another small twist of her mouth. 'They took it badly, but how else could they take it?'

He told her about finding Flic, who had been clearly upset but in control, which was, of course, one of her great strengths. He told her what she'd said about leaving Imogen alone but checking on Chloë.

'And have you?' Sylvie asked.

'Not yet. I wanted to see you first.'

She shook her head. 'It was a little odd, in a way. Distressed as they all were, I had the feeling they were angry too, as if the lump – the *cancer*' – she used the word deliberately, testing it – 'was somehow my fault.'

'I guess we often feel angry at things we can't control.'

'Like death,' Sylvie said.

Matthew held his tongue, waited.

'I told them,' she went on, 'that I'm not going to die, not just yet anyway. Which was, I hope, not a lie. The oncologist was very clear about saying that if he were concerned, he'd have recommended mastectomy – and he did not.'

Matthew leaned forward and knocked twice on the wooden table.

'I did the same thing when he told me that,' Sylvie said, 'though I'm not usually too superstitious.' She paused. 'Thank you, Matthew.'

'What for?'

'Being here. Being sensitive. For saying you won't leave us just yet.'

'No need for thanks,' he said. 'We're family now.'

'You can still change your mind, you know.'

'I won't.'


He went to call in on Chloë and saw from her still-damp cheeks that she had cried herself to sleep. He stood over her for a few moments, wishing he might stroke her hair, pull the covers up over her, act as a real father might. But he was not that, neither to her nor her sisters, and he didn't want to risk waking and perhaps startling her, so all he did was turn away, close the door softly behind him and go downstairs.

The study door was open, the room dark, Flic nowhere to be seen, so he assumed she'd gone up too. Matthew wandered into the drawing room, Kahli following, poured himself a finger of malt, found a half-eaten packet of potato crisps, sank into a chair and shared the crisps with the dog.

'Easy pleasing you, guy, isn't it?' he said softly as the animal sidled close, wagging his tail. 'Not the rest of your family, God knows.'

Except Sylvie, of course. Though even she, he suspected, might not be placing so much faith in him were it not for this new crisis. Had she, Matthew wondered yet again, completely dismissed Imogen's insinuations? Or had she just decided that, being *almost* sure of his innocence, it was wiser in the circumstances, certainly less traumatic, to stash any lingering doubts on some mental back-burner?

Pointless dwelling on that now.

He downed the rest of his malt in one, took his glass and empty crisp wrapper into the kitchen, put fresh water in Kahli's bowl, bade him goodnight and went back upstairs to do what he usually did on these still-new lonely nights: watch American sit-coms on the Paramount Comedy Channel until he finally dropped off to sleep.

A voice woke him. Shrill and unmistakably afraid.

He threw off the duvet and stumbled in T-shirt and shorts into the corridor. The lights were on, and Flic was standing outside Imogen's bedroom, apparently engaged in preventing Chloë from entering.

'What's happened?' Matthew heard Sylvie's tread on the stairs from the second floor.

'What's wrong with Imo?' Chloë wanted to know.

'She's all right.' Flic was unconvincing, ashen-faced and trembling. 'Can you keep her out, please.' She pushed Chloë towards Matthew, then turned to Sylvie, who was still fastening the belt of her robe. 'Groosi, Imo's bleeding,' she said. 'I've already phoned for an ambulance.'

'A haemorrhage, you mean?' Sylvie was horrified.

'Not that kind of bleeding.' Flic's voice shook.

'*Why's* she bleeding?' Chloë wanted to know.

Matthew had hold of her right arm. 'It's okay, honey.'

'I want to see her!'

'It's her wrists,' Flic told her grandmother.

194

'Oh, my God.' Sylvie ran into the room.

'Let me *go!*' Chloë pulled away from Matthew.

'Chloë, no.' He grabbed at her arm again, but she yanked herself free and, afraid of hurting her, he let her go.

She entered the room and screamed.

'For God's sake!' Flic turned on him. 'Can't you do *anything* right?'

'Stop it, Flic.' Sylvie bent over Imogen, who lay on her bed, flat on her stomach, moaning softly, blood spreading from her wrists over the sheets and pillows.

'Let me see.' Matthew stepped forward.

'Get *out*,' Flic snapped.

'She's going to die too, isn't she?' Chloë wailed.

'Let me take a look.' He brushed Flic aside. 'I've had first-aid training.' Sylvie stepped aside, let him squat beside the bed. 'It's okay,' he told Imogen calmly, 'you're going to be fine.' Gently he tried to look at her left wrist, but she pulled it away. 'Come on, honey, you have to let me see.'

'How bad is it?' Sylvie asked, while Flic put both arms around Chloë and watched impotently. 'What should we do?'

'It's not arterial,' Matthew said, checking the other wrist.

'Are you sure?' Sylvie asked.

'Positive. Do you have a first-aid kit?'

'In the kitchen,' Flic said.

'Get it,' he told her.

'I'll go.' Chloë ran, relieved to have something to do.

Matthew held both wounded arms. 'We need to keep them raised.' Imogen had stopped fighting him off, her dullness almost more worrying than the cuts themselves, which he saw now were fairly ragged attempts.

'Let me help.' Sylvie knelt beside him. 'Flic, go and see if Chloë—'

'Here it is.' Chloë ran back into the room with the box.

'Good girl,' Matthew said. 'Sylvie, I need two sterile dressings and some bandage. Dressings first.'

Sylvie tried to open the box, but her hands were trembling.

'I'll do it.' Chloë took it back from her, found what was needed. 'Do I need to wash my hands first?'

'No, just unseal them carefully and try not to touch them too much.'

195

She opened the first dressing, passed it to him, and he pressed it to the slightly deeper wound on Imogen's left wrist. 'Sylvie, can you hold that firmly in place for me?' He waited till she had it, then, with Chloë's help, did the same for the right, and had her hold that dressing while he wound and secured the bandages.

They heard the doorbell from below.

'Thank God,' Sylvie said.

'Flic, go let them in,' Matthew said.

Flic didn't move.

'Flic!' he said, more sharply.

She ran.

# 30

It was just after ten next morning before Flic was able to get Imogen to herself.

She was in a private room on the top floor of the Royal Free Hospital, where, once she had finally been moved from A&E, they had insisted she stay for assessments. The whole family had been there until almost five, but then Matthew had seen that Sylvie and Chloë were both out on their feet and had persuaded them to go home, leaving him there with Flic, who had refused to go.

'Why are you still here?' she asked him, without particular hostility, as they drank coffee in the twelfth floor waiting area.

'I promised your grandmother I'd stay till she gets back.'

'I don't mind staying alone,' Flic said. 'I'm hardly helpless.'

'I do know that,' Matthew said.

'Thank you,' she said quietly.

'What for?'

'For what you did for Imo last night.'

'It was nothing much,' he said.

'It was exactly what needed to be done,' Flic said.

'You're very welcome.'

'Would you be offended if I had some time alone with Imo?'

'She's probably still sleeping.'

'Maybe, but I'd still like to sit with her on my own.' She hesitated. 'I didn't realize how bad she was feeling. I should have known.'

'You can't always read other people's minds, no matter how close you are.'

'Maybe not,' Flic said. 'But I'd still like to be with her for a while.'

'Take all the time you need,' he said. 'I'll stay here.'

The lights had been dimmed in Imogen's room and all was quiet, her sister still sleeping soundly. Her face was even paler than usual against the dark of her spiky hair and thick lashes, but she looked calm, peaceful even, with no signs – other than her bandaged wrists – of the torment that had to have led her to harm herself in the way she had just hours before.

Flic walked over to the bed, waited a moment, listening for approaching footsteps, then, hearing none, bent and prodded Imogen's left shoulder. 'Wake up, Imo.'

Imogen stirred, gave a small moan.

Flic shook her. 'Wake *up*.'

Imogen opened her eyes, squinted up at her sister, groaned. 'What?'

'I want to talk to you.'

'Not now.' Imogen shut her eyes again.

'Yes, now.' Flic shook her again. '*Now*, Imo.'

The brown eyes opened again, puzzled, hurt-looking. 'Flic, I'm really tired.'

'So am I, believe it or not,' Flic said fiercely. 'So's Groosi, and so's Chloë, though I don't suppose you give a stuff about any of us, do you?'

'Of course I do.' Imogen sat up a little, then flopped back against the pillows. 'Honestly, Flic, can't this wait till later?'

'No, it can't. I need to talk to you before anyone else comes back.'

'Okay.' Imo saw the intensity on her sister's face. 'Okay.'

Flic sat on the side of the bed. 'Why did you do it?'

'Why d'you think?' Imo said sulkily.

'Because you're a stupid selfish little cow?'

'Fuck off,' Imogen said.

'Not till I've finished.' Flic shook her head. 'I don't know if you botched it on purpose or not, but either way, have you forgotten?'

'What?'

'That I need you,' Flic said. 'We *all* need you, you silly bitch.'

'Are you crying?' Imogen was startled.

'No, I'm not crying,' Flic said angrily. 'Just shut up and listen.

198

All you've achieved is that some strange shrink is going to come and prod around your fucked-up head to find out why you cut your wrists. And if you even start telling them a *quarter* of the truth, you'll ruin everything.'

'Everything's already ruined.' Imogen's eyes were dull. 'Mum and Dad are both dead, and now Groosi's going to die, too.'

'Groosi is *not* going to die,' Flic said firmly. 'She's had a lump cut out, and she's going to have treatment and she'll be fine.'

'And Matthew's going to stay forever and be our fucking father.'

'Stepfather,' Flic amended. 'And anyway, maybe that's not all bad.'

'Not bad? Are you *crazy*?'

'Not crazy at all.' Flic looked down at her sister's outraged expression and relented a little. 'Punishment, remember? *That's* what could be good about him staying. You're the one who's been growling on about his not being punished if he got to skip off back to New York or wherever. So now, because Groosi's ill, he can't go without looking like a complete bastard, so we're going to use that, aren't we?'

'If you say so,' Imogen said.

'And we're also going to turn *this* thing around,' Flic told her. 'You having done this bloody stupid thing.' She heard voices outside and stopped talking for a moment till they'd gone. 'You're going to tell Matthew that you want him to stay.'

'Don't be so fucking ridiculous,' Imogen said.

'Listen to me, Imo.' Flic's eyes were steely. 'You're going to *beg* him to stay with us, and so am I, and we're both going to make sure that Groosi and Chloë and Isabella *hear* us doing it, or at least get to know about it.' She took a breath. 'And if anyone asks you why you did this seriously stupid thing, you tell them you just couldn't take any more of losing everyone you love. It's true, after all, isn't it?'

Imogen shrugged.

'Nothing more than that, you hear?' Flic had a new flash of inspiration. 'Except maybe you can tell them that you and I sometimes used to act up a bit with Mum and Matthew, and since Mum died you've been blaming yourself for being difficult – and you've read that stress can cause cancer, and so now you're blaming yourself for Groosi being ill too.'

'Shit,' Imogen said, and shook her head. 'You're amazing.'

Flic didn't care if that was a compliment or not. 'If that's what you stick to as long as you're in here, you'll get the sympathy vote, no problem.'

'What do you mean, as long as I'm in here?' Imogen looked alarmed.

'They'll probably keep you here till the shrink says you can go.' She paused. 'So have you got all that?'

'I don't want to stay here. And I want a cigarette.'

'Well, you can't have one. Imo, concentrate, for God's sake. You have to tell them you couldn't bear the thought of losing Groosi too, and you've been blaming yourself, and that's *it*. Okay?'

'Okay.'

'And then, once you're home, you ask Matthew to stay. Yes?'

'If you say so.'

'I do.' Flic started to get up, then stopped. 'You could try telling someone you'd rather talk to Susanna than another shrink, but they probably won't let you choose. Whoever it is, make sure they know you realize now that it was a stupid thing to do and you're going to get over everything and you'll never do it again.'

'You're doing my head in, Flic,' Imogen said wearily. 'Can't you at least smuggle me in some ciggies?'

'I'll try. But you have to get this right.' Flic looked at her. 'You know you will get over it all, don't you, Imo? You really will feel better.'

'Maybe. If we ever get rid of him.'

'There's no maybe about it,' Flic said.

'Yeah,' Imogen said.

# 31

'They asked you themselves?'

Ethan – in London for five days just before Thanksgiving for an accountancy convention that had to do, so Matthew vaguely understood, with differences between European and US taxation laws and collection methods – looked surprised.

'First Flic, then Imo – which really got to me,' Matthew confirmed.

They were having dinner together at an Italian restaurant in St John's Wood, not far from Ethan's hotel.

'Got to you how?' Ethan enquired.

'Emotionally.' Matthew shrugged. 'I'd already decided to stay, and of course, the girls knew about that. But they seemed to want me to know they were actually pleased I was staying.'

'Staying because of Sylvie?'

'Probably. Mostly, I guess. But their coming to me that way was really something, Ethan. Flic was quite calm about it, of course, but Imogen seemed pretty churned up when she asked me, and that's definitely not her style where I'm concerned.'

'She's been through some terrible ordeals,' Ethan said, 'even since Caro. That open verdict must have been so tough on everyone.'

'It was.' Matthew still found it hard to think about, tried not to.

'Still, I must say I am surprised.' Ethan seemed about to say more, then changed his mind.

'And?'

'Not so much "and",' Ethan said slowly. 'More a case of "but".'

Matthew wound some fettucine around his fork and waited.

'Are you sure,' his brother began, 'that this is right for you? Staying, I mean.'

'Oh.' Matthew laid his fork back on his plate.

'Does that mean you're not sure?' Ethan asked.

'Not at all,' he said tersely. 'It means that I realize I'm about to get pulled into another negative conversation.'

'I don't mean to be negative.'

'Don't you, Ethan?' Matthew felt real irritation edging to the surface. 'It just seems to me that you're always second-guessing my decisions, always feeling you have to play big brother.'

'That's what I am.' Ethan smiled.

The irritation lessened only slightly. 'So go on.'

Ethan looked at him for another moment before continuing. 'I'm concerned that you're being sucked into a life that you just don't belong in now Caro's gone. Largely through obligation.'

'I am obligated,' Matthew agreed. 'That's part of life, isn't it?'

'It's not a good basis for a decision as major as the one you're making.'

'I haven't told anyone I'm going to stay forever.' Matthew picked up his fork again. 'You can't tell me, Ethan, that you of all people would advocate my walking out on this family now.'

'No,' Ethan admitted. 'I guess not.'

'Well then.' Matthew began eating again.

'Just . . .'

'Just *what*?' Irritation resurfaced.

'Just make sure that Sylvie really understands it might not be forever.'

'She does understand it.'

'I hope so,' Ethan said.

It was like a kind of dance, Matthew thought sometimes. Something between a stately, well-mannered minuet and a change-partners barn-dance. Like Ethan, Karl (now the happy new father of a baby girl named Trudy) seemed wary, almost distrustful, not of Flic or Imogen, but of his own ability to make wise decisions.

'They really piss me off,' Matthew confessed to Kat over lunch on the Friday after Ethan had gone home.

They had fallen into a habit of lunching together at least twice a week since that unplanned meeting in Hampstead, and any awkwardness he had felt that evening had evaporated, mostly because Kat was still involved with her problem boyfriend.

'Sylvie's planning to go back to her flat,' Matthew told Kat now, sitting over their smoked salmon sandwiches in the bar of the Kenilworth Hotel. 'And Isabella and Mick have agreed to take over the top floor, which is already pretty much self-contained. Which all seems sensible to me, because Sylvie's having her treatments, and the stairs are too much for her, and everyone loves Isabella, so I don't see a problem.'

'Who does?' Kat asked.

'Apparently Ethan and Karl see all kinds of problems.' He shook his head. 'Do they think I don't know there could be – almost certainly *will* be – pitfalls? Do they think there's anything about Caro's daughters they have to warn me about that I couldn't work out for myself?'

'They're probably just trying to protect you.'

'I'm sure they are, but it seems to me they've picked a lousy time to start paying attention to what I spent so long trying to get them to listen to.' Matthew took a bite of his sandwich. 'Of course I wish Sylvie could stay on at the house – it's been great having her there as peacekeeper. But she's a sick woman right now, and I'd say she's earned a little peace of her own.'

Kat smiled. 'You're very fond of her. That's nice.'

'She's a terrific person.'

They both finished their sandwiches and ordered coffee.

'So how do you see your role now?' Kat asked.

'Long-term?' He shook his head. 'Impossible to say. Short-term, it seems very simple to me. They've told me they want me to stay; I feel they may actually *need* me now, at least for the time being. Sylvie certainly needs my support.' He paused. 'And I know it's what Caro would have wanted me to do.'

'Simple, as you say.'

'So you don't think I've made a bad decision?'

'I think,' she said, 'that as a decent man, you're making the only decision you really can in the circumstances.' She smiled. 'And as to the long-term picture, as they say, time will tell.'

For the next week or so, life seemed to smooth along. Sylvie went home, though she continued to spend as much time as she felt up to at Aethiopia. Isabella and Mick moved into the attic, Isabella running the household while Mick lounged around composing and playing. At VKF, the church project was finally getting underway, and Matthew's chances of working on it under MacNeice were looking good. And Caroline's daughters appeared the greatest wonder of all: grief-softened, almost compliant young women, treating their still-startled stepfather considerately and with something approaching affection.

'Transference,' Susanna told Matthew during one of her regular phone calls to check on their progress. 'Caro's gone, Sylvie can't be with them all the time, so, apart from Isabella, you're their only remaining in-house guardian.'

'I'd rather hoped,' Matthew said drolly, 'it might be because my public-enemy-number-one status is finally becoming a memory.'

'Well, it is, isn't it?' Susanna was matter-of-fact. 'That stage is over now.' She paused. 'Which doesn't mean, of course, that you'll never encounter problems with them again.'

'I never heard of teenagers and adults who didn't have problems.'

'Of course not,' Susanna said. 'Just as long as you're ready for them.'

Each Sunday morning, they took flowers to the cemetery, sometimes with Sylvie, sometimes with Isabella, after which they adjourned to Aethiopia for lunch, much as they had in the past. It was a ritual that Matthew felt no need of, since he felt far closer to Caro at home than at her graveside, but he knew it comforted the girls, so he went along with it. Routines in general seemed to bring some solace, and though occasionally Matthew might have preferred to shake loose a little, he never did so. From being the rank outsider, he was coming to feel enfolded, even, sometimes, a little smothered by the new, almost unnatural kindness of his stepdaughters, yet he allowed it to go on, to roll over him, still too relieved by the end of hostilities to want to fight any part of it.

His energies were, in any case, limited. The months of battling, his fears for the marriage and then the numbing horror of loss and the need to cope, for the sake of others, had left him drained, with little left over after work for anything more than fitting in with the world according to the Walters.

A few smooth lines on his personal graph chart, without spikes of either more pain or pleasure, seemed just what Matthew needed for now. Anything that broke the calm felt unwelcome. Like the Sunday when, returning from the cemetery, they found Susanna waiting for them, having invited herself to lunch. His hackles had risen instantly and unjustly, for Susanna had been fair to him both at the inquest and since, but he couldn't help himself. She was tactful during lunch, warm to the family, cordial to him, but afterwards she took a handful of visiting cards from her bag, explained that she'd changed her number because of a crank caller, and then distributed them – one card for each family member – which made Matthew want to retrieve the little white cards and rip them up, though he was not at all certain why he felt like that.

*Curb it*, he told himself. No room for irrationality, not now. Smooth and straightforward.

*Simple*.

# 32

'There's no one here except me,' Mick told Susanna as she stood on the doorstep of Aethiopia on the Wednesday afternoon after she'd gatecrashed Sunday lunch.

'Where's Isabella?'

'Out.' Mick wished he hadn't bothered answering the doorbell. He'd been in the family kitchen making himself a sandwich because their own fridge upstairs hadn't had any cheddar and he particularly liked the pickle that Isabella bought for Imogen but always forgot to buy for him.

'Do you know when she's due back?' Susanna knew he wanted to shut the door on her, but chose to be thick-skinned about it. 'I could wait.'

Mick sighed and stood back to let her in, not prepared to waste any energy arguing with a heavy like Snoozanna – his name for the shrink who was, to his mind, self-obsessed and always banging on about something. 'She went to town – then she was going to pick up the girls.'

Susanna closed the door behind her. 'Are they coming straight back after school, do you think?'

'Couldn't tell you.' Mick headed back towards the kitchen. 'Wait if you want, though it could be quite a while.'

She followed him. 'I don't want to impose.'

'You won't be.' He picked up his sandwich, tucked the Budweiser he'd taken from the bottom of the fridge, and gestured towards the kettle. 'Help yourself to a coffee, whatever. I'm working upstairs.'

'Don't worry about me,' Susanna said.

'I won't.' He called from the hall, halfway to the staircase. 'Dog's in the garden, by the way. Do me a favour and let him in when he's ready.'

'No problem,' she called back, then muttered: 'Lazy sod.' She had little time for Mick Bates, who was, she felt, a sponger.

She went to the door, opened it and looked for Kahli, saw him, in the fast fading afternoon light, at the far end of the garden. Susanna glanced to her left, towards the terrace, then quickly averted her gaze and shut the door. She had not been here on that day, had not actually seen Caro lying there, yet her imagination had conjured up the image all too graphically, and it was hard for her to bear.

She picked up the jug kettle, took it to the sink, filled it and switched it on, then wandered out of the kitchen and into the drawing room. Nothing, she'd observed on previous visits, had been physically greatly altered since Caro's death. Photographs stood where they had before, furniture, ornaments and plants still arranged exactly as she had placed them.

*Still early days*, Susanna thought, conscious that the changes, when they did come, would very probably be subtle and gradual, but no less insidious for that.

In the attic, three floors up, Mick's synthesizer began droning, and, on sudden impulse, Susanna left the room, quickly climbed the stairs, went directly into her friend's old bedroom and turned on the light.

The dressing table made her catch her breath. Caro's things were still in place: her perfume bottles, mirror, antique silver hairbrush and comb, photographs – two of each child, one of Sylvie, one of her and Richard, the last addition of her and Matthew.

Susanna walked over to the table, picked up the Guerlain bottle, one of Caro's favourites. She took off the stopper, held it to her nose, inhaled; instantly her eyes filled with tears, and swiftly she put the stopper back and replaced the bottle.

An intense surge of desire swept over her, the urge to go through her dear friend's bedside table drawer and touch anything of hers still left there. Not Matthew's. The only thing that had made him remotely interesting had been Caro's love for him.

She conquered the impulse, switched off the light, left the room and moved along the corridor, past Chloë's room and the bathroom, to Flic's.

207

Nothing here she might not have expected, at least not on the surface. A world of infinite fascination *beneath*, almost certainly, in a young woman as intriguing as Flic, and if Susanna had had time to browse through that world safely, to broaden the art of investigation that was, after all, part of any psychotherapist's work, she would have loved to delve more deeply. Except that Flic was not her patient, and it was the myriad of unanswered questions about her sister that had long been vexing Susanna, and so once again, she controlled her inquisitiveness and moved along.

She half expected to find Imogen's door locked, but it was open, and she wondered if that meant the teenager might be more relaxed than she had been, or maybe she had simply been in a rush that morning . . .

'All right down there?'

Mick's voice calling from the attic stopped Susanna in her tracks. She hadn't noticed the music ceasing, had been too absorbed.

'Fine, thank you,' she called back.

'Found all you need?'

She ignored the sarcasm. 'Yes, thank you.'

She waited a moment to be sure he wasn't going to come down. The music began again.

'All right,' she said softly, and switched on the light.

A teenage girl's bedroom. Plenty of photographs, of the family as it had been, one whole wall filled with pictures of Richard Walters, some with Imo, some on his own or with Caroline. Not a shrine, exactly, Susanna was glad to see, nothing too unnatural, in the circumstances. No pictures of her stepfather, not even with her mother. No surprise there.

Susanna's remaining scruples retreated. This was in a good cause. As a therapist, she knew she had been failing Imogen, not getting through. Not reaching the real, deeply unhappy person behind the prickly exterior, and, by the same yardstick, failing Caro too.

*Invasion of privacy.* A small, surviving reservation flickered into life.

Not just wrong, of course. Appallingly so.

Yet was it so very different from prying into a young woman's psyche?

*Entirely different.*

But it might, possibly, help her understand Imogen a little more. For her sake and Caro's.

Swiftly, methodically, carefully – aware of the time constraints and of Imogen's fury if she realized that anyone had gone through her private things – Susanna checked through the wardrobes and came upon three shelves of neatly stacked Astrid the Cow T-shirts, sweatshirts and other assorted junk from Richard's commercially glorious period. Imo's father-worship, of course, already well-known, and nothing else of tremendous interest . . . Two sealed packs of Marlboro concealed in a tampon box – Susanna already knew about Imogen's smoking, had, during one stressful session, allowed the girl to light up in her consulting room. A packet of condoms, not concealed at all. That, too, was sealed, might have been bought for show while out with friends, though Susanna had never found Imo the kind of girl to care much about peer pressure. She had claimed, during another session, to be a virgin, and Susanna had believed her. Perhaps, the next time – if there was a next time – she would try to probe a little deeper . . .

There was nothing else, and self-disgust pricked at her again. Harder to justify this trespass – *betrayal* – if she found nothing of real use.

She glanced up at the lamp, then at the windows. If Isabella and the girls returned now, they'd know right away that someone was, or had been, in the room. She thought of drawing the curtains, but that might be even harder to explain away . . .

*Hurry.*

She closed the drawer that held the condoms, checked to make sure she'd shut the wardrobe doors completely, then got down on her knees and looked under the bed. Nothing but the usual rubble down there, stray slippers, tights, tissues . . .

Something was stuck to the underside of the bed itself.

Susanna's heart skipped a beat. She waited a moment, listening, then, hearing nothing but Mick's music, she wriggled closer, stretched out her arm and carefully pulled at the thing, drawing it out.

It was a small plastic bag, attached with ordinary sticky tape. Looking around, Susanna saw a Scotch tape dispenser over on the table beside a dictionary, which meant she'd have no trouble putting it back as she'd found it.

Though suddenly that seemed the least of her problems.

The bag was a commonplace transparent food bag, fastened with one of the white ties that came with most such bags.

Except that this bag was filled with white powder.

Susanna had asked Imogen about drugs, and Imo had sneered at the question and refused to answer, and Susanna had hoped that her bravado meant she was into nothing worse than tobacco.

'Silly, *silly* girl.'

Very cautiously, she untwisted the tie, opened the top of the bag, held it close to her nose and sniffed.

And laughed out loud.

Baby powder. Bloody *Johnson's*!

'Well done, Imo,' she said.

Last laugh for the teenager, even if setting a trap like this for anyone searching her room did indicate a rather high level of distrust of those in the household.

Susanna refastened the tie, got up to snap off two strips of Scotch tape of exactly the same length as those she'd just eased off the little package, then got down on the floor and stuck it back, even going so far as to feel for the tacky places on the underside of the bed, so that she could replace it as accurately as possible.

She was about to stand again, still chuckling gently, when she felt a slight bulge beneath the carpet under her left knee. A floor-board out of place.

*Ignore it.*

And she might have stopped then, had she not noticed, abruptly, that one corner of the fitted carpet over by the wall was not as firmly tacked down as the rest.

If Imogen were to find her doing this . . . It didn't bear *thinking* about. If even Mick were to discover her, he'd be in his rights to call the police, let alone tell the family.

Susanna wavered, found she was perspiring, her pulse racing, uncertain *why* she should feel this way, why an uneven board should mean anything, but this was instinctive now, something was pushing her on to keep looking . . .

Caro's face flew into her mind. Caro was the reason she was behaving this way. Caro, who would have been so anguished if she'd lived to see her middle daughter slash her wrists, see her taken to hospital and quizzed by strangers.

This was for Caro, too, Susanna told herself as she eased up the carpet a little way, then realized she was going to have to move a chair and the bedside table if she was going to reach that odd little bulge in the floor.

Quickly, she straightened up, went to the door, opened it a crack, listened again.

Mick was still definitely upstairs working.

She looked at her watch. Even if Isabella was bringing the girls straight back from school, she ought to have a little longer. The traffic up East Heath Road was always awful at this time, and the room faced the road, so she'd almost certainly hear the car . . .

The bedside table was quite light and easy to move – and there it was, the cause of the bulge. A floorboard not quite in place.

The ease with which the board lifted told Susanna she was right. She propped it carefully up against her own upper body, then lowered her right hand into the dark space beneath.

'Bingo.'

Her fingers had touched on something that felt like plastic. Another bag? She gripped it gently, raised it slightly to feel its weight. Heavier, larger too, than the little bag beneath the bed, something metallic-sounding clanking slightly inside it. Sweating more profusely, Susanna lowered it again, felt around the space, touched something else. Leather? A book? Larger, flatter . . .

She withdrew her hand, wiped it against her skirt, listened one more time, then put down her hand again and withdrew the plastic bag – plain white, unmarked – set it down on the carpet, then inserted her arm back down through the gap to pull out . . .

A folder of cream-coloured leather, old and dusty, its edges folded closed in the manner of a cardboard office wallet, fastened with black velvet ribbon tied in a bow.

Susanna's heart beat faster and her fingers shook as she untied the bow and opened the folder and saw that it was an artist's miniature portfolio.

Containing drawings. Pen-and-ink sketches.

Susanna stared down at the top one, feeling sick.

The girl in the drawing had no head to speak of, just an impression of fair, straight hair falling across the face, but it was abundantly clear that she was young, in fact, pre-pubescent. She was lying on a couch, simply that, *doing* nothing, nothing being done *to* her, yet there was no mistaking the obscenity of the work,

211

which stemmed not so much from the fact that she was almost naked, but from the single garment that she wore. If it could be called a garment.

Susanna had seen photographs of chastity belts, had read something about them in a book on sexual domination games while treating a patient whose fantasies were threatening to destroy his marriage.

Something creaked, upstairs. She froze for a second, realized she was running out of time. Swiftly, having to fight to stay careful, afraid of creasing the thick cartridge paper – her real desire to crumple it, rip it to shreds – she looked through the small sheaf of drawings, saw that some were far viler: the model – *child* – on all fours in one, sitting on a chair in another, legs spread as wide as the revolting contraption would allow her. Variations on a theme. Unmistakably. Child pornography.

All signed with initials. *R.W.*

She put them back, took a couple of deep breaths, folded down the leather edges and retied the bow, used another second or two to blow gently over the whole to try to resettle the dust more evenly, then lowered the portfolio back into its hiding place.

And saw again the plastic bag.

'God,' she said, softly.

She didn't want to look inside, had a great urge just to stuff it back under the floor, finish up and run. But she knew she'd come too far for that.

She reached for it. It was not sealed in any way, though the bag was much larger than what it held, had been folded several times to make a neater package.

She opened it, already knowing what she would find.

It was made of black leather and metal. A belt to fit around the waist, with narrower strips leading to a broader leather section designed to cover the genitals. The belt buckle comprised of metal rings and a small, but strong-looking padlock. And with it, wrapped in a wad of tissue paper, a key.

There was no doubting that it was the same contraption as in the drawings.

And she had recognized the girl with no face.

The broad shoulders, unusually broad for a child, and the long legs.

Imogen. Almost certainly, Imogen.

212

'You bastard,' she said. 'Oh, Christ, you complete *bastard*.'

She heard a car pulling off the road, eyes opening wide in horror, heart hammering, but she contrived to wrap the tissue paper back around the key and place it back into the bottom of the bag, then the *thing*, sickened now simply by its feel, and then she folded the top of the bag down again to form the same kind of neat package, and lowered that back down too.

She heard voices, heard car doors banging.

'Christ.'

She flew over to the light switch, flicked it off, then hurried back to push the floorboard down, did it perfectly – *too* perfectly – tried to remember which edge had been not quite down, got it right, then scrambled to her feet, ignoring the cramp and numbness in her legs, got the carpet back, then the bedside table and chair, and that wasn't too hard, because the indentations from their weight were still visible, even in the dim light – and then she crept over to the window and peered down.

And saw that it was not Isabella and the girls at all, but another carload of strangers who'd driven their big black car up onto the kerb right outside the house and parked it there, and who were now crossing the road presumably for a walk on the Heath, though why they were doing so, in the dark, was beyond her.

She wiped her hands on her skirt again, turned the light back on for just a second to check that all looked as it had, then opened the door.

Music, of a kind, still came from above.

She stepped out into the corridor, quietly shut the door, walked to the top of the staircase, then called loudly upwards: 'I'm just leaving, Mick!'

The music paused, she heard footsteps.

'What?' He sounded irritated.

'Just telling you I'm going to leave now, Mick.'

'Fine.'

'Give them my love, would you, please? And tell them I'm sorry I couldn't wait any longer.'

'Yeah, sure.'

More footsteps, and then the music began again.

Susanna took a deep breath, walked down the staircase, found her bag where she'd left it in the kitchen, let Kahli, who was now sitting patiently outside the back door, back into the house, and left.

She had never been a heavy drinker, but she poured herself a large glass of red when she got home and soon followed it with a second.

She didn't have a clue what to do.

'Nothing,' she told herself. 'Nothing you can do.'

If Imogen found out what she had done, she would fly into a rage, perhaps report her to the BPA or maybe the police, and if either Sylvie or Matthew got to hear about her ferreting around the house, they'd almost certainly never let her near the house or, more importantly, the girls, again. Worst of all, Imo would never, ever *trust* her again, and that would be the most terrible betrayal by her of Caro.

On her third glass of wine, she found herself trying to find alternative explanations for what she had found. The pen-and-ink drawings were unarguably Richard's and indisputably, loathsomely pornographic, but there was no certainty that they had, as she'd instantly assumed, been of Imogen. It had, after all, only been the colour of hair – Imo's *real* colour – and the girl's physical build that had made her feel it had been Imogen.

Not to mention the fact that the drawings and the ghastly *thing* had been under her floorboards.

Someone else might have put them there, of course.

'Why would they do that?' Susanna asked herself out loud, scornfully.

Perhaps because it was the only loose floorboard in the house?

'Rubbish,' she said.

Even if that were true – and she knew it wasn't – who else could it have been? If Richard himself had wanted to hide those things, he could have stashed them in a hundred different places anywhere in the world.

She devised another scenario. Richard's private line in porno-art might have had nothing whatever to do with his daughters (someone else's child, then, which was hardly a huge improvement). Maybe Imo had just happened upon the drawings and chastity belt after her father's death, and buried them beneath her floor to protect his memory?

Susanna's thoughts were mercifully starting to fuzz as she

poured herself a fourth glass of wine. Nonsense, all of it, she realized that. The drawings *had* been of Imogen, she was as good as certain, the child-model's build had told her that. Imo had always been more athletic than her sisters, had, she remembered Caro saying, been chosen for the netball team at The Grange because of her height and strength, though that had only lasted one or two terms, because Imogen couldn't be bothered with it, it hadn't been her 'thing' . . .

'It was Imo,' Susanna said aloud, slumping into a chair.

Which meant any number of hideous, nightmarish possibilities needed to be examined, faced, from sexual abuse to Electra complex to incest or God alone knew what might have befallen and affected that child, and even if Susanna had come upon the evidence in a less reprehensible fashion, she doubted now if she would be the right therapist to deal with Imogen's problems.

And anyway, in these circumstances, what could she do about it?

'Nothing,' she said again.

*Nothing.*

The worst, the most frustrating answer of all.

# 33

'Have you been in my room?' Imogen demanded in a hiss just after eleven that night.

'When?' Flic had just climbed into bed and had been on the verge of turning out the light when her sister had barged into the room.

'I don't know when. *Have* you?'

'I don't know what you're talking about.' Flic yawned. 'And would you mind not yelling at me?'

'I'm not yelling.' Imogen sat down hard on the side of the bed. 'Someone's been poking through my Astrid things.'

'Probably Isabella tidying up.'

'She knows better than to touch Astrid stuff.'

'Have you checked your fake stash?'

Flic had been the only person Imogen had confided in when she'd laid that trap about three years ago, soon after the first major eruption of her privacy obsession. Flic had called her neurotic at the time, but she'd admired Imo's originality, almost wishing she'd thought of it herself.

'That seems okay,' Imogen answered thoughtfully.

'So what's the big deal?'

'I don't know.' Imogen shook her head. 'Just a feeling. Like someone's been snooping.' She paused. 'If it's him, I don't know what I'll do.'

'You haven't been locking up lately, have you?'

'Because Groosi didn't like it, but I'm going to go out tomorrow and buy a great big padlock.'

'Wouldn't work on your door.' Flic yawned again. 'Don't be such a drama queen. All you have to do is remember to use your key.'

'Do you think he has been poking around?'

Flic shrugged. 'I don't think it's really his style.'

Imogen shifted on the bed. 'When are we going to start again?'

'Start what?'

'You know what.'

Flic sighed. 'Soon.'

'You're being really weak,' Imo told her. 'Procrastinating.'

'Go to bed, Imo.'

'You know I'm right, don't you?'

'Go to *bed*.'

The trouble was, Flic thought after her sister had gone, Imogen was right. She *had* been procrastinating, and she had also been feeling profoundly weakened lately, had told herself it was prudent for them to bide their time, rest up for a while before starting again.

Just a *little* longer. That was all she needed to steady herself, prepare the groundwork and get underway. And she *was* right to feel she needed to get back her full strength before beginning, because once they did start again, there would be no going back.


The following Sunday morning, Phil Bianco himself telephoned Matthew asking him to come into Bedford Square for an urgent planning meeting.

'More than my job's worth to refuse,' Matthew told Isabella in the kitchen after the call. 'But it's the first time I'll have missed going to the cemetery, and I don't like letting down the girls.'

'Don't worry.' Isabella was making coffee. 'If Sylvie can't take them, I will.'

'Are you sure?' He was grateful. 'Don't you and Mick have plans?'

She shook her head. 'Nothing till later.'


When the family got back from the cemetery for lunch, Matthew was still out.

'Start of things to come,' Flic said as they began eating.

'What things?' Chloë asked.

It was just the three of them, Sylvie having stayed home and Isabella now upstairs with Mick.

'The start of Matthew dumping us,' Imogen said.

'Why d'you say that?' Chloë asked.

'It's the truth,' Imogen said.

'You talk such rubbish sometimes, doesn't she, Flic?'

Flic put a sprout in her mouth and said nothing.

'You're pathetic when it comes to Matthew,' Imogen said.

'And you're a cow,' Chloë said.

'You are a bit pathetic about him, actually, Chloë,' Flic agreed. 'And he really isn't worth it.'

'I bet he isn't even really working,' Imogen said.

'Of course he is,' Chloë said.

'Bet he's not.'

'Why are you starting all this being nasty to Matthew stuff again?' Chloë asked.

'I've never stopped,' Imogen said. 'And I don't trust him a single centimetre.'

Chloë stood up. 'I'm going to phone him at the office, show you he's there.'

'They won't answer on a Sunday,' Flic said.

'I'll call his mobile,' Chloë said.

'That won't prove anything,' Imogen pointed out.

Chloë knew she was right, but didn't feel like admitting it. Anyway, she liked standing up to Imo, and if she wanted to phone Matthew on his mobile, she would, and her sister could just jump - in the lake.

Kat was all alone on the second floor catching up on overdue paperwork when she heard ringing.

Matthew's mobile sat on his desk, its owner upstairs, working with MacNeice on some ideas that had come out of the church planning meeting. She left it for a few more rings, expecting voice-mail to pick up, but the ringing just went on, so finally she got up and answered.

'Matthew Gardner's phone,' she said.

'Who's that?' The voice at the other end sounded startled.

'This is a colleague. Can I take a message?'

Chloë put down the receiver.

'Who answered?' Flic asked.

'A woman,' Chloë said.

'Who was she?' Imogen wanted to know.

'She didn't say her name. She said she was a colleague, and then I hung up.'

'Bastard,' Imo said, almost spitting the word.

'Could *be* a colleague,' Flic said.

'Of course it was,' Chloë said, 'or why would she have said it?'

'So why'd you hang up on her, dope?' Imogen asked.

On Tuesday, as Kat, Matthew and Robert Fairbairn were leaving the building together at lunchtime, Kat remembered that she hadn't bought a gift for a friend's fiancé's birthday whose dinner party she was invited to that night.

'I'll have to go to Selfridges,' she said.

'Why go all the way there?' Fairbairn asked. 'Plenty of shops round here.'

'Go to Heal's,' Matthew suggested.

Kat shook her head. 'He works near Marble Arch and I know he hardly ever has time to go shopping. If I get him something from Selfridges, at least it's no big hassle for him if he wants to change it.' She looked at them. 'Don't suppose either of you fancies helping me choose?'

'Not me,' Fairbairn said. 'I detest shopping.'

Matthew looked at his watch. 'We'll have to move it.'

They went to the tie section on the ground floor, where Matthew held up a succession of the more light-hearted silk ties over his own for Kat to inspect.

'Matthew, I thought it was you.'

He turned and saw Susanna, laden with bags. 'How are you?'

'Staggering along.' She looked at Kat with unconcealed curiosity. 'Aren't you going to introduce me to your friend?'

He did so.

'We work for the same firm,' Kat said.

'Of course you do,' Susanna said.

She sat behind her writing desk early that evening, staring at her telephone, trying to rationalize what she was about to do. She felt she had explored every other avenue, ransacking her mind and conscience, fretting almost incessantly since making her discovery in Imogen's room.

219

The person she *wanted* most to speak to about that was Sylvie, but of course she could not do so, which meant that she now had no choice but to talk to Flic. Not about the drawings, of course, or the chastity belt. But Matthew and his redheaded friend had at least provided her with a means to start talking again.

She had felt shocked, quite horribly so, when she had seen them laughing together over the ties, so clearly intimate. A part of Susanna had lately begun to feel that Matthew might have been worthier of Caro's love than she had first believed, but now those feelings had been well and truly squashed. And the realization of how atrociously swiftly the young widower had put his loss behind him made it seem all the more urgent for Susanna to find a path back into regular, in-depth communication with all three Walters sisters, Imogen most of all.

It was, of course, a highly questionable way to proceed. Deliberately pouring salt into wounds that had seemed, of late, to be starting to heal. Yet still it was, she was almost certain, in the best possible cause. For what Imogen had been hiding had surely to be a most painful, suppurating kind of wound, more than probably the deep underlying cause of her past depression and perhaps her recent suicide attempt. And even if that had been a mercifully half-hearted effort, the next one might not be.

Susanna shivered at that prospect, picked up the phone and dialled the number, holding her breath as she heard it being answered.

By Flic.

Imogen was in the garden with Kahli when Flic came to find her. Old John had asked them all to keep watch on the dog as much as possible to try to curb him of his new habit of digging holes in the lawn.

'Behaving himself?' Flic peered at the retriever in the pale floodlight.

'Being a pain,' Imogen answered. 'Won't pee or crap while I'm watching, but the minute I turn my back he starts digging.'

Flic motioned to her sister to walk with her further from the house.

'What's up?' Imogen asked.

'It's time,' Flic said.

Imogen knew instantly what she was talking about. 'How come?'

220

Flic reported what Susanna had said. 'The woman said they were *colleagues*,' she ended, meaningfully.

'Like Chloë's woman on Sunday.'

'Almost definitely,' Flic said. 'Chloë told me she had an accent, and Susanna said this Katrina Dunn is Scottish.'

'I suppose,' Imogen said slowly, 'they might have been working. I was only winding Chloë up on Sunday.'

'Even if that's true,' Flic said harshly, 'it's obviously just a matter of time before he does forget all about Mum.'

'Bastard,' Imogen said.

'So I'm ready now. For some action.' Flic glanced back at the house. 'Starting as planned.'

Imogen gazed down at her feet, dug her left heel into the grass.

'Problem?' Flic enquired.

'Only about Chloë.'

It was the one aspect of their strategy they had argued about several times. 'We have no choice now,' Flic said. 'Chloë has to get involved, like it or not.'

'But she still thinks he's great,' Imogen pointed out.

'So we'll change her mind,' Flic said. 'We'll make it sound like a prank, a little bit of payback for all he's done.'

'What if she won't?' Imogen asked.

'Then we'll say that means she obviously didn't love Mum enough.'

'Susanna says emotional blackmail's a very low way to get what you want.'

'She's right,' Flic said. 'But needs must.'

# 34

'This is your big chance, Chloë,' Flic told her youngest sister.

'So don't blow it,' Imogen said.

'I still don't see why *I* have to do it.'

'Because you're the only one of us who can,' Flic said, patiently. 'We've told you that. We've explained it all to you.'

'It's not as if it's going to be really hard for you,' Imogen said.

'You've already proved you can,' Flic said.

'No one sussed it when you did the note for getting out of P.E.,' Imogen pointed out.

'Exactly,' Flic said. 'It was perfect.'

'It was forgery,' Chloë said. 'It's a crime.'

It was early Saturday afternoon, five days before the shortest day of the year, and they were on the Heath with Kahli, having pleasantly surprised Matthew and Isabella by volunteering to go together, rather than, as was usually the case, having to be coerced.

Flic and Imogen had waited till they were well out of sight of Aethiopia before outlining the plan to Chloë. She had, as they had both expected, not taken it well.

'It's not a *real* crime,' Flic told her now.

'Forging people's signatures *is* a real crime.' Chloë knew that, had seen a forger arrested for it in *The Bill*. 'If I get caught, I'll go to prison.'

'You won't get caught,' Flic said. 'And if you were, you definitely wouldn't go to prison.'

'But if you did,' Imogen teased, 'we'd come and visit you.'

'Shut up, Imo.' Flic saw anxiety and anger on Chloë's face.

'It was your idea to get Chloë involved.'

'Because she's the only one of us talented enough to do it.'

The mention of her talent mollified Chloë for a moment.

'You've got to remember this is for Mum,' Flic capitalized.

'Because of this other woman?' Chloë shook her head, dismissing the notion. 'I don't believe he's in love with someone else.'

'We do,' Flic said, glancing at Imogen. 'And there's more, about *her*.'

'What?' Chloë looked from one to the other. '*What*?'

'We're pretty sure now that he was with her the day Mum died,' Flic said. 'We knew she was unhappy before that, didn't we?'

'Only because you and Imo were being such pigs to him.'

'Why d'you think we were like that?' Imogen asked.

Chloë frowned. 'You knew about her?'

Flic shrugged. 'More or less.' She paused. 'That's not the point now, Chloë. The point *now* is that because you're the only one of us with Dad's talent, the only one who's going to be an artist—'

'Or a forger,' Imogen added.

'Shut *up*, Imo.' Flic glared at her. 'The bottom line, darling, is that you won't be doing anything wrong. On the contrary, you're the first of us who can really make a difference, for Mum's sake. All you have to do is practise Matthew's signature for a while, get it absolutely right, then we'll show you what to do.'

Chloë was still wavering. 'But what if I do get found out?'

'You don't really think I'd let you take the blame, do you?' Flic was soft now, gentler. 'I'd never let you get into trouble, Chloë. If the worst came to the worst and someone did find out – which they won't – I'd say I did it.'

'Would you really do that for me?'

'I'd do anything for you, Chloë,' Flic said.

Flic stood over Chloë for the next three evenings while she practised, Imogen staying out of the way in case she rubbed Chloë up the wrong way and put her off. With her natural flair for calligraphy and almost uncannily accurate copying, Chloë found Matthew's forward sloping, looped hand easy to master.

'You're really good, you know,' Flic said, full of admiration.

'Do you think so?' Chloë was flattered.

'I know so.' Flic picked up the piece of paper her sister had been practising on. 'Frankly, if I didn't think you were up to this, I'd never let you do it. It's much too important to take any risks.'

Chloë was still torn. 'How much trouble is this going to make for Matthew?'

Flic looked down into her worried eyes. 'Worst case, he'll have some aggravation.'

'Okay.' Chloë put out her hand for the paper. 'One more go, and if you think it's good enough, I want to do the real ones now.'

'Are you sure?' Flic was dubious. 'You're going to have to get them totally right.'

'If I don't get it over with now, I might change my mind, and I'm fed up with Imo going on at me.'

'Actually,' Flic said, 'I had to talk Imo into agreeing that we should ask you to do it in the first place. She didn't want to upset you.'

'Really?' That both surprised and pleased Chloë.

'Absolutely.' Flic picked up the Mont Blanc ballpoint that she'd pinched from the desk in the study, a pen that their mother had given Matthew during the summer and which she knew he liked using. 'Okay,' she said. 'Have one more go with this.'

Chloë took the pen, steadied herself, and wrote, smoothly, swiftly:

*Matthew Gardner.*

'Perfect,' Flic said.

# 35

Christmas came, was survived, followed – on Boxing Day – by Flic's birthday and then by New Year's Eve. Sylvie was present for the most part, but Isabella and Mick were staying with his family; any friends the girls might have hoped to see were also out of London; and to cap it, a cable fault had taken out both Aethiopa's telephone lines.

It was the third evening of 2001 before the phones were restored and Matthew thought about checking his messages.

'The gift was great, Matt.' Ethan's voice. 'Way more than we expected. Susan and I and the boys were all pretty damned impressed, I can tell you.'

'I couldn't *believe* it when it arrived.' Kat's voice. 'And you really, really shouldn't have, but I *loved* it.'

'You could have knocked me down with a feather and no mistake' – John Pascoe's voice – 'though I think it'll take me till Easter to finish it.'

Matthew noted down all the calls, scratched his head, then decided to call Kat. VKF was closed till Monday, but he had her home number.

'Sorry I'm not here to take your call,' her voice said.

Matthew cut off the call, decided, after all, to wait till they were back at work to ask her what exactly she had thanked him for in her message. He looked at his watch, figured Ethan might just be home, and dialled New York.

'He's still at the office,' Susan told him, 'but I'm so glad you called, Matt. That was such a fabulous surprise – it's hard to say what my absolutely favourite thing was, but if I *had* to, I guess it would be the hot mustard.'

Matthew was on the verge of telling his sister-in-law that he didn't have a clue what he was supposed to have given them, but something stopped him.

'How were the holidays?' he asked instead.

'Wonderful,' Susan said. 'All my guys together, though we missed you.'

'I miss you too,' Matthew said.

He'd just asked her to have Ethan call him when he heard Isabella and Mick arriving back from their holiday, and Matthew said how about pizza, which got the thumbs-down, and then Isabella suggested Thai, which everyone liked, and they could have had it delivered, but Matthew had an urge to get out, so he volunteered to go and pick it up. And when he got home, Ethan had already called and left word that he thought he was coming down with the flu, so he didn't want Matthew calling back.


'Just what,' he asked Kat after the nine o'clock general meeting on Monday, 'am I supposed to have given you?'

She looked confused. 'The gorgeous little food basket.'

Matthew shook his head. 'Not from me.'

'You didn't send me that wonderful basket full of goodies?'

'Afraid not. Wish I had.' He walked beside her towards the staircase. 'Did this gift come with a card? Or do you know any other Matthews?'

There had been no mistake, at least not from Kat's perspective. The card that had accompanied the present had read: *To dear Katrina, wishing you a Merry Christmas, with love from Matthew.*

'Sounds very nice,' he said, back in their office. 'I really do wish I could say it came from me, Kat, but as it is, I didn't get you anything.'

'Why should you?' she said. 'We bought each other drinks before the holiday.' She was clearly embarrassed. 'I wasn't going to get you anything either.'

'Oh, God, you did,' Matthew said. 'Because you thought I sent you this thing. Can you take it back?'

'I don't want to take it back. It's no big deal, not in the same league as yours.' She grinned. 'Or not yours, as it turns out.'

It was evening before he finally got around to speaking to his brother, to whom he had apparently sent a small hamper from Fortnum & Mason, and to John Pascoe, who had received a gift box from Selfridges. And then Karl phoned, just back from his holiday in Garmisch-Partenkirchen, and thanked him too.

'What exactly did I send you?' Matthew asked.

'The marvellous basket of coffee and chocolates from Harrods.'

'Great,' Matthew said, and went on to tell his friend what was going on.

'Someone playing a joke,' Karl said.

'Apparently. Though I can't see the funny side of it.'

'Who?' Karl asked.

Matthew glanced at the study door, checked it was closed. 'Who'd be your first guess? With their track record of hoaxes.'

'I thought that was all over.'

'So did I.'

'Surely this is a rather complicated hoax for young girls.'

'I haven't really begun to think it through.'

'So how many of these are you supposed to have sent?'

'Four, so far,' Matthew answered, 'though the girls' grandfather has left a message for me too.'

'So he could be number five.' Karl paused. 'Do you have an account with these stores? Have you checked with them?'

'Not yet.' Matthew shook his head. 'Tell you the truth, I'm not much looking forward to finding out the extent of this thing.'

'I don't blame you.' Karl thought again. 'Is there anyone else it could be?'

One other person had come to mind, just a while ago. Susanna Durkin was the only person Matthew could think of who regularly made him bristle with irritation. But it was, he supposed, an absurd notion, and one he'd probably only dredged up because of his reluctance to suspect Flic and Imo.

'Matt?' Karl prompted.

'No one I can think of right now.'

By morning, having established that Gabriel Walters had received a fruit basket from Marks & Spencer, Matthew's anger was steadily mounting. He had to wait till ten, after the morning meeting, to try phoning any of the stores, but with the January sales in full flow, it took a long time to get anywhere; and then, while he was holding on for the right department at Harrods, Phil Bianco walked into the office and Matthew had to hang up. Trying the store again at lunchtime, he finally found someone able to look into the matter, who told him quite swiftly that there were no related purchases logged on his account, and suggested that while they attempted to track down the items at their end, Matthew might like to check to see if any of his credit or charge cards had been used or were, perhaps, missing.

Arriving home that evening, adding insult to injury, he found a note from Susanna thanking him for his beautiful gift and thereby ruling her out as a suspect. He called her immediately and explained that there had been some kind of mistake.

'I admit I was a bit surprised,' she said. 'I mean, it was delightful, but I wouldn't have expected you to be so extravagant.' She paused. 'Would you like to have it back? Though I'm afraid there's only the little wicker basket and a jar of chutney left.'

'No, thank you,' he said. 'You might as well enjoy it.'

'That's very kind of you, Matthew.'

He didn't feel kind, putting down the phone.

Anything but.

'Is everything all right?' Flic asked him over dinner.

'Fine,' he said. 'Why wouldn't it be?'

'I don't know. You just look a bit . . . Cross, I suppose.'

Matthew shook his head. 'A few headaches at work.'

'Poor Matthew,' Chloë said.

'Sure you're okay?' Imogen asked.

He managed to smile at her. 'Perfectly.'

'Not coming down with anything, I hope?' Flic said.

'Not that I know of.'

'Perhaps,' Isabella suggested, 'if you all leave Matthew in peace . . .?'

'It's fine,' he assured her, then smiled at his two older step-daughters again. 'It's kind of you all to be so concerned about me.'

'Actually,' Isabella said, 'you do seem a little preoccupied.'

'Not preoccupied at all,' he said.

Seeing all four of them regarding him so quizzically, he found himself, as he had once before very briefly, wondering about Isabella's deep-down allegiances. He remembered those other, far more trivial, pranks – his mail, messages, that kind of thing – and asked himself if there was, after all, any possibility that Isabella might have been behind some of those pieces of trickery.

Or just helping, perhaps?

He took another look at her, at the calm, nut-brown eyes.

*Nah.*

He arrived at VKF next morning to a summons from Phil Bianco.

'He wants you to go down right away,' Gary Higgins told him.

Bianco, sitting behind his enormous gleaming desk beneath the beautiful, creamy ceiling, seemed even more cold-eyed than usual.

'I would like to believe,' he began without preamble, 'that this was a simple mix-up by you – just picking out the wrong credit card – but try as I may, I can't see that as being very probable, so I'd like to hear your explanation.'

'What am I meant to be explaining?' Matthew asked, though a bad feeling was already gnawing at his gut.

'Do the names Harrods or Fortnum's or Selfridges help you at all?' Bianco's tone was scathing.

The gnawing turned into a hefty punch.

'I see they do,' Bianco said.

'I'm afraid so.' Matthew looked at the sleek leather chair in front of the MD's desk. 'Could I sit down, try and make some sense of how far this thing has gone?'

'I would infinitely prefer it,' Bianco said, 'if you would simply come clean.' He paused, but did not invite Matthew to sit. 'As it is, I've already spoken with New York, and they've agreed that with your previous good record, so long as you meet the bill instantly and in full, they're prepared to give you the benefit of the doubt and take no action.'

'The bill?' His stomach was lurching now.

'On your company VISA card,' Bianco said with helpful sarcasm. 'The card that Wolf Brautigen told me you should have because that had been the deal in New York and Berlin – against my better judgment, by the way. The card you apparently elected to use for your Christmas shopping.'

'Okay,' Matthew said, quietly. 'This is starting to make some kind of sense.'

229

'I'm sure it is.'

'Not the kind of sense you mean.' Matthew ceased waiting to be asked, and sat down in the leather chair.

'*This* kind of sense is what I mean.' Bianco picked up two sheets of paper, stapled together, and passed them across the desk to Matthew. 'The statement for your card and a copy of an order form from from one of the stores.'

Matthew looked at the figures on the top sheet, outrage growing.

'The form, as you see, was signed by one Matthew Gardner.' Bianco paused. 'That is your signature, is it not?'

'Not,' Matthew said.

'Sure looks like it.'

'I agree. But I didn't sign any such form.'

'With respect,' Bianco said, 'you would say that.'

'With equal respect' – Matthew fought to hold down his anger – 'given what you've already said about my good record—'

'What New York said,' Bianco amended.

'If I were going to switch architecture for crime, do you honestly believe I'd do something as damned stupid as this?'

'You might,' Bianco said, 'given the number of officially sanctioned gifts purchased at that time of year.' He shrugged. 'As I said, Gardner, I really would much rather you just admitted the whole thing.'

'There's nothing to admit *to*.' Matthew took a deep breath. 'If you would just listen to me, I was trying to tell you that for the last few days, people have been thanking me for gifts I know nothing about.'

'I've already told you the firm is prepared to overlook the matter so long as you pay up.' Bianco's smile was chilly. 'The gifts are, I understand, non-returnable, and you're not denying that your friends have received them, and at least all the items seem to be under fifty pounds – luckily for you, since clearly they must be paid for.'

'Of course they must,' Matthew said, 'so long as it goes on the record that none of this was down to me.'

'Prove that, and I guarantee it'll go on the record.'

'So you see,' Matthew said to Karl later, calling him on his mobile from outside the office, 'if I want to keep my job, let alone my good name, I have to prove that someone else did this.'

'But you're afraid of what you might prove,' Karl said.

'Oh, I want to prove it,' Matthew said, 'for my own peace of mind if nothing else. But if it is Flic or Imo, it isn't something I'd want to shout from the rooftops.'

'Of course not.' Karl sounded uncomfortable. 'Except . . .'

'Except what?'

'Are you so sure that it is them?'

'Not completely.'

'Last time we spoke,' Karl said, 'you hesitated when I asked if it might be anyone else who had done this thing.'

'I did hesitate.' Matthew remembered that he had been thinking of Susanna. 'But then the person I was thinking about called to thank me for the same kind of gift.' He didn't bother to add that he had, since then, added Isabella – albeit half-heartedly – to his list of suspects.

'I see.' Karl paused. 'Might they have been covering up?'

Matthew laughed faintly. 'Too many movies, my friend.'

It was just himself and his stepdaughters at the table that night, since Isabella was upstairs with Mick. He was tempted, momentarily, to feign a bad headache in order to absent himself, but then he decided he'd be damned if he'd back off that way.

The phone rang while they were clearing the table. Flic stood up to get it, asked who was calling, then passed the cordless phone to him.

'For you,' she said. 'A person named Katrina.'

Matthew took the phone, almost amused by Flic's stuffiness. 'Hi, Kat.'

'Hope you don't mind my calling you at home?'

'Of course not. What can I do for you?'

'I was just wondering if you were okay. Only you looked so awful after your meeting with Bianco, and after that we never had a chance to talk.'

He told her that he was fine, thanked her, said he'd see her next day at the office, and all the while he was aware of Flic, Imogen and even Chloë watching him, naked accusation in their eyes.

Looking at him that way, he realized with a jolt, because he was speaking to a woman.

Another woman. Not their mother.

He could hardly believe the guilt he felt.

It was time, he felt, to speak to a lawyer. Not to William Standish, Caro's stuffed shirt of a solicitor, he decided, but during the single evening he'd spent at Selsdon Park Hotel, Matthew had chatted with an attorney from Manhattan now practising in London. The man, he recalled, had given him his business card.

The thought of a fellow New Yorker, at this particular moment, seemed vaguely comforting. Matthew looked in his wallet and, behind a photograph of his nephews and his Organ Donor card, he found the card still there.

Jack Crocker was out of his office when Matthew called first thing Thursday morning, but phoned back within the hour. Matthew asked him to hold on while he took his mobile outside into Bedford Square, after which the American listened attentively to his predicament. His response, when Matthew had finished, was sympathetic but practical, his advice to first settle the bill – since his credibility at VKF was clearly on the line – and then to try to ascertain who was responsible.

'I believe I may already know that,' Matthew told him. 'I would very much like to be wrong about it, but I think it's unlikely.' He went straight on. 'If I'm right, I don't plan to take any legal action, but what I'm after is some solid proof.'

'Do you want to tell me who you suspect?' Crocker asked.

'Not at this stage. If you don't mind.'

'It's your business.' The lawyer paused. 'It's not really my field, but I'd imagine it mightn't be too tough to nail the culprit, especially if the gifts were ordered via mail order. Half the people in this country receive Christmas gift catalogues, at their homes and offices, and as I recall, some, if not all of them, have a reference number. So if those order forms were used, it should at least be possible to trace the recipient of the catalogues concerned. If they register as having been sent to you, then it's a question of who else would have had access to the catalogues.'

'But those things can be picked up in the stores, can't they?'

'I think I even saw one in my dentist's waiting room.'

'Not so straightforward then,' Matthew said.

'Perhaps not, if you want absolute proof.' Crocker thought for another moment. 'I'd suggest hiring a private investigator, but given that you already have some idea of who's behind this—'

'Possibly,' Matthew said swiftly.

'And you hope to be wrong, yes, you said.' There was a shrug in Crocker's tone. 'I was going to say that you'd probably be throwing good money after bad by using a detective. Frankly, I think you'll find that with time and patience, it's a job you could probably do yourself. And if you're not planning to take legal action, you certainly don't want to pay my fees.'

Matthew thanked him, after which they chatted for a few moments about life in London versus New York City.

'It's a mean kind of a trick,' Crocker said, as they were about to end the conversation. 'I understand your not wanting to name names at this time, but can I just ask whether you think this is personal or business-related? I've never regarded architecture as a particularly cut-throat world.'

'Not at my level, at least,' Matthew said.

'Personal then?'

Matthew didn't answer.

'Nasty,' Crocker said.

# 36

Early on Saturday afternoon, Flic answered the doorbell to find Susanna on the step, weighed down with shopping bags.

'I seem to have bought half of Waterstone's and I was gasping for a cuppa, so I thought rather than sit alone in a café, wouldn't it be much nicer to spend a little time with my friends?' Susanna stepped into the entrance hall. 'Hope you don't mind?'

'Of course not.' Flic smiled. 'Don't you have bookshops in Muswell Hill?'

'You know we do,' Susanna replied amiably, 'but since I was in Hampstead anyway, seeing a client . . .' She set the bags down, leaned them against the wall beside the umbrella stand. 'Sure you don't mind, Flic? Only I seem to have been trying to get to see you all for ages.'

'We've been busy.' Flic walked towards the kitchen.

'I know. I'm not complaining, I've just missed you.' Susanna fished in a bag for a package, then followed. 'How's Imo?'

'Fine,' Flic said. 'She and Chloë are both out. Isabella and Mick are in the garden with Kahli, and Groosi's at her flat.' She picked up the mug of coffee she had just made herself and took a sip. 'And Matthew's in the study.'

'Shall I make my own?' Susanna looked at the mug.

'No, of course not. Sorry.' Flic put down the mug again, filled the kettle and switched it on.

Susanna, at the window, was watching Isabella and Mick standing in the middle of the lawn, deep in conversation, Kahli close by, digging a hole and being ignored.

'They're having a row,' Flic said.

'I'd better not go out then to say hello.'

'Not unless you're in the mood for marriage guidance.'

Susanna smiled at her. 'You're becoming a cynic, Flic.'

Flic took a second mug down from the cabinet and spooned Nescafé into it.

'I think maybe I should just say hi to your stepfather.' Susanna still held the package in her right hand.

'Be my guest.'

Susanna left the kitchen, walked towards the study and then, hearing Matthew's voice from beyond the door, waited for several moments, listening with great interest before tapping softly and going straight in.

'So you honestly think I should just let the whole damned thing go, whatever the firm thinks of me?' Matthew stopped, still holding the phone to his ear, staring at her, perplexed.

'Sorry,' Susanna mouthed.

'Ethan, I have to go now. Unexpected guest. We'll speak soon.' He put down the phone.

'More Christmas gift problems?' she asked.

'I didn't hear you arrive,' Matthew said coolly. 'Or knock, for that matter.'

'I did, actually,' she said. 'Flic let me in.'

'Where is she?'

'I couldn't help hearing what you were saying,' she said sympathetically. 'It must be unpleasant for you. Having people think—'

'Where's Flic?' Matthew cut her short, standing up.

'She's making me a coffee,' Susanna said.

He came around the desk and ushered her inhospitably out of the room, following close behind, heading her into the kitchen. Flic was standing near the fridge, drinking her coffee.

'I'd appreciate it, Flic' – Matthew was curt – 'if you would let me know when we have visitors.'

'Announce them, you mean,' Flic said coldly, 'like some old-fashioned servant?' She gestured to the mug on the table. 'Your coffee, Susanna,' she said, and left the room.

'Not like you, Matthew,' Susanna remarked, 'to be so grouchy.'

'Did you want something in particular?' he asked her.

'I *wanted*,' she said, 'to give you a little present.' She held up

235

the package. 'To make up for eating almost everything in your lovely basket – but since you're in such a bad mood, perhaps I'd better just leave it . . .'

The garden door opened and Mick came in with a face like thunder, ignoring Matthew and Susanna and walking straight out of the kitchen on his way upstairs. Three or four seconds later, Isabella came in, looking tight-lipped, pausing to wipe the soles of her shoes on the mat just inside the door.

'Is this a kitchen or a train station?' Matthew demanded.

Isabella looked at him, startled.

'He's still very upset,' Susanna said in a hushed voice, 'about these presents.'

'I would thank you,' Matthew said, 'not to discuss my private business.'

He stalked out of the room, back to the study.

'It must be very embarrassing,' Susanna said to Isabella, still conspicuously quietly, 'having one's hand caught in the proverbial cookie jar.'

'What are you talking about, Susanna?' Isabella asked.

'The Christmas gifts,' Susanna said. 'The freebies?' She shrugged. 'A lot of people do that sort of thing, I suppose, if they think they can get away with it.'

Isabella eyed her with undisguised dislike. 'Why are you here, Susanna? Did someone invite you?'

'I brought Matthew a present,' Susanna replied with dignity, and placed her package on the table. 'And I was hoping to see Imogen.'

'She's not here,' Isabella said.

'Will she be back soon?'

'Not until very late.'

Susanna looked sceptical. 'Surely if she's with Chloë, it won't be that late?'

'She isn't with Chloë, and she will be late.' Isabella stood her ground.

'I'd better go then,' Susanna said, resigned, 'before I catch the foul mood that everyone in this house seems to be in.'

She walked, slowly and pensively, through the small, attractive back roads, making her way to Perrin's Lane and Sylvie, with whom she'd been seeking an excuse to speak ever since her find in

236

Imogen's bedroom. The call she had made to Flic in December, after seeing Matthew with his Scottish 'colleague' in Selfridges, had not resulted in the rapprochement with Caro's daughters that she'd hoped for, yet the discovery still haunted Susanna.

Obviously, she reaffirmed to herself, turning into Flask Walk, she still could not – would *never* be able to – share the results of her snooping with Sylvie or anyone else, but if Caro's mother was home now, she would try to raise this just-gleaned possibility of Matthew's dishonesty. Frankly, Susanna didn't see him as the fraudulent type, but she *was* a great believer in all roads leading – at least potentially – to Rome.

'How, may I ask,' Sylvie asked, 'do you know about this trouble at Matthew's firm?'

'I eavesdropped,' Susanna replied, with what she hoped would be seen as refreshing honesty. 'Reprehensible, I know, but in a good cause, I'm sure you'll agree.'

'I don't agree,' Sylvie said. 'And I don't want to talk about it.'

'But don't you think you should? For the girls' sakes?'

'If Matthew chooses to discuss his private problems with me, that's one thing,' Sylvie told her. 'Otherwise, it's his business, not mine, and certainly not yours.'

'Surely where his problems affect your granddaughters, they become your business?' The older woman said nothing, so Susanna bulldozed on. 'He's patently worried that this may cost him his job, and naturally enough, I suppose, it's making him unreasonable with the girls.'

'In what way?' Sylvie asked.

'He was very moody with Flic while I was with them. And with Isabella, too.'

They were seated in the living room, and Sylvie, who had decided not to offer Susanna a cup of tea, began to wonder if perhaps she ought to do so now. 'Surely this Christmas gift nonsense is just a storm in a teacup?'

'I hope it is,' Susanna said, 'for everyone's sake. But in the unlikely event that Matthew did succumb to temptation—'

'Of course he didn't,' Sylvie said decisively.

'I expect you're right – you know him far better than I do. But just supposing, for a moment, that he *did*, that would mean Caro's girls are being brought up by—'

'Matthew's hardly bringing them up.'

'They're in his care.' Susanna saw the older woman glaring at her. 'I just wanted to be sure that you knew about this, Sylvie.' She took a swift breath. 'And I also wanted to say that I think it might be wise for us to keep a more careful eye on the girls.'

'Us?' Sylvie was ironic.

Susanna pretended not to notice. 'I haven't seen Imo professionally for a while now. It occurred to me that all this unpleasantness may have added to her burden. After all, we both know how vulnerable she is, don't we?'

'Is business so poor' – the words sprang from Sylvie's lips before she had time to consider them – 'that you're having to tout for customers now?'

Susanna flushed deeply, but still held her ground. 'I trust you don't really believe that, Sylvie,' she said, 'but just in case you do, suffice it to say that I'd be glad to see Imo for no fee at all.'

'I'm sorry.' Whatever Susanna's faults, Sylvie was sure she'd never been motivated by greed. 'I didn't mean that, and I shouldn't have said it.'

'That's all right.' Susanna's flush paled a little.

'And I will think about what you've said.'

'I hope you will,' Susanna said, 'for Imo's sake.'

From Matthew's standpoint, one of the few real blessings in the weeks that followed – an especially painful period, with his first wedding anniversary to endure – was that Sylvie was again spending more time at Aethiopia. He was invariably glad of her presence, was always the first to suggest she stay overnight when she came for dinner, though Sylvie generally rejected that idea, preferring to go home to Perrin's Lane. Her treatments were over, and she claimed, for now at least, to have been given the all-clear by the oncologist, but Matthew was aware that she still tired more easily than she had before and worried about her, even broaching the possibility of installing a stair-lift so she might stay with them for longer periods. Sylvie said that was a ghastly idea, told him, only half joking, that if he was trying to turn her prematurely into an old woman, that would be going the right way about it.

The VISA bill having been settled, the company had dropped the matter, though Matthew had been transferred from the church project to another shopping centre, this time in Dagenham. Since

238

MacNeice had appeared well pleased with his work before Christmas, this was clearly Bianco's personal punishment, which rankled deeply with Matthew.

Almost as deeply as the hoax itself, which he had now decided to put down to experience. Proving that the girls were behind it would have been time-consuming and probably costly, but more to the point, if he *had* obtained the proof he would have had to decide what to do with it. More confrontation, more distress for Sylvie, more misery all round.

'I told you,' Flic said to Chloë quietly during a morning break at The Grange, having followed her into the students' cloakroom, 'that nothing terrible would happen to him. He's just had some aggravation, as I said, and he'd never believe in a million years that you had anything to do with it.'

'He's been awfully grumpy,' Chloë said, 'and I think he's quite unhappy.'

'He deserves to be,' Flic reminded her. 'Have you forgotten the other woman? Have you forgotten he left Mummy alone, to be with *her*, the day she died?'

Chloë shook her head. 'I still don't think that's true.'

'It's true,' Flic said. 'Believe me.'

# 37

'Have you heard the news?' Mark Loftus asked Matthew the instant he got into the office after lunch on the first day of February. 'Kat got fired.'

'Not fired,' Fairbairn amended. 'Made redundant.'

'Where is she?' Matthew had been on site in Dagenham since Monday.

'Home, I suppose,' Loftus said. 'Licking her wounds, poor cow.'

Nick Brice walked in. 'Talking about Katrina?'

'Have you seen her?' Matthew asked.

Brice nodded. 'First thing, coming out of Bianco's office, looking like hell.'

'Bastard,' Matthew said with feeling.

'Careful,' Fairbairn cautioned. 'Walls and ears.'

Matthew called her first chance he had to be alone. Her machine was on, but he thought she might be screening calls, so he told the machine he was going to hold in case she picked up, and two seconds later she did.

'You okay?'

'I've been better.' She sounded rueful.

'What are you doing later?'

'No plans.'

'Have dinner with me?' He figured she might be feeling lonely, knew she'd finally told her on-off boyfriend to take a hike.

'I'll be lousy company.'

'That's usually my line, isn't it?' Matthew paused, remembering she'd told him she lived in Earl's Court. 'There's a nice bistro at Queen's Gate – that's close enough to you, isn't it?'

'Of course it is.' Kat hesitated. 'Are you sure?'

'I'll pick you up and we can walk together.'

He'd been unable to reserve at that restaurant, and Kat said she had no appetite anyway, so they went instead to a small, unpretentious, dimly-lit Italian closer to her flat. It was, she said, exactly what she needed, but Matthew saw that she was close to tears as she spoke, and it was so completely out of character that he was really concerned.

'What did Bianco say to you?' he asked, pouring from the carafe of red he'd ordered as soon as they'd sat down.

Kat shook her head. 'It's not really him, or the firm. They've been quite fair. Last in, first out, you know?'

'Except that you're talented and hard-working.'

'So's everyone else there.'

'But this has still left you in a mess, has it?' Matthew asked gently.

Kat nodded. 'I need to earn good money,' she said quietly, 'for my family.'

That was news to Matthew. She had spoken periodically of her family in Edinburgh, had mentioned her mother and brother with warmth and affection, never giving any hint that everything in their garden wasn't rosy.

'It's a fairly common tale, I suppose,' Kat told him now. 'My dad walked out on us years ago – my mum, brother and me.' She drank some wine. 'But the thing is, Harry, my brother, is Down's Syndrome, and so it's been tough on our mum.'

'I'll bet.'

'She's always had this thing about nothing being allowed to hold me back. She pushed me to leave home, get my qualifications, come to London, because it was what I wanted, and she wanted me to do well and be happy and independent. So *I've* always been equally determined to make sure I can earn enough to keep on helping her and Harry. But now . . .'

Matthew watched her fight back more tears, then down more wine, and he refilled her glass and decided it might be as well if they ordered some food.

241

'Might a loan help at all?' he asked a little later over mine-strone, going straight to the point, knowing prevarication wouldn't go down well with Kat.

'Definitely not,' she said, decisively. 'Thank you, but so long as I get a job quite soon, I'll be all right.'

'Okay,' he said. 'Hope you didn't mind my asking?'

'Don't be silly,' Kat told him.

'If I thought it would be any use at all, I'd offer to have a word with Laszlo King in New York.' He grimaced wryly. 'But where Bianco's concerned . . .'

'Your own downgrade to Dagenham.' Kat tried to smile back. 'Perhaps I should be grateful to him for simply firing me.'

'You've been made redundant, not fired.'

'Feels like the same thing.'

'You need to get that out of your head fast,' Matthew told her. 'You're good, and you will get a new job – a better job – where they'll appreciate your talent.'

She shrugged. 'That's more or less what Bianco said.'

'Make him put it in writing,' Matthew said.

By the time they got up to leave, Kat was more than a little unsteady on her feet, and Matthew had intended to walk her home and leave her at her front door, but first she had trouble fitting her key in the lock, and then, as soon as she got over the threshold, she had to bolt through her living room into the bathroom, knocking over her drawing board en route, and so he figured he ought to stay a while to make sure she was okay.

'I'm so sorry,' she said when she emerged to find him in the kitchen, having found some mugs and coffee. 'I never inherited my dad's capacity for drink – I should have known better.' And then the smell of the coffee reached her, and she was gone again.

Matthew glanced at his watch, saw it was almost eleven, considered calling home in case anyone worried. But then he remembered that since Sylvie was at her own flat and Isabella was probably upstairs with Mick, there was no one at Aethiopia likely to worry about him – except perhaps Chloë, who was presumably already fast asleep – and so he settled down to wait for Kat, who was, it seemed, going to be in need of a little TLC when she did finally come up for air . . .

\*

Flic was still awake when he came home a little after one o'clock; she heard the front door close, heard his attempts to subdue Kahli's greeting, then creep up the staircase and into his room.

Her mother's room.

Their *parents'* room.

'You came in very late,' she said next morning at breakfast.

'Yes,' he said.

'Go anywhere nice?'

'Out to dinner.'

'With a colleague?' Imogen asked.

Her hair had been cut and dyed again, the colour and style this time a degree or two less aggressive. A raven crop now came to mind, Matthew felt, rather than ink-black retro-punk. He had, without thinking, told her he liked it when he first saw it, and in the instant or two before she remembered how much she hated him, Imogen had looked pleased.

'Yes, as a matter of fact,' he answered now.

'Long dinner,' Flic commented.

'Long nose,' Isabella remarked.

Chloë looked at her sisters and said nothing.

'It was actually quite helpful of him,' Flic told Imogen later outside the chemistry lab. 'Just what we needed to persuade Chloë to do her thing again.'

'On what?' Imogen was puzzled.

'I told you I've been checking out his mail when I can.' Flic paused as two teachers approached, waited till they'd passed. 'You know there's still all sorts of stuff that comes addressed to Mum.'

'So?'

'I've found the perfect thing,' Flic said softly. 'It came on Tuesday, and I've been working out what exactly to do with it ever since. I didn't want to tell you till I'd got it quite right, but I have now. The only snag was that we needed Chloë on board, and I wasn't sure she was ready. But now . . .'

# 38

The telephone call from David Munro – Caro's accountant, and, since Matthew's arrival in London, his – came on the morning of Valentine's Day.

It was cold, wet and bleak in the way only February knew how to be, and the cold he'd been nursing for over a week had turned into a nasty cough, and Sylvie had sent Howard Lucas to see him yesterday, and now Matthew was on a short course of antibiotics and supposedly spending a day or two in bed.

'I never stay in bed,' he'd said.

'I expect you prefer to hang around other people, infecting as many of them as possible,' the doctor had pleasantly said.

And in fact, the first few hours of this Wednesday morning, after another bad night of coughing, had seemed almost enjoyable with all the appalling weather *outside* his windows and Isabella willingly bringing him cups of tea.

Until he'd answered the phone.

'I'm sure there's no cause for concern,' Munro told him in an accent that reminded Matthew faintly of Kat's, 'but the Revenue seems to be querying something regarding Caroline's estate.'

'Something I can help with?' Matthew was surprised, since most of those details had been dealt with by Sylvie, with Munro's assistance.

'So they seem to think,' Munro said, 'though I suspect there may have been a mix-up.' He paused. 'Do you know anything about a garage in Maidenhead?'

'Not a thing.' Matthew thought about it. 'Though I think I've heard Sylvie mention a house there. Presumably that might be connected?'

'I'd have said so.' Munro sounded relaxed. 'Anyway, I just wanted to call and let you know that I'd heard from the Inspector, and assure you that as soon as I have any more information or questions for you, I'll be in touch.'

Matthew got up after that and had a shower, then wandered down to the kitchen, treated Kahli to a dog biscuit, made himself a cup of instant soup, took it back up to bed and switched the TV on, volume low, just for company.

He thought, when the phone woke him, that he'd only just dozed off, but the clock on the bedside table told him he'd slept for almost two hours.

'Mr Gardner, it's William Standish.'

Caro's solicitor, the one Matthew had chosen not to consult after the Christmas gift fiasco because he'd found him stuffy.

'What can I do for you, Mr Standish?'

'Your secretary tells me you're unwell.'

'Just a virus, nothing serious.'

'I'm glad to hear it.'

Matthew figured this call was no coincidence. 'Does this have something to do with my wife's estate and some garage?' He coughed, then went straight on. 'Only I talked with my accountant a couple of hours ago, so whatever it is, he should have it under control.'

'Did Mr Munro explain the nature of the problem?'

'Not exactly.' Matthew coughed again. 'I don't mean to be rude, but couldn't this wait?'

'I don't think it would be wise to let it wait,' Standish said.

Matthew sighed, tugged a man's size tissue out of the box resting on his duvet and mopped at his nose. 'Okay,' he said. 'So what exactly *is* this problem?'

The solicitor explained that, as Matthew had already surmised, the property Caro had inherited from Richard had included a garage which had been rented out, first by Richard himself, then by Caroline.

'Since her death, rent has continued to be paid.'

'Is that a problem?' Matthew asked.

'Not in itself,' Standish replied. 'So long as the rent were being paid into the estate, as it were. Being declared as *part* of the estate, that is.'

'And it hasn't been?' Matthew longed to go back to sleep.

'Apparently not,' the solicitor said. 'Though there's only been one payment, since the arrangement has always been biannual.'

'And?' Matthew tried to be patient.

There was a moment's silence.

'I'm sure this was just an oversight on your part, Mr Gardner. Pressures of work and family responsibilities. This must have been a very difficult time for you.'

'I don't understand,' Matthew said, though the first prickles of unease were tickling at his back. 'Are you asking me if *I've* received the rent on this garage?'

'I believe that you have,' Standish said, clearly.

'Not that I know of.'

'The cheque was dated the twenty-fifth of January, made out to M.C. Gardner – your wife's full initials, of course – and was paid into *your* bank account on the fifth of February.' The solicitor paused. 'I'd have thought it unlikely you'd have forgotten about it – though perhaps, if you were already unwell . . .'

Less than an hour later, Matthew called Jack Crocker and told him about the calls.

'I've checked with the bank and it seems the money really is in my account – or at least it was, very briefly, since I've been working on an overdraft for a while.'

Crocker took a moment to absorb the information. 'First step,' he said, 'is to get sight of the paying-in slip.'

'Already requested,' Matthew told him. 'And I've written a new cheque, in the same amount, to the solicitor's firm, so that the money can be properly redirected.'

'Do you know who the payee on the cheque was?'

Matthew explained about Caro's seldom used first name. 'Same initials.'

'So it would be an easy mistake for you to have made,' Crocker said.

'If I'd made it, I guess so. But I didn't.'

'You're sure about that? You might have had a bunch of cheques that arrived the same week, paid them all in together.'

'I wish,' Matthew said dryly. 'I'm a lowly architect, Jack. I don't work as a freelance, and people just don't send me cheques. The only property dealings I have are connected with my New York sublet that more or less takes care of itself.'

Crocker took a moment, then asked: 'How did they find out?'

Matthew's mind felt fogged. 'Who?'

'How did the Revenue find out?' Crocker clarified. 'How did anyone find out that the cheque was paid into your account as opposed to your wife's estate's?'

'I don't know.'

'Seems strange to me, Matthew. The guy who wrote the cheque would only have known that it had cleared.'

'I guess so.' More unease.

'So what would you like me to do for you?' Crocker asked.

'I don't know. Find out the answer to that question, I suppose.'

'Couldn't your wife's solicitor do that?'

'He isn't my solicitor,' Matthew said.

'Okay,' Crocker said. 'Give me some details, and I'll do what I can.'

Matthew had struggled back into the office next day when Crocker called him, and again he felt compelled to head out into the street with his mobile.

'I've talked to the garage tenant.'

'And?'

'He says he was tipped off in an anonymous phone call, believe it or not. Female voice telling him that the rent had been paid into your account rather than the estate's. He tried dialling 1471, but of course the number had been withheld.'

A host of ugly thoughts crowded into Matthew's mind.

'Have you seen the paying-in slip yet?' Crocker asked.

'A copy,' Matthew said. 'Looks just like my signature.'

'Another forgery then, you think?'

'Not much doubt about it.' He felt chilled.

Crocker was silent for a moment. 'Does the female voice slot in with your suspicions over the Christmas gifts?'

'It might.'

'Do I take it you still don't want to pursue this legally?'

'I'm not sure.'

'I think you should at least consider it,' Crocker said.

'Easier said.' Out of the corner of one eye, he saw Stephen Steerforth walking towards the VKF building, and quickly he turned away and strolled a little way along the pavement.

'Does anyone in your household do banking chores for you?' Crocker asked. 'Do you have a housekeeper?'

Isabella again. *Nah*, he decided again.

'She's never been to the bank for me,' Matthew answered. 'And if I'd asked her to, she'd have signed her own name on the paying-in slip, not mine. Cash and cheques can be paid in by anyone, after all, can't they?'

'Sure can.' Crocker paused. 'Are you quite certain you didn't do this yourself when you were maybe exhausted or coming down with this flu?'

'How about,' Matthew countered sarcastically, 'when I felt like illegally appropriating my late wife's income because my own bank account was running a little low?'

'Just asking.'

A large delivery van screeched to a halt close to where he was standing, and the driver of the black taxi behind hooted loudly.

'Where the hell are you?' Crocker asked.

Matthew told him. 'This wasn't a conversation I particularly wanted to share with my colleagues.'

'Can't say I blame you.' The attorney thought again. 'What's the position, probate-wise, on your wife's estate?'

'If you were the Revenue, you'd know the answer.'

'Humour me,' Crocker persisted.

Matthew filled him in swiftly and succinctly, told him about asking Caro to leave him out of her will till they'd been married for several years, and about her insistence on specifying that he be allowed to stay in the house, rent-free, for as long as he wished.

'Any major conflicts with the family about that?'

'Have I said anything about conflicts?' Matthew asked.

'Comes to mind.'

'I have a question for you.'

'Go ahead.'

'Do you believe what I've told you?'

'I have no reason not to,' Crocker answered. 'One more question from me?'

'Okay.'

'How many females in your household?'

'I don't want to go there right now, Jack.'

'I guess I can understand your reluctance,' the lawyer said, 'but I'm not sure it's the smartest reaction.'

'In your opinion,' Matthew asked, 'is this something the Revenue might make a big deal about?'

'I can't predict what the Revenue might or might not do. It would be good to think that so long as this was a one-off misappropriation, they might not worry about it too much.'

'But we can't be sure of that.'

'You can't have this both ways, Matthew.' The other man's tone was mildly reproachful. 'Unless you're prepared to implicate the person or persons I'm now assuming you suspect in your own home . . .' He left the rest unspoken.

'Can't I deny this without implicating anyone else?' Matthew asked. 'The money's being redirected, as I told you. Can't I just let it drop and hope the Revenue does the same?'

'Sure you can, so long as you realize it is just a hope. Theoretically, I guess this is a fraud, though obviously a very minor one.' Crocker paused. 'But minor or not, I can assure you that if it were me these things were happening to, I wouldn't just be sitting there with my thumb up my ass. I'd be taking some action.'

'I'll think about it,' Matthew said.

'Off the record, who are we talking about here? Family member?'

'Off the record?' He was wavering.

'Strictly.'

'Possibly a family member. Possibly more than one.'

'This is your late wife's family, presumably?'

'Possibly,' Matthew said again.

'May I ask you a very undiplomatic question?'

'Okay, and then I need to get off this phone.'

'You're a New Yorker. You only came to live in London because of your wife, right?' Crocker didn't wait for an answer. 'Reading between the lines, there must be some pretty significant conflicts between you and her family. So my question is: why are you still here?'

Matthew told him, very briefly, about Sylvie's illness and his commitment to Caro's daughters, at least for the time being.

'Very noble,' Crocker said. 'You're a decent man.'

'But?'

'But if it were me, I'd get the hell out of there.'

He needed someone else to talk to, someone who would be on his side yet straight with him, but the two people who most fitted that bill were Ethan and Karl, and this was not the stuff of phone calls.

He considered flying to Berlin for the weekend, but when he called Karl, he and Amelie were packing to go to Spain for a few days' break.

'Come to Marbella instead of Berlin,' Karl suggested. 'We can hit a few golf balls, have a few beers, talk properly.'

It was tempting, but with his friends clearly planning a free-and-easy weekend, he didn't feel right about burdening them. Besides which, it smacked a little too much of running away.

*Isn't that what your own lawyer more or less told you to do?*

He'd hardly needed Crocker to start those thought processes running again. But the more he thought about getting out, the more he decided he'd be damned if he was going to be run out of town by his stepdaughters. More compellingly still, he had no intention of leaving London or VKF with mud sticking to his name.

'Another time,' he told Karl.

There *was* one other person, he realized suddenly, he felt he could talk to. He was surprised, in fact, by how much he wanted to see Kat again, and he wasn't wholly certain that it was the best idea he'd ever had, but there could be no denying that he badly needed a friend right now.

She was home when he called, getting changed to go to the theatre.

'I don't have to do that though,' she said, hearing the tone in his voice.

'Of course you do,' Matthew said quickly.

'No, actually, I don't. I was going on my own, and I know someone who'd love my ticket, so where do you want to meet?'

They met in Café Flo in St Martin's Lane after she'd handed over her ticket outside the Duke of York's Theatre, ordered steak and *frites* for two, and talked things through. Kat was shocked, told him he ought to speak to Sylvie about what had happened.

'Not yet,' Matthew said. 'She's been through enough.'

'Don't you think she has a right to know?' Kat asked gently.

'She has a right to a little peace, a right to recover.'

'And what about your rights, Matthew? You have to think about yourself too. You have to find a way to put a stop to this. Don't forget you're the outsider here, the foreigner, the one they're most likely to pin the blame on unless you do something.'

'I know,' he said, softly. 'Believe me.'

'Jack Crocker was right, you know, about telling you to leave that house.'

'I know that too.'

'You have to talk to Sylvie,' she said again. 'I know what you've said, and I respect you for caring about her, but I think you might be making a bad mistake if you wait too long.'

'I won't wait too long,' Matthew said.

Kat thought for a moment. 'There is one thing you *can* do right away – tomorrow, if not tonight.'

'What's that?'

'Get a new lock put on your study door.'

# 39

'Nothing's happening,' Imogen said the following Thursday night.

'Not yet,' Flic said. 'Or not so far as we know. Except he's locking his study.'

'Dad's study.' Imogen on automatic.

'He's looking very fed up, so I think we can assume *something*'s happening.'

'No police. Nothing *real*.'

'Not yet,' Flic said again. 'Though this is probably too small for the police to bother with.'

'I just want to get *on* with it,' Imogen said frustratedly.

'That's why we're moving straight on to the next thing.' Flic smiled grimly. 'Which is exactly your cup of tea. It won't be easy, because it's really going to have to be all down to you. But if you get this right, there's absolutely no *way* we won't be getting rid of him big-time.'

Imogen was intrigued but apprehensive. 'What the hell do I have to do?'

'What do you like most in the world that you're not supposed to? Other than smoking.'

Imogen considered for a moment. 'Sex?'

'In one,' Flic said.

'I'm not doing that,' Imogen said after Flic had told her.

'You'll be great.'

'It's disgusting.'

252

'But in such a good cause. And nothing much will actually *happen*.'

'If you like it so much,' Imogen said, 'you do it.'

'It wouldn't work with me,' Flic said.

'Why not? Because I like boys more than you do?'

'Because I'm seventeen. Over the age of consent. It has to be you, because Chloë really couldn't do it, and neither of us would want her to, would we?'

'I still hate it,' Imogen said.

'What do you hate more?' Flic challenged. 'The idea or him?'

'Him, I suppose.' She shook her head. 'Him, definitely.'

'And do you want this to be over or not?'

'You know I do.'

'Then you'll do exactly what I tell you. Right?'

'Do I really have to, Flic?'

'You really do.'

'When?' Imogen asked.

'Tomorrow,' Flic said.

# 40

Sylvie came to dinner on Friday, bringing two whole bagfuls of new paperback novels for everyone and cakes from Maison Blanc, her mood upbeat and infectious, gladdening Matthew on one hand because she clearly felt so much better, saddening him on the other because that meant he might, sooner rather than later, be compelled to share recent events with her.

*Not tonight, at least.*

The evening went on with the same pleasurable quality. Isabella had honey-roasted a pair of ducks for them, which they all loved, and Matthew opened some wine, and even Chloë was allowed a small glass, and Kahli was given titbits by everyone at the table. And after dinner they all sat around the fire chatting, no one even suggesting they switch on the television, and then Sylvie began yawning, and Matthew called a cab to take her home because he thought he might be over the limit, and when Flic volunteered to make hot chocolate, he actually felt able to almost delude himself, just for a short while, that theirs was, after all, a normal, contented family . . .

'Good chocolate,' he told her after his first sip.

'I whisked the milk,' Flic said, tucking *Ralph's Party* under one arm and carrying her mug to the door. 'And sprinkled Flake on the top.' She looked at Imogen, sprawling in one of the armchairs. 'Coming up?'

'Yeah, okay.' Imo picked up her own mug. 'Night,' she said.

'Would one of you please check on Chloë?' Matthew asked.

'I will,' Flic said. 'Sleep well.'

He thought he might, for once, after the good food and wine and now, with the added relaxing aid of the nightcap, and he debated for a moment getting up to pour a little cognac into the drink, but suddenly he realized he was too tired to do any more than finish the chocolate and get upstairs to bed . . .

He dreamed, *knew* he was dreaming, yet knowing made it no better.

Awful dreams, darkly abstract, yet filled with physical sensations. Softness, like flesh, pushing against his own, his hands being dragged at, his fingertips, finger*nails*, gouging into something . . .

A voice, crying out.

*Awful* dreams . . . Violent, sexual dreams.

Flic, lying awake in bed, heard Imogen's soft tread in the hallway, then the sound of her bedroom door closing, and she was about to get up and go to her, but then she heard the key on the inside of the door being turned, and knew she would have to wait.

The sounds began, soft, steady, insistent, growing swifter.

Flic knew what Imogen was doing, had heard those sounds many times before, had always hated them, but tonight they seemed to her to be infinitely more disturbing than they had *ever* been, and she covered her ears with her hands and squeezed her eyes tightly shut, until – finally – she fell asleep.

It was almost four o'clock when Imogen came in to wake her.

'Least you can do is stay awake with me.' Her tone was carping, yet her eyes glittered.

'You did it then?' Flic asked, feeling sick.

'Of course I did,' Imo said. 'You'd have been proud of me.'

'You managed to use his hands?' She was surprised how difficult she found it even to ask the question.

'That's what you told me to do.'

'Good,' Flic said. 'Good.'

'Want to see?' Imogen lifted up the hem of her Astrid shirt.

'God.' Flic covered her mouth. Her sister's thighs were covered in scratches, some still bleeding.

'There'll probably be bruises by morning,' Imogen said.

Flic took her hand from her mouth, her mind at work again.
'Did you scratch him?' she asked.

'No. I wanted to, but I thought that really might wake him.'

'You were right,' Flic said.

'Pity, though,' Imogen said.

# 41

He woke just after eight to a sick headache and the muffled sounds of voices and activity overhead. Pushing back the covers, he headed blearily for the shower, noticing as he turned on the water that there was dirt on his hands and beneath his fingernails.

Not *exactly* dirt, he realized, trying to wash it away.

It looked, as it eddied in the hot water and vanished down the plughole, pink.

Like blood.

The dreams came back to him then, that bizarre sensation of his nails gouging into something soft, like flesh, and quickly he checked over his body to see if he'd maybe scratched himself.

Nothing.

He got out of the shower, dried himself, saw some of the dark traces lingering under the nails and used his brush to finish the job. Then, still too sluggish to think about it, he put down the nail brush on the edge of the basin, threw his towel into the washing hamper and went to get dressed.

He came out of his bedroom just as Isabella and Flic were walking down the stairs from the floor above, Mick behind them.

'Morning,' he said.

If their expressions hadn't told him something was badly wrong, the fact that they were all fully dressed at that time on a Saturday morning ought to have alerted him. Sylvie flashed into his thoughts and his stomach clenched.

'What's happened?'

'You tell us.' Mick pushed ahead of Isabella and stood right in front of him. 'You dirty bastard.'

'What's up with you?' Matthew stared past him at Isabella and Flic. 'Would someone like to tell me what's going on?'

'Don't look at *them*.' Mick poked him in the chest with two fingers. 'Look at me, you piece of garbage, look at a *man*.'

'Mick, stop that.' Isabella had one arm around Flic. 'That's not the way.'

'I know his sort.' Mick wasn't in the mood to stop, poked him again.

'You want to cut that out.' Matthew stepped to the right.

'I'd like to cut *something* out.' A push this time, both hands against Matthew's chest. 'Or *off* – you'd understand *that*, wouldn't you, you pervert!' A shove.

'*Hey!*' Matthew shoved him right back, stared in angry bewilderment at Isabella, saw that Chloë had come out of her room, looking scared, saw that Flic had moved away to Imogen's bedroom door. 'What the hell is going *on* here?'

'It's okay,' Flic told Chloë from along the corridor.

'It's bloody well *not* okay,' Mick said loudly.

Matthew saw the other man's right hand move again, bunching into a fist and coming his way, and instinctively he grabbed Mick's arm and drove him away hard enough to send him crashing into the wall. 'That is *enough*.'

'I haven't even started, man!'

'Mick, you *stop* that.' Isabella, slender in T-shirt and jeans, but startlingly forceful, pushed between them. 'Matthew, will you please go downstairs and wait for me so we can talk?'

'About *what*?' Matthew, shaking with anger, stared at her again, then over at his two stepdaughters, now standing close together outside their sister's door. 'Flic? Chloë? What's this about?'

'Don't talk to me!' Flic's arms were around Chloë now, protectively.

'If you won't let me thump him,' Mick told Isabella, 'at least call the cops.'

'No police.' Isabella was still restraining her husband, both hands up against his chest. 'Think what that could do to Imo.'

'What does Imo have to do with this?' Matthew was still seething at Mick's unprovoked assault, fighting to stay under control. '*Will* someone please *talk* to me, tell me why this man's gone crazy?'

Mick shrugged himself free of Isabella, then turned swiftly and gave Matthew another aggressive shove. Matthew punched him, a hard, clean blow to the jaw, and Mick reeled backwards.

'*Stop* it!' Chloë screamed. 'Stop it, both of you!'

'Mick, please go *upstairs.*' Isabella's voice was shaky but clear. '*Please.*'

'You're nuts,' Mick told her, nursing his jaw. '*Nuts* not to call the cops.'

'For God's sake,' Matthew bellowed, 'what is this talk about calling the *cops?*'

'We're not staying here any more,' Mick told Isabella.

'Good idea,' Matthew agreed loudly. '*Great* idea.'

'We can't leave,' Isabella said to Mick. 'We especially can't leave now.'

Mick shot Matthew one more filthy look, then began to move towards the stairs. 'Any bother,' he told his wife, 'and you yell, right?' He paused. '*Right?*'

'Okay.'

Matthew started towards the girls.

'You stay away from us,' Flic said sharply.

He stopped dead in his tracks.

'What's *happened?*' Chloë, in tears, asked her sister. 'Why are they fighting?'

'We're fighting' – Mick, halfway up the stairs, answered her loudly – 'because your sick fuck of a stepfather—'

'Mick, will you be *quiet!*' Isabella yelled at him.

'—has been interfering with your sister,' Mick finished.

'*Mick!*' Isabella was appalled.

'Kid's better off knowing,' he said over his shoulder, 'before he does the same to her.' He stomped on up the stairs and disappeared.

Matthew felt violently sick. He leaned against the wall.

'Matthew?' Isabella looked at him warily. 'Are you all right?'

'Great,' he said. 'I'm just great.' The shaking was worse now. 'I've just been told I'm . . .' He had to stop, couldn't get the words out, didn't *want* to.

Isabella went to the girls, shepherded them into Imogen's room, then came out again, closing the door behind her.

'I really think it would be best,' she told Matthew, 'if you go downstairs. I'll come in a few minutes. We can talk then.'

'What exactly am I being accused of?' His voice was trembling.

'Go down,' she said again. 'I'll come.'

She came to the study about fifteen minutes later. She was carrying a mug of coffee in one hand, a plastic bin bag in the other. She gave him the mug, then opened the bag and showed him what was inside.

'Your towel has blood on it,' she said quietly.

He stared at her, struggling to absorb unspoken implications.

'I want to let you explain,' Isabella said.

'Explain *what*?' he said. 'I don't have a clue what's going on.'

'You could start with the blood.'

Matthew held the mug of black coffee to his lips, tried to take a sip, but the trembling was too bad, he had to set it down on the desk. His mind was doing strange things, slipping back and forth over other bad moments during the past year, other times when he'd experienced lurches of dismay, bad gut feelings. There was quite a collection of those times.

Nothing to compare with this.

'I can't explain the blood,' he said. 'I can't say I cut myself, because I didn't.'

It came to him then, abruptly, chillingly, that maybe he ought not to have this conversation with Isabella, that he ought perhaps to call Jack Crocker. But the act of doing that, of actually calling a lawyer, it seemed to him, would take this instantly out of the realms of bizarre-morning-nightmare to the nastiest kind of reality. Besides which, he thought he could trust Isabella. And he had nothing to hide.

He told her exactly what he had woken to. Told her he'd only noticed the blood – if that was what it actually had been – when he'd got under the shower.

'What's Imogen been saying?' He came back to it, finally, had not wanted to ask, did not really want to know.

'Nothing,' Isabella said. 'Not really, not yet. But . . .'

'But?' The word was quiet but harsh.

'She's covered with scratches, Matthew.'

Horror seemed to grip him, to actually *seize* him, by the throat, in his gut. He felt unable to speak.

'On her thighs.' Isabella paused, swallowed. 'And there are bruises.'

'Bruises,' he repeated, his voice deader now, his mind trying hard to shut down, to absent itself from what he was hearing.

'She told Flic it was you.'

'I thought you said she hadn't said anything.' Clutching at straws.

'Just your name.'

'According to Flic.'

'Yes,' Isabella said. 'But I have seen her legs.'

Matthew looked at the mug on the desk, tried to fasten his eyes on it, to stay focused, as if that might help anchor him somehow, keep him from going out of his mind. And then, after a long moment, he looked back at Isabella.

'Surely,' he said, 'I don't have to tell you that I would never touch a hair on those girls' heads?'

She said nothing.

'For God's *sake*, Isabella.'

'I don't know what to think,' she said, helplessly. 'Of course I find it hard to believe you would do such a thing—'

'I would *die* before I'd do anything like that!' Shock was building again, more mightily than before, any numbness dwindling. 'You've lived with me for a long time now, Isabella. You *know* me.'

'It's very difficult for me,' she said. 'I can't ignore what Flic told me – I can't ignore the bruises and the scratches.' She paused. 'Or this.' She held up the bag with the towel.

Matthew told himself to hold on, to *think*.

'Have you tried talking to Imo yourself?'

'She won't speak about it.'

'Maybe because there's nothing to say. Nothing real.'

His dreams came back to him again suddenly, their *content*, abstract and vague as they had been. 'I dreamed that—' He stopped abruptly.

'What did you dream?' Isabella asked curiously.

It hit him.

'The chocolate,' he said. 'The hot chocolate Flic made last night.'

'What about it?'

'You didn't have any, did you?'

She shook her head. 'I don't know about chocolate. Maybe I was upstairs.'

261

Matthew stood up, suddenly. 'God.'

'What?' Isabella looked perplexed. 'What, Matthew?'

'Flic brought me my hot chocolate specially – she never does that kind of thing for me, does she?'

'Sometimes she does,' Isabella said.

He didn't answer, his mind working overtime. 'My mug.' He saw her looking at the mug on the desk. 'Not this one. The one with my chocolate. I left it . . . I *think* I left it in the drawing room. Have you cleared it away?'

'Not yet. I haven't done anything yet.'

'Thank God.' He went past her to the door, moving fast, out into the hall and into the drawing room. The mug was gone. He roamed around the room for a moment or two, scanning book-shelves, end tables, even the floor. No mug.

He passed Isabella again, in the hall, and went into the kitchen. Two mugs stood in the sink, together with the milk pan and a spoon. He looked at the dishwasher. Its door was shut tight, the glow of the ON indicator dim in the morning light.

'Sure,' he said under his breath, then turned around and saw that Isabella had followed him in and was looking at him quizzically. 'Think I'm nuts talking to myself?' He smiled wryly. 'Not as nuts as you'll think when I tell you what I figure happened here.'

He turned the switch to OFF and opened the door a little way, let steam swirl out for a moment, then opened it fully and pulled out the upper rack.

'Okay,' he said, harshly, and pointed with his right index finger into the sink. 'One mug for Flic, one for Imogen.' He stepped back with a touch of bitter theatricality and pointed into the machine. 'And one for Matthew.' He looked at Isabella. 'See that?'

'Yes.' She was mystified, humouring him.

'I didn't put it in there. Did you?'

'No.'

'I didn't switch on the machine last night, or this morning. Did you?'

'No, I didn't,' Isabella said.

'I left my mug in the drawing room last night and went up to bed, *after* Flic and Imo had gone up.'

Isabella said nothing, still perplexed.

'Someone, therefore, had to have come downstairs, collected my mug, put it in the dishwasher and switched it on.' Matthew

262

knew how he had to be sounding, but he was past caring. 'You're thinking "big deal", right?' He nodded. 'Right. I don't blame you.'

'I'm trying to understand,' she said, gently.

'You know what?' he said. 'Don't bother. But maybe Mick is right about one thing. Maybe you should call the police. In fact, maybe I should call them myself, tell them what *I* think happened.'

'And what is that?'

'That someone – Flic – put something, some kind of drug – maybe a crushed-up sleeping pill, I don't know . . . But *something* in my mug of hot chocolate, just enough to combine with the wine and the scotch I had with Sylvie before dinner, so I wouldn't wake up . . .'

'Matthew?' Isabella sounded anxious.

'Except, of course, if I did tell the cops that story, without the remains of my chocolate to give them for testing – if they were even remotely *interested* in listening to my side of things, which is doubtful – they wouldn't believe me, would they?' He paused. 'Especially not when my stepdaughter has scratches on her, and you have my towel with blood on it, which is probably hers.'

He heard a sound, from the staircase.

'Isabella?' It was Flic, calling quietly.

'Coming.' Isabella looked at Matthew. 'I must go upstairs.'

'Of course,' he said. 'Go see to my stepdaughters.'

'And I have to talk to Mick. He's going away this morning, remember?'

Matthew did remember vaguely, something about some gigs in Ireland. 'I expect he won't want to go now,' he said. 'Not if it means leaving you with a suspected . . .' He stopped, turned away, gripped the edge of the sink.

'Are you all right?' Isabella asked.

'No,' he said. 'Far from it. But go up and see the girls.'

She started out of the room.

'Isabella?' he called her back.

'Yes?'

'Do one thing for me, please. Tell Chloë it's not true.' His voice was choking up. 'Please do that for me.'

Isabella was pale, her dark eyes full of dismay. 'If I tell her that, it's the same as telling her that her sisters are liars.'

Matthew shook his head. 'Can't have that,' he said.

\*

263

He went back to the study, sat down, stared at the telephone. He thought about calling Sylvie, getting to her before the others did – if they hadn't already – but then he figured that would be pure selfishness, dragging her into new misery simply to get in the first blow. Time enough for that later.

He made a decision, leaned forward, flipped through his address book and dialled Jack Crocker's number. Being a Saturday morning, a machine picked up, but the message included a mobile number for emergencies. He scrawled the number down and dialled again.

Voice mail. He left a message.

*Now what?*

He couldn't stay here. Not unless they were going to call the cops. If they were going to do that, he *had* to stay or risk being perceived as a possibly guilty runaway. But if they weren't, if they were going to maybe sit on it for a while, talk to Sylvie, as they would surely need to, then he was not prepared to sit it out here in the enemy camp.

He thought of his office. Not always the most comforting of places either, but suddenly the thought of his drawing board, and even the paperwork that had been piling up all week, seemed halcyon by comparison with this.

He went to talk to Isabella.

# 42

'Where's he gone?' Mick asked Isabella.

'To work.'

'Is he coming back?'

'Of course. He lives here.'

'Then I can't go to Ireland.'

'You have to go – you can't let down the band.'

Mick looked at his bags and instrument cases, all ready packed in the middle of the floor of the attic apartment. His aggression was mostly spent now, the rest of his personal weekend coming back into focus. 'I still think you should call the cops, baby.'

'Not unless Sylvie says so,' Isabella said. 'As soon as you've gone, I'll phone her, tell her what's happened, and then we'll see.'

'Make her come and stay,' Mick told her. 'I don't want you staying here unless there's another grown-up with you.'

'I won't need protecting from Matthew.'

'I suppose not,' he agreed, darkly, 'if he's into kids.'

With Mick gone, Isabella tried phoning Sylvie, but got no answer. She went to check on Chloë – who was, thankfully, getting ready to go to Beatrice's for the day – and then on Imogen, who was lying down after a warm bath. Isabella had told her *not* to wash in case the police were called in, but Imo had replied, quickly, harshly, that she was sure that sort of advice only applied to rape victims, and rape was not what had happened to her. She wanted a bath, *needed* to try and relax, she had said, and Isabella, glad that she was, at least, speaking about it, had not felt equipped to argue the point.

'How are you feeling now?' Isabella sat on the edge of her bed.

'Not so bad,' Imo said. 'Sleepy.'

'That's good.' Isabella stroked her hair. 'I still think you should let me phone Dr Lucas.'

'I don't want to be poked about.' Imogen was instantly tearful.

'All right,' Isabella soothed her. 'Though your grandmother may call him anyway when she comes.'

'Have you talked to Groosi yet?'

'Not yet.'

'Tell her I'm okay when you do. I don't want her upset.'

'I'll tell her, don't you worry.'

The office was quiet, deserted so far as Matthew could tell but for Steerforth and MacNeice, who had been on their way up to the third floor with polystyrene coffee cups as he had arrived.

'Looking for overtime?' MacNeice had asked.

'Just some catching up,' Matthew said.

'Sucker for punishment,' Steerforth remarked.

Wasn't *that* the truth?

He attempted some work, but was abjectly failing when he heard a sound and looked up to see Phil Bianco standing in his cubicle doorway, watching him.

'Good morning,' Matthew said.

'Glad to see you,' Bianco said. 'I was going to let this wait till Monday, but since you're here . . .'

'What can I do for you?' Matthew stood up.

'Be in my office in ten,' Bianco told him.

In Aethiopia, Isabella had tried Sylvie again, then gone to talk to Flic, finding her in the kitchen brushing Kahli by the open back door.

'Your grandmother's still not answering.'

'I think she's having her hair done.'

'It's early for her,' Isabella said.

'Highlights today,' Flic said. 'They take longer.' She stopped brushing the dog, who whined and pawed at her for more. 'Thought any more about the police?'

'I thought we agreed we'd wait for your grandmother.'

'I suppose.'

'I think it's better.' Isabella paused. 'Did you switch on the dishwasher last night or this morning?'

'No. Why? Isn't it working?'

'It's working fine,' Isabella said.

'Good,' Flic said, and went on brushing the dog.

Matthew knew there was another problem when Bianco failed to invite him to sit.

'I've had a visit,' the MD told him. 'Two officials from the Inland Revenue, asking questions about you.'

For one second, weakness and defeat struck Matthew, then renewed anger took over. A cold, fortifying kind. 'What kind of questions?'

Bianco didn't answer directly. 'I guess it's only fair to tell you that I felt I had no choice but to tell them about the Christmas gift *confusion*.' He stressed the word with a thin smile. 'You should also know that VKF is starting to have a few doubts about your employment.'

The anger kept Matthew's mind sharp. 'If they didn't come about the gifts, why were they here?'

'I didn't call them, if that's what you mean.' Bianco paused. 'If I were you, Gardner, I think I'd be getting myself a lawyer.'

Chloë had just been picked up by Beatrice Lang's mother when Isabella told first Flic – watching *Now, Voyager* in the drawing room – and Imogen, still in bed, that she was going up to the attic for a while to take care of some chores.

'If you want me,' she told Imogen, 'just call.'

'I'm going to sleep some more,' Imo said.

'Best medicine,' Isabella agreed.

Back in his office, Matthew was finding it impossible to concentrate. Not that, after Bianco's parting shots, there seemed much point in working overtime.

He tried Crocker again, left a second, more urgent-sounding message, then, on impulse, called Kat.

'You just caught me,' she told him. 'I've got an interview first thing Monday, so I'm going shopping with some friends for something to wear.'

'Enjoy,' he said, loath to bring her down. 'Find something to knock 'em dead with.'

\*

Isabella had stripped their bed and emptied Mick's dirty washing sack that hung on the back of their bathroom door, so while the skylight window was open, airing the place, she decided to put a load into the washing machine.

On her way down, she paused on the landing.

Sounds of activity came from Imogen's room.

She tapped on the door and went in. The teenager was on her knees, stuffing something into a black bin bag.

'What are you doing, Imo? You should be resting.'

Imogen twisted the top of the bag, held on to it. 'I couldn't sleep.'

'No need to clean your room.' Isabella smiled. 'Of all times.'

'I feel better doing something.' Imo seemed defensive.

'So go for a walk, maybe, with Kahli.' Isabella went towards her, began to reach for the bag. 'Give me that and I'll throw—'

'I'm not finished yet.' Imogen held onto it.

'No more work.' Isabella was firm. 'Tomorrow, if you like, you can clean every room in the house, but not today.'

She put down her laundry, reached for the bag again, made a light-hearted grab for it, but Imogen yanked at it unexpectedly and one of the plastic seams ripped, emptying the contents out over the carpet.

'Now look what you've done,' Imogen snapped, scrabbling to try to stuff a leather portfolio and some loose sketches back into the bag. 'Why don't you mind your own business?'

'Leave it, Imo.' Isabella knelt down to help.

'No! Just go away and leave me *alone*!' Imogen clutched something close to her chest.

Isabella looked at her. She was very pale, with two splashes of high colour on her cheeks. She looked intensely guilty.

A stab of misgiving struck her.

'Show me that, please, Imo,' she said, quietly.

'No.' Imogen was breathing hard, almost panting. 'Go away.'

'I'm not going anywhere.' Isabella looked more closely at what the girl was grasping so tightly, saw that it was another plastic bag, smaller and white. 'What's in there?'

'It's private,' Imogen said, harshly, close to tears. 'It's *mine*.'

Ordinarily, Isabella was a great respecter of privacy. But something was going on in this room right now, she felt, something different and significant. And in view of all that had happened earlier, and in view of the manifest and complex emotions – guilt high among them – in Imogen's eyes right now, she felt instinctively that giving in and turning away would be wrong.

'Whatever it is,' she said, 'it's making you very upset.' She held out her hand. 'If you prefer, we can wait for your grandmother.'

'Bitch,' Imogen said.

'Thank you,' Isabella said. 'Which is to be? Me or Groosi?'

Imogen sagged, let the white bag fall. 'It's nothing, anyway. Have it if you want, you nosy cow. Mick might like it.'

Isabella picked up the bag, looked inside, frowned, reached into it and withdrew something strange and ugly. It was leather and metal, a belt of some kind . . .

She made a small noise of shock, dropped it, stared at Imogen.

'It's not mine,' Imo said.

'That's not what you said a moment ago.'

'It *isn't* mine.' Desperate now. 'I'd forgotten it was there.'

Suddenly, the contraption on the floor between them ceased to be uppermost in Isabella's mind. Something else, however, seemed painfully clear.

'It wasn't true, was it?' she asked softly. 'What you told Flic about Matthew?'

Imogen said nothing, just stared at her, tears still in her eyes, unshed.

'Imogen, tell me the truth. Please.'

'We made it up.' Imo said it so quietly it was almost inaudible.

'What?' Isabella asked.

'We made it up,' Imogen repeated, loudly, defiantly. 'Flic and I. We made it up to get back at him.'

'Shut up, Imo.'

They both turned at the sound of Flic's voice.

'He hasn't had any *punishment*,' Imogen went on.

'Imogen, shut *up*.' Flic came into the room, looked down at her sister, barely holding onto her anger. 'Have you no sense at all?'

'It's only Isabella,' Imogen said. 'She's family.'

'No,' Flic said. 'She isn't.'

Isabella stared up at her. 'How could you do such a thing?' She remembered the scratches, the bruising, the blood. 'How . . .?' She felt nauseous, got to her feet, wanting, *needing*, to get out of there.

'Why don't you leave us for a bit?' Flic asked her, coolly polite.

'Don't blame Imo for telling the truth.' Isabella was finding it hard to speak to her normally. 'Don't hurt her.'

'Why should you say that to me, Isabella?' Flic enquired.

Isabella had to swallow before she could answer. 'Her legs.'

'I didn't do that to her,' Flic said.

Isabella stared at her again, and then the nausea hit with a vengeance, and she ran from the room, heading for the bathroom – then, abruptly, jerkily, she changed her mind, took a deep breath, brought herself back under control, and went downstairs.

Matthew was still in the office. Didn't know where else to go. A hundred places or more beckoned – he was in London, after all. But none of them would make him feel any better, so for the moment, while he still *had* an office, he figured he might as well stay in it.

Bianco had left a little while ago, and Steerforth a few moments afterwards. It had occurred to Matthew for a moment that Bianco might ask him to leave too, that he might no longer trust him to remain on VKF premises alone. But MacNeice had not left, so maybe that was why Bianco had said nothing, or maybe he was just being paranoid.

That word again.

'Just because you're paranoid . . .' Matthew muttered, leaving the rest of the axiom unsaid.

He couldn't face the Dagenham project, so he hunched over his drawing board and began to doodle. Back home in New York, in his apartment on Fifty-second Street, he had often spent Sunday mornings – after the obligatory journey through the *Times* – doodling on a big sketchpad, and sometimes, though not often, the scrawls had turned into something more promising.

He didn't anticipate anything like that today, but at least with Bianco out of the building he could allow himself the luxury of a little freestyle sketch-therapy, something to vent his inner feelings on. And it did help, just a little, there was a smidgen of liberation in those strong, downward and horizontal thrusts of charcoal . . .

Until the charcoal snapped, and Matthew leaned back in his chair and saw that he had indeed graduated from the freedom of abstract doodling. Though there was little comfort in what seemed to have suddenly appeared on the paper before him.

It looked, undeniably and uncompromisingly, like a jail cell.

Downstairs, Isabella was pacing, ignoring Kahli's plaintive whines and scratches at the back door as he begged to be let out.

She needed, badly, to talk to Matthew, but this was definitely not a conversation for the telephone. Nor, even if she could reach Sylvie now, was it something she was keen to burden her with, certainly not without Matthew present for back-up.

She looked at the sleek silver watch Mick had bought her for Christmas. She knew where Matthew's office was, knew she could take the Northern Line to close by. If she left now, right away, if she was lucky with the trains, she could be there in half an hour or so.

What if she missed him, she asked herself as she walked quickly up the stairs, deliberately averting her eyes from the girls' rooms and going directly up to the attic? What if he'd already left?

Her boots lay on the floor, high-heeled and impractical, but Isabella had never had any difficulty walking or even running in high heels, had been wearing them since she was sixteen, and anyway they were *there*, and she didn't have time to think about sensible shoes now, and her coat was down in the hall cupboard, and here was her bag – and yes, her purse was inside – and she was heading back down the stairs, not looking back, and Kahli was running back and forth in the hall, and if no one let him out soon he'd probably pee in the house, but that was too bad, that was the least of her worries now. And even if Matthew had left the office, even if she didn't get to speak to him, even if she was not, for once, doing the perfectly correct, most responsible thing – and she had always been *very* responsible, hadn't she, ever since she had first come to Caroline so long ago, had always put the needs of the girls before her own . . . But right now, right this minute, only one thing seemed to matter.

She wanted, *needed*, to get out of the house.

At Imogen's window, Flic watched Isabella leave, saw her hurry along the path, debate for a moment which way to go, then saw her turn left.

271

'Right.' She turned around, spoke to Imogen, still on her knees on the floor. 'I'm going out.' She walked to the door, moving fast. 'You stay here, clean up this mess, get rid of it.'

'Where are you going?'

'Put it all in another bag and go and dump it in someone else's wheelie.'

'Okay,' Imogen said.

'Don't go anywhere else, don't even answer the phone.'

'What if Groosi calls?'

'Don't answer, pretend you're asleep.'

'What are you going to do?' Imogen looked scared.

'Whatever I have to,' Flic said.

# 43

Isabella was on the southbound platform at Hampstead station, waiting for the next train. It was very crowded with shoppers, tourists, all kinds of people, everyone looking so normal that she envied them.

Usually, when she took the tube, Isabella went to Belsize Park because it was a downhill walk from the house, but Hampstead was closer, so she'd come here, and now her legs were aching, and it *had* been silly of her to wear the boots, but all that had seemed to count at that moment had been getting out, and maybe, if she was lucky, she would find a seat on the train when it finally came, though she doubted it with all these people waiting . . .

She looked up at the sign for about the fifth time.

CHARING CROSS        4 MINUTES

She still felt a little sick, and her heart was pounding uncomfortably hard, but at least she was out of there, and she'd made up her mind that she would not go back unless she knew that someone else would be there with her, and she didn't care if that was Matthew, or Sylvie – poor Sylvie – or someone else, even Susanna, and when had she ever felt that she would actually be glad to see *her*?

When Mick got back from Ireland, Isabella thought that perhaps she might suggest it was time to consider moving on. It was all so dreadfully different now, with Caro gone. Nothing was the same, nothing felt right any more, it was all so unhappy, and now, after *this* . . .

'Sick,' she muttered, and felt the woman to her right cast a glance at her. But it *was* sick, that horrible, disgusting thing that Imogen had been trying to hide from her. That, and the wounds on her legs . . .

*'I didn't do that to her.'*

What exactly had Flic *meant* by that?

Isabella shook her head vehemently, trying to push the thoughts away, and the woman beside her eyed her again, then moved a little way along the platform, putting several people between them; and the realization that a stranger thought her odd, perhaps even crazy, made Isabella smile for just an instant or two – though, in the circumstances, it was hardly surprising that someone should think that . . .

CHARING CROSS      **2** MINUTES

Still more people were coming onto the platform, and Isabella, who quite often went into the West End on Saturdays, couldn't remember it ever being as busy as this, and there must have been a long gap since the last train, and the crowd building up around her, behind her, was increasing her sense of anxiety, and her heart was beating even more rapidly, and she wished now that she had walked down to Belsize Park, though that would, of course, be just as busy being one stop down the same line . . .

CHARING CROSS      **1** MINUTE

She thought, suddenly, of home, and of her family. Of her parents, who had been so upset when she'd first told them she was coming to London to work as an au pair, but who had nonetheless supported her decision, bestowing on her a thousand cautions about big city life, and men, and exploitative employers. And then she had met Mick, and they had reacted with almost as much horror as if she had fallen in love with a murderer, just because he'd been working as a waiter.

If her parents had so much as an inkling of what had happened over the past twenty-four hours, she thought now, ruefully, they would probably fly over to England and drag her back home by her hair . . .

At last the train was coming . . . there was the familiar rumble, growing louder, the rush of wind, the movement of people all around her.

The push – the sudden hard shove in the small of her back – was so startling, so *violent*, that Isabella cried out as she stumbled. She

274

tried to stop herself, steady herself, but the heel of her right boot tipped sideways, and the stumble turned into a fall, and she was falling forward, and she knew what was coming, and the train's sound was a roar now, and she saw faces, blurring, horrified eyes, open mouths . . .

Her arms reached out, hands clawing, and for an instant she caught at a man's coat, tried to grip it, but reflexively the man yanked himself away from her, and Isabella saw the fear in his face, then, a half-instant later, his terror for *her*, and his arms were outstretched then, but it was too *late*, and she was still falling, forward and down, and the track seemed to be flying towards her, coming to meet her, and the train thundered into the station, horn blaring, and she could hear screaming, her own and someone else's, and then she hit the rails sideways on, and the world exploded right inside her body and inside her head . . .

On the platform, people gasped with horror, some wordless, some shrieking or sobbing. Some fled from the sight, a few pushed closer, craning their heads to see for themselves. A man in a business suit was bent over, retching; an older, elegant woman nearby sank to the ground, her face very pale. And another passenger, a young woman with long blond hair, was being held back by two shocked men to stop her from trying to climb down onto the track . . .

'I have to help her!' she screamed. 'I have to *help* her!'

'You can't help her,' one of the men told her.

'It's too late, love,' the other man said.

'No,' she screamed. 'Oh, God, it *can't* be!'

'Don't look any more,' the first man advised.

'Nothing you can do for her,' the other man said.

They were still holding her, still restraining her, she was still screaming when she saw an old, white-haired man, about fifteen yards along the platform, watching her. Staring at her in horror. A different kind of horror.

John Pascoe.

For one moment, Flic stopped struggling, stopped screaming, and froze, and then she broke loose and hurtled towards him, sobbing, flinging herself at him, and she felt Pascoe's brief hesitation before his arms went around her, held her.

'Oh, John,' she sobbed against his chest. 'It's so awful.'

'It's all right,' he told her, still holding her. 'It's all right.'

Flic drew back just a little, and looked into his familiar, craggy, grey and sick-looking face.

And saw a strange and dreadful expression in his eyes.

There one second, gone the next.

But it had, most certainly, been there.

# 44

They went to hospital together in a black taxi, an eternity later, after the power to the line had been cut, and the paramedics had come, and the transport police – blocking the exits so that names and addresses could be taken before those remaining on the platform could leave; after a young man leaning against the wall beside Flic had pointed to the CCTV cameras and sagely told her that they hardly needed witnesses these days, not with everyone and everything being filmed, though on the other hand, with the station such a mob scene it might be impossible for the cops to actually *see* much that was useful on the tape.

'I wouldn't mind a look myself,' he said.

She had stared at him, her eyes still wet. 'That's so sick.'

'I don't know,' he said. 'Depends.'

'On what?'

'On the old chestnut, you know. Did she fall or was she pushed?'

The police had taken Flic's details, seen she was in shock, then observed that the old man with her was unwell. They had offered an ambulance to take them both to the Royal Free, but old John had become agitated by the suggestion and Flic had told them she was sufficiently *compos mentis* to take him in a taxi.

'Helping him,' she told them, 'would help me a bit, I think.'

'Would you be happier with that, sir?' the officer had asked.

'I don't need to go to hospital,' old John had said. 'I just want to go home.'

'It might be as well to get checked out.' Flic had gently tucked her arm through his. 'And I know I could use the company.'

'Better for you both then,' the policeman had said.

Old John had said nothing.

Poor Isabella had been lifted up, covered and taken away. To the morgue in St Pancras, Flic supposed silently, knowing that was where her mother had been taken.

*Don't think about that.*

'I thought,' she said to old John in the taxi, 'you always said you hated the tube.'

'I do,' he said, his voice still a little quavery, 'but we all have to use it sometimes, don't we?'

'It was so crowded today,' Flic said. 'Not like a weekend at all.'

He didn't answer.

'Shoppers, I suppose.' She paused. 'Like us.'

'It's the dark I hate.' John withdrew a large, neatly-ironed white handkerchief from one of the outer pockets of his green down jacket and wiped his damp forehead, then mopped swiftly at his eyes. 'I'm scared of the dark,' he said. 'Always have been, can you credit that? Foolish old man.'

'You're not a bit foolish, John,' Flic said.

'I'm always afraid the lights will go out.'

'They have emergency lighting,' Flic said.

'I know that,' he said. 'There's no logic in my kind of fear.' He paused. 'Never thought I had to be afraid of the trains themselves.' He shuddered, glanced sideways at her for a second, then looked away again, out of the window. 'Always the unexpected that gets you though, isn't it?'

Flic watched him for a moment or two, saw him wince, suddenly, then clamp his lips together as if he was in pain.

'What's wrong?'

He winced again.

'John, what's the matter?'

'I'm all right.' He fumbled inside his jacket.

'Your spray?' Flic knew, they all knew, that he had a bit of a dicky heart, and sometimes – usually when he thought no one was looking – they'd catch him taking swift drags from some kind of spray medication.

'In my pocket.' He felt inside the jacket again. 'Oh, blast it.'

'Let me help,' Flic said.

'It's all right.' More fumbling.

278

'Let me *help* you, John.' Quickly, Flic slipped her hand inside the jacket, located a pocket and the little spray, gave it to him, watched him use it. 'Okay?'

He nodded, shut his eyes for a moment, then opened them and nodded again. 'Better,' he said. 'Thank you, Flic.'

'You're welcome,' she said.

'My hands,' he said. 'I couldn't seem to . . .'

'It's the shock,' she said. 'I'm feeling it too.'

'Are you?' old John said. 'You seem quite calm.'

'Not a bit of it,' Flic said.

And thought about the CCTV cameras.

And then about the expression she'd seen in his eyes on the platform.

Sylvie was home in her flat when Flic phoned from the hospital with the news.

'Can you come?' Flic was crying. 'Please, Groosi.'

'Of course I'll come. Is Matthew there?'

'He went to work,' Flic said.

'I'll try and find him.'

'Just come,' Flic begged her. 'I need you, Groosi.'

Two road accidents and an overdose had meant that Flic and John had sat in the Accident and Emergency waiting area on the lower ground floor for what seemed an age, so when Sylvie arrived, the old man was still being attended to.

'My poor girl. What a terrible, terrible thing.'

For just a moment or two, being held by her grandmother, Flic felt safe again, *normal* again, and then old John emerged from wherever they'd taken him, and Sylvie drew away from Flic and went to talk to him, and it was purest agony for Flic to have to watch them, yet not *hear* what was being said. And then they both turned around to look at her, and she, who had never had so much as a dizzy spell in her life, thought she might be about to faint.

'What an awful ordeal for you both,' Sylvie said, coming back to her.

'It was so *horrible*,' Flic said. 'Poor, poor Isabella.'

'I can hardly bear to think about it,' her grandmother said, then shook her head. 'Why were you both at the station? Where were you going?'

'Shopping.' Flic paused. 'Isabella wanted new boots.'

279

'But why were you with her?'

And Flic began to cry again.

'It's all right, darling.' Sylvie put her arms back around her. 'It's all right. You don't have to think about it now. They've told John he can leave, and we're all going to go home together and I'm going to call Howard Lucas and have him take a look at you both.'

Matthew reached Aethiopia to find a shattered household, with Dr Lucas attending to both Flic and John Pascoe, who was looking white as a ghost.

'I can't believe it,' he told Sylvie. 'I can't take it in.'

'Neither can we,' she said. 'It's too terrible.'

'Isabella wanted new boots,' Flic was telling the doctor, her voice rising almost to hysteria. 'She said hers weren't safe in wet weather because the heels were so high, and she asked me to come with her to help her choose, and Imo wanted to be left alone, so I went.' She raked her hair with her hands, her gestures jerky. 'I'm not sure, but I think those awful boots might have been what made her stumble, but I couldn't really *see* because there were so many people at the station – far more than usual, weren't there, John?'

Pascoe nodded, but said nothing.

'I always try and stay behind the line on the platform, especially when it's crowded' – Flic's voice edged ever higher – 'but Isabella was in front of me, and there were just so *many* people, and they got between us, and the train was coming in, and it just *happened*, out of nowhere, and it was so horrible, so *horrible*, I'll never be able to forget it as long as I live.'

'It's all right, Flic,' the doctor told her gently.

'No, it's not,' she said. 'No, it's *not* all right, and I can still see her, right after, the way she . . .' Her voice rose shrilly into the air and she stared at Pascoe. 'Can't you, John? Can't you still *see* her?'

The old man nodded, averted his eyes, gazed down at his feet. 'I can still,' he said quietly. 'I can still see all right.'

'Is Chloë still out?' Matthew asked Sylvie.

'Yes, thank God.'

'Maybe she should stay at Beatrice's overnight?' he suggested.

'There's no point,' Sylvie said. 'She'd only want to know what had happened, and if we didn't tell her, she'd worry more.'

He nodded, looked at Flic, whose right hand was now being held by the doctor. She was still very agitated, had not spoken to

Matthew since he'd arrived, had scarcely glanced his way, and as he had just told Sylvie, he was having great difficulty taking in what had happened to Isabella, *more* so, of course, in view of the morning's trauma.

Except that it seemed that Sylvie didn't know – she was certainly *speaking* to him as if she didn't – what had gone on here just a matter of a few hours ago.

He was loath to ask, but he knew he had to.

'Where's Imogen?'

'Upstairs,' Sylvie told him. 'Too upset to come down.'

'Has Dr Lucas seen her?'

'She's refused to see him,' Sylvie said. 'We'll have to keep an eye on her.'

Matthew looked at Flic again, waited for her to say something, but she was too distraught, too obviously in shock, and he supposed he could understand that only too well.

Except that one thought kept going around and around in his head. He found it very hard to believe that Isabella would have gone shopping for boots, of all things, after what had happened.

Not just hard. *Impossible.*

Which meant, of course, that Flic was lying, and that in itself was certainly nothing new, though why she should be lying about Isabella going out to buy boots was something he couldn't begin to comprehend.

Not that it mattered now. When Isabella was dead.

A new thought jolted him. 'Does Mick know?'

She nodded. 'Poor man phoned a while back, from Dublin.'

Matthew heard the sudden unsteadiness in her voice, looked at her sharply. 'How are you doing, Sylvie? Can you cope with this?'

She looked at him bleakly. 'I'll have to. We all will.' She shook her head. 'It's Mick we have to think of. And Isabella's parents, of course.' She paused. 'I haven't phoned them yet. I was . . .'

'I could do that,' Matthew said. 'If you wanted me to.'

'Oh, yes, please,' Sylvie said gratefully. 'That is one thing I would very much prefer not to have to do.' Her mouth trembled a little. 'I suppose I know all too well how they're going to feel.'

By night, the house was running mechanically, engulfed again in the strange, dull, unreal aftermath of sudden death. Chloë had returned, Matthew had seen John home, and Sylvie had brought some belongings from her flat; but now, feeling suddenly too unwell to struggle up and down stairs, she had asked Matthew to make her up a bed on the drawing room couch.

'Are you awake?'

Imogen, coming quietly into Flic's room soon after eleven, asked the question in a low whisper, half-hoping to find her sister deeply asleep.

'What do you want?'

No reprieve there, which meant that Imogen was going to have to ask the next question, the *real* question, the truly dreadful, nightmarish one that had been burning inside her since she'd heard about Isabella.

'What do you *want*, Imo?' Flic's voice was soft but harsh.

Imogen sat near the foot of the bed. 'I have to ask,' she said.

'What do you have to ask?'

Imo licked her dry lips. 'Did you do it?'

'Do what?'

'Isabella,' Imogen whispered. 'Did you do that to her?'

'Push her, you mean?'

Imo nodded, said nothing.

'Of course I didn't,' Flic said, her voice almost, but not quite, matter-of-fact.

'Are you sure?' Imogen paused. 'Only you said, before you went out – before you followed her – that you were going to . . .' She hesitated again, had to take a deep, shuddering breath. 'That you were going to do whatever it took.'

'I did not push Isabella under the train,' Flic said. 'It was providence. Pure dumb luck, that's all.'

'She's *dead*, Flic.'

'I know. I saw it happen.' Her voice was dull. 'It was one of the worst things I've ever seen. Not *the* worst, though. *Uglier* than Mummy or Daddy, but not nearly as bad.'

'I really liked Isabella,' Imogen said.

'So did I,' Flic agreed. 'You know that, Imo. And you know I'd never have wished her harm in normal circumstances, don't you? But thanks to your big, stupid mouth, it's just as well it did happen, isn't it?'

Imogen didn't answer.

'*Isn't* it?' The dullness was gone.

'I suppose,' Imo said, and paused. 'Groosi still doesn't know about this morning.'

'Not yet, no.'

'What do we do now?'

'Now I'm going to sleep,' Flic said.

'And then?'

'Then we go on with the plan.'

Flic slept for two hours, then lay in bed rigidly awake, reliving it all over and over again. The agonizingly slow build-up as they'd waited for the train, the platform filling up.

*Thank God for the crowd.*

The young man at the station had said the mob would make it almost impossible for the police to see much when they looked at the recordings.

She'd forgotten about the cameras.

*Don't think about them now.*

But when she stopped thinking about them, the replaying began again. The sights and smells and sounds of Isabella's long and ghastly fall. Of her actual death. Old John's face. His eyes, staring at her, *into* her . . .

Flic got out of bed and began to pace. She wished she had another of those pills, *more* than one, wished she could have had an injection, the kind Imogen had been given after she'd cut her wrists, wished she could simply go *on* having injections for a long, long time, just stay asleep and dreamless.

*Not possible.*

She had to do what she had told Imo. Go on with the plan, or else everything that had happened would be wasted.

She managed to stop pacing, after a while, and sat in a chair near her window. She did not close her eyes, did not look out at the night. Just sat. Thinking. Not thinking. Thinking again.

For a time, she thought about her mother.

Then her father.

About her childhood.

And then, about Matthew.

It was five-thirty when she picked up the phone and made the call.

'Susanna, it's Flic.'

# 45

It was Matthew who opened the door when Susanna arrived at nine am.

'I'm here to see Sylvie.'

'She's still asleep.'

'I'll wait till she wakes up.'

He saw from her eyes, from the way they regarded him, why she had come, knew that one of the girls must have called her, felt an instant, curious pang of something like consolation. Resignation, he supposed. And a kind of sickening relief. Because finally, surely, this would represent the beginning of the end.

*After this, even Sylvie will want me to go.*

He stepped back.

'Come on in,' he said.

'I know how you must feel,' Susanna said, 'but we can't ignore this.'

'Obviously,' Sylvie said.

'You're still trembling.'

'Yes.'

They were in the drawing room, alone, sitting close together on the couch, Susanna with her arm around the older woman's shoulders, all too aware of the new and dreadful shock she had brought her.

'I'm so very sorry,' she said for the third time. 'I had to tell you.'

'Of course you did.'

'The worst possible timing, I realize,' Susanna said, 'with poor,

284

poor Isabella, but still, we have to think of the girls above all, don't we? In the long-term, I mean.'

'*I* have to think of them, yes.' Still shakily, but firmly, Sylvie drew away.

'I'm not here to tread on your toes,' Susanna said. 'I just want to help.'

'I know you do.' Sylvie was reeling, finding it almost impossible to absorb what the younger woman had told her. 'I'm grateful to you for coming.' She began to rise from the sofa. 'I will talk to the girls, and take appropriate steps.'

'Do you mean the police?' Susanna asked.

'I don't know.' Sylvie sat down again.

'That could be very hard on Imogen,' Susanna said. 'Gentle as I'm sure they would be . . .' She trailed off in doubt.

'I have to ask you something,' Sylvie said. 'In confidence.'

'Of course. Strictest confidence.'

'Do you believe what Flic told you?'

'I don't know,' Susanna said evenly. 'Do you?'

'Please,' Sylvie said. 'No therapy games – I'm not your patient. I know you're aware that other accusations have been made, over the last year or so.'

'Nothing like this,' Susanna said.

'No. Of course not.' Sylvie shook her head. 'I just can't believe it of Matthew. I've come to know him very well.'

'But you can't be sure.'

'No, I can't. And I can't begin to imagine the girls making up something so horrendous. It would be . . .' She stopped, unwilling to verbalize the thought that came to mind.

'Flic sounded very disturbed, absolutely wretched, in fact,' Susanna said. 'I would stake my reputation on *her* believing what she told me.'

'Which was what Imo told her,' Sylvie followed the train of thought.

'I do have reason to . . .' Susanna stopped. 'I do believe that Imogen still has serious, unresolved problems.'

'Imo had problems long before Matthew came on the scene.'

'Yes, she did, but that doesn't mean he may not be responsible for intensifying those problems, whether deliberately or inadvertently.'

'Nothing inadvertent about assault.'

285

'*Sexual* assault,' Susanna added.

Sylvie felt very sick.

'It occurred to me that you might like me to speak to Imogen first.' Susanna paused. 'Professionally, that is.'

'I don't think so.'

'Not immediately, perhaps, but in a day or so?'

'Maybe.' Sylvie was noncommittal. 'I do know you mean well, Susanna, but I think this is something I have to deal with myself.'

'Whatever you learn,' Susanna persevered, 'Imogen will need counselling.'

'Then if she does' – Sylvie got up – 'she will have it.'

Susanna rose too. 'Sylvie?'

'Yes?'

'Don't you find it rather disappointing that Matthew chose not to tell you himself about Imo's allegation?'

Sylvie answered steadily. 'Given what's happened to Isabella since then, no, I don't really think I do.'

'It is something, though, that the police might regard as quite damning, don't you think?' Susanna said. 'If you were to decide to call them.'

'I don't know,' Sylvie answered wearily.

Susanna regarded her with real sympathy. 'It's all too much, isn't it?'

'I expect we'll cope,' Sylvie said.

Susanna stooped to kiss her swiftly on one cheek. 'If you can't, call me. Any time at all. Please.' She turned and opened the door. 'I'll see myself out.'

Sylvie stood quite still for several moments after the door had closed behind Susanna, staring into space. From beyond the door, she heard sounds. Water running in one of the bathrooms upstairs. Chloë on a phone somewhere. Light, female footsteps on the first floor. Kahli barking in the garden.

Life going on.

She had a tremendous urge to lie down, to sleep, preferably for a long time, but she knew, of course, that she would not allow herself to do that, would not, in any case, *be* allowed to do that.

*Take a minute*, she told herself.

She turned, walked to the armchair closest to the window, sank down and closed her eyes.

There was a knock on the door.

Matthew was the only member of the household who would knock.

Sylvie sighed and opened her eyes.

'Come in,' she said.

# 46

'What are you going to do?' he asked, after they had talked for a while.

'I'm not sure,' Sylvie said. 'Talk to the girls, of course.'

'Would you like me to leave? At least while you get to the truth?'

'Not really.' She shook her head, distractedly. 'Oh, Matthew, I don't know.'

'Nor do I.' He spoke openly, found talking to her a relief, as he always did. 'I've been asking myself for the past twenty-four hours whether I should stay or go. Frankly, going would be by far the easiest option. But you and I talked once about my not wanting to run out on the family. This would be running *away*, and I'll be damned if I'll let anyone accuse me of that.'

'You're only talking about leaving the house, not the country. Aren't you?'

'I do think it might be easier for you if I weren't here, maybe just while you talk to the girls. And then afterwards . . .' He paused. 'I can go to a hotel, someplace nearby. It's your call, Sylvie.'

'Not just mine,' she said, softly, sadly. 'I have to listen to my granddaughters.' She was finding it very hard, just now, to look into his face. 'Perhaps you're right about finding somewhere, just for tonight.'

Matthew took a moment, forced himself to swallow the brief gust of pain and rage that rocked him.

'Perhaps I should,' he said.

\*

288

She had not, this time – for the *first* time – told him right away that she believed him. He understood that, of course, was even able to empathize with her to some extent. She was their grandmother, after all, was, with Caro gone, the person closest to them. And whichever way she chose to go, whatever or whomever she chose to believe, ultimately, it would be Caro's daughters who would remain in greatest need of her protection and defence. If she believed Imogen and Flic, then she would, almost certainly, inform the police, and he would be facing the unthinkable. If she decided that he had been speaking the truth, then that would mean *her* facing something potentially much harder, from her perspective.

Either way, he did not envy her.

As to his own situation, unthinkable was an understatement.

And Jack Crocker had still not returned his calls.

'She hasn't called the police,' Flic said to Imogen upstairs, while Chloë was taking her bath. 'Neither of them have. I thought Susanna might do it off her own bat after I told her, but now Groosi will want to talk to you and decide for herself.'

'I don't want to talk about it.' Imogen's eyes were filled with fear. 'Not to Groosi, not to anyone.'

'You won't have to actually *say* anything much about it,' Flic told her. 'We've gone over this, Imo, you know what to do. Just act too freaked out to talk, *refuse* to talk. It'll be okay, they'll all just figure you're traumatized, so worst case, they'll make you see Susanna again or another shrink.'

'They?' The fear was heightening.

'The cops,' Flic said.

'You said they haven't called the cops.'

'I don't think they have.' She paused. 'So I'll have to, won't I?'

'Flic, you can't.'

'Of course I can. You've been assaulted by your stepfather. Who better to call for help than your older sister?'

Fear was turning to terror. 'They'll find out I was lying.'

'No, they won't.' Flic managed a smile. 'It's good that you're so scared, Imo, it'll help convince them.'

'They'll know what I did.' Imogen's voice was half whisper, half shriek.

'Shut up.' Flic's smile was gone. 'Don't you dare talk like that. Not ever again, do you hear me?'

289

'I won't. Just please don't call them, I can't stand it.'

'I have to. It's the plan. It's the way it has to be now.'

'But he'll *go* now, anyway, police or not. He'll have to.'

'Maybe, maybe not,' Flic said. 'This way, we make sure.' She relented a little. 'You won't have to testify in court or anything, Imo. There's no real evidence left. You did all the things you're not meant to, took a bath, washed your nightie.'

'What about his towel? The one with blood on it.'

'Isabella was the only one who knew about that, and I've hidden it.'

'You could get rid of it,' Imogen said.

'Don't be stupid,' Flic said. 'I'm going to keep it in case.'

'In case of what?'

'In case he *doesn't* go. In case they don't kick him out of the country.'

'Maybe we shouldn't have done this,' Imogen said, scared again. 'Maybe it was too much.'

'We did what we had to do. *You* did what you had to.' She stood up. 'Now I'm going to do the same.'

Sylvie had taken a little time to compose herself before what would, inevitably, be a deeply distressing conversation with her granddaughters. She had considered, briefly, taking one of the tranquillizers that Dr Lucas had given her after Caro's death, and which she thought she'd left in her room on the second floor; but tempting as that had suddenly seemed, she knew she needed all her wits about her, so instead she had made herself a strong cup of coffee and then gone for a stroll out in the chilly garden to try and calm herself down. Matthew had come to find her a while back, had told her that he had packed a bag and was going to check into one of the small hotels he'd noticed around Swiss Cottage and would telephone her from there to give her the details. And then, almost as soon as he had gone, just as she had decided she was now ready to talk to the girls, Mick had arrived back from Ireland, and thoughts of accusations and confrontation were pushed – almost mercifully, Sylvie guiltily realized – to the back of her mind.

Mick looked shattered, seemed to have aged a decade.

'I'm not staying,' he said, after accepting her words of condolence and horror. 'I've just come for some of my stuff.'

They were in the entrance hall, just inside the front door.

'This is still your home,' Sylvie pointed out gently. 'At least until you decide what you want to do.'

Mick shook his head. 'Like I said, I just want to pick up a few things.' He paused. 'And I think I'd like to talk to Flic, if you don't mind. About what happened to Isabella.'

'I thought she'd told you.' Sylvie hated the thought of Flic being put through that again. 'On the phone.'

'Not the same, on the phone, is it?' he said. 'And there were things she said that I didn't – don't – understand.' His darkly shadowed eyes were fierce with pain. 'Like why Isabella was at the station. Do you know why she was there?'

'She was going shopping,' Sylvie said. 'For shoes, or boots, I believe.'

'That's what Flic told me,' Mick said. 'Only it doesn't make sense. Not after what . . .' He looked away, chewed at his bottom lip, then looked back at her again. 'Do you know about what happened here yesterday morning?'

'Yes,' Sylvie said. 'I do.'

'That's the bit I don't get, you see? I wanted to call the police – about what Imo told Flic – but Isabella wanted to wait till she'd talked to you. When I left, that's what she was waiting to do, talk to you.' He paused, thinking back, the anguish visible again in his eyes, in the set of his mouth. 'I told her I didn't want her staying here with *him* unless another grown-up was with her.'

'There you are then,' Sylvie said. 'That's probably part of why she went out.'

They heard a sound behind them and turned to see Flic hurrying down the staircase, and then she was in Mick's arms, sobbing out her sorrow, telling him how terrible it was and how much she had loved Isabella, and he was comforting her; and seeing that the bereaved young man was clearly going to be gentle with her, Sylvie guided them both through into the drawing room and said she would leave them alone while she made some tea.

'Call if you need me.'

'We'll be fine, Groosi,' Flic said.

The kettle was just boiling when she heard the doorbell.

'Now what?' she murmured, going to answer it, Kahli running from the kitchen, barking at her heels.

A man in a raincoat and a woman in a navy blue suit stood on

291

the doorstep. Sylvie could not have said exactly why, but even before the man dug beneath his coat and took out his warrant card to show her, she knew they were police officers.

Detective-Sergeant Malloy – the male officer – and Detective-Constable Riley, to be precise, from Hampstead Police Station.

They had come, Malloy – a thin, middle-aged man with a sharp nose, pale face and light-brown, rather deadpan eyes – explained to Sylvie after she had identified herself, in response to a report of an alleged assault against a minor, Miss Imogen Walters, to whom they now hoped to speak.

They also wanted, if he was on the premises, to speak to Matthew.

'Who reported this?' Sylvie felt shaky again, out of control.

'You are Miss Walters's grandmother?' Detective-Constable Riley was a young, round-faced, pretty brunette with a London accent.

'I am.' Sylvie paused. 'Was it Miss Durkin who called you?' It seemed to make little sense given what Susanna had said.

'I called them, Groosi.'

Flic had emerged silently from the drawing room.

Sylvie turned. 'You phoned the police? Without mentioning it to me?'

'I thought you had enough to deal with, after Isabella,' Flic said. 'And I thought you might not want anyone to know.'

'She did right.' Mick came out behind her.

Sylvie turned away from them both, back to the visitors still on the doorstep. 'You'd better come in.'

Chloë came down as they moved in a group towards the drawing room, and Sylvie, acting swiftly and instinctively, instructed her to go back upstairs and stay with Imogen until further notice and, perhaps because Chloë was afraid of the goings-on, or perhaps because the whole scene reminded her all-too terribly of the day of her mother's death, she complied without argument.

Sylvie shut Kahli into the kitchen, then, gathering her wits as best she could, she joined the others, introducing the police officers to Mick and explaining the tragedy that had just befallen him, and the atmosphere in the room seemed to soften as condolences were extended.

'Why don't you go upstairs, Mick,' Sylvie suggested to him quietly, 'and collect the things you wanted?'

292

'They might want to talk to me,' he said. 'I was here, wasn't I?'

Malloy understood Sylvie's wish for family privacy. 'We can have a chat in a while, Mr Bates, if that's all right with you?' His voice was calming and courteous, yet its firmer undertones left no one doubting that the detective-sergeant was in charge.

'Fine.' Mick glanced at Flic. 'All right, love?'

'Yes,' she said. 'Thanks, Mick.' Her eyes filled again. 'And I'm so, so sorry.'

'I know you are.'

Malloy waited until he had left the room and the door had closed behind him. 'I take it Imogen is here?'

'Yes, she is,' Sylvie said. 'She's been resting.'

'And Mr Gardner?' Riley asked.

'Is out.' Sylvie felt, rather than saw, Flic's sharp glance.

'Can you tell us where he might have gone?' Riley asked.

'No, I can't,' Sylvie answered. 'Though he's due to telephone me some time soon.' She paused. 'I can ask him to get in touch with you when he does.'

Malloy thanked her.

'I would like to be present,' she went on, 'when you speak to Imogen.'

'Of course,' Malloy said. 'Your granddaughter's under sixteen, so the law requires a parent or responsible adult to be present.'

'Imo doesn't want to talk about it,' Flic told them abruptly, 'not to anyone. She hasn't even said anything much to me since she first told me what had happened.'

'Our rape counselling team,' Malloy told her, 'is very experienced at dealing with cases such as your sister's.'

'Imo wasn't raped,' Flic said.

'Indecent assault comes under much the same banner, Miss Walters,' Riley said.

'I still doubt they'd get much out of Imo.' Flic was adamant.

'We will need your sister to make a statement,' Malloy said, 'before we can properly pursue the matter.' He paused. 'They'd talk to her very carefully, in a special interviewing suite. She would be made to feel quite comfortable and safe.'

'I don't want Imogen to have to go anywhere,' Sylvie said, 'unless it's absolutely unavoidable.' She explained. 'My granddaughter has been through a great many ordeals, and has found it quite hard to cope. She's received treatment for depression. Which is why,' she added, glancing at Flic, 'I would so much rather have had a chance to speak to her by myself first.'

'You haven't spoken to her about this yet?' Clearly, Malloy was surprised.

'I didn't learn about it until about an hour ago.' Sylvie realized how strange that must sound. 'I was – we've all been – terribly shocked by Isabella's accident.' She paused again. 'I rather think my family were trying to spare me.'

'I see,' Malloy said.

'So who did tell you about it, Mrs Lehrer?' Riley enquired.

'Susanna Durkin, a family friend.'

'The person you first thought had told us,' Malloy said.

Sylvie nodded. 'Flic – Felicity – had phoned her late last night.'

'Susanna's my sister's psychotherapist,' Flic explained.

'And also a friend?' Riley referred to Sylvie's words.

'She was a close friend of my late daughter's.' Sylvie was struggling to keep up with everything, to focus on what was immediately best for the girls. 'Would you mind if I at least tried to have a few words with Imogen before you see her? This all seems to be happening so quickly, getting out of control.'

'Quickly might be the best way of keeping things *under* control,' Malloy said. 'Better than trying to sweep something like this under the carpet.'

'Especially with it being her stepfather she's accused,' Riley added.

'All the more reason,' Sylvie said.

'Would you mind explaining that, madam?' Malloy asked.

'If I'm honest . . .' She glanced at Flic, and stopped.

'Go on, please,' Malloy encouraged.

Sylvie hesitated again, then went ahead. 'I do have to say that I find it very hard to believe that Matthew – Mr Gardner – would do such a terrible thing.'

'My grandmother thinks our stepfather's the cat's whiskers.' Flic sounded flippant, but bitterness sparked in her eyes. 'But he's not. I wish he was.'

The two detectives seemed to take a moment, absorbing the atmosphere.

'Best all round, I'd say,' Malloy ventured, 'if we do have a word with the young lady sooner rather than later.'

'But I'm not at all sure that is best,' Sylvie persevered. 'If you insist, perhaps I could call our GP?'

'Imo cut her wrists a few months ago,' Flic said. 'She's very vulnerable.'

Malloy glanced at Riley. 'I think,' he said, 'we'll ask our own doctor to join us.' He paused. 'If that's all right with you, Mrs Lehrer?'

Sylvie took a long, unhappy breath. 'I suppose it will have to be.'

The interview, once the woman police doctor had arrived at Aethiopia, was as much of a nightmare of frustration as Sylvie had feared. While Flic waited, like a sentinel, with Chloë outside their sister's bedroom, Imogen, silently weeping much of the time, allowed her scratches and bruising to be examined, then sat hunched over on her bed, hugging her legs, trembling but steadfastly refusing to speak.

'I told you,' Flic said outside, when they'd given up.

'Can I go in now?' Chloë asked.

'Good idea, darling,' Sylvie told her. 'Just sit with her quietly.'

'Seems you were right,' Malloy said as they made their way downstairs. 'Perhaps you might be able to persuade her to open up later, Mrs Lehrer. When things have settled down a bit.'

'Perhaps,' Sylvie said tiredly. 'Naturally I'll try.'

'Otherwise, without a formal statement' – he reiterated his earlier words – 'our hands may be tied.'

'But you will talk to my stepfather, won't you?' Flic asked sharply. 'I mean, you've seen the scratches.'

'Most certainly,' Malloy assured her. 'If he's willing to speak to us.'

'What if he doesn't phone?' Flic said agitatedly as they reached the entrance hall.

'I'm sure he will,' Sylvie addressed the detective evenly, 'and I'll ask him to contact you.' She remembered abruptly what he'd said earlier. 'Do you still want to speak to Mr Bates?' She glanced at Flic. 'Mick is still here, isn't he?'

Flic nodded.

'Actually,' Malloy said, 'I'd like a bit of a chat with Felicity first.' He smiled at her reassuringly. 'All right with you?'

'Perfectly,' she said.

'Are you sure about this?' Sylvie asked Flic.

'Why not? I've got nothing to hide.'

The doctor having departed, Malloy, Riley and Flic adjourned to the kitchen, leaving Sylvie free to return to Imogen and Chloë.

'Would you like a drink?' Flic offered, after pushing Kahli into the garden.

'No, thank you,' Malloy said. 'But you go ahead.'

She took a Coke from the fridge, poured it into a glass, sipped it, then sat at the table with the officers. 'Do you want me to tell you what my sister told me?'

'Yes, please,' Malloy said.

She told them slowly, carefully. 'It's difficult for me, obviously,' she said when she'd finished, 'not having been there.' Her smooth forehead creased. 'Imo said she actually thought she was having a nightmare, and by the time she realized, it was too late.'

'Your bedroom's next door to Imogen's, isn't it?' Riley asked.

'Yes.' Flic shook her head. 'And no, I didn't hear anything. If I had . . .'

'Naturally,' Malloy said.

'I asked her why she hadn't screamed. I thought perhaps he'd covered her mouth or something.'

'But he hadn't?' Riley said.

'Imo said she supposed she didn't scream because she was so sure she was dreaming.' Flic shuddered. 'And then, when she realized, she said all she cared about was getting him *off* her.'

'Surprising, though,' Malloy said, 'that she didn't scream for help.'

'Yes,' Flic agreed. 'I would have.'

'So the scratches happened,' Riley said, 'when she was fighting him off?'

'That's what she said.'

'Did she tell you if she'd scratched him?' Malloy asked.

'I asked her that. She said she didn't think so. *I* would have,' she said again, and shut her eyes. 'I still can't believe I didn't hear anything.'

'Take it easy, love,' Riley said.

Flic took a moment, opened her eyes, bit her lip. 'At least,' she said, 'it sort of proves that all the other things were true.'

'Other things?' Malloy asked sharply.

'Nothing like this,' she said. 'But he has been in trouble.' Flic hesitated. 'You should probably talk to my grandmother about that.'

'We will,' Riley said. 'But if you could just give us a hint now, Flic?' She paused. 'You don't mind if I call you that, do you?'

'Not at all,' she said. 'Everyone does.'

'So,' Malloy said. 'These other things?'

When the phone rang, Sylvie – in Imogen's room – picked up the cordless extension and carried it out into the hall to speak, keeping her voice low. 'The police are here.'

'Right,' Matthew said. 'Do you want me to come?'

'No, I don't think so,' she said. 'I told them I'd ask you to get in touch with them. It's a Detective-Sergeant Malloy and a woman named Riley. They're from the station in Rosslyn Hill.'

'I know it,' he said. 'Not much point my calling them now, is there, if they're at the house?'

'I'll tell them you'll contact them later,' Sylvie said. 'Say in about an hour?'

'Sure.' Matthew felt his stomach quake.

'I think it would be best if you do go of your own accord.'

'Yes.' He remembered why he had phoned her. 'All the small hotels I tried were full, so I've checked into the Marriott.'

'Is it very expensive?' It was a relief for her to think of something else. 'Would you let me help?'

'Absolutely not.' He paused. 'Besides, I may not need a hotel.'

'I don't know,' Sylvie said anxiously. 'I do think it was the right thing for you to do, just while I sort things out with the girls.'

'I didn't mean because I'd be coming back to the house,' Matthew said wryly. 'I meant that the police may have something else in mind.'

'I'm sure *that* won't happen.' Sylvie tried to sound positive.

'I guess it depends on what Imo told them, doesn't it?'

'I can't talk about that. I'm sorry, Matthew.'

'I wouldn't expect you to tell me, Sylvie.'

'I mean that I'm sorry about everything,' she said. 'It wasn't me who called them, you know.'

'I wouldn't blame you if you had,' he said.

\*

297

The detectives left a short while later, after going up to the top floor for a few words with Mick.

Chloë came downstairs as soon as Sylvie had closed the front door on them.

'I want to know exactly what's going on,' she said.

'All right, darling,' Sylvie said. 'Later.'

'Not later.' Chloë, whose hair had recently been cut quite short, erasing even more of the remnants of softer childhood, was determined. 'I'm fed up with having to stay upstairs and not being told anything. I'm not a bloody baby any more, and I'm not budging till you tell me.'

'Take it easy,' Flic said. 'I'll tell you.'

'No,' Chloë said. 'I want Groosi to tell me.'

'Groosi's very tired,' Flic said. 'She needs to rest.'

'I'm sorry,' Chloë told her, 'but she'll have to rest after she's told me.'

For almost the first time that weekend, Sylvie smiled.

'It's all right, Flic,' she said. 'Chloë's absolutely right.'

'Thank you,' Chloë said, and turned her back on Flic.

# 47

The unthinkable, it seemed to Matthew, sitting in the small, stuffy, claustrophobic interview room, was already well underway.

He had come to the police station of his own accord, had not been arrested, but that made the nightmare no less real or appalling.

Detective-Sergeant Malloy and Detective-Constable Riley had both been civil enough to him since he had arrived on the dot of four o'clock. Jack Crocker had, finally, surfaced from the golf course and was on his way. Malloy had told Matthew that he was free to leave at any time and was, of course, entitled to wait for his solicitor, but Matthew had found the prospect of waiting any longer unendurable.

'You understand, Mr Gardner, why we've asked to see you?'

Malloy still sounded civil enough, Matthew thought, but colder – as they said in his own, oh-so-distant and, at that instant, yearned-for country – than a witch's tit.

He nodded. 'I think so.'

'In your own words then,' the detective-sergeant said. 'What happened yesterday morning?'

Matthew shook his head, gazed unseeingly down at the plastic cup of coffee that a uniformed police woman with a shiny, eager face had brought him earlier, but which he had not yet touched.

'Mr Gardner?'

'I'm sorry. It's just that you said yesterday,' Matthew explained, 'and it feels more like a week ago to me.' He paused. 'You heard what happened to Isabella – to Mrs Bates?'

'We did,' Malloy said. 'Very tragic.'

'Yes,' Matthew said.

'So,' Malloy prompted. 'Yesterday?'

'There isn't that much to tell you.' Matthew shook his head again. 'I came out of my bedroom first thing and found what felt like a lynch mob outside my door.'

He told them all he remembered about what had gone on, about his fight with Mick, about learning from Mick and Isabella that Imo had accused him of assaulting her.

'I couldn't believe it.' He shook his head again.

'Couldn't you?' asked Malloy.

'No. It was the most enormous shock.' He paused, abruptly uncertain of whether or not to continue this way, without Crocker or some other lawyer at his side.

'Go on, please,' Malloy said.

'When I say it was a shock' – Matthew began to choose his words more carefully. – 'I'm talking about the *kind* of accusation that was being made against me.' He paused. 'It wasn't the first time that my stepdaughters – the older two, not Chloë – had falsely accused me or tried to make trouble for me.'

'What kind of trouble?' It was the first time Riley had spoken since the start of the interview.

'All kinds,' Matthew said, ironically. 'All sizes. Small, medium and pretty damned large. Nothing as big, as *disgusting*, as that though. So it was a hell of a shock.' He looked at both detectives for a moment. 'If we're going to have to get into this properly,' he said slowly, 'then I'm going to have to tell you a whole bunch of stories that I'd much sooner not have to. About things that have gone on; things my stepdaughters have said to me, done to me, or done in my name. Things that, for Caro's – my wife's – sake, I never wanted to speak about outside the family.'

'Can't hurt your wife any more,' Malloy pointed out.

'No.' Matthew paused. 'But they're still her children, and strangely – and probably, mostly for Caro's sake – I do still care about what happens to them.' He paused. 'I also care, very much, about my mother-in-law's feelings. She's been rather ill in the past few months. She's had more than enough to cope with, without this.'

'Sounds as if you've had more than your fair share too,' Malloy said.

300

'I guess so.' Matthew wondered if the touch of sympathy was genuine.

There was a knock, the door opened, and the shiny fair-haired policewoman popped her head round. 'Mr Gardner's solicitor is here, sir.'

'Show him in,' Malloy said.

# 48

Just before five, unable to bear the suspense any longer, Susanna telephoned Sylvie and was brought up to date.

'You sound exhausted,' she said.

'I suppose I am,' Sylvie said.

'Anything I can do? Try talking to Imo? Or just come to lend you a hand?'

'I don't think so,' Sylvie said. 'Not today, at least.'

Susanna came away from the phone with a feeling of dread, diluted only very slightly by relief. Flic had at least passed the burden on, and even though Susanna knew that Caro would have been desperately unhappy about the whole mess, probably it was better that a halt be called. Even a halt as ugly as this.

Poor Matthew.

She was startled by the wave of pity, wondered what exactly it meant. If it meant that she believed him innocent, then that also meant she thought Imogen guilty of the most appalling and vindictive lies. Though if the teenager was guilty, then a large portion of the blame for that surely lay on someone else's shoulders.

Susanna thought about the awful cache beneath that floor, the almost irrefutable evidence of something deeply unhealthy in Imogen's past, something leading right back to her father. No tremendous surprise there for Susanna. Shock, certainly, and disgust, but no *real* surprise, for her periods of therapy with Caro had taught Susanna more than most about Richard Walters.

First Richard. Then Matthew.

For whether or not Caro's second husband was directly responsible for Imo's continuing downward spiral, he had certainly been a catalyst. At least this horrible allegation was bound to get him out of his stepdaughters' lives, which had, Susanna felt, to be a good thing. And if Matthew was innocent, so long as Imogen refused to talk to the police, they would surely have to let him go, and as disagreeable as the whole experience would be for Matthew, Susanna could not muster too much concern. After all, he had a built-in escape hatch in America. Even if his name was sullied here, he could skulk off home, where he belonged.

If only he'd never come. If only he'd never met Caro in Switzerland. If only he'd stayed in Berlin or gone back to New York. If only . . .

If it weren't for Matthew, Caro would still be here.

So no pity for him.

*Save your pity for Caro's girls.*

And the good news, hopefully, was that involving the police might just lead to Imo's being pushed back into counselling, and whether or not that was with her or another therapist didn't really matter. What mattered was Imo's health.

And to hell with Matthew Gardner.

# 49

Matthew and Crocker were having the private consultation to which they were, by law, entitled. If he wanted to leave, Crocker reminded his client, he could, but the fact was that, tempting as the thought of getting the hell out did seem right now, Matthew also wanted it over with, all questions asked and answered.

'You do realize,' the lawyer had told him right away, 'that this is way out of my field?'

'I didn't know who else to call.'

'They'd have called someone for you,' Crocker said. 'They still would.'

'No,' Matthew said. 'At least you know what went on before this.'

'I trust you haven't told them about that.'

'I was starting to, when you arrived.'

'You shouldn't even have *begun* to mention that stuff,' Crocker said. 'You should have stuck to what they asked and volunteered nothing further.' He paused. 'Do I take it now that your step-daughters were your suspects in the other matters?'

Matthew nodded wearily. 'Surely if I'm claiming that one or both girls set me up for this thing, they're going to need to know what grounds I have for thinking that way?'

'Set you up?' Crocker asked. 'Or made up the whole thing?'

As succinctly as possible, Matthew told him about all the events of Friday night and Saturday morning. About the drinking chocolate that he thought had probably been laced, all evidence washed away. About the bizarre dreams. About the blood on his fingers and beneath his nails. About the towel that poor Isabella had taken from his bathroom.

'I guess,' Crocker said, 'you could have a blood test. Toxicology tests to prove that you'd been doped.'

'It's almost Sunday evening,' Matthew pointed out. 'Would stuff like that still show up in blood tests?'

'I don't know,' Crocker admitted. 'Do you know if they have the towel?'

'They haven't mentioned it. Nor have I, by the way.'

'Thank heaven for small mercies.' The lawyer paused. 'I wish you'd gotten the hell out while you could.'

'I wish you'd find something more constructive than that to tell me, Jack.'

'It's what they're going to be thinking,' Crocker said flatly. 'If you tell them about all the other troubles between you and your stepdaughters, they're either going to think you're nuts for staying with them – no matter how much you loved your wife – or they're going to think you're a Grade A liar.'

'Wonderful,' Matthew said.

'I take it they haven't cautioned you?'

'You mean, did they Mirandize me? Nothing like that. Not yet.'

'What about fingerprints or DNA?'

Matthew shook his head.

'I made a call on my way here,' Crocker said, 'to a colleague who does deal with this kind of work. He said they may ask if you'll consent to being printed and maybe giving a DNA sample – nothing much to that, I guess you know?'

'I've seen it done on TV.'

'He also said they might want your consent to having the police surgeon examine you.'

'To see if she scratched me, is that it?' A new wave of nausea gripped Matthew.

'I'd imagine so,' Crocker said. 'My colleague said that at this stage you have a perfect right to refuse all or any part of it – and they may not even ask.'

'But if I want them to believe I have nothing to hide?'

Crocker shrugged. 'Then I guess you might be wise to cooperate.' He paused again. 'Maybe your instincts were on the money about mentioning the fraud business. If they don't already know about it, it's probably only a matter of time before they do find out

305

and at least you'll have been straight with them.' He paused. 'And if letting them know that you see yourself as the victim blurs their focus a little, that's all to the good.'

'I am the victim,' Matthew said tightly.

They were both silent for a moment.

'Anything else to tell me before we face them?' Crocker asked.

Matthew pondered for a moment, then told him about the time, just days before Caro's death, when Imo had told Sylvie that he had been 'looking' at her inappropriately. 'Her own grandmother didn't believe her,' he said, 'if that helps.'

'Not much,' Crocker said grimly. 'If I were you, I'd keep that to myself.'

Within minutes of the interview recommencing, DS Malloy – as Crocker's colleague had surmised – asked Matthew if he would consent to being fingerprinted and giving a DNA sample. Matthew glanced at Crocker, who made the merest of gestures, which might have been encouragement or might not, and then told Malloy that he would consent. When the question came, seconds later, about the physical examination, Matthew commented that he had the strongest objections to it, but was prepared to undergo it, if it would help convince them of his innocence.

'You're perfectly in your rights to refuse,' Malloy said.

Matthew looked him in the eye. 'I won't refuse.'

The questioning began again. Malloy asked about Matthew's relationship with all his stepdaughters, and Matthew answered each question as calmly as he could manage to. Crocker found a suitable moment to clear the way for Matthew to raise the subject of the Christmas gifts and garage rental cheque, but whether or not Malloy or Riley had already known about the issues, they seemed wholly disinterested in them now.

The most unnerving line of questioning came right out of left field.

'On the day that your wife died, Mr Gardner' – Malloy's voice was smooth and even – 'you were away, weren't you?'

'I was at a golf weekend organized by my firm,' Matthew said, startled.

Malloy looked down at some notes. 'At Selsdon Park Hotel in Surrey.'

'That's right.' Matthew glanced at Crocker, who said nothing.

'I don't suppose you happen to remember exactly where you were at the time of her death,' the detective asked, 'and who, if anyone, was with you?' He looked down again. 'To refresh your memory, Mrs Gardner was estimated to have died between two and three o'clock that Saturday afternoon.'

'My memory doesn't need refreshing,' Matthew said sharply, despite his reeling senses.

'Do you remember where you were at that time?'

Matthew shook his head, still confused. 'I don't know exactly. At a guess, I'd say I was either in the restaurant or lounge.' He paused, glanced at Crocker again, and again got no help from him. 'Why are you asking me questions about my wife's death? One of your own colleagues, a detective . . .' He cast around for the name, but came up blank.

'Detective-Sergeant Ross was one of the officers involved in that investigation,' Riley supplied.

'That's right,' Matthew said. 'He gave evidence at the inquest.'

At last, Crocker laid a hand on Matthew's left arm, stopping him. 'I think I'm as confused as my client, Detective-Sergeant, as to why you're asking these questions.'

Malloy nodded, closed the file on his desk, smiled comfortlessly. 'I don't think we need detain you or your client any further for now, Mr Crocker.'

Riley rose without a word.

'Mr Gardner is free to go?' Crocker asked.

'Quite free.' Malloy paused.

'What about the prints and the sample?' Matthew asked.

'If you still have no objections.' The detective paused. 'Just one more question, Mr Gardner,' he added, as if it were an afterthought, 'if you don't mind?'

'Not at all.' Matthew gritted his teeth.

'An easier one this time. Much more recent.' Another chilly smile. 'Do you remember where you were at approximately twelve-thirty yesterday afternoon?'

The time of Isabella's death. Matthew stared at Malloy, then sideways at Crocker.

'I was in my office. At Vikram, King, Farrow in Bedford Square.' He paused, swallowed hard. 'That's in Bloomsbury.'

'Could anyone confirm that?'

'I don't know. Probably not.' Matthew was still staring at him, a hard bubble of anger rising painfully in his chest. 'My boss, Philip Bianco, was there a little earlier. And two other colleagues. Would you like their names?'

'Yes, please,' Riley stooped to pick up a pen.

'Stephen Steerforth,' Matthew said tightly, 'and Andrew MacNeice.'

'What time did they leave?' Malloy asked.

'I don't remember. You'd have to ask them.'

'All right.' Malloy made a couple of notes. 'That's it for now, Mr Gardner. Thank you for your cooperation.'

Matthew had learned, years before, during a lengthy visit to the dentist in New York, that it had helped to mentally absent himself, to close his eyes and remember something pleasurable. He already knew, as he signed the consent forms in the custody suite, that no attempt at fantasy would help him today. The fingerprinting was easy enough, and the giving of the DNA relatively simple. But the indignity of the physical examination was so great that it took all Matthew's self-control not to withdraw his consent and demand to be let out there and then.

He had been told that if a decision was arrived at not to proceed with the case, or if, at some later date, he was found innocent of any charges, he could, if he applied to so do, witness the destruction of any samples taken.

It was impossible for Matthew to picture any circumstances in which he would ever volunteer to return to this place again.

Crocker had waited for him. They walked out of the building together. It was dark, the fresh, cold air very welcome.

'Okay?' Crocker asked.

'Not really.' Matthew took a couple of deep breaths, then pushed away the memory of the examination and returned to one thing that had been exercising his mind since the interview had ended. 'What the hell does Caro's death have to do with all this?'

'Beats me,' Crocker said.

'They held an inquest, Jack – we were all so scared in case the Coroner decided Caro might have killed herself.'

Crocker said nothing.

'The verdict was open, because no one could work out exactly how she'd fallen, but the Coroner ruled out foul play – there was never the slightest *question* of anything else, of anything suspicious.' A whole new kind of horror was beginning to grip him. 'And then those questions about Isabella.'

'I can't help you there either,' Crocker said.

'I told them it was Isabella and Mick who told me what Imo had said.' Matthew walked on a couple of feet along the broad pavement, then turned around as a fresh thought struck him. 'I'll bet Flic told them I was there at the tube station – *she* was there, you know, when it happened – I'll just *bet* she's trying to link Isabella's accident to me.'

'Maybe.' Crocker's breath misted as he shifted his weight from one foot to the other. He looked awkward again. 'I told you before we started in there, Matthew, this isn't my field. You're going to have to find a good criminal lawyer.' He scratched his right eyebrow uneasily. 'I'll be more than glad to try and help with that, if you'd like me to.'

Matthew felt abruptly colder. He took a step closer and looked into the other man's face. 'You're not quite sure about me, are you?'

'That's not at all what I'm saying,' Crocker said.

'You don't need to,' Matthew said.

# 50

'Are you all right?' Sylvie asked Matthew on the telephone.

She had gone into the study to take his call, was speaking quietly, feeling deeply disloyal to her grandchildren for wanting to speak to him at all, let alone with the very real sympathy she seemed still to be feeling for him.

'As well as can be expected,' Matthew said, 'is the expression that springs to mind. How about you?'

'I've been better,' she said.

In truth, as evening drew in at Aethiopia, Sylvie felt that she was barely hanging on. She felt conflicted about Flic's call to the police, angry and frustrated, yet at the same time filled with a certain respect. At least Felicity was no ditherer, had never faltered in her bad opinion of her stepfather, even if she had, for some time, given the impression of being willing to compromise. Though whether that had been an act of peace, or a total sham, Sylvie was no longer sure.

'Flic's going to bunk with Imo for the time being,' she told Matthew now, 'so I can have her bed rather than hike all the way up to the spare room.'

'Good idea,' Matthew said. 'Better than the couch too.' He paused. 'Are you okay with the stairs to the first floor?'

'I seem to have been up and down non-stop for the past twenty-four hours or so,' she pointed out, 'so the answer would appear to be yes.'

'How's Chloë?' Matthew asked.

'Livid,' Sylvie said. 'With Flic, mainly, for—' She winced, not having intended to disclose who had turned Matthew in.

'It's okay.' He was gentle. 'I more or less figured it out.'

Sylvie didn't speak, did not, still in deference to her grand-daughters, know what she *could* say.

'I'll leave you in peace,' Matthew told her.

'Not quite the word I'd use.'

'Let me know,' he said, 'if you need me.'


He put the phone down, looked around at his hotel room, appointed with everything the traveller could possibly need.

Except those things that *he* needed right now. Companionship. Loyalty. Love. Peace of mind.

He had, a while ago, checked his voice mail and heard Kat apologizing for having been in such a rush the last time he'd phoned her. It would be good, he thought with something approaching longing, to talk to her now.

*And tell her what?*

That he was in exile in a hotel room? That he had just spent hours at a police station because one of his stepdaughters had claimed he'd indecently assaulted her – but that just in case suggesting that he was some kind of paedophile wasn't *enough*, the detectives had wanted to know where he'd been at the time of both his wife's and his housekeeper's deaths? (And, of course, Kat didn't know about Isabella, didn't know about any of the horrors that had unfolded since yesterday morning.)

Hardly stories to tug at the sympathies of a decent young woman.

*I have to talk to someone.*

Karl or Ethan? Not yet. He couldn't face telling them, not until he had no choice, was maybe instructed by his lawyer to look for character references or maybe even bail money.

*Christ.*

If he sat here alone much longer, he was going to go nuts.

He picked up the phone and dialled.


'Why the *hell* did you drag up Mum's death again to the police?'

Imogen was close to hysteria. Flic had just brought her up some supper on a tray and had, for the first time, told her what she'd said to Malloy and Riley.

'You know damned well why.' Flic stood over her sister, between her bed and the camp bed she'd put up earlier.

311

'But it wasn't part of the *plan*.'

'I've made it part.'

'Without asking *me*.'

'I don't have to ask you, Imo.'

'No, all you want to do is *use* me.' Imogen's face was still the same sickly hue it had been all weekend.

Flic's hands clenched into fists. 'You've got a bloody cheek to talk to me like that.' It was an effort keeping her voice down. 'I'm doing this for you – for all of us, remember?'

'But surely we've done enough now,' Imo protested. 'There was no *need* to bring Mum into it.'

Flic's anger fizzled out. 'I know.' She sat down heavily on the camp bed, felt the springs twang beneath her. 'I couldn't seem to stop myself. I was talking to them, answering their questions, and it just seemed to come naturally.' She shook her head. 'I just hate him so *much*, Imo. I just want us to be rid of him.'

'You don't hate him any more than I do.'

'I know.' Flic paused. 'Groosi's upset with me for calling the police without asking her, and Chloë's furious too.'

'Think we can still trust her?' Imogen asked.

'I think so,' Flic said. 'She's still too scared of being found out about the forgeries to shop us.' Her smile was wan. 'And when the chips are down, she's still our little sister. She loves us.'

Imogen was silent for a moment.

'I still wish you hadn't mentioned Mum.'

'I know,' Flic said again.


'I can't believe all this,' Kat said on the phone. 'I just can't take it in. It's monstrous. *They're* monsters.'

'I shouldn't have called you,' Matthew said.

'You most certainly should have,' she said decisively. 'And now that you have, you're going to come here for dinner.'

'I don't want to put you out, Kat.'

'The only way you'll put me out is if you don't come.'

'Don't you have an interview first thing tomorrow?'

'So what? I can still boil water and throw pasta into it.'

'Are you sure?' Matthew asked.

'Get over here,' Kat answered.

\*

Her flat, simply decorated and furnished as it was, felt like a safe haven. She'd opened a bottle of wine, lit an aromatic candle that she said contained lavender and something called ylang ylang, both of which were supposed to promote relaxation, and the water was already bubbling on the stove beside a pan of sauce.

'Smells great,' Matthew said. 'Arrabiata?'

'Waitrose's best,' Kat told him. 'And there's some really good herby bread to go in the oven.'

Matthew sank down into one of her chairs, shaking his head.

'What?' Kat asked.

'I think I must be delusional,' he said. 'For a moment there, I felt normal.'

'You are normal,' she told him. 'It's the things that are happening to you that aren't.'

'I could be arrested any minute.'

'Think you were followed here?' She handed him a glass of red wine.

'I doubt it.'

'Then I don't expect you'll be arrested this evening.'

He grinned up at her. 'What a cheery soul you are.'

Kat shrugged. 'Just climbing down to your wavelength.'

Flic had a headache. A bad one. It had begun a couple of hours ago, shortly after she had answered the phone and heard John Pascoe at the other end.

'How are you feeling?' She had sounded calm, even warm, but her entire body had tensed at the sound of his familiar voice.

'Much better, thank you.'

'Taking it easy, I hope?'

'I'm not much good at that, Flic, you know that. And if you take it too easy, stop for too long at my age, everything seizes up.'

'Still,' she said. 'After that awful shock.'

'Is your grandmother there?' Pascoe asked.

'I'm not sure where she is,' Flic said, though she knew, in fact, that Sylvie was in the kitchen making herself some tea. 'Can I give her a message, John?'

'Tell her I'll be there for work in the morning, if you don't mind.'

Her headache had begun then.

'Isn't that a bit soon?' she asked, casually.

'Not for me. I miss my garden.' He'd paused. 'And my chats with your grandmother, of course.'

And the pain in her head had tightened.


'I should go,' Matthew said, at about ten-thirty.

'Why?' Kat asked from the sofa she'd rescued from the binmen a month back, and which she'd perked up with a red and mauve throw from the Reject Shop.

'It's getting late. You have your interview.'

'It's okay,' she said. 'So long as I get about six hours sleep, I'm usually fine.'

'Are you a good sleeper?'

'My mother claims two gas canisters once exploded in our neighbour's house and I slept through the whole thing, fire brigade and all.' Kat grinned. 'Nothing's changed.'

'I used to sleep pretty well too,' Matthew said.

Kat stretched, got up, came over to his armchair and knelt on the floor beside him. She was wearing a vivid green sweater over black jeans that brought out the colour more intensely in her eyes, and her short, layered red hair was rumpled.

Matthew had a sudden urge to reach out and touch that hair.

'You know what?' Kat said softly.

He shook his head.

'I don't think you should go back to that hotel, however much it's costing.'

'Don't you?'

'I think,' she said, 'that you should stay here.'

He hadn't noticed before that her nose, which was small and rather sweet, had a scattering of freckles. 'I never realized you had freckles,' he said.

'That's because I usually cover them up with make-up.'

'You shouldn't,' he said. 'They're lovely.'

Kat looked at him for a long moment, met his eyes, then looked away.

'What's up?' He felt the shift.

'It just occurred to me,' she said, awkwardness creeping in, 'that maybe it might *not* be all that wise, after all – from your perspective, not mine – for you to stay at another woman's flat just now.' She paused. 'Last thing I want to do is make things worse for you.'

He thought about it. 'Might as well be hung for a sheep.'

She smiled. 'Might as well.'

It struck him then, suddenly, painfully, that perhaps she did not, after all, believe his side of the story.

'What?' she asked.

He shook his head.

'I saw that look,' Kat insisted. 'Tell me. If we're friends.'

'I was thinking,' he said, slowly, 'that I wouldn't blame you if a part of you was wondering if my stepdaughters might be telling the truth.'

'You are joking, aren't you?' Kat said.

Her tone was blunt, matter-of-fact, as if what he had said was absurd, and his doubts vanished as swiftly as raindrops on a hot pavement.

'Thank you,' he said.

Their eyes met again, and this time neither veered away.

'Would it be too soon,' she asked, softer again, 'for you to kiss me?'

*Yes.* A voice inside his head. *Much too soon.*

Yet he kissed her anyway.

Could not stop himself. Did not *want* to stop himself.

Her lips, her mouth, tasted of red wine.

He wanted to go on kissing her, wanted to drown in kisses, to have her wrap him in her arms, to do the same for her, to go on and on and forget everything else.

*Too soon.*

He drew away.

'It's okay,' Kat said, gently.

'I'm sorry,' he said.

'You don't have to be sorry, Matthew.' She smiled at him. 'Nor do you have to go back to your hotel.' She stood up, stretched her legs. 'The couch is a wee bit short for you, but I think you'd be quite cosy, if you'd like.'

'I'd like very much,' he said.

'I'll fetch you a pillow and a blanket then, shall I?'

He nodded. 'Please.' He felt a little dazed, but it was a pleasant feeling, mixed with a tremendous tiredness, and he had no wish for it to leave him. 'Can I help?'

'Just sit there,' she said.

She didn't have to tell him that twice.

# 51

He woke stiff and aching, muzzy-headed for one almost pleasurable moment – before reality descended like a full-scale demoli-
tion job.

Kat was in her kitchen, wearing a dark pin-striped suit with a
long-line jacket and neat, short skirt that displayed her slim legs to
fine effect.

'You look terrific,' Matthew told her.

'I bought it on Saturday.'

'Good purchase.' He looked at his watch. 'You're very early.'

'It's somewhere up in Highgate. I don't want to be late.' She
dumped a coffee cup in the sink. 'Help yourself. Anything I have
is yours, okay?'

'Okay. Thank you.'

'Did you get any sleep at all?'

'More than I've had in a while.'

She checked her Swatch watch. 'Got to go.' Her mind was already
halfway to her interview. 'The phone's yours too, bathroom, whatever. Clean towels on the top shelf of my bedroom wardrobe.'

'Kat, just go. I'll be fine.'

'And unless you want to go back there, feel free to check out of
the hotel.' She hesitated. 'Unless you want to go back home, of
course.'

'I doubt that.' Matthew paused. 'Way things are headed, I might
end up being accommodated by Her Majesty.'

'Don't even *joke*,' Kat said fervently.

He went with her to the door, saw that her portfolio was

propped against the wall, ready and waiting. 'Are you sure you don't mind leaving me here like this?'

'I never say things I don't mean, Matthew.'

'No,' he said. 'I imagine you don't.'

She unlocked the door, stepped out, turned back. 'Are you going to the office? After what Bianco told you, I mean?'

'I don't know,' he said. 'Depends on how long it takes me to find myself the right kind of lawyer.' He smiled at her. 'Scoot, Kat. Break a leg.'

Flic woke in the camp bed, saw that Imogen was still asleep, and lay there, not moving.

Her head was still aching.

But her mind was functioning better.

*No school today.*

Not for her or Imo. Chloë could go – probably already had, since the clock on her sister's bedside table said it was almost eight-twenty.

Groosi must have decided to let them both sleep.

She wondered if old John had arrived yet.

Quietly, carefully, she got out of bed.

Kat's flat, without Kat in it, was alien territory. Matthew had folded up the blanket she'd given him the previous night, had thought about putting it back onto her bed, then thought that might be presumptuous, and had left it instead in a neat square on the couch. He took the slip off the pillow, felt he should wash it, but there was no washing machine, and anyway, washing a single pillow slip would have been wasteful. He considered taking it to a launderette, wondered if there was a pile of dirty washing some-where in the flat that he could take along with it on her behalf, but again that might smack too much of interference in Kat's private life, so he simply folded the slip, too, and placed it on top of the pillow on top of the blanket.

Procrastination was driving him nuts. What he wanted to do was get dressed and go to work, bury himself in dreary Dagenham or in whatever Bianco now deemed him fit to do as lowest-guy-on-the-totem-pole-yet-again. Anything was better than hanging around yet another home in which he did not belong, wondering what to do next, what was going to *happen* next.

Eight-thirty. Too early to call Crocker, the lawyer who at best believed him a fool, but who was, nevertheless, still the only person he knew in this town who could recommend him to a decent criminal defence specialist.

He made himself more coffee, switched on Kat's television, sat in her armchair, only vaguely aware of some young woman being interviewed about a case she was hoping to bring against her local authority, his own mind back in north London, in the slender white house on East Heath Road.

The female house, as he had first thought of it; a house made for women. As it would be again now, after Mick left, as he surely would.

Once *he* was gone. Whether to a jail cell or back to the States.

Back home.

*They might deport me.*

It was the first time that thought had occurred to him. It sent a sick chill through him, made him shudder.

He looked at the time on the screen. Almost eight forty-five.

Perhaps Crocker was an early bird.

His mobile was in his jacket pocket. He remembered the number without checking it, got no answer for several rings, then the message telling him the office was open from nine until five-thirty and asking if he wanted to leave a message.

Fifteen more minutes. No point saying anything to the machine.

He wondered if Kat had reached her appointment yet, realized he hadn't asked her nearly enough questions about the firm she was hoping to join – a small, successful, creative practice, she'd said, looking for a junior associate with AutoCAD skills, all of which could mean anything or nothing. He certainly wished her all the luck in the world, knew he'd miss her if he went back to New York, wondered idly if she would visit him if he went to jail.

*Cut that out.*

Twelve minutes.

Chloë had gone to school, and Sylvie, having seen her off, was resting in Flic's bedroom.

Flic was in Chloë's room, waiting at the window overlooking the garden, when old John arrived. He looked weak, doddery, certainly not well enough for work. She watched him for a while, walking slowly around the garden inspecting the still wintry beds, contemplating what she knew he thought of as his domain.

318

*Foolish old man.*

She had always been fond of him though. John Pascoe was such an integral part of her life, she could not remember a time when he had not been a part of it.

Flic wished that he had stayed at home this morning.

Matthew experienced a dash of comfort when he tried Crocker's office again, for although the lawyer had gone straight into a meeting, he had left word for Matthew to be put through to him if he called.

'I've found you a guy,' Crocker told him. 'Got a pen?'

Matthew saw a wipe-down board on Kat's kitchen wall and, grabbing the felt-tip pen attached to it by a piece of string, he noticed in one corner of the board a clever little drawing of a thin, upstanding wolf in a suit, wearing glasses that sent off cartoon-style sparks into the air. *Bianco.* Matthew made a mental note to tell Kat that, if she chose, she might consider a change of career.

'Okay,' he said, taking the cap off the pen.

'Jasper Hughes, of Reeves & Hughes, in Camden Town, which should be convenient, though more to the point Hughes is reputed to be very good.' Crocker swept right on. 'I've already talked with him, and he's waiting to hear from you.'

Matthew scribbled down the details. 'I owe you.'

Flic took a long, slow, thoughtful bath, trying to calm herself.

It was crystallizing now. She hated *it*, but it was growing clearer nonetheless with every passing minute.

She stepped out of the bath, wrapped herself in a robe and went back to Chloë's room, back to the window.

Her grandmother, who she'd believed was still resting, was outside in the garden, talking to Pascoe.

'Damn,' Flic said softly, and, very quietly, opened the window a little way so that she might hear what was being said.

'. . . no need for you to have come.' Sylvie's voice.

She hadn't missed much then.

'. . . better doing than sitting.' Old John's.

A repeat, almost, of the conversation Flic had had with him the previous evening. She began to relax again. Sylvie was still wearing a dressing gown, and her arms were folded across herself against the chill, so she was bound to come inside again any second now.

Her grandmother glanced upwards. Flic froze, edged back a little way.

'I think it's going to rain soon.' Sylvie's voice floated up to the window quite clearly. 'You'd probably be better off getting on with that little job in your workshop.'

'Good idea,' old John said.

Flic supposed that her grandmother must have turned away, for her voice became less audible, but she heard her say something about seeing John later and not overdoing things. Then she heard the old man saying something that sounded like: 'Don't you trouble yourself.' And then she heard the sound of the back door closing.

She looked out again, saw the old man walking, definitely more slowly than usual, up towards the old shelter. He had two workbenches, one above ground under the strip of corrugated iron roof near the wooden door, one down below. He would, Flic guessed, probably do what he usually did in bad weather: hang up his jacket on the hook on the outer wall of the shelter beneath the roof, turn on the light from the switch on the same wall, then give the old warped door a kick and a yank to open it, and make his way down the stone steps. He kept a kettle down there, and two battered old biscuit tins, one filled with PG Tips tea bags, the other with granulated sugar – old John liked his tea horribly sweet. In the past, Isabella had brought him drinks from the house, and sometimes, at weekends or during school holidays, Flic had taken a cup for herself and they'd had one of their chats under the willow tree, but now there was no Isabella, and if Sylvie had offered to bring him something . . .

*Don't you trouble yourself.*

Flic nodded to herself. She felt rather strange suddenly, and very cold. There were butterflies in her stomach, and her skin felt as if insects were crawling over it . . .

'Get dressed,' she told herself softly.

Doing normal things would help her. *Doing* always helped Flic, she found, especially at times of self-doubt. Her father had taught her when she was just a little girl about actions speaking louder than words, and she had learned through the years since then that he had been right.

There were things now that needed to be done. *Had* to be done. And she was the only one who could do them.

# 52

Reeves & Hughes's offices were on the ground floor of a terraced house off Camden High Street, their waiting room small and square and slightly shabby, all the magazines on the low end-table dog-eared, out-of-date and mostly free, with one *Evening Standard* left over from the previous Thursday. The pretty, bespectacled receptionist yawned widely, then grinned apologetically, as she brought Matthew coffee in a pottery mug, after which a stylish, long-legged black woman – who turned out to be Louise Reeves, presumably Jasper Hughes's partner – came in to pick up her messages. And then the man himself appeared to fetch Matthew.

'The beleaguered Mr Gardner, I presume?'

Matthew stood up. 'That about sums me up.'

'Come through.'

Hughes was stocky, bow-tied, in his early forties with curly dark hair, a little overweight and a touch foppish and brisk in manner, but as he bade Matthew take a seat and stood surveying him for a moment or two before sitting down behind his own paper-strewn desk, Matthew saw that his brown eyes were velvety soft and warm.

'First,' Hughes said, 'I need you to tell me everything you feel may be significant, however trivial or foolish it may sound.'

Matthew wondered, very briefly, which part of the country Hughes came from. As an American, he still found it impossible to differentiate Manchester accents from those emanating from, say, Leeds, and this man, with his slight brush of something northern, was confounding him completely.

Not that it mattered a scrap.

'I take it from that,' he said, 'Jack Crocker's given you a hint or two?'

'Naturally.'

'How much time do you have?'

'We,' Hughes amended. 'We have as much time as we need.'

Sylvie found Flic in the bathroom brushing her hair and told her that she'd decided there was one thing she needed on this miserable Monday morning above all else.

'A hairdo.' Flic scrutinized her grandmother. 'Not that it needs it.'

'I need it.' Sylvie reached out and stroked Flic's sleek hair. 'Now if I had beautiful hair like yours, I could do it myself.'

'But that would be no fun.' Flic smiled. 'Or rather no escape.'

'How astute you are.' Sylvie paused. 'John's here – have you seen him?'

'From the window,' Flic said. 'How is he?'

'He should probably be home in bed, but you know John.'

'He'd rather be gardening.'

'I've suggested he sticks to pottering under cover – I think he's been mending one of the dining chairs in the shelter. Do you think, while I'm out, you could keep an eye on Imo – still sleeping – and maybe see if John wants a sandwich a little later?'

'No problem, Groosi.' Flic held up her brush, ready to continue. 'And I'll make sure he doesn't overdo things.'

'Good girl,' Sylvie said.

Matthew had related his tale quite swiftly, surprising himself with his ability to speak coherently and almost crisply about his mounting pile-up of horrors.

'That's it?' Hughes asked when he had finished.

'Isn't it enough?'

'Certainly seems to be.' The lawyer leaned back in his swivel chair. 'I can only begin to imagine how immensely distressing this must be for you, Mr Gardner.'

Matthew said nothing.

'It could, of course, be much worse.'

'Could it?'

322

'They haven't charged you or even arrested you,' Hughes pointed out. 'Still, all in all, it does seem a particularly *disagreeable* mess.' He tapped the lobe of his right ear with his gold Cross pen. 'However, if we keep our wits about us and work through one potential allegation at a time, I feel reasonably optimistic about our ability to disprove them all.' He smiled. 'After all, we're hardly dealing with major criminal brains, are we?'

'I wouldn't be too sure,' Matthew said, without humour, 'if we weren't dealing with the makings of at least one.'

'Felicity, you mean?'

'Flic. Yes.' Matthew noticed a small gleaming gold clock on the mantel and saw that he'd been talking for more than ninety minutes.

'Penny for them?'

'Fees,' Matthew said. 'I just realized that this is going to be expensive.'

'Nothing we can't work out,' Hughes said reassuringly, and stood up. 'After a spot of lunch, perhaps.'

'Shouldn't we just go on?' Matthew asked. 'Maybe contact the police?'

'Nothing that can't wait till after a good steak and a glass of wine.' Hughes smiled. 'Both of which you look as if you could use, if you don't mind my saying so.'

Matthew didn't mind at all.


Imogen was, as Sylvie had told her, still asleep, and Flic knew that, like Groosi's hairdo, it was probably more a means of escape than a symptom of exhaustion, and as such, in view of Imo's history, it meant they all needed to be vigilant. It was also, however, for the moment, extremely useful, leaving Flic free to go about her business.

*Doing.*

She had made a plate of ham sandwiches, covered with cling film for protection against the rain, and then she had put on a parka and left Kahli in the kitchen, closing the door behind her, and now she was walking through the garden towards the willow tree and the shelter, where old John was gently working at repotting some plants, resting them on his outdoor workbench.

She saw him look up as she approached, saw the startled look in his eyes as he saw that it was her, and knew that she was right. That there could be no doubt.

'I've brought you some sandwiches, John.'

'That's kind of you.'

'Plenty of mustard, just the way you like them.'

'Lovely.' He went on working the earth in one of the pots with his fingers.

'How are you feeling today?'

'Not too bad,' he said. 'Not too good either, I suppose.'

'It's still the upset, I expect.' She put the plate down on the work-bench. 'Groosi thought you were going to work down below today.'

'I'm better up here, in the air.'

Flic walked a few paces away from him, reached up and fingered one of the branches of the willow. 'How about we have one of our cuppas together?'

'In this weather?' he said.

'I never mind a bit of rain.' She paused. 'And I could use one of our chats, John. If you can spare the time, that is?'

He stopped potting. 'Course I can, if you like.'

'Only being in the house seems to be getting me down at the moment.'

'Perhaps you should have gone to school with Chloë?'

'I would have,' she said, 'but I woke up with a bad head. And anyway, Groosi wanted to go out, so she needed me to stay with Imo.'

John glanced towards the house. 'How's she doing?'

'Sleeping.' Flic smiled at him. 'So I've got time for a cuppa.'

The gardener nodded again. 'I'll go down then, put the kettle on.'

'If you don't mind,' she said. 'Or I could do it?'

'Already on my way.' He walked the few steps to the open door, wiped his right hand on his ancient corduroy trousers and turned the light switch on the outside wall. 'Mind, my mugs have seen better days, bit like me.'

'Won't bother me,' Flic said. 'I'll wait here then, if that's all right.'

'Make yourself at home,' John said. 'I'll bring up another chair.'

And he started down the steps.

There was no difficulty to it. No unpleasantness, even. Not like Isabella. Just a matter of flicking the light switch and of closing the door – the door that was never fully closed these days because it was so badly warped and if it was properly, completely shut, it took a strong man to heave it open again.

She had planned it out in the dark, sleepless hours, had envisaged this scenario among several other possibilities. She knew the old air-raid shelter well, had played in it with Imo as a child, knew that the light switch on the inside had not worked for years. She also knew that the torch that John kept on a shelf down there was, at this minute, standing in a corner of the garage. And that his box of candles and matches were in a wheelie bin several houses down the road.

Which meant that it was very, very dark down there.

And old John Pascoe, who was frail these days, and whose heart medication spray was in the inside pocket of the green down jacket now hanging above ground on the hook on the outside wall of the shelter, was afraid of the dark, had talked to Flic about that fear in the taxi on Saturday on their way to hospital.

So all that Flic had to do now was to ignore his voice calling out to her. She would, instead, walk back up to the house, clip Kahli's lead to his collar, and chivvy Imogen out of bed and into some clothes so that they could go to pick up Groosi at the hairdressers and have a little late lunch or tea together at Starbucks or the Coffee Cup . . .

And if, by chance, old John's weary, frightened heart did *not* give up the ghost down there in the dark, Flic was perfectly prepared to say that she had heard the phone ringing in the house and had known Imo was asleep, so she had gone to answer it, and the wind must have slammed the door shut, and she couldn't imagine why the light was off, unless maybe the old, forgetful man had forgotten to switch it on . . .

# 53

Jasper Hughes's considered advice regarding VKF was that Matthew should return to work next morning.

On the subject of home, he felt that, if Matthew could stand it, he should go back to the house directly after their meeting to try and have a quiet, private chat with Sylvie about the future. He was, after all, guilty of nothing, was being atrociously dealt with, and surely, by now, could be in no more doubt that he was ready to leave Aethiopia for once and for all.

'Given the situation you've been placed in, you have no real alternative. Your mother-in-law sounds a sensible woman, so I'm sure she'll understand.'

'She'd have understood if I'd gone a long time ago,' Matthew said.

'You could ask her what will be easiest for her and, perhaps, the youngest girl,' Hughes suggested. 'That way, she'll see you're still trying to do the right thing.' He paused. 'Just don't allow yourself to be left alone with any one of those young women, even for a minute.'

He arrived in a taxi to find Susanna just parking her blue Mini Metro in the driveway behind Sylvie's car. They walked silently up the path together in the pouring rain, and already Matthew knew that there was now little hope for the quiet chat with Sylvie that Hughes had recommended.

He still, of course, had keys, but he allowed Susanna to ring the bell. Sylvie opened the door, all three girls behind her in the entrance hall, all wearing coats and jackets.

'What a surprise. We've just come in ourselves, back from meeting Chloë at the station.'

Kahli came bounding to greet Matthew. Behind him, an invisible frost seemed to rise and fill the hallway.

'Needless to say,' Susanna said quite brightly, 'we didn't come together.' She paused, spoke in a more confidential tone to Sylvie. 'I'm not sure you ought to let him in, in the circumstances.'

Sylvie took a step back. 'Come in, please, both of you.'

'Groosi,' Flic said, 'I think you should call the police.'

'Nonsense,' Sylvie said. 'I said, come in.'

For a moment, at the foot of the staircase, Imogen vacillated, then bolted.

'See?' Flic said. 'Groosi, please call the police!'

'Bloody *hell*.' Chloë looked at Matthew, eyes loaded with accusation, and followed Imogen upstairs.

Matthew looked at Sylvie. 'I was hoping for a private word.'

'I don't think that's a very good idea,' Susanna said.

'No one here wants to talk to you,' Flic said.

'Flic, that's quite enough.' Sylvie closed the front door. 'Matthew, it might have been better if you'd phoned first.'

'This is still, to the best of my knowledge, my home,' he answered coolly, 'as you've often reminded me, which means that I do not, as a matter of fact, need to make an appointment to come here.'

'You're absolutely right,' Sylvie said. 'Please forgive me.'

'If you are going to talk to him, Groosi,' Flic said, 'I'm going to listen. I want to hear whatever lies he's going to tell you.'

'I do think everyone should keep calm,' Susanna said.

Sylvie eyed her with intense irritation. 'What I just said to Matthew really *does* apply to you, Susanna. I would like you to telephone before barging in.'

'I have been phoning,' Susanna said without rancour. 'There was no answer and no machine, so frankly, I got a little anxious.'

'There was no need,' Sylvie said shortly.

'You're looking very tired,' Susanna said. 'Since I am here, why don't you go and lie down, and I can help with dinner?'

'I don't need or wish to lie down.' The aggression in the atmosphere was getting to Sylvie. 'I realize you probably can't help yourself after a lifetime of bossiness, Susanna, but I really would prefer it if you stopped trying to organize this household.'

327

'Why don't you both just go?' Flic said.

'Why don't you learn some manners?' Matthew replied.

'Groosi, please tell this creep to go.'

'Shut up, Flic.' Sylvie took off her coat and dumped it in Flic's arms. 'Tired and fed up as I am, I am also, regrettably, the adult in charge here, and what I want right now is for all of you to be quiet and listen.'

Everyone did, remarkably, fall silent.

'Imogen and Chloë' – Sylvie raised her voice so that she would be heard upstairs – 'I'd like you both to change out of your wet clothes.' She lowered her pitch again. 'Susanna, if you insist on staying, I'd appreciate it if you would wait for me in the drawing room.'

'If you'd rather I went—'

'I don't actually care, at this precise moment.'

'Very well.' For the first time, Susanna looked offended, but did as she was asked, making a point of firmly closing the drawing room door behind her.

'Flic, I'd like you to go and check that old John's all right, because the Austin's still outside in the road, and he should have left hours ago.'

'Maybe he did go,' Flic said. 'Maybe he didn't feel like driving.'

'Maybe, but I'd still like you to go and check.'

Flic headed for the back of the house. 'I'll be right back.'

'Switch the floodlights on,' Sylvie called after her, then managed a weak smile for Matthew. 'Meantime, you and I can have our chat. Where would you prefer? Study or kitchen?' She paused. 'Perhaps you'd like a cup of something?'

He shook his head, mustered a smile of his own. 'I have to tell you, Sylvie,' he said, 'that if only my life weren't going to hell in a handbasket quite so damned fast, and if I didn't know that one of your granddaughters would appear as soon as I laid so much as a finger on you, I would give you the *biggest* hug right now.'

Suddenly, Sylvie looked perilously close to tears.

'And I would let you,' she said.

Chloë was with Imogen in her room. Imo had retreated to her bed, was sitting on the bedspread, legs drawn up, hugging her knees the way she often did when agitated, and rocking to and fro.

Chloë watched her for a few moments. 'Did he really do what you said?'

Imogen nodded, went on rocking.

'But if he did that,' Chloë said, 'how come Groosi still likes him?'

'She's always liked him.'

'But she wouldn't, surely,' Chloë reasoned, 'if she thought he'd hurt you?'

Imogen stopped rocking. 'What are you going on about?'

Chloë was still watching her. 'He didn't do it, did he?'

'I've told you he did.'

Chloë said nothing, but her expression was wary, uncertain.

Imo's eyes narrowed. 'Think I'd make up something like that?'

'I'm not sure.' Chloë paused. 'I hope not.'

Flic had made sure that Kahli stayed in the kitchen again, and was out in the garden, making a good show (in case anyone was watching her in the floodlighting) of checking around all the less immediately visible nooks and crannies beyond the willow tree and the shelter.

It hadn't been long enough. Not to be sure.

The door was still shut. There were no sounds, no cries for help or knocking. No audible signs of life. But that didn't mean he *wasn't* alive. Even if he had suffered some kind of attack, he might simply be unconscious, or perhaps he'd just fallen asleep from exhaustion.

His jacket still hung on the hook.

No way she could pretend not to see that.

She couldn't believe she hadn't thought about his old Austin, she couldn't *believe* that. She had reckoned on no one thinking of looking for him until tomorrow, or maybe tonight at the earliest in the event that someone, some friend or relative, maybe, had missed old John and got in touch . . .

His damned *car*.

How could she have forgotten something so *obvious*?

'Stress,' she said out loud.

Too much pressure on her, too many demands. Matthew still here, not in custody, presumably because Imo hadn't given the police a statement. Too *much*.

Not her fault.

*

329

Sylvie had told Matthew to sit at the kitchen table while she boiled the kettle and got out the tea things, and he had glanced at her near-ashen face and had wanted to tell her to sit and let him do it, but he understood that, having made such a considerable concession to him in the circumstances, she needed to keep control of the situation. Letting *him* make the tea would be tantamount to high treason in the eyes of her granddaughters.

The back door opened, Flic came in and Kahli, who'd been waiting to go out, pushed between her legs and escaped.

'Kahli, come back!' Flic called agitatedly.

'Let him go,' Sylvie told her.

'It's so wet,' Flic said.

'He needs to pee,' Matthew said from the table.

Flic ignored him. 'I couldn't see John,' she told her grandmother. 'But his jacket's still there.'

'Where?' Sylvie asked.

'Hanging outside the shelter.'

'Did you look down there?' Matthew asked.

Again, she ignored him.

'Flic, please answer the question,' Sylvie said sharply.

'The door's shut,' she said. 'I couldn't get it open to look. You know what it's like when it's shut all the way.'

'Is it the jacket he was wearing when he came this morning?'

'The old green one,' Flic said.

Sylvie looked at Matthew. 'We'd better get that door open.'

He was already on his way.

'It's really jammed tight,' he called over his shoulder to Sylvie, who'd followed with Flic. 'I need something for leverage.'

'There may be something in the garage,' Sylvie said.

'I'll go,' Flic offered.

'Hurry, darling.'

Chloë had come outside too, was now being followed by Susanna. 'What's going on, Groosi?'

'We're worried that John may have got himself stuck in the shelter.'

'The door's jammed,' Matthew told her.

'Anything I can do?' Susanna called.

'Flic's gone to get something to help jemmy it open,' Sylvie told her.

330

Kahli started barking excitedly, turning in circles, and Chloë ran to the shelter and banged on the door. 'John! Are you in there?' Kahli went on barking.

'Kahli, be quiet,' Sylvie told the dog.

Chloë shook her head. 'I can't hear anything.'

Flic reappeared, waving something in one hand. 'I found a sort of crowbar.' She ran past her grandmother, gave it to Matthew. 'You'd better hurry – he might have had a heart attack!'

Sylvie stepped forward to take Chloë's arm, draw her out of Matthew's way. 'Let's give him space to work.' They all backed off, stood anxiously watching.

'It's a real bastard.' Matthew heaved at it, grunted, got the crowbar into a narrow space where the door had warped, worked to get the position right. 'Almost there, I *think*.' He gave one big push, then hauled at it, and the door jolted open. 'Wait up here. I'll take a look.'

'Is the light on?' Chloë called.

'No, it's pitch dark.'

'There's a switch outside.' Flic ran forward, flicked the switch, then returned to her grandmother's side as Matthew descended the steps.

'You're trembling, darling,' Sylvie said. 'Try not to worry too much. John's a tougher old bird than he looks.'

'Do you really think so?' Flic asked.

'I don't know,' Sylvie answered.

'Is he there?' Chloë called to Matthew.

'Not so far as . . .' There was a pause, and then they heard his steps coming back up. 'No one down there.' He fingered the jacket on the hook. 'But this is a little weird – and the car being outside.' He looked at Sylvie and the two girls. 'I'm going to do some more checking around, but I think you should all get back into the warm.'

'Are you sure he's not down there?' Flic asked.

'Not a trace.'

'I want to look too,' Chloë said.

'No, honey,' Matthew told her.

'You can't tell me what to do,' Chloë snapped.

'Chloë, don't be rude. Come inside with us, please,' Sylvie said.

'Come on.' Flic tucked one arm in her grandmother's, the other in her sister's. 'Might as well be Matthew catching cold rather than us,' she said.

331

'Flic, please,' Sylvie rebuked.

Imogen came downstairs as they were all standing around in the kitchen, waiting for Matthew to return. 'What's going on?'

Chloë brought her up to date.

'Matthew's gone to look around,' Susanna told Imogen.

'You mean he's still here?' She looked appalled.

'He's trying to help,' Sylvie said.

'If he's coming back in here' – Imogen looked panicky – 'I'm going back upstairs.'

'Why?' Chloë asked quietly. 'Can't you face him?'

Flic glared at her. 'I'd say it's the other way round.'

'Maybe,' her youngest sister said, softly but boldly.

'Calm down, girls,' Sylvie said.

Susanna watched Imogen for a moment, but said nothing.

'Why are you looking at me?' Imo asked.

Matthew came in from the garden, hair and clothes soaked through. 'Nothing. Car and other keys in his pocket.' He closed the door behind him and held something up. 'And this.' He looked at the label. 'I just hope he doesn't need it too badly.'

'That's the spray he uses for his heart problem,' Sylvie said, newly alarmed.

'He used it on Saturday, after the accident,' Flic said.

'Poor old John,' Chloë said anxiously.

Imogen didn't speak, just leaned against one of the kitchen units.

'Are you all right, Imo?' Susanna asked.

'Of *course* she isn't all right,' Flic erupted suddenly. 'None of us is, though maybe we might be if *he* would just go.'

Matthew ignored her, looked at his mother-in-law. 'Anything else I can do, Sylvie? Is there someone we should contact about John?'

'*We* can do that,' Flic shouted, and suddenly her eyes were filled with furious tears and she was trembling violently. 'I'm telling you, Groosi, I really, really can't take him *being* here any more.'

'Flic, this isn't helping,' Sylvie told her.

'Please tell me you're not going to let him come back and live here again, *please* tell me that, because if you are, then I'm going to take Chloë and Imo out of this house and find—'

'Flic, sweetheart.' Susanna tried to put her arm around Flic.

332

'Get *off* me!' Flic pulled away from her, went to her grand-mother, seized both her hands, utterly distraught. 'I *mean* it, Groosi – we'll go to a hotel or to a friends' or *anywhere*. Haven't we all been through *enough*?'

'I don't want to go anywhere,' Chloë exclaimed.

Imogen covered her face with both her hands. 'I can't stand this.'

'I'm going,' Matthew said, looking at Flic, almost believing that this was no performance, that either Caro's oldest daughter was seriously disturbed or a budding Oscar winner. 'I'm going, Sylvie, before this gets any more out of control.'

'Matthew, please wait,' Sylvie said.

'All I came for was a quiet conversation with you about the future,' he went on, 'because I figured the least I could do was consult with you over a few things.'

'There's no *way* you're having a quiet conversation with our grandmother.' Flic clutched at Sylvie's right arm. 'You're not to talk to him alone, Groosi, you're *not*! He's dangerous, for God's sake!'

'Stop being so melodramatic,' Sylvie said, quietly.

'How can you *say* that?' Flic shrieked.

'Flic, stop it!' Imogen's hands were still covering her face. 'Please!'

'I want him out *now*!'

Susanna stepped forward anxiously. 'This isn't helping anyone.'

'For once,' Matthew said, 'I have to agree with you.' He put John Pascoe's medication spray down on the table. 'Sylvie, you have my number if you need me.'

'She won't need you,' Flic said.

'Everyone please stop being so *horrible*!' Chloë was in tears.

Matthew put out his hand to gently touch Sylvie's arm. 'Call me?'

'Don't touch my grandmother!' Flic slapped his hand away.

He looked at her with the most intense dislike, was amazed at himself for managing to control himself now, when what he had a profound and shocking urge to do was to slap her face very hard. Instead, he began to walk towards the kitchen door.

'Keep *away* from me!' Imogen cried out, and ran out ahead of him.

'You bastard,' Flic said. 'You bloody *bastard*.'

The sound that came from Sylvie shocked them all.

A groan, deep and despairing, transforming, in the most distressing way, into a cry of pain.

'Groosi?' Chloë said.

Sylvie slumped and fell to the floor.

'Oh, my God,' Flic cried out.

Susanna got down on her knees, felt at Sylvie's neck for a pulse. 'Get an ambulance,' she said sharply, and unfastened the top button of her blouse. 'Dial 999,' she ordered. '*Now*!'

Chloë ran to the phone and dialled.

'Let me help.' Matthew got down on the floor beside Susanna.

'You get away from her!' Flic screamed.

'Shut *up*, Flic,' Chloë shouted, 'I'm trying to hear.'

'I don't want you touching her!'

Matthew looked up, stared Flic straight in the eye. 'Have you done a CPR course?' He took her silence for a negative. 'Then if you want your grandmother to live, get the *fuck* out of the way.'

'I've done a course,' Susanna said.

'Good,' Matthew said quietly. 'We can work together.'

And Flic, terrified and beaten, fell silent.

# 54

Imogen and Chloë, fear having rendered them both incapable of argument, had, as recommended by the paramedics, remained at home. Flic had wanted to travel in the ambulance, had become almost unhinged when Matthew, as the calmest adult in the family, had been asked to go in her place, but Susanna had reminded Flic that what counted now was Sylvie's safety, and that if Flic got into her car without any more fuss, they would very likely reach the Royal Free at the same time as the ambulance.

'We'll call you, darling,' Susanna told Chloë, 'as soon as we know anything.'

'Thank you,' Chloë said in a numb, suddenly very young voice.

'What I need you to do for the moment is to take very good care of Imo.'

'Imo's fine,' Chloë said.

'No,' Susanna told her firmly but softly. 'She is not at all fine.'

It felt, to Matthew, like the bizarrest of nights.

'It's getting hard to choose worst experiences these days,' he told Kat on the phone during the evening after realizing they hadn't spoken since early morning.

'But they think she's going to be all right?' Kat asked.

'They're not exactly committing themselves yet,' Matthew said, 'but she's looking better than she was.'

'Was it her heart?'

'I can't make it out,' he said. 'Seems almost like her system just crashed.'

335

'You said she'd had chemo recently, didn't you?'

'Cancer, chemo, losing her only daughter, and a total absence of the peace and quiet she needed to recover.'

Sylvie remained in the Intensive Therapy Unit for the night, conscious but sedated, with Flic by her side most of the time. Susanna stayed at the hospital, impressing Matthew with a calm professionalism he hadn't observed before, making him wonder exactly why he had taken such a dislike to her from the beginning.

He stayed too, partly from a lingering sense of responsibility, but mostly because he *wanted* to be there, for Sylvie, of course, and, in a way, for Caro.

Even – bizarre though it was – for Flic. For he had seen her terror when her grandmother had collapsed, and her awful defeat when she had been forced to let him help Sylvie. And he had stood for a while and watched her sitting with the sick woman, and been reminded of the way Flic had first seemed to him, back at the very beginning, in Switzerland. Beautiful, calm, mature for her years. Even now it was hard to believe, looking at her, that she could be capable of the things she had done to him during the past year.

*Who would a jury believe?*

The thought rocked him, chilled him, made him turn away and return to the waiting area, to Susanna and their temporary truce, and to the machine coffee and grave faces and the passing chatter of night nurses and visitors and doctors and orderlies.

By morning, Sylvie was out of danger, though still weak, and being transferred by her consultant to the coronary care unit.

They were told to go home.

'I'm not leaving,' Flic said.

'You're completely exhausted,' Susanna told her gently. 'You won't be any use at all to your grandmother unless you get a few hours' sleep.'

Matthew, a few feet away, kept silent, knowing that if he backed Susanna up, Flic would never leave.

They walked in silence to the car park. Susanna unlocked the doors of the Mini Metro, Flic got into the passenger seat and Susanna tilted forward the driver's seat so that Matthew could climb into the back.

'Why's he getting in?' Flic asked.

'I'm coming back to the house to get some things.'

'*Just* to get some things?' she asked.

'For the moment,' he said.

Flic said nothing more, but when they reached Aethiopia, she marched quickly up the path ahead of them and blocked Matthew's way into the house.

'We can fetch whatever you want,' she said.

Fresh anger surged. 'I'm too tired for this.'

'Come on, Flic,' Susanna coaxed. 'Let him in, there's a good girl.'

'Don't speak to me as if I were a child,' Flic snapped.

'Then don't behave like one,' Matthew told her.

'I suppose,' Susanna said to him, 'if you tell me what you need, I could try and find it for you.' She looked apologetic. 'It might save a lot of fuss.'

'Unbelievable.' He shook his head. '*Really* unbelievable.'

'She's very upset,' Susanna said.

'And I'm *not*?' It took another major effort to step back rather than force his way past. 'Pushing women out of my way's not something I care to do,' he said tightly, 'so I guess I'll wait.'

'I'm sorry,' Susanna said.

He began to walk back up the path, then turned around. 'Will you be staying with them, Susanna?'

'Absolutely.'

Flic was opening the front door, and Matthew raised his voice so she would hear. 'Then I'd be glad if you'd make sure that no one touches my property or interferes with my mail in any way.'

Susanna nodded. 'Of course,' she said.

'I'll be in touch,' he said.

Chloë and Imogen were awake, the younger girl in pyjamas, her sister in one of her Astrid sweatshirts, both pale with fearful, shadowed eyes, having spent the night scarcely able to sleep or even settle, wandering around the house, turning TVs on and off, nerves ragged, imaginations running riot. Imogen, who'd been steering clear of her friends again for the past several days, had suddenly felt a most intense need for comradeship and had fired off a series of text messages to Annie and Nicola, divulging nothing but her wish to hear from them, and getting no replies for the simple reason that they had, almost certainly, been sleep-

337

ing. With the advent of dawn, Chloë had badly wanted to go to the hospital but Imo had said she couldn't face it, and Chloë had remembered what Susanna had told her about Imo not being okay, and had remembered her cut wrists and said no more about going.

Now, in the kitchen, after their return, she was avid for hard information. 'I want to see Groosi, even if Imo doesn't.'

'And you shall,' Susanna, filling the kettle, assured her. 'As soon as I've had a short rest, I'll take you.'

'I don't need taking,' Chloë said.

'Perhaps not, but they may not just let you in.'

'If they don't, I'll sit outside and wait till they do.'

'Chloë, give it a rest.' Flic looked at Imogen, slouched at the table. 'How are you doing, Imo?'

'How d'you think?'

'I'm shattered,' Flic said, 'so I'm going to bed.' She started for the door, then halted. 'Where do you want to sleep, Susanna?'

'Why's she sleeping here?' Imogen asked.

'Because apparently we're too young to be left on our own.'

'Isn't Matthew coming back?' Chloë asked.

'No,' Flic said.

'Not ever?'

'Certainly not today.' Susanna got out some mugs.

'Never,' Imogen said, 'if we can help it.'

'Imo,' Flic said, 'will you sort Susanna out some clean linen for my bed? I'll go on camping with you, okay?'

'Don't bother about changing linen.' Susanna found some camomile tea. 'I'm much too tired to care.'

'When can we go to the hospital?' Chloë wanted to know.

'Give me a couple of hours,' Susanna said.

'I don't *want* to wait a couple of hours.'

'Well, you're going to have to.' Flic opened the door. 'By the looks of you both, I think we could all use another hour or two.'

'Has Imo told you about Mick phoning?' Chloë asked suddenly. 'About poor old John.'

Flic froze in the doorway, made herself turn around slowly. 'What about him?' She looked at Imogen. 'When did he phone?' Her tone was sharp. 'Why didn't you tell me?'

'You weren't here,' Imogen said. 'Do you want to hear, or yell at me?'

338

'Come on, Imo, love,' Susanna soothed. 'We're all tired and edgy.'

'John's in hospital too,' Imogen said.

'What happened?' Flic had grown paler.

'Mick said he came back here yesterday afternoon for some more stuff – must have been while we were meeting Chloë. Anyway, he saw John's car outside, so he went out to see how come he was still working.' Imogen saw that Flic's face had gone from pale to chalky, and frowned. 'Mick said he heard funny noises from the shelter – banging and someone calling out.'

'So John *was* stuck in there after all,' Chloë said.

'Poor man,' Susanna said.

'Go on,' Flic said.

'That's it,' Imogen said. 'Mick got him out, drove him to the Royal Free.'

'Was it his heart again?' Flic asked.

Imogen shook her head. 'Mick said they thought his heart was okay, but he was really cold – hypothermic, he said – and in a hell of a state, so they kept him in.'

'But he's okay?' Flic asked. 'Or going to be?'

Imogen gave her another curious glance. 'Hope so. Mick said John told him the light went out and he's scared of the dark, so it must have been bloody awful for him down there.'

'School,' Susanna said suddenly and irrelevantly.

'I'm not going to school,' Imogen said quickly.

'Me neither,' Chloë confirmed.

'I'm not suggesting you do,' Susanna said. 'But oughtn't we to phone them?'

'Could you?' Flic asked. 'It would sound better coming from you.'

'The number's in the blue book by the phone,' Chloë said.

'I'll call in a minute.' Susanna stifled a yawn. 'Then we'll all get a bit of rest.'

'Are you sure Groosi's okay?' Chloë asked again.

'Absolutely,' Flic said.

'Touch wood,' Imogen said.

'I think,' Flic told Imogen upstairs a little later, 'you're going to have to give the police a proper statement now.'

339

'No.' Imogen shook her head. 'No way.'

'We've got to keep the pressure on him or we might be back to square one.'

'I'm not talking to them – I've *told* you.' The wild look was back in her eyes. 'You said I could just refuse to talk, you *promised* me.'

'And I meant it, but he's still walking around, isn't he? Still free as a bird.'

'I'm not talking to them, Flic.' Imo was unyielding. 'You can't make me.'

Flic was silent, thinking.

'Why were you so freaked out just now, downstairs?' Imogen used the silence to change the subject. 'When you heard about John?'

'I was shocked, not freaked out.'

'You went white as a ghost.'

'Did I?' Flic shrugged. 'Maybe because I was with him on Saturday when he had his turn.' She walked over to the window, gazed out unseeingly at the grey morning. 'It's awful to think of him getting locked in like that.'

'At least he didn't have a heart attack.' Imogen yawned.

'Yes.' Flic turned back to face her. 'Go to sleep.'

'What about you?'

'I'm going to have a bath. I don't think I'll get to sleep unless I relax first.'

'What about—' Imogen bit her lip.

'Forget about the police,' Flic said. 'I've changed my mind.'

'Honestly?' The relief was immense. 'Only I'd be so scared of screwing up.'

'I know.' Flic paused. 'Go to sleep, Imo.'


Back in his room at the Marriott, Matthew hung his trousers in the press, made some coffee, showered and checked his voice mail: one message from Ethan, two from Karl, and the last from Kat, asking for news and sending love.

'Not to worry if you don't have time to call,' she'd said. 'I just wanted to let you know I'm thinking of you.'

He phoned the Royal Free first, managed to elicit the information that Sylvie was improving, then called Kat back and got her machine.

'Sylvie's holding her own,' he told it, 'and I'm going to go to VKF and try doing some work – unless Bianco throws me out. Hope you hear good news soon about the job. Call you later.'

Bianco was nowhere to be seen when Matthew arrived, and with Brice, Fairbairn, Loftus and Gary Higgins all asking him where he'd been the previous day in their normal, generally disinterested fashion – and, therefore, he presumed, unaware of his problems – it seemed reasonable to assume he still had a job.

*For now.*

With a sense of release, however fleeting, Matthew sat down at his drawing board and immersed himself in work.

Dagenham had never looked lovelier.

Susanna, Imogen and Chloë slumbered on till noon, then jerked into wakefulness with a collective sense of shame for having been able to sleep so soundly while Sylvie remained in hospital.

Flic was in the kitchen when Susanna came down for coffee.

'Goodness, you're already dressed.'

'I had things to do,' Flic said, 'and anyway, I couldn't sleep.'

'You really should have tried to at least rest,' Susanna told her. 'It won't help your grandmother if you make yourself ill too.' She paused. 'Have you phoned the hospital yet?'

'Of course. They wouldn't let me speak to her, but they said she's doing well.'

'You could have come and told me.' Chloë came in, wearing jeans, pulling a turquoise sweater down over her short hair. 'Can we go now? I didn't mean to sleep this long.'

'Soon,' Susanna said, spooning Costa Rica into a filter bag.

Chloë looked at Flic. 'You're ready. Why can't we go ahead?'

'No reason.' Flic looked at Susanna. 'You don't mind, do you?'

Susanna hesitated, then thought about the rare chance of time alone with Imogen. 'Not at all. So long as you both remember to stay calm around Groosi. It's important not to worry her.'

'We're not stupid,' Chloë said.

'I know that,' Susanna told her.

She drank a strong cup of coffee, then went upstairs, listened at Imogen's door, heard nothing, so went to freshen up and get dressed again. Then she went back down to the kitchen, let Kahli in from the garden, toasted two slices of granary bread, poured a glass of orange juice, set them with a pot of honey on a tray, and carried them upstairs.

She balanced the tray with one hand and knocked on Imogen's door.

'What?' The voice sounded ratty.

'Only me,' she said, opening the door. 'Thought you might like a little something. Hope you don't mind.'

Imogen was lying on top of her bed, still in the same Astrid sweatshirt, her dark-dyed hair spiky and her face pasty.

'It's chilly in here.' Susanna brought the tray to her, put it down on the bed. 'Can I fetch you a robe or a sweater?'

'No, thanks.'

'Do you think you can manage to eat something?'

'Sure.' Imo shrugged. 'I'm not ill.'

Susanna sat down near the foot of the bed. 'Let's keep it that way.'

Imogen sighed, pulled the tray disinterestedly towards her, picked up a half-slice of toast, nibbled at one corner.

'Flic phoned the hospital. Your grandmother's doing well, apparently. She and Chloë have gone ahead to see her.' Susanna smiled. 'Chloë refused to wait any longer. She's grown up a lot lately, don't you think?'

'Mm.'

Susanna glanced down at the floor. Aside from the extra bed, everything looked very normal, belongings strewn around haphazardly: socks, trainers, a Bridget Jones paperback, a bottle of black nail varnish – though neither Imo's finger nor toenails were currently painted – an open Coke can and a pair of jeans. It was hard and unpleasant to remember what lay beneath.

'I was wondering,' she said, 'if you might feel like talking.'

'About what?' Imogen looked irritated.

'I don't know. Things in general.' Susanna trod carefully. 'So much having happened. You having been through so much.'

Imogen put down the toast. 'I don't want to talk.'

Nothing Susanna had not expected. 'I know you didn't want to talk to the police,' she said, 'and I think I can understand why not.' She paused. 'But surely I'm a bit different?'

'Why?'

'Because you've often been able to talk to me. Because we've

342

always got on pretty well – at least I hope you feel we have. And because you should know by now that anything you tell me is in complete confidence, if you want it to be.'

'I do know that,' Imogen said. 'But I still don't want to talk.'

Susanna swallowed her disappointment and tried a different tack. 'Then how about eating that, getting dressed and coming to the Royal Free with me?'

'I don't think so.' Imogen felt her lower lip tremble. She didn't want to start crying, not now, with Susanna there. 'I can't face that,' she said. 'I don't want to go anywhere, but especially not there.' Her eyes filled with tears, and she clenched her fists. 'I just can't stand the thought of seeing Groosi like that, not after . . .'

'No,' Susanna said. 'I understand.' She stood up, her eyes drawn, despite herself, to the section of carpet over by the wall that she had pulled up that awful day.

'What?' Imogen asked.

'Nothing.'

'You were looking at something.'

'Not really.' Susanna shook her head and managed a smile. 'Just gazing into space, you know? The way one does some-times.'

Imogen nodded, picked up the glass of juice, and drank some.

'I'll leave you in peace then, shall I?'

'Please,' Imogen said. 'Thanks for this.'

'Don't forget what I said, though, will you? About talking. And I don't just mean about recent things. We can talk about anything you like – the past, whatever.'

'Yeah. Okay.'

'Promise?' Susanna said, clutching at straws.

'Yeah,' Imogen said. 'Sure.'

Matthew, just rising from his drawing board to go to the men's room, sat down again to answer his mobile.

'It's me,' Kat said. 'Sorry I wasn't here when you rang.'

'Any news about the job?'

'Not yet. Fingers crossed.' She paused. 'How's Sylvie?'

'Doing better, they say.' He paused. 'I'm at the office.'

'How are things there?'

'Okay, so far. Early days.'

'And on the war front?'

343

He wandered casually to the door of his cubicle, saw that Loftus was the only other person in the office and that he was engaged on his own phone. 'I haven't been arrested yet,' he said, 'so I guess that's good news.'

'Want to come over later for dinner?'

'Sounds great.' Abruptly he remembered his awkwardness after their kiss. 'But let me take you out, okay?'

'Whatever you feel like,' Kat said easily. 'Decide later.'

The realization struck him – followed instantly by that increasingly familiar stab of guilt – how utterly different she was from Caro, how much more clear-sighted, for one thing.

*Too soon.* That came again, too, almost like a refrain.

But then he thought of Kat's cropped red hair and her unmade-up freckled nose.

And smiled.

Sylvie was on a drip and still attached to a monitor, but she was in a good-sized room with large windows overlooking Primrose Hill and beyond, and only one other patient, a silent, sleeping woman.

Flic and Chloë felt relieved that the other inmate was asleep.

'I thought you'd be in a private room,' Flic said softly.

'I don't mind,' Sylvie said. 'It's quite nice to have company.'

'Not much company,' Chloë said.

'Shush,' Flic said. 'You'll wake her.'

'I'm so sorry,' Sylvie said.

'What for?' Chloë asked.

'For being such a worry to you all.'

'It's hardly your fault, is it?' Flic said. 'It was mine, wasn't it, for kicking up such a fuss about Matthew.'

'My collapsing had nothing to do with that,' Sylvie said firmly.

'I'll bet it didn't help,' Chloë said.

'All sorts of things haven't helped, darling.'

They sat in silence for a moment.

'When are you coming home?' Chloë asked.

'Soon, I hope. I'm certainly feeling much better than I was.' Sylvie was still too drained to be properly convincing. 'I don't want any of you fretting about me.'

'As if we would,' Flic said dryly.

'I would,' Chloë said.

Sylvie reached for her hand. 'Flic's just teasing, darling.'

344

'I know,' Chloë said, 'but I'm not in a teasing mood.'

Flic stood up. 'I'm going to find some coffee,' she said. 'Can I get you anything, Groosi?'

'Not for me, thank you, darling.'

'Chloë? Want a Coke?'

'Please.'

'Why don't you go with Flic?' Sylvie asked.

'Because I want to stay here with you,' Chloë said. 'If I hadn't been told I had to stay at home with Imo,' she added pointedly, 'I'd have been here last night.'

Sylvie squeezed her hand. 'You're here now. That's what matters.'

Susanna sat in the drawing room at Aethiopia and mulled over her failures.

She thought, sitting there surrounded by Caro's possessions, about the depths of her feelings for her friend. She thought about Richard Walters, about things she had learned about him during her therapy sessions with Caro – things that paled into insignificance beside the probable implications of what she had since unearthed. She thought about the intensity of her early dislike for Matthew, perhaps irrational, she realized now, for she had long since accepted that the American was neither the fortune hunter nor the chauvinist she had first believed him to be. But then she thought about Imogen's horrendous allegations – and then, perplexingly, remembered the fine manner in which Matthew had responded to Sylvie's collapse and, before that, to the drama surrounding John Pascoe. The way he had remained with them at the hospital, despite Flic's obvious loathing, patently because he really cared about Sylvie.

Not that any of that rendered him incapable of what Imo had accused him.

Her mind strayed back yet again to the items beneath Imogen's floorboards, to the teenager's refusal to speak to her about past and present troubles.

'Useless,' she said aloud, and saw herself, suddenly, as Matthew and even, far more importantly, Sylvie probably saw her. As a judgmental, meddlesome, ineffective woman trying to impose herself on them and Caro's daughters.

She had, assuredly, failed Imogen and, consequently, her

sisters. Most of all – and of greatest importance to her, right or wrong – she had failed Caro.

'*Useless*,' Susanna said again.

Flic had been trying – before she'd left Sylvie and Chloë in the hospital room to go in search of John Pascoe – to calculate what she would do when she came face-to-face with him.

Part of her wanted to run away, to avoid ever seeing the old man again, but that was, of course, impossible. She was going to *have* to face him, to see for herself what condition he was in and how much he recalled of what had happened to him. She was going to have to try to persuade him – if he began making accusations – that he had been imagining things; and if she could not persuade him of that, she would have to summon the inner strength to act the sweet, concerned visitor, shocked and upset at the things he was saying. And hopefully, in view of his being old and sick, anyone in earshot would suppose that his mind was wandering, that he was probably suffering from early Alzheimer's . . .

Except that when, after some stressful searching – since he was not, as she'd expected, in the coronary care unit – she finally located his ward on the lower ground floor near Accident and Emergency, old John was not there.

He had been discharged.

'How could you let him go like that?' Flic asked a nurse.

'Not my decision,' the young man said. 'But he was much better, and I heard him say he had someone at home to take care of him.'

'But he's not *well*,' Flic said agitatedly. 'He has a bad heart, and his mind is going. I heard he was in an awful state when he came in.'

'He did seem distressed when he was admitted, but he soon perked up.' He smiled. 'Nothing much wrong with his mind that we noticed. A lovely gentleman, quite on the ball, I thought.'

'Did he say anything? About what happened to him?'

'About getting trapped in that old shelter, you mean?' The nurse pulled a face. 'Death traps like that should be pulled down.' He touched Flic's arm reassuringly. 'He really was quite well, considering. If you're worried, why not pop round to see him at home, set your mind at rest?'

Flic was shaking as she made her way back towards the lifts,

346

her hands still trembling as she slid some coins into a vending machine and pulled out Chloë's can of Coke.

*Why not pop round to see him?*

Why not indeed?

Except that the nurse had also said that John had someone at home to take care of him. Someone whom he might, at this very moment, be talking to about what had happened to him in the shelter.

And to Isabella.

*Nothing to be done.*

Except wait.

The can felt icy in her hands.

She couldn't remember old John ever mentioning anyone at home.

And there was no way she could *bear* to simply wait.

*Why not pop round to see him?*

She looked to her left, then to her right. A nurse, some visitors, a woman in a violet-coloured bathrobe, shuffling in slippers. No sign of Chloë, looking for her.

Slowly, thoughtfully, Flic put the Coke can down on the floor.

A freebie for someone.

And went to find the exit.

# 55

The house in West Finchley was a small terraced wedge of drably coloured brick, with a garden gate that squeaked loudly upon opening. Only the tiny plot of front garden – grass perfectly mown, edges trimmed, soil tidily turned, rose bushes neatly pruned – declared it as belonging to old John.

Flic's heart had pounded as she'd asked the taxi driver to wait, and now, as she rang the doorbell, her palms felt damp. Hearing footsteps approaching, she wiped her hands quickly on her parka, and composed herself.

'Can I help you?' A woman wearing a sari, black hair beautifully fastened into a bun, dark eyes enquiring but friendly, stood looking at Flic.

'I've come to see John Pascoe.'

'And you are?'

'Felicity Walters. A friend.'

The woman's face broke into a warm smile. 'Felicity, I've heard so much about you.' She stepped back to allow Flic to enter the narrow hallway. 'Please do come in. John will be so happy to see you, though I know he's sleeping right now.' She shut the door, held out her hand, kept her voice low. 'I'm Gita Khan, one of John's neighbours.'

The warmth of the stranger's greeting told Flic all was well.

*So far.*

'How is he?' Flic asked. 'We were all so upset when we heard what had happened to him. I went to visit him in hospital, then found he'd been sent home.'

'Too soon,' Mrs Khan said disapprovingly. 'After such a terrible thing.'

'But he's all right, isn't he?' Flic glanced down, saw to her right a pair of boots, caked with mud, she supposed, from her own back garden, standing on the opened centre pages of the *Radio Times*.

'I'm not really sure.' The woman spoke confidentially. 'He seems very quiet to me. I think he's still shaken. My husband and I have always found John a contented man, but suddenly he seems rather anxious.'

Flic braced herself. 'Hasn't he told you what he's anxious about?'

'Not really.' Gita Khan gave a small, expressive shrug. 'He allowed me to wait while he put himself to bed, and to bring him a cup of tea – and none of this is in character, Miss Walters.'

'Please call me Flic.'

Another smile. 'I know that's what John calls you.'

'It's what everyone calls me.'

'A pity, in a way. Felicity is such a lovely name.'

'Thank you.'

Flic thought about the taxi waiting outside, about Sylvie and Chloë back at the hospital, surely wondering by now what had become of her. Much more of this graciousness, and she thought she might implode with tension.

'He's a very independent man, don't you find?' the Indian woman asked.

'I suppose he is,' Flic agreed.

'Rather proud, too, I would say. So he was most embarrassed, I could tell, letting me bring him tea while he lay in his bed, yet he did let me do it. That's what I meant by not in character.'

'I'm sure he's very grateful for your help.'

'It's a pleasure to be able to repay him a little.' Mrs Khan smiled again. 'My husband is a very poor gardener, and John has helped to make our flower beds quite beautiful.'

'I'm sure,' Flic said. 'Do you think he's up to a visit?'

'I think he would welcome it, though as I said, he's sleeping at the moment.' Mrs Khan paused. 'As a matter of fact, I was just going next door to fetch some sugar, because John has run out.'

'He does like his tea very sweet, doesn't he.'

'So perhaps, if you wouldn't mind waiting in the living room till I come back? Then I can make a fresh pot of tea, and perhaps we can see if he's awake.'

'That would be lovely,' Flic said.

She bore the suspense as the neighbour insisted on seeing her into the living room, told the woman that there was no need to hurry on her account, said that she was very tired because her grandmother had also been taken ill, and so she was, therefore, quite glad of the chance to sit down to wait. And that, of course, was a mistake, because the courteous older woman seemed to feel compelled to ask a whole series of concerned questions about her grandmother, and to tell Flic how *especially* kind that made her for taking time to visit John.

'What about your taxi?' Belatedly, Mrs Khan realized that the black cab waiting outside was connected with Flic. 'Won't it be terribly expensive?'

'It's all right,' Flic said. 'We made a deal on the price.'

It wasn't true, and she supposed the meter was shooting up by the second, and she didn't have much cash on her, but she couldn't worry about that now, couldn't *think* about money when all that really mattered was that there was a man lying upstairs in bed, an old man whom she really liked, but who might, any time now, recall exactly what had happened to him in the garden at Aethiopia, and worse, start talking about it, either to Gita Khan or maybe even to the police . . .

At last, the other woman left.

Closed the front door. Walked up the path, turned left and left again. And vanished from sight.

Flic turned from the window out of which she had been watching, her palms sweating again.

She seldom perspired.

*Now or never.*

She walked out of the room and to the staircase, so much smaller and narrower than theirs at home, its carpet dingy and threadbare, smelling slightly of damp.

Flic went up the stairs.

A small landing and four doors. Two ajar. Bathroom and lavatory. She put her hand on the knob of the door nearest to the bathroom, twisted it open and peered inside.

Old John was lying very still, eyes closed, snoring gently. He was wearing paisley pyjamas, his left arm under the covers –

sheets, blankets and an old-fashioned blue eiderdown – his right on top, the hand looking very gnarled and smaller than usual. Flic had always thought his hands immensely big and strong-looking.

Now, idiotically, they made her want to weep.

He looked very weak, much more so than the last time she had seen him.

*Has to be done.*

She hadn't felt like this either before or after she'd shut the shelter door.

Nor even at Hampstead tube station, before or after Isabella. Though the horror of *that* had been almost too much to bear.

This, somehow, seemed worse.

He gave another snore, louder this time, and then a small moan.

Flic stopped breathing.

And noticed the photograph on the dresser near the window.

It was one of a group of three pictures in narrow wood frames. One was of a woman, probably his wife, who had died many years before. One was of a young boy, his son, Flic supposed, who she knew now lived in Florida with his own wife and children.

The third photograph was of Gabriel and Richard Walters. Her grandfather and her father, taken when Richard was no older than she was now. Gabriel was grinning at the camera, but her father looked grave. He looked – now that her hair was so short and dark – amazingly like Imogen.

Flic licked her dry lips. She had never realized that old John had felt close enough to her father and grandfather to keep their picture beside his own family's in his bedroom.

And then she saw the pillow.

On the floor beside the bed, as if it had fallen or been thrown out.

Asking to be used.

Flic turned her back on the photograph, took three steps forward, stooped and picked up the pillow.

*Has to be done.*

She closed her eyes.

Thought about doing it.

About placing it over his face.

Pressing down. *Pushing* down.

She heard the muffled cry, felt his shock, his terror, reverberate through her arms and into her body, felt the legs beneath the covers jerking, felt the free hand clutching at her arm, and then falling away.

She pressed harder.

Waiting.

Felt him grow weaker.

Felt the struggle stop.

Felt *everything* stop.

'Here we are then.'

Gita Khan's voice came warmly from just outside the door.

Flic opened her eyes and dropped the pillow onto the floor.

In the bed, old John, safe and sound, stirred, began to wake up. The door opened.

'Here you both are.' Mrs Khan came in, holding the tea tray.

Flic opened her mouth to speak, but no sound came out.

'Isn't this a nice surprise, John?' The Indian woman set down the tray on the dresser top, close to the photographs. 'Your Felicity coming all this way specially to visit you.' She chuckled. 'Or your Flic, I should say, shouldn't I?'

'Hello, John,' Flic managed to say. 'How are you feeling?'

'Not so bad,' he said.

She could hardly bring herself to look into his face, could feel his eyes boring into her. Her arms felt like wood, heavy, useless. She stared down at the pillow on the floor by her feet and wondered at the power of her imagination.

'I've brought you both a nice fresh pot of tea,' Mrs Khan said, unnecessarily. 'How do you take yours, Flic?'

Flic forced a smile. 'I won't, thank you.' She raised her left arm, made a show of looking at her watch. 'I really need to get back to the hospital. I didn't realize how long I'd been away.'

'What a shame.' Gita Khan bent, picked up the pillow, put it on a chair near the bed. 'Isn't it a shame, John?'

'Yes,' he said.

Flic felt heat sear her cheeks.

'You're quite sure you can't stay?' Mrs Khan asked.

'Quite sure,' Flic said. 'I'm so sorry about what happened to you, John.' She made herself look at him, at the old blue eyes that were piercing her own, seeing through her. 'I do hope you feel much better soon.'

'Thank you,' old John said.

She turned and walked out through the door. She heard Gita

Khan asking her to wait so that she could see her out, but she *couldn't* wait, not a second longer, and if she didn't get out into the fresh air now, right now, she thought she might start screaming or, at the very least, that she might pass out . . .

She wrenched at the front door, got it open.

The taxi was still there.

She stepped outside, pulled the door shut behind her.

Took a deep breath.

And walked up the path.

# 56

They came after lunch.

Matthew had gone out to buy a sandwich and had brought it back to his desk, had just phoned the hospital again and had, to his great pleasure, found it possible to speak to Sylvie when Gary Higgins buzzed through on the intercom to say that two gentlemen wanted to see Matthew in reception right away.

'Sylvie, I have to go.'

'Is everything all right?'

He knew she'd heard the shock in his voice.

'Everything's fine,' he told her and hung up.

He had known instantly that it would be the police, had expected Malloy, but the two men were strangers, in plain clothes, and their manner – even as they informed him they were placing him under arrest – discreet enough, yet as he exited the building with them, Matthew felt that they might as well have had flashing blue lights glued to their heads, and hell was opening up again beneath his feet.

Jasper Hughes, a jaunty pink carnation in his buttonhole, arrived less than forty minutes after Matthew's call from the station.

'No panicking,' Hughes told him calmly. 'You've been arrested, as you know, on suspicion of indecent assault, because they are now in possession of some evidence.'

'What kind of evidence?' Matthew asked, with dread.

'A towel. Presumably the towel that Mrs Bates showed you on Saturday morning.'

354

Flic again, Matthew guessed.

'Still, no one's said anything yet about charges,' Hughes went on, 'so it's simply a matter of answering their questions and keeping your head.'

'But I can't just leave like last time?'

'Afraid not.'

'Just checking,' Matthew said.

'If things get too much at any point, let me know and I'll try and make sure we take a breather.' Hughes paused. 'Ready?'

Matthew's stomach felt as if the quarter sandwich he'd eaten for lunch had been made of lead rather than ham.

'As I'll ever be,' he said.

The men who'd delivered him were nowhere to be seen, and with Malloy seated opposite him, asking the questions, Riley once again at his side, it might have felt like a case of *déjà vu* had it not been for the presence of Jasper Hughes beside him instead of Crocker, for the twin cassette tapes in a machine at the edge of the table recording the interview, and for the fact that his own position was clearly more precarious than it had been first time around.

The questioning seemed endless, and for much of the time Matthew felt nauseous, afraid and despondent, bolstered only occasionally and fleetingly by Hughes's nods of encouragement. The detectives' focus was much more tightly concentrated today on the alleged assault against Imogen, yet some questions did deal again with the events of the past year, and several times Hughes checked Malloy, suggesting that they were straying well away from the crime of which Matthew was suspected; but on most of those occasions DS Malloy responded by assuring Hughes that his line of questioning was relevant. Matthew was just beginning to feel that he couldn't take much more when his lawyer requested time out, to which Malloy acceded immediately, and Matthew sent a silent message of gratitude to Jack Crocker just for finding him Jasper Hughes.

'It's very early days and they're still fishing,' the lawyer said as soon as they were alone, 'so don't allow yourself to get too rattled.'

'Easy to say.' Matthew hadn't realized until the break that he was shaking again.

'If you agree, I'd like to raise the Christmas gift issue again, and the business with your wife's garage rental cheque.'

355

'Why?'

'Because now that this is official, Malloy is less likely to raise either of those topics since they're unrelated to the assault, and I think that reminding them – from our perspective – that this isn't the first time someone has attempted to frame you, may work for us in the long run.' Hughes gave one of his gentle smiles. 'I think Malloy may realize that this rather odd string of alleged offences simply doesn't ring true.'

'What if he thinks they just prove I'm an all-round scumbag?'

'Bringing up petty crimes may not make you instant man-of-the-year, but a touch more or less popularity won't matter in the long run.'

'So what is going to matter?' Matthew asked tensely.

'Walking out of here today, and then *staying* out.'

*Amen to that*, Matthew thought, then remembered the subjects that had not, thus far, been raised this afternoon. 'Might this still be leading back to the crazy questions they were asking me last time about where I was when Caro and Isabella died?'

'I can't see it,' Hughes shook his head. 'It's patently all bunkum, and Malloy's a sensible man.'

'If it's all such bunkum, why am I here?'

'Because they have just a little more under their belts than when you first came here.' He looked at Matthew. 'The good news is that Imogen still hasn't made a formal statement.'

'That's only a matter of time,' Matthew said morosely.

'They're extremely unlikely to take this further unless she does,' Hughes said.

'Flic gave them the towel.'

'Possibly.'

'Then she'll make Imogen give the statement.'

# 57

'Where have you *been*?' Chloë demanded.

'What happened to you, darling?' Sylvie was looking very anxious.

'Have I been gone ages?' Flic bent to kiss her grandmother's cheek.

'You've been *hours*,' Chloë said.

'Just over an hour,' Sylvie amended.

'Groosi's been really worried – I phoned the house *twice*.'

Flic sank down onto one of the chairs. 'I'm sorry.'

'So what happened?' Chloë wanted to know.

'Give your sister a minute,' Sylvie said. 'She looks worn out.'

Flic managed a smile at her grandmother. 'I'm sorry. Both of you.' She knew she was still trembling, realized she'd better use that. 'I was going to get the drinks, but then I decided I wanted some fresh air, so I went out for a walk, and then suddenly, out of nowhere, I felt really sick, so I ran back inside and had to make a dash for one of the ground floor loos – I suppose I lost track of time.' Not total fiction since, after the journey back – which had incorporated a stop at a cashpoint to enable her to pay for the taxi – she had indeed had to go to a lavatory downstairs for a cool wash and to compose herself before getting another Coke and coming back up to the twelfth floor.

'Poor darling,' Sylvie said.

Flic felt in the deep pocket of her parka, handed over the can to her sister.

'It's not cold enough,' Chloë complained.

'So get a colder one,' Flic said.

'I will.' Chloë stood up.

'Here.' Flic opened her bag, fished out some coins for her.

'Anything for you?' Chloë was already at the door.

'Same, please.'

'Do you think maybe you should see a doctor?' Sylvie asked as the door shut.

'Of course not,' Flic said. 'I'm fine. Just a bit upset.'

'My doing,' Sylvie said.

'Hardly,' Flic said wryly.

'You must go home,' her grandmother told her. 'I think I'm going to have a nap anyway, so there's no need for you to stay.'

'I'd like to, if you don't mind.'

'Of course I don't mind,' Sylvie said, wearily, and closed her eyes.

Flic bit down a sudden desire to cry. Nothing had actually happened, she tried to convince herself. She had dropped the pillow before John had woken and before Mrs Khan had come into the room. Neither of them could have read her mind. Which meant that she was no worse off than she had been before her visit to West Finchley.

*Except for his eyes, boring into me.*

Though maybe that, too, had been her imagination.

Chloë came back in, saw that Sylvie was sleeping, quietly handed Flic her Coke and sat down on the opposite side of the bed, while on the other side of the room, the female patient slumbered on.

Flic wondered, briefly, if she was actually sleeping or comatose.

And then her mind returned to John Pascoe. And the ramifications of his telling what had happened to Gita Khan.

And of Gita Khan passing the information on.

She looked at Chloë, tipping Coke out of the can into her mouth, and imagined the way her little sister's big blue eyes would change if she heard.

Maybe Mrs Khan wouldn't believe John. Yet even if she did not, even if she and others decided that the old man was not, as the nurse had said, 'on the ball', there would still be ugly question marks over how he had come to be trapped in the shelter and, infinitely more horrifyingly, over Isabella's death.

358

Flic looked at Sylvie.

Her grandmother loved her very much, but she was a realist, not some cuddly, doting granny who would hear nothing bad said about her grandchildren.

*Oh, God.*

How would it be if it all came out? Groosi would collapse again, maybe even die. Imogen would crash over the edge she was always so worryingly close to, and that would be her fault, too. Grandfather Gabriel, who'd been close enough to old John to merit a photographic position beside his wife and son, would never understand.

No one would understand.

*It doesn't matter, so long as we're rid of Matthew.*

That wasn't true, of course. It did matter, terribly, because it would signal the end of her world, her family's world, and it would all be down to her, all her fault.

*Not true.*

Not *true*, Flic.

His fault. All of it. None of it would have happened but for him.

*His* fault.

'Flic, darling, are you all right?'

She blinked, saw that her grandmother was awake and watching her. 'I'm fine.'

Sylvie reached for her hand. 'You're cold.'

Flic pulled her fingers away, irrationally but horribly afraid that her grandmother might sense something via her touch, might actually read her mind.

She stood up. 'I have to go.'

'All right, darling.'

Chloë was staring at her.

'Chloë, darling, you go too,' Sylvie said.

'I don't want to go.'

'It's time you went home,' her grandmother insisted. 'I need to rest, and much as I love having you here, I can't sleep properly if I know you're sitting, waiting.'

Flic bent, kissed her grandmother's warm cheek. 'I've got a headache, Groosi. I'm sorry for worrying you before.' She picked up her jacket, her bag. 'Come on if you're coming, Chloë.'

'Go on, darling,' Sylvie urged.

Chloë got up reluctantly, gave her grandmother a hug, mindful of the drip and wires attaching her to the monitor. 'Can I phone you later?'

'Of course you can.'

'Come *on*.' Flic was already at the door.

'I'm *coming*.' Chloë kissed Sylvie again. 'I love you, Groosi.'

'I love you too, darling.' Sylvie looked towards Flic. 'Wish you better.'

'Thank you,' Flic said, and went out.

'What's going on with you?' Chloë had to walk fast to keep up.

'Just shut up, can't you, and give me some peace and quiet?'

'Something's the matter,' Chloë persisted.

Flic stopped in her tracks, turned, her eyes glinting with sudden anger. 'I mean it, Chloë. I've got a lousy headache, I'm exhausted, and I want to go *home*.'

'All right,' Chloë said, startled. 'Keep your hair on.'

'Are you going to keep quiet?'

'Yes,' Chloë said. 'Okay.'

'Good,' Flic said, and went on walking towards the lifts.

In his bedroom in the little house in West Finchley, John Pascoe was sitting up against the pillows Gita Khan had just plumped up for him, staring into space.

'Are you all right, John?' his neighbour asked.

He nodded, then drew the eiderdown more closely up around himself.

'Are you cold? Would you like me to bring you a heater? We have a spare one, and it's quite good.'

He shook his head. 'No, thank you. I'm not cold.'

Mrs Khan eyed him solicitously. She had hoped the visit from the young woman might cheer him up, put a little colour and strength back into him, but if anything, the old gentleman seemed to look worse than he had.

'Perhaps I should telephone the doctor?'

'No need,' he said. 'I'm all right, Gita. Just a bit . . .'

'Yes?'

'Old,' he said.

Gita sagged for a moment, then rallied again. 'How about a nice cup of tea?'

'Yes,' he said. 'Thank you, Gita.'

She went to pick up the pot on the tray that still stood on the

360

dresser, about to take it downstairs to boil fresh water, and then she turned back to look at him again. 'You seem worried, John.'

'I'm all right,' he said again.

'If there's something you would like to speak about . . .'

He shook his head. 'Nothing. Thank you,' he added again, as an afterthought.

He saw her sigh, then watched her carry the pot out of the room.

He would not really have minded talking to her about things, would have found it a comfort to unburden himself to someone. He had, in fact, almost decided a while ago that he would do just that.

And then he had woken up and seen Flic standing there.

He knew now that he could not talk to anyone about it. Not, at least, until he was feeling stronger. More like his old self.

He looked over at his photographs. At Gabriel and Richard Walters. Thought about them, and about poor Caroline and her mother, of whom he was very fond.

And was not at all sure that he would *ever* be able to talk about it.

# 58

Jasper Hughes had been right. They had not locked Matthew up. They had shown him the towel, had asked him about it, and he had done his best to answer calmly, and they had, finally, let him go. Though his troubles were clearly not over, not by a long chalk, as they both agreed. For now, it was police bail pending further investigation and questioning.

'At least they didn't ask for my passport,' Matthew said out in Rosslyn Hill, still holding the sheet of paper that the custody sergeant's computer had issued him, detailing his bail date, time and place.

'Thinking of going somewhere?' Hughes asked.

'Just in no mood to go back to the house to fetch it.'

'Can't blame you for that,' the lawyer said.

In Aethiopia, Susanna had been doing her best, since Flic and Chloë had returned from the Royal Free, to ease the strained atmosphere. But Imogen was still spending most of the time skulking in her room, and Susanna felt sure that the other two sisters had had an argument, which was, so far as she knew, a rare event in their case.

*Food*, she decided.

'I'm going to make some supper in a while,' she said, finding Flic and Chloë in the drawing room, both staring at a soap opera on the television. 'Any ideas?'

'I'm not really hungry,' Flic said.

'Chloë? What do you fancy?'

'Nothing, thank you.'

'We have to eat,' Susanna said.

'Why?' Chloë said. 'We're not starving.' It was the sort of answer Imogen gave when she was being stroppy, and she found that talking that way helped, just a bit, to release a little of the knotted-up feeling that seemed to be filling her chest and stomach.

Flic shifted restlessly in her armchair. 'Where's Kahli?'

'In the garden again.'

'Poor Kahli,' Chloë said. 'He knows Groosi's ill.'

'Animals do sense tension,' Susanna agreed.

Flic stood up, suddenly, the TV remote control that had been on her knee clattering onto the floor. 'How much do the police *need* before they arrest someone?'

Susanna tried not to appear disturbed. 'Quite a lot, I imagine.'

Flic didn't say any more, just walked over to the fireplace and stared into the grate.

'I hope they don't come back here again,' Chloë said, fretfully.

'If they do,' Susanna said, 'it won't be anything for you to worry about.'

'What do you know?' Chloë said rudely.

'Enough to know it doesn't help to get all wound up about things that may never happen,' Susanna replied, still calmly.

Chloë turned away from her and regarded her sister for a long moment, and then, very abruptly, she turned and ran out of the room and up the staircase.

'What's the matter with her?' Susanna asked Flic softly.

'Stress. Groosi being ill. Everything else. Getting to us all.'

'I suppose so,' Susanna said. 'At least your grandmother's out of danger, thank God.'

'Yes,' Flic said quietly. 'Thank God.'

In need of a stiff drink after parting from Hughes outside the police station, Matthew had gone into the nearest pub, bought a whisky and sat in a corner to drink it.

It was after six-thirty when he arrived back at the Royal Free. He met no difficulties in discovering where his mother-in-law had been moved to, and there were no signs at her door discouraging visitors, but when he entered the room, Sylvie was sleeping.

He stood by the door for several moments in case she woke, then, when she did not stir, quietly let himself out again.

Sylvie had not, as it happened, actually *been* asleep. She had been lying on her side when Matthew had entered the room, had seen him reflected in the dark, uncurtained portion of the window, and had simply decided, on the spur of the moment, that she was not up to speaking to him.

She was still much too troubled by what she had seen in her granddaughters' faces prior to the end of their visit. Flic had seemed a million miles away, had looked dreadfully burdened, almost frightened, such a rarity in her that Sylvie had herself experienced a deep, resonant fear. And Chloë, too, had not been her usual self, had seemed quite resentful of Flic, and so it had, frankly, been a relief when they had both left.

Then there was Imogen, still staying away. Imo, the most difficult, the most troubled, yet still in her way, a loving girl, in many respects the most passionate of Caro's daughters. And yet she had not come to see her grandmother. Why not? Because she feared hospitals, or because she couldn't face Sylvie? And if the latter, *why*? The answer to that, among so many other questions, a list growing steadily longer in her mind, was what Sylvie could not face, not yet at least.

Illness was quite interesting in that respect, she mused, lying with her eyes still closed in case anyone else decided to arrive. Alarming as her attack had been, it had, in a way, given her some respite from unpleasantness and perhaps her body had been protecting her from something worse than her family's ugly behaviour, something even more fearful – though right now, feeling as she did, she could not quite put her finger on *exactly* what that might have been.

Something very bad, she suspected, but that for the time being, thankfully, she did not have to deal with, and there had been too *much* to deal with for such a long time, and all she really wanted to do now was to sleep, *really* sleep . . .

Emerging from the hospital, Matthew had turned right into Pond Street, for no good reason, since left would have brought him to Rosslyn Hill and thus closer either to one of the Northern Line stations or to the Marriott Hotel. He had crossed the muddle of roads near Hampstead Heath Station and had aimed himself instinctively away from East Heath Road and home and Hampstead in general, pointing himself instead onto Parliament

Hill, vaguely aware that if he managed to walk in a comparatively straight line, he ought to find his way to Highgate, where he thought he might take another breather in a pub or bar, before heading back to Earl's Court and the consolation of Kat.

It had been a curious, somewhat bizarre impulse, given his previous experience of wandering on the Heath after dark, but perhaps, he wondered, it might also have been a kind of escape bid; perhaps he had almost been hoping to lose himself for a while, and to cease, therefore, having to confront reality; perhaps if he fell into one of those murky, freezing ponds or pools, or ran into a low-hanging tree branch and got a concussion . . .

Nothing so simple.

It began to rain. At least, at *first* it rained, and then, when he was too far onto the Heath to make it worth turning back, the wind picked up, blustering bone-chillingly from the east, and the rain turned into a downpour. In minutes, Matthew's clothes were soaked through, his hair dripping into eyes that were already stinging from the wind's whipping, and his shoes – worst of all, if it was possible to place *anything* at the pinnacle of his discomfort list – filled with water, mud and, so it felt, stones.

He emerged, finally, having contrived not to fall into any of the Highgate Ponds, to find himself a long way from the High Street, with no bars or pubs in sight, though the way he felt now, he doubted that any respectable establishment would allow him in.

He wanted to weep – hell, he wanted to *howl*. He wanted, suddenly, to go back to East Heath Road, to Aethiopia, to the slender white house, and to put his wet, icy hands around the slender white necks of either Flic or Imogen – either neck would do right now – and throttle them at *least* until they turned blue and had to beg him for mercy.

But instead, all he did, all he *could* do, was go on walking, trudging until he found the tube or a bus route or – please God – a taxi with its For Hire sign glowing, or even just a public phone – the battery on his mobile having died again, and what *use* were the damned pieces of junk if their batteries always ran down exactly when they were needed most?

The girls all came to the kitchen when Susanna called them, all sat down at the table to make a show of at least trying to eat the poached eggs and mashed potatoes she'd laid out for them.

'Would you prefer something else? I don't mind.'

'We're not helpless,' Imogen said. 'We can make whatever we want ourselves.'

'I know that,' Susanna said.

'I just don't think we're very hungry,' Flic said.

'Sorry,' Chloë said.

'No need to apologize,' Susanna told her.

Flic got up and began to clear the table, and Susanna said it was all right, that she was glad to be kept occupied, after which Imogen stood up and left the room, followed, a moment later, by Chloë.

'It's very nice of you to stay and help us,' Flic said. 'But Imo's right in a way – if you want to go home, we'll manage perfectly well.'

'I'm happy to stay,' Susanna said, 'if you don't mind.' She paused. 'I didn't offer to stay just because Matthew asked me, you know. I would have anyway.'

'I know,' Flic said. 'You've always wanted to help.'

Matthew had climbed aboard a bus, finally, had sat near the front, exhausted and cold, but relieved just to be sitting, barely able to summon the mental strength to plan the rest of his journey. Hopes of a comfortable cab ride had vanished when he'd realized, close to Highgate Village, that he had hardly any cash on him.

So instead it was this bus to Liverpool Street, and after that the Circle Line to Earl's Court, and be damned glad to be out of the rain, and of the many aimless thoughts that had passed through his brain that evening had been the knowledge that he was definitely not the stuff that the truly homeless were made of; that if he ever hit rock bottom and all doors were slammed in his face, he would either rapidly become a hypothermia statistic or lose his mind.

*Already losing it, Gardner.*

God, he was so damned *cold*.

# 59

They all sat, lay, paced in different rooms.

Susanna sat in the kitchen, Kahli by her feet, drinking camomile tea, alternately thinking and trying *not* to think.

Something, she believed, was going to happen. Something significant and, she feared, bad. Emotions were running too high, the three sisters too agitated, too unhappy and afraid in their own individual ways.

'It can't go on like this,' she said softly to the dog.

Flic was in the study. Their *father's* study. Everyone considered Imo the hypersensitive one about that kind of thing, and it was true that Imo tended to go overboard about their dad's territory, his old studio, his work, the Astrid T-shirts and the like. Yet she had always felt it all too, every bit as piercingly. It was just that she had always been better equipped to deal with the pinpricks and the blows, with the emotions. With the pain.

She recognized that her own outer shield had thinned over the last few nightmare days and nights. The shocks of what she had been forced to do to Isabella, and what she had tried to do to John, had taken their toll, of course. But worse than that, if she was honest – and Flic preferred, if possible, to *be* honest with herself – had been her *failure* to silence John. Twice over. It was those failures, she thought now, which had enfeebled her earlier in Groosi's hospital room, when she'd felt such awful fear creeping over her, taking her over, threatening her and everything, every*one* important to her.

367

*No more.*

It was time to rebuild her defences, to toughen up again. If old John had told his neighbour what she'd done, and if Mrs Khan had actually *believed* him, Flic thought she might have heard about it by now. But even if he had not said anything yet, because he was either too weak or shaken, and if he tried to accuse her later on, then no matter how many doubts such an accusation might raise, she still felt that John's age and poor health would speak against him and for her. Imo might be the better actor in the short haul, but Flic had the inner steel to carry through the long-haul performance, and would do so.

So all she had to do now was toughen up, and wait.

It was only the waiting that was unnerving her.

Nothing she couldn't cope with though.

Imogen was in her own room, staring into space.

This room was the only place she felt safe in now.

Halfway safe, at least.

Away from prying eyes.

Even Flic was making her afraid now. Spending so much time with her, sleeping in here. That was why she felt so tired, she supposed, because she was scared to close her eyes at night, in case . . .

In case *what*? She surely couldn't really be afraid of Flic, of *all* people. But that was the thing, wasn't it? She *was* growing afraid of her sister; was, increasingly, becoming afraid of everything, everyone. Even herself.

Especially herself.

She felt best in here, on her own, with her father's things around her. She felt best sitting hunched over on her bed, wearing one of his Astrid shirts, knees drawn up, arms around her legs, holding herself, rocking herself. Rocking felt nice, reminded her of happy, comfortable times.

Innocent times.

Long, long ago.

Chloë, too, was in her bedroom. It was a room that, in some ways, she no longer really liked, and yet she could not envisage wanting to change it, because Caroline had been responsible for most of it and so the thought of having strangers in here scraping off wall-

368

paper or pulling down curtains that her mother had chosen, or the idea of putting any of her stuffed animals and dog-eared books into boxes and taking them to a hospital or the Oxfam shop was all too much.

*Too soon.*

Except that being in here lately seemed to make her sad, rather than comforted. Sad, and a bit lost. And scared. She was so awfully, horribly scared, and it just seemed to keep on getting worse, the way *everything* was getting worse. Everyone was dying, and her sisters were still doing everything they could think of to get Matthew into trouble; perhaps even, the way things were going, into prison.

That was what was scaring her so much. Not the fact that he might go to prison, because she knew that was not really going to happen, because she could not allow it to.

*That* was what was scaring her.

The fact that she was going to have to tell the truth. About what *she* had done. Her part in all this.

She had no way of knowing, for *sure*, that Matthew had not done what Imogen claimed, and it was terrible thinking that her own sister – *sisters* – might tell such hideous lies. Yet she knew better than anyone how clever they were at inventing and plotting. So yes, of course, she *did* know that Imo was telling lies now too.

And she was going to have to tell.

Not just for Matthew's sake either. Because of how things *felt* now, here in Aethiopia. And outside, too, wherever she was. There was no escaping it, nothing was peaceful. Imogen was worse than she'd ever been. She'd always been grouchy, of course, and depressed sometimes, but now she was either horrible or somehow not quite *there*. And suddenly Flic, too, seemed off in another world, unreachable and harder than Chloë had ever known her. And frightened, too, which alarmed Chloë almost more than anything.

And Groosi was lying there in hospital, might have *died*, and this truly *was* the worst thing of all. Chloë was so desperately afraid that her grandmother's attack might have been a punishment for *her* sins, for what *she* had done to Matthew, who her mother had really loved.

*I could have said no.*

She'd learned about saying no, to drugs and sex and smoking

and alcohol – not to forgery, no one had taught her that. But they had taught her about free will. She could have stood up to Flic and Imo, but she had not, had been too much of a wimp.

So now here she was, pacing around in the little girl's room that no longer felt like home, and what she needed to do, more than anything, was to tell someone the truth. And Chloë knew that she would be punished, because she had done those things, had committed *forgery*. And the prospect of being taken away by the police, maybe having to stand up in court and be cross-examined, maybe being sent away to some detention centre, was too horrific to think about. Yet if she *didn't* tell someone, if she didn't just open her mouth and let all this out to someone very, very soon, she was sure, she was absolutely and completely *certain*, that she would go mad.

# 60

Matthew had finally reached Kat's.

It had never occurred to him until he was fifty yards away that she might, not having heard from him, have gone out, but then, abruptly, that thought had struck him, and he'd almost yelped out loud with the pain of it.

But she had been there.

'Matthew,' she'd said at the door, staring at him. 'What's *happened* to you?'

'I got a little wet,' he had answered.

'Wet?' she'd said. 'You look three-quarters *drowned*.'

He'd hesitated, muttered something about taking off his shoes for the sake of her carpet, but Kat had grabbed his hand and dragged him through the door. To hell with her carpet, she had said, and he'd realized then that he was still shivering, and Kat had laid a cool hand on his forehead and said he was very warm, and what he needed to do, what she was *ordering* him to do, was take off all his wet things, *all* of them, no arguments. She was going to fetch him her towelling robe, she'd said, which would be much too small but better than nothing, and then she was going to put him to bed and bring him hot soup and two paracetamol.

'No arguments, do you hear me?'

Not a single one.

He was in her bed now, alone, tucked up like an overgrown boy. Kat had brought him a big mug of steaming tomato soup and a hunk of soft white bread, and then she'd left him alone while she went to make herself some supper, imagining, Matthew supposed, that he might prefer to be alone.

Which was not, as it happened, at all true.

He had, he suddenly felt, been alone for far too long. However many people there might have been around him, in Aethiopia, or at VKF, or out and about, or in the police station, he had still felt, he realized, utterly alone. And he wasn't quite sure now why he'd stopped returning his brother's and Karl's calls, whether it was a shame thing, or embarrassment.

That was over now, he decided, drinking his soup. When Kat came back in, he was going to share with her all that he'd been through since he'd last seen her. And then, if she was willing, what he wanted, more than anything (too soon or not, and Caro would have understood, he thought, he *hoped*) was to lie beside her in this bed, holding her and being held, and he doubted that he'd be up to anything more than that, and he hoped she wouldn't mind, but he did need, very badly, to be held.

Except that before that, right *now*, in fact, just as soon as he could set down the mug, move the tray safely out of the way and get his head down on her pillow, he knew, with what little was left of his strength, that he was going to sleep.

# 61

Chloë had waited for what seemed a very long time, listening to the sounds of the house until she had heard Flic come upstairs and go into Imogen's room. And then she had waited a few more minutes, to be sure, before very, *very* quietly opening her door and going downstairs to find Susanna.

She was in the kitchen, sitting at the table, Kahli by her feet, a mug of something cupped in her hands.

'Can I talk to you?' Chloë asked her softly.

'Of course you can.' Susanna put down the mug. 'Sit down.'

'Not here,' Chloë whispered. 'You can sometimes hear from upstairs what people are saying in here.'

Susanna regarded her for a moment. 'Where would you be comfortable?'

'Nowhere,' Chloë said. 'But I think the safest place might be the Quiet Room.'

It was hard, Susanna thought afterwards, to know quite how she felt.

Dazed. Shocked, of course. Horrified, not so much by poor Chloë's forgeries – for there was no question that the child had been under awful duress to have done such things – but by the dreadful implications that her confession had thrown up. Which she badly needed to think about, thoroughly.

After she had dealt with Chloë.

They were sitting on Caro's couch, the girl beside her trembling and red-eyed.

'You've done the right thing in telling me, darling.'

'Have I?' Chloë still looked scared.

'Yes.' It was hard to sound and appear calm. 'You've handed over your problems to me now, and that's a very sensible thing to have done – the only thing you could do, by the way.'

'I could have kept quiet,' Chloë said.

'And do you honestly think that would have done anyone any good at all?'

'I don't know.'

'It would not.' Susanna paused, wanted to be straight with her. 'Darling, I'm not going to pretend that I automatically know exactly how best to deal with what you've told me.'

'Are you going to tell the police?' Frightened blue eyes.

'No.' Susanna considered for a moment. 'At least, I'm certainly not going to tell them now – and I won't tell them anything at all *ever* without letting you know first. All right?'

Chloë nodded.

'And I think you're right about not telling your sisters that we've had this chat – not yet anyway.' She saw the child's relief. 'I have a lot of thinking to do. I need to work out the absolutely best way to proceed with this, for all your sakes. Yours, your sisters', Groosi's, and Matthew's too. Does that sound all right, Chloë?'

'Yes.' A whisper.

Susanna reached out and tenderly stroked the golden hair, a wave of empathy rolling through her for Caro's youngest. 'For now, darling, I really believe there's no need for you to be too scared of the consequences of what you did.'

'Forgery.' Very white-faced.

'Yes,' Susanna agreed. 'But you're still very young, and yes, of course it was very wrong, but you know that, and you're trying to put it right now, aren't you?'

'I suppose,' Chloë said.

Susanna looked at her, then stood up slowly.

'Where are you going?' Fresh alarm.

'To make you a nice warm drink, to help you relax, maybe sleep.' She paused. 'If that's all right with you, Chloë? If you want to stay up, talk some more, that's fine. It's entirely your decision.'

Chloë shook her head. The idea of relaxing, sleeping, was exactly what she wanted. And, she thought, perhaps even more

374

than that, the opportunity to make her own decisions. *Not too many decisions though*, she thought, *not yet*.

'I'd like the warm drink, please,' she said. 'Thank you.'

Susanna brought her the drink, saw her safely to bed, encountered Flic coming out of Imogen's room, kept her wits about her and explained that Chloë was exhausted, feeling the after-effects of Sylvie's collapse, that she'd given her a mug of milky cocoa and that she was now nice and sleepy.

'Good,' Flic said.

'If you want to check on her, she seems about ready to drop off.'

Flic shook her head. 'I'll leave her for now.' She hardly seemed interested.

'Only I don't want you to feel I'm taking over, Flic.'

'I don't feel that. I'm grateful.'

'Do you need anything from your room?' Susanna asked. 'Only I think I might have a bit of a rest myself.'

'That's fine,' Flic said. 'I'm going downstairs anyway.'

Susanna waited, as the young woman went towards the staircase, and then she went to her temporary bedroom. Flic's room, available because its usual inhabitant was still sharing with Imogen. Though they did, of course, have a spare room on the second floor that Sylvie had used till she'd become ill, but Susanna supposed that the two older sisters had felt the need to stay close . . .

*Grateful*, Flic had said just now. The word seemed to grind in her head as she shut the door quietly, firmly, then went to sit in the chair near the window.

*Thinking time.*

Having hung up Matthew's clothes to dry and plugged in his phone, Kat went to check on him.

'Kat?' he said, fuzzily.

'Sorry,' she said. 'I didn't mean to wake you. Go back to sleep.'

'That's okay, I'm awake now.'

'For about three seconds, from the look of you.'

He knew she was right, at least he knew it with the fragments of his consciousness still fully functioning. 'Sorry, Kat,' he said.

She smiled at him. 'Close your eyes.'

'I wanted . . .'

'Just close your eyes, Matthew, and give in for a bit.'

He closed them.

All evening Susanna had quietly observed the three sisters, fancied herself almost able to *see* their secrets seething in their minds, had found herself visualizing for a few moments at supper time sausages in a pan, skins stretched too tautly over simmering flesh until they split apart, spilling their insides . . . Unusually unattractive visualization for her, she realized, for Susanna preferred her imagery graceful and serene, sometimes used her imagination as a tool of self-protection to steer her own mind away from patients' torments.

She had not expected Chloë to be the one to break it to her; mostly, of course, because it had not occurred to her that Caro's youngest child might be capable of doing the kind of thing she had now confessed to.

'Why *did* you do it?' Susanna had asked, upstairs in the Quiet Room, striving to comprehend. 'Why did Flic and Imo *want* to do such things to Matthew?'

'Because they said it was his fault Mummy died.'

It had taken Susanna moments to absorb the full impact of that statement. She had reacted stupidly at first, had pointed out what they all already knew, that Matthew had not even *been* here on the day of Caro's death, and that the Coroner had ruled out foul play.

'That wasn't what Flic and Imo meant,' Chloë had explained to her. 'They meant that he made her unhappy. That Mummy and Matthew had a row before he went away, but then he still went off and left her, even though she was going to have a baby. They said he was in love with this other woman, that he went away to be with *her*.' Her eyes had filled with remembered horror. 'And then, of course, Mummy died, and that was why they blamed him.'

Susanna thought she could at least begin to comprehend their motivations for those earlier actions – for hadn't she experienced similar lines of suspicion? They had been wounded and young, while she was an adult, an experienced psychotherapist . . .

If only it had all stopped there. But there was this other terrible thing, Imogen's latest accusation against her stepfather, the dreadful thing that no one seemed to know quite how to deal with. Perhaps because they hadn't felt quite able to believe it, for if

376

Sylvie had *really* thought it true, Susanna knew that she would have stopped Matthew from coming within a mile of her grand-daughters.

Now that too seemed to be clarifying. Because if Matthew had not been guilty of those other lesser things, if he had, in fact, been set up by Caro's daughters – *set up* – oh God, such cold-blooded words to contemplate – then it was suddenly horribly clear that the assault allegation was definitely another, infinitely graver, fabrication.

But Flic had described Imogen's scratches, had mentioned blood and bruises. And though Imo had refused to talk to the police, she had, Sylvie had admitted, been examined by their doctor. And if that allegation had been bogus, if there had been no assault, then . . .

Susanna's head reeled with it all, the loathsome leather and steel contraption coming back to her yet again. And the drawings. Foundations enough, perhaps, she now wondered, upon which to build a disturbed young mind; a mind sufficiently obsessed with hatred for Matthew – perhaps for all men – to endure self-mutilation as a means to punish the object of her hatred?

Except that, according to Chloë, *Flic*, not Imogen, had been the planner, the leader of the campaign against Matthew, and Susanna could believe that, not just because she was older, but because Flic had always possessed the sharper, clearer brain. But if Flic was behind these plots, then surely that meant she had countenanced, if not encouraged her younger sister to physically harm herself . . .

Sitting in Flic's bedroom now, Susanna felt violently sick. It was hard, too hard, to think about this.

*Remember your training.*

She had to find a way through, to detach herself. These things had happened, and she, who had so wished to remain involved with Caro's daughters, had now to find the best method of dealing with them. On the psychiatric front, this was now beyond her, but there were certainly professionals available who could help the sisters. And though she had told Chloë she would not speak to the police (not *yet*, that was what she'd promised, wasn't it?) ultimately, unless she was prepared to allow an innocent man to . . .

*You have to talk to Flic.*

Who was still downstairs. Alone.

Susanna wanted a drink badly, something to calm her, but on

the other hand, she supposed she needed a clear head more than she needed her senses dulling.

*Go on.*

Still, she sat, not moving.

*Now. Before she goes back to Imogen.*

Now.

*No more procrastination.*

Susanna stood up.

# 62

'It's not true.'

Flic's words, flat, stark, underpinned with anger.

'Which part isn't true, Flic?'

'All of it. None of it.'

They were in the drawing room. Just the two of them. The other sisters, if they had heard any of the conversation, had chosen to remain off-stage up in their rooms. Kahli was over by the door, lying down, muzzle between his paws.

'I know,' Susanna said, 'that some of it is certainly true.'

She was sitting in one of the armchairs. Flic was standing. She had changed, a while ago, into a navy blue tracksuit with *FW* embroidered in red over her left breast. Her long hair was fastened back in a pony tail, her eyes were narrowed, her mouth set. She looked, Susanna thought, athletic, strong. *Dangerous*?

That was absurd, she told herself. Flic's mind might have become sadly twisted of late, engaging in complex, damaging and probably, alas, sordid strategies, but the young person standing here now was, fundamentally, still Felicity, Caro's beloved first-born.

'You *think* you know that,' Flic said, 'because Chloë's given you a few facts.'

'That's part of it, yes.' Susanna was managing to remain calm, her training finally kicking in, some of that vastly useful, albeit spurious, detachment assisting her. 'But only part. I've been troubled for some time.'

'You've been *nosy* for some time, you mean,' Flic said.

'You've been troubled, too.' She ignored the insult.

'You've spotted that, have you, Susanna? How clever of you.'

'Not especially.'

'No, you're right. It's *not* especially clever to notice that I've been *troubled*, as you put it.' She paused. 'Let me see. My mother met a creep of an American, took about five minutes to forget our father and marry him, and then she *died* and left us with him. Our dear stepfather, who has thicker skin than a rhino, stayed on in our house – *our* house, not his.'

'Because your mother wanted him to,' Susanna said. 'Because he wanted to help you all.'

'He's committed crimes,' Flic went quickly on. '*He's* committed them, not me, not Imo, not Chloë, whatever she's told you. He even got into my sister's bed and tried to *rape* her – and now you're saying even *that's* supposed to be down to *me*—'

'This isn't the way to—'

'I don't know what you're *talking* about.' Flic's anger was building. 'And you think *I'm* troubled? I think you must be crazy.'

'Try and calm down, Flic.'

'Calm *down*?' Flic came closer, glowered down at Susanna. 'Who the hell do you think you *are*? Moving in on us like a member of the family.'

'I was asked to stay.'

'By *him*,' Flic snapped. 'And didn't you jump at it?'

Susanna was experiencing a growing wish to escape, but she stayed. *For Caro*. 'We need to talk this through, Flic,' she said. 'For Chloë's sake, as much as yours and Imo's. She's been distraught, that's why she came to me.'

'Chloë still acts like a little girl.' Flic turned away, crossed to the windows, looked out into the night. 'She gets upset when we leave her out of things, so she imagines them instead. She's told you a pack of *lies*. I'm surprised you could be so gullible.'

Susanna looked at the young woman's rigid back, and licked her dry lips. 'I believed Chloë when she told me,' she said. 'I still do, I'm afraid.'

For another moment, Flic stood still, the only sounds in the room the dog's soft panting and the ticking of the mantelpiece clock. And then she turned round. 'I want you to go.'

'I'm not going to do that.'

Flic came a few steps closer. 'I said I want you to *go*. I don't want you here any more. We don't *need* you here, accusing us, plotting against us.'

Susanna saw the rage in her eyes, could almost feel it coming off her in hot waves, and again she longed to leave. 'I'm not plotting, Flic, you must see that. The last thing in the world I want is to hurt any of you. Your mother was my dearest friend.'

'She didn't think of you that way.' Flic's eyes grew colder. 'She thought you were a bore, always hanging around.'

Susanna felt as if she'd been spat at. 'That isn't true,' she said. 'And it's beside the point now, in any case. We're talking about *you*, Flic. About the things you've done, and how we can best deal with them.'

Flic came even closer, stopped just two feet away. 'I've told you how we can deal with them. You can leave. Right now. Get out, Susanna.'

'I've told you, I'm not leaving.'

'Get *out*.' Flic's voice rose, shaking. 'Get up and get out of my house!'

'No, Flic.' Susanna's hands gripped her chair tightly, as if afraid Flic might try to drag her from it. 'I'm not one of your younger sisters,' she said. 'You can't bully me out of saying what I think, or of trying to help you.'

'How can you call this *help*?' Flic was shouting now. 'How *dare* you? You sit there like the dense cow you are, accusing me of actual *crimes*, when you know perfectly well that *he* did those things.' Her cheeks grew pink, her pupils enlarged, she looked quite wild. 'Fraud? Injuring my own sister? Why not go all the way and accuse me of pushing—'

She stopped, suddenly and jaggedly, her face contorting with pain and fury and something more – *horror* – and then she made a sound, half-shriek, half-wail, and turned and ran out of the room, her left foot catching Kahli's side as she went, making him yelp and jump, startled, to his feet.

Susanna sat very still. Her hands continued to grip the armrests, her knuckles white. Her whole body was trembling, her heart pounding. She felt very sick again, as she had upstairs earlier, only more so. The nausea was worse, *every*thing was worse. Than she could ever have imagined.

She knew – *thought* that she knew – she had to hold onto that,

381

because she didn't really *know* – how Flic's last, unfinished sentence might have continued.

*Pushing.*

'Why not go all the way and accuse me of *pushing* . . .' Flic had said, and then her face had frozen in that ugly, horrified way.

It could have meant anything. She could have been talking about Susanna's accusation that she had *pushed* Chloë into forging Matthew's signatures. Or about her *pushing* Imogen into making the assault allegation. Of course it could have meant that.

It *could* have.

Yet Susanna knew, instinctively, that it had not.

The horror on her face meant that Flic knew she had caught herself just in time, just before her own rage had betrayed her. Before she had given herself away.

*Pushing.*

A picture came into Susanna's mind. An imagined picture of ferocious, terrifying vividness.

Of Isabella falling from the platform at the tube station.

Of the seconds before that.

Hands against her back.

*Pushing.*

Flic had been there, hadn't she? With Isabella. Had said they'd been separated by the crowd, that Isabella had stepped over the line, that she had stayed back. That Isabella had stumbled because of her high-heeled boots.

That Isabella had wanted to go shopping for boots.

Which had seemed odd to everyone, after that morning's events at home, hadn't it? *Hadn't* it?

'Ridiculous,' Susanna said aloud. She was being utterly idiotic, utterly *mad*. What reason on earth would Flic have had to want to hurt – *kill* – Isabella?

Unless Isabella had found out the truth about the assault.

'Oh, my God,' Susanna said softly.

Over by the door, Kahli whined.

'Oh, my *God*.'

Susanna's heart began to pound wildly and she felt her eyes open wide, though she was staring at nothing, into space, into her own mind, her imagination, her thoughts, speeding inexorably now, unstoppable as that tube train had surely been, except that *her* thoughts were moving back. To last Saturday. And beyond.

To last September.

To the most hideous, most monstrous, most *unthinkable* suspicion of all.

Caro's death.

Flic had been there too – *here*, too. In this house. Ill in bed.

And the verdict had been 'open'.

*Stop it!*

Susanna was starting to feel faint. What was she *thinking* of? Flic had adored Caroline, all the sisters had loved their mother, there had never been the slightest, tiniest suggestion of anything else.

*They could have had a fight.*

No, it was Imogen who'd been the moody one, the depressive, the daughter who had given Caro a degree of grief. Flic had always been the sensible one – Caro had often told Susanna how easy it was to communicate with Flic, how astute and wise she could be.

Yet that same young woman had just towered over her calling her a 'dense cow' and telling her that her mother had found her a bore.

*Hardly grounds for this, Susanna.*

She shook her head fiercely, impatient with herself. This was no time to allow her own sensitivity to overwhelm her judgment skills. Flic had said those things out of anger, *after* she'd been accused of dreadful things.

Nothing compared with what Susanna was thinking now.

*Imagining.* Just imagining. She had no proof, didn't *want* any proof. It was the very *last* thing she wanted.

Yet she had seen Flic's face, her wildness, her fury.

And her horror as that word had slipped out. *Pushing.* And then the awful sound she'd made as she'd run from the room.

Susanna closed her eyes, and at last her hands let go of the chair and fell limply into her lap.

Kahli whined again, stood up, padded across to her.

She opened her eyes again, trying to get her thoughts back into some semblance of normality. They were all upstairs now, all three sisters, and Flic had gone up in a fury, and Chloë was up there, wasn't she, fresh from betraying both her older sisters?

'Oh, God.' Susanna stood up. Kahli wagged his tail. 'It's all right,' she told him softly.

*Liar.*

Her legs were like jelly.

Shock.

She eyed the drinks cabinet, decided that a brandy might be the best short-term medicine, made her shaky way over, found a bottle, a glass, pulled the stopper, poured, spilling some over one hand and onto the carpet, not caring . . .

She carried the glass back to the chair, sat down again, heavily, used both hands to raise the glass to her lips, and took a sip.

Never, in her life, could she remember needing a drink more.

Except, of course, the day she'd heard about Caro. She had come very close to fainting then, had thought she might die, too. Had, in fact, wanted to die.

*Think about her daughters, not yourself.* About Chloë, first and foremost.

What to do next?

*Talk to someone.*

But who? Not to Sylvie, in her condition. Nor to the police, not after she'd promised Chloë, not unless she was left with no other choice.

There *was* only one other person now.

If anyone was entitled to know about this now, it was Matthew.

Susanna swallowed some more brandy, felt it beginning to work. The blue address book was on the kitchen counter near the phone. Matthew's mobile number was bound to be in it. She would ask him to come, and she would be helping him, after all, and he would tell her that shock was making her imagination run riot. After all, if there had been any grounds for suspecting Flic, the police would have realized, knowing she'd been at both deaths. Except they were only investigating the assault allegation, and they knew that people fell under tube trains with awful regularity – you were *always* hearing those gruesome announcements about 'incidents' on the line causing delays . . .

*Tell Matthew to come.*

# 63

Flic was sitting on the camp bed in Imogen's room.

Had been sitting there since she'd come upstairs.

Imo was sleeping again.

She had woken for a moment when Flic had come in, had stirred, mumbled something, and then, when Flic had not replied, had gone straight back to sleep.

Better that way, Flic had decided. She did not think she could have coped, just then – *nor now, nor perhaps ever again* – with more of Imo's hysterics. She felt too drained, too exhausted, too afraid.

She'd paused, just for a second or two, outside Chloë's room, before she'd come in here, had considered going in and telling her what she thought of her, of what she'd done to her and Imo, to them *all*, but then this great weariness had overwhelmed her, and she'd felt she had nothing left, that there was no point in attacking her little sister, even if she had so startlingly and comprehensively betrayed her.

*No point.* Not now, not after what had happened downstairs. No point in doing anything now, not after the way Susanna had looked at her just before she'd run out of the room.

What Flic wanted, suddenly, more than anything, was to be like Imogen. To have the ability to shut out the world that way, in sleep. And maybe now, after all that ghastliness, she *might* be able to do that. She could crawl into this little bed and curl up in a ball, and forget, for a while.

*Go on then.*

She stood up, began to pull off her clothes, quietly, carefully.

Enough, she'd had enough, could bear no more, not now. Maybe tomorrow, when she knew what Susanna was going to do, or if John Pascoe had decided to tell Gita Khan or anyone else about . . .

*Enough.*

She began to walk towards the wardrobe to fetch a hanger, then changed her mind and dropped her tracksuit on the floor. She thought about going to the bathroom for a wash, but that seemed too much effort as well, and besides, she might wake Imo or encounter Chloë or Susanna . . .

*Get into bed.*

The springs creaked, but Imo didn't stir, and Flic lay down, rested her head on the pillow.

*Blot it out.*

Susanna's words, her shocked face. Other things, other concerns, other fears. About old John, about Sylvie, about Matthew. Other uglier memories. *Blot it all out.* But it was easier said than done, and Flic didn't know which was more painful, the awful sadness she had now begun to feel, the sense of being cornered and shockingly alone, or her sudden urge to start screaming. She really felt that she could do that, just scream and scream and go *on* screaming until they all came running – and for several moments she actually had to hold both her hands over her mouth to stop herself from doing it, and then the violent urge began to leave her, and she was just so glad that Imo was asleep . . .

Except that Imogen – lying so absolutely still in her own bed, eyes closed, breathing even – was not asleep at all.

She was wide awake. Intensely awake.

Intensely *alive*.

Flic had always been the *doer* in their twosome. And it always had been a twosome, with Chloë excluded, but Flic had always been the leader, the pacesetter.

Not tonight. Not any more. Tonight, for once, Imo knew exactly what she was going to do.

*Had* to do.

There was nothing else left now. Not after what had been said this evening, by Chloë, by Susanna, by Flic herself. They had all believed that she was sleeping, out of the way, but she had listened, had heard all the fear, all the anger, all the pain.

Now, suddenly, for the first time in a very long while, her path seemed clearly, perfectly defined. And one feature of that path rendered it almost beautiful.

It had an end.

# 64

Matthew heard faint ringing, put out his hand to pick up the phone, groped around in space, opened his eyes, peered through the semi-darkness and remembered that he was not in Aethiopia, but in Kat's bed.

He looked groggily to his right, knowing already that she was not with him, had not, judging by the appearance of the pillows, come to bed yet; or probably she was leaving him to sleep alone, feeling he might prefer it that way.

*Not true.*

Kat appeared in the doorway, the hall light behind her. 'Matthew, it's your phone,' She handed him his mobile.

He noticed the time on her alarm clock. Almost eleven-thirty. He felt a jolt of alarm. *Sylvie.*

'Matthew, it's Susanna, I'm sorry, but—'

'Is it Sylvie?'

'No. Not Sylvie.' She paused. 'I need you to come.'

'Come where?' His head ached. 'To the hospital?'

'No,' Susanna said. 'I told you, it isn't Sylvie.'

Matthew realized suddenly that she was speaking very softly. 'Why are you whispering, Susanna? What's going on?'

'I can't tell you on the phone. I really need you to come here, Matthew, to the house. I have to talk to you.'

'Since when?' He sounded cold, couldn't help it.

'Matthew, please.'

'It's late.' He looked at Kat. 'I think I'm coming down with something. Whatever it is can wait till morning.'

388

'No, it can't.' Susanna paused. 'Matthew, there's a nightmare happening here, in this house, and if I don't tell you about it very soon, *tonight*, I'm really afraid of what might happen.'

'To the girls?' A voice in his head said: *Who cares?*

'To the whole family,' Susanna said. 'To us all, maybe.'

He realized then that the fear in her voice was real. 'Okay.'

'You'll come?'

'I said okay.'

'How long?'

'I don't know. Long as it takes.'

'Make it very soon, please, Matthew.'

'I'm way across town.'

'If you come by car or taxi,' Susanna said, 'park away from the house. I'll be keeping watch for you, so don't ring the bell.'

'What the hell is going on, Susanna?'

'Don't even use your keys. I don't want Kahli to bark.'

'Jesus.' He put down his phone and got out of bed.

'You're not going out?' Kat said disapprovingly.

The robe Matthew had gone to bed in had come adrift and he fished for the belt to make himself decent. 'Something's very wrong.'

'This is at the house, do I gather?'

He nodded, looking around for his clothes. 'Susanna sounds scared.'

'Your things are hanging in the kitchen,' Kat told him. 'It's warmer in there, I thought they'd dry out better.'

'Thank you.' He looked at her. 'You look great, by the way.'

'Thank you too,' she said. 'I thought Susanna was in the enemy camp.'

'We've certainly disliked each other from the get-go,' Matthew said on his way to the kitchen, 'but I guess I'm developing a certain respect for her.'

'This was the woman who saw us in Selfridges and looked at me as if I was a bad smell, isn't it?' Kat asked wryly, following him. 'The woman who made you sit in on that awful family therapy session?'

'Susanna adored Caro,' Matthew said, already pulling on trousers. 'I mean I think she really loved her.' He zipped his fly, reached for his shirt.

'Are they dry enough?'

389

'Wonderfully, thank you.'

Kat filled the kettle, switched it on. 'So has all this been a jealousy thing, do you think? Her problems with you, I mean?'

'Maybe.' Left sock. 'Partially, I guess.' Right sock. 'She's been pretty great since Sylvie collapsed. Helping with the girls.'

'Not helping you though,' Kat reminded him. 'You said she wouldn't even let you into the house, remember?'

'Only because Flic was being such a bitch – and, I guess, she doesn't know whether to believe Imo or me.' Matthew pulled out the crumpled newspaper Kat had stuffed in his shoes, slipped his foot into the left one and grimaced.

'Still wet?'

'Hardly surprising.' He put on the right shoe. 'Not too bad.'

'If you're determined to go, I'm going to come with you.'

'No need for that,' Matthew said. 'It's late. You get into your own bed and get some sleep.'

'No.' Kat was quiet but decisive. 'You make us both a cup of something hot, and I'll go and get dressed.'

'I don't want to drag you into some ugly family scene, Kat.'

'I think, in the circumstances, you could maybe use a witness.' She spoke from the doorway. 'Especially if it gets ugly.'

Matthew knew she was right. 'Are you sure?'

She smiled at him. 'I couldn't sleep now anyway.'

'Some day,' he said, 'I'm going to get to make all this up to you.'

'Some day,' Kat said, 'I'll let you.'

Susanna had listened for several moments after finishing the call to Matthew and then, hearing nothing, had breathed a sigh of relief. He would come, had told her he would, and he was not the type to let her down, and she knew now just what a pity it was that she hadn't realized the kind of man he was a very long time ago, when Caro had still been here . . .

Too late for all that now.

*Check on Chloë.*

But Flic was up there. And Imo.

*Chloë trusted you. She's depending on you.*

Just what Susanna had always wanted these girls to do, have that kind of faith in her as a friend. *Be careful what you wish for.* Wasn't that what they said?

390

She climbed the stairs, telling herself to tread normally, not creep up like a burglar afraid of creaking boards. The doors on the first floor were all closed. No sound coming from Imogen's room, nor from Flic's – *her* room, for the moment, though she wasn't relishing entering in case Flic was in there, waiting for her.

She moved on to Chloë's, tapped gently, opened the door.

The curtains were not drawn, and though there was no moon, there was enough light for her to see the golden head on the pillow. Sleeping soundly, thank goodness. Poor, exhausted child.

Now her own room.

She hesitated outside, fingers on the handle, then opened the door, switched on the light, saw that no one lay in wait.

*A shower.*

That, she decided abruptly, was what she needed now. A nice brisk shower often calmed her better than a bath, and she obviously had more than enough time in hand before Matthew's arrival. There was only a hand-held shower in the girls' bath, but Susanna knew there was a walk-in shower in Caro's – *Matthew's* – bathroom, and even if it didn't exactly calm her down tonight, it might help her feel a little more normal, help her to organize her thoughts . . .

Matthew had assumed they would take a cab, but Kat had told him there was no guarantee they'd get one in this weather.

'My upstairs neighbour Sam has a car,' she'd told him. 'He's always telling me I can borrow it.'

Matthew had felt a small, absurd stab of jealousy, had doused it instantly and waited while Kat had hurried up to the next floor before returning with a set of keys.

'Was he sleeping?' Matthew asked.

'Oh, yes. But he didn't mind. Sam's a generous soul.'

The garage was three streets away, down a dark alley, and though one of the keys turned in the lock, the door refused to pull up, but then Kat remembered Sam telling her that it had to be kicked hard on the bottom right hand side, after which it obliged.

'Maybe this needs kicking too,' Matthew said as Kat tried starting the engine of the elderly lime-green VW Beetle for the third time.

'Sam says it always takes four goes.'

Sure enough.

'We'll have to stop for petrol.' She eyed the gauge.

'Couldn't we make it without?' Matthew was remembering how Susanna had sounded, and wondering just what they might find when they got there.

'I don't know,' Kat said. 'Are you up to pushing?'

'We'll stop for petrol,' Matthew said.

# 65

Susanna was in the bathroom drying herself when she heard the high-pitched sound.

Matthew could not possibly have arrived so swiftly, and, in any case, she'd asked him not to ring the bell. But then, listening to the sound as it continued piercing the air, she realized that it was not the bell at all . . .

'Oh, my *God*.'

She dropped the towel, grabbed a robe from a hook and ran out of the bathroom into the bedroom and over to the door.

The smoke alarms seemed to be sounding from *everywhere*.

Susanna opened the door, saw smoke, slammed it shut again, cursing herself, knowing she ought to have felt it first for heat, that had the fire been close it might have been too late to get it closed again.

*The girls.*

She stared wildly at the telephone by the bed.

*Everyone out first*, then *phone from another house.*

She ran back to the bathroom, grabbed a hand towel and soaked it, then ran back to the door, held it up over her nose and mouth and opened it.

The smoke seemed to be coming from above, and the way to the girls' rooms was growing foggier by the second.

'Fire!' she yelled, and saw that Imogen's door was open. '*Fire!*'

And then she heard screaming.

# 66

He was reminded, instantly, of the final chapter of *Rebecca*, the moments when de Winter and his wife see the glow in the night sky and know, with chilling certainty, that Manderley is aflame. There was no logic in this realization for Matthew, of course, as he spotted the reddish gleam on the Hampstead horizon, just a blush in the dark with a narrow plume of grey swirling upwards. *Something* was burning somewhere higher up on or around East Heath Road, but there was no reason to assume it had anything to do with Aethiopia.

Yet he did assume it, *knew* it.

'You see that?' he asked Kat starkly.

'Yes.' She accelerated up the long gently winding hill.

'Jesus,' he muttered, under his breath. 'What have they done?'

'I'm going as fast as she'll let me.'

'I know,' he said tightly. 'Thanks.'

The house came into view.

'Christ,' Kat said, and put her foot down even harder.

The fire was easily visible, the glow seeming to come from the rear, from an upper floor. Matthew was already punching 999 as Kat drove the last hundred yards and jerked to an abrupt halt.

'Fire,' he told the operator starkly, pushed the phone into Kat's hand and opened the passenger door. 'Tell them it's Aethiopia, halfway down East Heath Road.'

'You're not going in?' she asked, alarmed.

He was already out of the car. 'Go next door, wake the neighbours, anyone you can find. If the phone dies, use theirs.'

'Matthew, please don't go in!' Kat shouted after him.

'Talk to the fire people!' he yelled back over his shoulder, heading up the path, fumbling for his keys, praying that no one had taken it into their head to change the locks since yesterday morning. 'And go next door!'

His keys opened both locks, but the safety chain was in place, so he took a step back and then charged the door, yelling as he launched himself through into smoke.

'Susanna!'

He was pretty sure it was coming from above. He almost switched on a light, then stopped himself, realizing a spark might trigger an explosion.

'Flic! Imogen! Chloë! It's Matthew!'

He kept calling as he moved as swiftly as he could around the ground floor, checking a room at a time, forcing himself to be methodical, too hampered by smoke and darkness to run.

*No help to anyone if you crack your damned head.*

'Tell me where you *are!*' he yelled. 'I've called the fire department!'

'*Matthew!*'

Flic's voice, from above.

'I'm coming!' He coughed as the acrid smoke hit his throat.

*Wet cloths.*

He moved into the kitchen, banged into a chair, steadied his course, blinked his stinging eyes a few times to try to clear them.

From over to his right, Kahli barked.

'Hey, boy.' He saw the dog cowering near the back door. 'Let's get you out.'

He turned the key in the lock, hesitated for a second in case the wind exacerbated the fire, then took a chance, opened the door, hauled Kahli out by the scruff of his neck, and closed the door again. Then he found a stack of cloths, drenched them thoroughly, prayed that Kat was safely next door, got himself out to the staircase and up to the first floor.

The smoke was thicker, but there was still no fire to be seen. Matthew tied one of the cloths over his nose and mouth and wedged the others under his left arm.

'Chloë!'

'In *here!*' Flic's voice again.

Matthew hurried to Chloë's room, saw Flic struggling to get Chloë out of bed.

'She won't wake up!'

'I'll carry her.' He thrust a wet cloth at Flic, then scooped Chloë up – heavy with sleepiness, perhaps already drowsy from smoke inhalation – in his arms. 'You're okay, sweetheart.' He started with her for the door. 'Tie that over your mouth and nose,' he told Flic, 'and tell me where the others are.'

'I don't know.' Flic's eyes were wide and terrified. 'I don't *know*!' She coughed. 'Upstairs, I think—' She held the wet cloth over her face, fastened the ends as he had. 'But I think the *fire's* up there!'

'Let's get you both out, and I'll come back for the others.' Matthew paused in the corridor. 'Imogen!' he yelled again. '*Susanna*!'

'I woke up,' Flic said, 'and Imo wasn't in her bed!'

'You go ahead of us.' The girl in his arms was stirring, getting heavier by the instant. 'Go on, Flic.' She didn't move. 'Go *on*!'

'I'm going to find Imo!'

'No, Flic!'

'Please, Matthew, just get her out!' Flic headed for the second floor.

'Flic, *wait*!' Afraid of stumbling with the youngster in his arms, Matthew curbed his urge to run, got safely down the stairs, turned left towards the open front door and felt blessed cold fresh air on his face.

'Matthew, thank *God*!'

Through streaming eyes, he saw a cluster of people on the path and beyond, on the pavement, saw Kat calling to him, a man hanging onto one of her arms as if he thought she might run into the house.

Chloë was coughing, beginning to struggle a little.

'You're okay, honey.'

'The fire brigade are coming!' Kat broke free, ran to him. 'Are you all right?'

'Fine, but I need you to take care of Chloë.' Carefully, he set the girl down, and she was awake now, but shocked and coughing too badly to speak, and Kat caught her as she almost fell, and then quickly, a couple from a house just up the road – the Baileys, he thought – rushed forward to help.

'How bad is it?' the man asked, as his wife steered Chloë away.

'Bad enough,' Matthew told him, slipping the cloth down off his face and taking gulps of air. 'I'm going back in to find the others.'

'No, you're *not*.' Kat grabbed his sleeve.

'I have to.' He slipped out of her grasp and turned back.

'It's crazy to go back in there,' Bailey told him.

'Matthew, *please* stay out here!' Kat was aghast.

'I have to *find* them!' He fastened the cloth back over his nose and mouth and ran back inside, headed straight to the staircase this time, knowing he might only have moments. 'Flic!' he yelled halfway up.

'*Matthew*!' Susanna's voice from above. 'We're outside Caro's sewing room.'

'On my way!'

He moved faster, taking more chances now, with time running out, and the smoke was denser up here, but he made out two blurry outlines ahead of him in the corridor.

'Thank God!' Susanna was barefoot, wearing a bathrobe.

'Help me!' Flic called. 'Imo's inside!'

'She's locked the door,' Susanna said.

'Let me through.' Matthew tried the handle, swiftly snatching his hand away, shocked by its heat. 'Imogen!' he shouted, and hammered on one of the wooden panels. 'Imo, if you can hear me, open the door!' He turned to the other two. 'I want you both out now.' He pushed Susanna towards the teenager. 'You take her down now.'

'I'm not going.' Flic's voice was hoarse.

'*Do* it!' Matthew rapped out.

Susanna tried to take hold of Flic's arm, but the girl shook her off. 'Flic, come *on*. Matthew will get Imo.'

Flic ignored them both. 'She might be unconscious!'

'Imo, move away from the door!' Matthew stood back.

'Quickly!' Flic begged him.

'Will you get *out* of here!' he bellowed at her, then kicked hard at the door, splintering wood. Dark smoke billowed through and Matthew kicked again, making enough of a hole for him to bend and get his hand through, praying the key was still in the lock. *Small mercies.* He turned it, yelped with the pain of its burn, then braced himself, grabbed at the handle and flung open the door.

'*Imo*!' He could hardly see anything inside.

'Let me through!' Flic screamed from behind him.

'Flic, we have to go *down*.' Susanna dragged at her tracksuit top. 'Leave this to Matthew!'

'*You* go.' Flic shoved her away, and Susanna fell against a wall.

'Imogen?' Matthew was in the room, scanning left to right of Caro's couch, which was ablaze. 'Imo!'

Air. He felt cold *air*, squinted through the fog, saw that the glass doors were open and that Imogen was outside.

'I *see* her,' he called out. 'She's on the balcony and she's okay, so you can both get out right now!'

'Flic, you heard him – come *on*!' Susanna sounded desperate.

'You go, I've *told* you!'

'Just get *out*, both of you!' He wavered for a second, then moved fast, felt a rush of great heat to his left, saw that behind the burning couch the flames were licking around the edges of the rug, and how much longer did they *have*?

'Stay away from me,' Imogen cried out as he reached the balcony, 'or I'll jump!'

'Don't be so fucking *stupid*, Imo,' Flic said from behind Matthew.

'I *will*!' Imogen, wearing a big white Astrid sweatshirt and socks, huddled at the left of the narrow balcony, her breath misting in the cold air, mingling with the smoke. 'I mean it, Flic, I *want* to jump.'

'No, you don't,' Matthew told her. 'That's the *last* thing—'

'Don't you *dare* tell me what I want or don't want!' Imogen was weeping.

'But he's right.' Flic pushed between them, and Matthew let her, knew it was the only thing to do. 'Just this once, he's bloody well right, you stupid, *stupid* girl.'

'Of *course* he is,' Susanna called. 'Please listen to them, Imo!'

'But I can't *take* any more!' Tears rolled from Imogen's eyes. 'You should have let me end it back then, Flic.' She was sobbing. 'You should have let me *tell*.'

'It's okay, Imo. It's going to be okay.' Flic reached out to her.

'Stay away!' Imogen held onto the railing and kicked out with one foot to keep her at bay. 'It's not going to be okay. It's *never* going to be okay.'

'The fire's *spreading*!' Susanna let out a scream as flaming tongues began scorching multiple forked paths along the papered walls in her direction, driven by a shift in the wind.

398

'Susanna, get out here with us!' Matthew felt suddenly afraid for her. 'You'll be safer out here!' She didn't answer, and the smoke had thickened, and he could barely see her. 'Susanna, come *on*.' He didn't want to leave the girls. 'Just run straight through, don't look, just *come*.'

'I don't think she *can*,' Flic said urgently. 'I think she's in trouble!'

Matthew's mind was starting to fuzz. From a distance, he heard the sound of sirens, heard Kahli barking.

'Matthew, Susanna's in *trouble*!' Flic pushed at his back. 'You're going to have to *bring* her out!'

She was right, he *saw* that she was right, that the flames were on the move, that he had no choice, and he stepped back into the room – and oh, Christ, it was even hotter than before, and Susanna was starting to fold over at the waist as he reached her, about to fall down, and he was trying not to breathe, knew that if he took in much more smoke, neither of them would make it out, and he just grabbed at her arm, pulled her close and started back through the room to the balcony.

And Flic shut the doors.

'What are you *doing*?' Smoke poured into his mouth and nose and throat and seared his eyes. 'What the hell are you *doing*?'

Flic stared through the glass at him, eyes unreadable, gripping both door handles tightly, and Matthew knew that her hands had to be burning.

'Flic, for God's sake!' Susanna cried out, choking.

He held her close with one arm, used his free fist to pound at the glass, but that, too, was unbearably hot, and he knew he was weakening.

'Flic, open the *door*!'

'Flic, what are you *doing*?' Imogen had left the edge of the balcony. 'Open the *doors*!'

Flic's palms and fingers were scorching, but she couldn't let go, knew the pain had to be endured. 'Susanna's the only one who *knows*, Imo,' she said. 'She's the only one they'd listen to – the only one except him who can really *hurt* us!'

'You can't do this, Flic!' Imogen screamed. 'It's too much, too *bad*!'

'I *have* to do it.' Flic's voice lifted in agony as her flesh scorched, but still she held on. 'I have to, for you, for us *all!*'

Matthew half heard, half read her lips through the glass, saw the horror on Imogen's face and the total resolve on Flic's, and for the very first time, it came to him that he and Susanna were both going to die – and maybe that had been the plan all along – Flic's plan, not Imo's, that much was clear.

'Break the glass,' Susanna gasped beside him, kicked out at the door with her bare toes, cried out. 'We have to *break* it!'

Matthew looked around for something to use, but it was getting too hard to breathe, and his lungs were bursting, and the heat was growing too intense to bear, and he couldn't *see* anything, and he couldn't take any more . . .

Outside, voices shouted below in the garden, and the dog's barking became more frenzied, and a ladder clanged against the railing.

'Flic, they're coming, you *have* to open the door or they'll *see*.' Imogen pulled at her sister's hands. 'Flic, it's too late, and it's *wrong!*'

'But you started the fire!'

'Because I wanted to die.'

'But you weren't alone in the house, you must have *known!*' Flic knew she couldn't, really *couldn't*, hold on much longer.

'I was going crazy.' Imogen was sobbing. 'I couldn't bear any more, I couldn't see another way . . . I thought the alarms – I was sure you'd all get out without me – Flic, *please*, you have to let them *out!*'

The glass in one of the panels exploded outwards, a thousand tiny daggers flying through the air, and the doors blew open, Imogen screaming as Flic fell to her knees and Matthew and Susanna stumbled out onto the balcony, gulping in the air.

'Everyone okay up there?' a fireman yelled.

They heard the steps on the ladder, felt the railings shiver.

Matthew stared down at Flic, at her burned hands and the streaks of blood on her face and the glass fragments sparkling like tiny diamonds in her hair. He heard the voice of the man on the ladder, heard Susanna answer him, but he couldn't take in their words, was too transfixed by Flic's *hair*.

400

And then, without a word, Imogen pushed past them, back into the blazing room.

'*No!*' Flic was still on her knees. 'Imo, *no!*'

It felt like a dream now to Matthew, *looked* like a dream, like a surrealist painting. The couch had gone, and the roar of the fire was deepening, and Caro's rocking chair was being devoured, and the little chest that had held her sewing materials. And Imogen was standing in the heart of it, her head a black spiky crown against the brilliance of the flames.

'Imo, *no!*' Susanna's voice. 'Oh, my God, *no!*'

'Not like this, Imo!' Flic screamed.

'It's what I *want!*' Imogen cried back at her.

Matthew heard that, registered that, knew that she wanted to die.

And that he could not let her.

'Oh, no,' he said. 'No *way!*'

And even that seemed dreamlike, in its way, too unreal to be happening. The way he took one more huge, painful breath and flung himself back into the inferno, right *at* Imogen, like the half-back he'd never been at school or since, hitting her hard, bringing her down. And the fragility of her body beneath his startled him, *stopped* the dream, brought him back to earth, because Imo had always been the toughie of the bunch, and for one long moment he thought she had stopped breathing, thought he had actually *killed* her.

And then she cried out. A long, heartrending wail of despair.

Matthew tried to move, but he couldn't catch his breath, couldn't find any more strength, and the fire was circling them now, and there was no more air left, and he thought they would suffocate before they burned, and . . .

Strong hands grasped at his arms, dragged him off Imogen and outside into the air, and through streaming eyes, Matthew saw they had her too, saw her bundled across a hefty fireman's shoulder, being carried down the ladder. Flic had already been taken, and Susanna was next, and hard jets of water were cannoning over the parapet and into the house, rocking him, drenching him. And he took one final look back into the Quiet Room, saw that everything Caro had loved in there had gone forever.

'Come on, mate!'

He turned away from the room, and allowed himself to be helped onto the ladder and down to safety.

# 67

They gave him a blanket and oxygen, and shepherded him swiftly and smoothly to the front of the house past the fire vehicles and flashing lights and chaos to where three ambulances stood, a safe distance away. East Heath Road had been cordoned off in both directions, and Kat and the Baileys – holding Kahli by his collar, Matthew was glad to see – and a few others loitered behind incident tape some way off.

Kat was waving to him, urgently, and Matthew raised a leaden arm to wave back to her, found it a great effort, lowered it again and looked around. Chloë was inside one of the ambulances, sitting huddled in a blanket staring bleakly out above her oxygen mask, a female paramedic sitting beside her holding her hand.

'She'll be all right,' one of the men guiding him said.

Matthew tugged his own mask away from his face. 'I want to see her.'

'At the hospital,' the paramedic said. 'You'll see her there.'

'Now.' His voice was hoarse but intense.

The man was young, his eyes very dark. 'All right,' he said gently. 'A few more breaths of that, then you can have a quick word.'

Matthew looked around as he breathed and coughed – and oh, God, his chest and throat really *hurt* – and he saw that Flic and Imogen were being taken to a second ambulance, and that Susanna – blanket-wrapped and able to sit unsupported, he was glad to see – was already in the third. And then he dragged together his scrambled thoughts and made himself confront the fact that Flic had just tried to kill him and Susanna, and he wondered what he was supposed to *do* about that – nothing now, perhaps, not yet – but he was intensely glad that, for a while at least, she and Imogen were being kept apart from Chloë.

'They'll be off in a minute,' the paramedic told him, 'so if you want that word.'

Matthew found he could manage without the mask, could walk unaided if he took it slowly, and as he approached Chloë's ambulance, the woman taking care of her smiled at him and moved deeper inside the vehicle, giving them space.

'How you doing?' He looked up at her, trying to gauge the damage, physical and psychological.

Chloë nodded. She still looked deeply afraid, haunted.

'Everyone's okay, honey.' Matthew forced a smile. 'So you don't have to worry about your sisters.'

'How's Kahli?' Scarcely above a whisper.

'He's safe – he's with the Baileys.'

Something troubled him, even now, in this moment of post-horror calm, about her expression. There was none of the relief he might have expected, no animation at all, just fear.

'Chloë, sweetheart,' he asked gently, 'what happened before the fire?'

'Nothing.'

'Only Susanna called me, asked me to come.'

'Did she?' The wariness was unquestionable.

The paramedic came forward again then. 'Will you be coming with us?' She was in her thirties, with short fair hair.

'Is Chloë doing okay?' Matthew asked. 'Only it was pretty hard rousing her back in the house earlier. I wondered if—' He broke off to cough.

'She's had a bit of a shock,' the paramedic said, 'and she probably took in a little smoke. She smiled at Chloë, patted her arm. 'Otherwise I'd say she's in very good shape, aren't you, my darling?'

Matthew glanced back, saw that Kat was still behind the tape, agitating a police officer to let her through. 'I'm not coming just yet.' It was a strain to speak. 'I have to talk to someone else.'

'You need to get yourself taken care of, too.' The woman looked down at him appraisingly. 'You'll have inhaled a lot of smoke. There could be some damage.'

They heard a sudden, loud, protesting cry and turned to look.

A cluster of people stood near the second ambulance. Matthew caught a glimpse of long hair glistening silver in the flashing lights and headlamps of the other vehicles. Flic appeared to be fighting with someone, shaking her head violently, arguing . . .

And then he saw the reason for her agitation.

Imogen – white sweatshirt and socks like beacons in the darkness – was running across the road towards the Heath.

'*Imo!*' Chloë's voice was a painful gasp.

Matthew waited one more second – and then he began to run too, away from Chloë and the ambulances, after Imogen. He had genuinely believed his strength all used up, yet fear was driving him again, the awful conviction that if Imo got too far onto the Heath, something even more dreadful would happen and that, if it did, irrational as it might be, he would never forgive himself.

*Still Caro's daughter, Sylvie's grandchild, Chloë's sister.*

He was coughing more painfully as he crossed the road, his heart pumping too hard, and thoughts were tumbling, free-falling as he ran, chasing Caro's tormented, suicidal middle child, and if she had started the fire, he had to get to her before she did something even crazier . . .

'Imogen, *stop!*' He could still see the patches of white bobbing up and down as she ran, but at any moment he knew the Heath's black wildness would swallow her up. 'Imo, please just stop *running!*'

Lights blazed suddenly, startlingly, illuminating the landscape around and ahead of him. Momentarily disoriented, Matthew thrust a hand up over his eyes to protect himself from the glare and turned to see that a line of vehicles had been turned to face the Heath, headlights and searchlights on full beam – and there were other people running too, towards them . . .

He turned back again and saw her, fifty or so yards ahead, her arms stretched wildly, frantically before her as she ran, her movements jerky, and he began running again, yelling her name, trying not to stumble, and his chest was even more painful than it had been, but something was still driving him, and he was almost on her now . . .

'Imo, *please!*'

And then he had her, and it was almost as it had been in the Quiet Room, only now there was no fire, just wet, squelching, uneven ground and the wind, and the strange, shifting light-show as headlamps played through the tall grass and shrubs. And suddenly, all the fight went out of Imogen, and she just lay there beneath him, spent and sobbing and coughing, breath rasping in her throat, both arms thrown out sideways so that, bizarrely, she resembled a penitent sweatshirted nun prostrating herself.

Matthew released her, sank down beside her, also fighting for breath, his limbs quivering and heavy. Looking back, he saw that the other chasers had stopped a distance away, were now watching, waiting – saw that Susanna was with them, thought that maybe she had asked them to wait.

For what?

'*You should have let me tell.*' Imogen's words to Flic out on the balcony, when she'd talked of jumping, of suicide, came back to him. And maybe that was why Susanna and those people were waiting, holding back.

To give Imogen the chance to tell him the truth.

He wasn't at all sure that he wanted to know the truth.

*No choice.*

Her shoulders had stopped heaving, and slowly, painfully, Imogen was beginning to move, to get to her knees, and for once, as he helped her to sit up, she made no attempt to push him away.

'I guess we've done running for tonight,' he said huskily.

Someone approached from behind, a uniformed policeman holding out two blankets, and Matthew raised his right hand. 'Can we have a few minutes?' His voice carried on the wind.

'Not really the spot for a chat, is it, sir?' the officer said. 'Bit nippy.'

'*Please,*' Imogen said violently, breathlessly, to the man. 'I won't run away again. I swear. I have to talk to him now, or I never will.'

'Please, officer,' Matthew said. 'Just a few minutes.'

The policeman looked back, perhaps seeking assent from someone, then bent and handed Matthew both blankets. 'Just a couple of minutes. Don't want hypothermia on top of everything else.'

'No,' Matthew said. 'Thank you.'

He waited till the other man had turned away, then passed both of the blankets to Imogen, who snatched at them, wrapped them around herself, huddled in them.

'So,' he said. 'Tell me, Imo.'

Her eyes were large and very dark and tortured.

'I killed my mother,' she said.

He was aware, as he listened to those words, that the greater part of his mind had shut down, protecting itself, could almost picture it – the part that felt love and loss and fear and confusion and pain – curling into a ball to take refuge.

How else could he have heard those words and not struck the girl who uttered them? How else could he not have gone insane?

*I killed my mother.*

'What do you mean?' he said.

'Not killed, exactly,' Imogen said.

*Not exactly.*

He sat for another moment, steadying himself, he supposed, readying himself. For whatever was coming next.

He looked into the huge agonized eyes.

'Come on, Imo,' he said. 'Just tell me.'

They both became aware of movement, heard the squelching of feet behind them, and turning, Matthew saw that Susanna and the policeman and a pair of paramedics were on the move again, and he knew there was nothing he could do to stop them.

'Later,' he said, urgently. 'When we're alone, okay?'

Imogen said nothing.

'Okay?' he said again.

They helped them both to their feet, gave Matthew another dry blanket, and Susanna – her own teeth chattering with cold and shock – put an arm around Imogen's shoulders, and Imo let her, allowed herself to be led back over the grass and mud to the road and the one remaining ambulance, the other two having departed with Chloë and, Matthew presumed, Flic on board.

'Flic didn't want to go,' Susanna told Matthew as Imogen was helped away, 'but they made her.'

'Good.'

They regarded each other, her bold brown eyes questioning, yet there was no irritating characteristic inquisitiveness in the gaze, he realized. This Susanna was too shaken for that, too sad.

'And Kahli's still with your neighbours,' she added.

'Good,' he said again.

*Good.* He didn't know what else to say. His mind was too blasted.

He saw Kat then, still waiting behind the tape. No longer waving or smiling.

'Would you mind going ahead with Imo?' he asked Susanna.

Susanna saw where he was looking. 'Of course.'

He helped her up into the ambulance, and they both glanced at Imogen, who had not spoken since they had come and stopped her. The teenager's eyes seemed almost blank now, and Matthew knew there was no point his travelling with her, knew she would not be drawn again while there were others there.

If at all.

'Don't be too long, will you?' Susanna said softly.

'I'll be right behind you.'

He waited till the doors were shut and the engine running before he turned around and began walking, very slowly and wearily, towards the tape and Kat.

She looked very shocked, her imagination probably conjuring up all kinds of explanations for what had just happened on the Heath.

Nothing that would compete with reality, Matthew thought.

407

# 68

Getting time alone with Imogen at the hospital was not as difficult as Matthew had anticipated. He had, after a while, persuaded Kat to go home, had just about managed to convince her that he was okay and would call her soon. As to the others, Chloë had already been allocated a bed for the night, Susanna was being treated for shock and exposure, as well as smoke inhalation, and Flic was, and would for some time, be receiving treatment for her splinter-cut face and neck and for her burned hands.

'You've all been incredibly lucky,' a nurse had told Matthew while he was waiting, yet again, in Accident and Emergency.

A man from the fire brigade had told him earlier that what he'd done had taken a lot of guts, but then another man had countered bluntly that he thought he'd been a bloody idiot, and when Matthew had remarked that he seemed to be pretty good at that, the man had looked at him as if he thought he might be demented.

'I need somewhere quiet,' he'd told another of the nurses a while back.

'Don't we all?' She'd smiled at him.

But then he'd made her see that he really meant what he'd said, that one of his stepdaughters had told him she needed to speak to him alone, and that it wasn't too long since they'd lost their mother, and all he needed was a room, an office, even a *broom* cupboard, for just a little while.

'There's a visitors' room around the corner,' she'd told him. 'If you're lucky, that might be empty.'

He'd remembered then, with a fresh rush of horror, that only the

previous afternoon he had been arrested on suspicion of indecently assaulting Imogen, and sweet *Jesus*, if Malloy knew that
he'd just requested a private room with Imo, he'd probably have
him dragged away in handcuffs or worse. But right now, right here
in this place, where chaos seemed, amazingly but only narrowly,
kept at bay, no one yet seemed to know about any accusations.

The visitors' room was empty, and the same kindly nurse had
brought Matthew a cup of tea, and had promised to try and find
Imogen to tell her where he was, and if she was up to coming for
their chat, then she'd see to it she found him.

*She won't come*, he thought, drinking his tea.

But she did.

# 69

'Flic was in bed with the flu.'

Imogen's eyes flickered as she said that, Matthew noticed, for perhaps her capacity for lying had suffered one blow too many, and he was fairly sure that they both knew Flic's 'flu' that September day had been a sham to keep Caro from accompanying him on the company's golf weekend.

But she talked of flu now, and he didn't challenge her because it wasn't really important anymore, and because he might not have long to listen, not if someone told DS Malloy or some other policeman that he and Imogen were alone.

*I killed my mother.*

He looked at Imogen, sitting on a visitor's chair wearing a navy blue, too-large dressing gown and a pair of bottle green woolly socks that someone had found for her, and those words she'd spoken on the Heath seemed to resonate in his head.

'I went out,' she said, 'to Nicola's, and Chloë and Isabella went out with Kahli so Mum could work in peace on her sewing. But Nic had a bunch of friends over, and anyway, I wanted to come back and see what Flic was up to.'

Matthew noted another tell-tale flicker. Truth and fabrication side by side. Uneasy bedfellows.

When she got back to Aethiopia though, she went on, Flic had been in bed listening to some book on tape on her earphones, and hadn't wanted to talk to her. So Imogen had decided the time had come to use her own brain, and with him away, it seemed the perfect opportunity to tackle their mother –

410

*really* tackle her, just tell her straight about how they all felt about *him*.

'We wanted you gone so much,' she told him. 'More than *anything*.'

He was so desperately tired, and his chest hurt, his whole body hurt, and yet at the same time he was utterly focused, *riveted*, on what she had to tell him, and so he just remained sitting quietly, listening.

Hearing how his wife had died.

'That's what I was going to do,' Imogen went on. 'Just go and tell Mum. Except first – I don't know why – I went into her – your – bedroom and had a bit of a mooch-around. Not really *looking* for anything, it was just because I still hated your things being in there, where my dad's things used to be. And then I . . .'

He waited a moment. 'Then you what?'

'I went into the bathroom. And I saw it.' Imogen's voice cracked, and she coughed for several seconds before she could go on. 'She'd thrown it away with the rest of the kit.' She paused again, her eyes filled suddenly with tears. 'You didn't know she was pregnant, did you? Before you went away?'

'No,' he answered. 'I didn't.'

'I wasn't sure,' Imogen said, 'if you knew or not.'

Matthew was horribly conscious again of time passing, perhaps running out. 'What happened, Imo?'

'I think I went a bit crazy,' she said. 'Not shouting or screaming or anything like that. I went to find Mum in the Quiet Room, told her I'd found the testing kit, that I *knew*. Mum saw my face, and then she asked me why I looked like that when surely it was *good* news?' Imogen wiped at her eyes with a crumpled bit of tissue in her right hand. 'I told her that it was the worst news in the whole world, because it was your baby. Because even if it was going to be my sister or brother, I'd always know it was half *yours*.'

Matthew felt sick.

'Mum looked at me as if she really wanted to hit me. I'd never seen her look like that, and that made me even angrier. I told her that she was as bad as you, *worse* in a way, because she'd dumped on my dad and me and Flic and Chloë by choosing you.' The tears were flowing now, and her nose was dripping and her face was twisting with pain and the ugliness of truth and memory. 'I said that other things had probably been her fault too, like my dad's stroke, and—'

411

Again she had to break off to cough, and in the pause Matthew became aware of movement outside the room, and braced himself for an interruption, maybe even for the police, coming for him again.

'Imo, tell me,' he said urgently. 'Tell me what *happened*.'

'I told her I really, really hated her, and I was so depressed I couldn't bear any more, and it was time she decided who was more important to her, her children – her real, *live* children – or an outsider she'd hardly known for five minutes.'

*Poor Caro.*

'Mum told me I was being childish and selfish.' Imogen's voice became querulous. 'She said she had a right to be loved and we'd never given you a proper chance. She said you were such a *lovely* man and you'd made her very happy, and it was *beautiful* that she was going to have your baby.' The outrage of that moment seemed to fill her again now. 'She hadn't listened to a word I'd said, not a *word*, and at that minute I really *believed* I hated her, and I told her that if she was any kind of a mother, she'd have an abortion.'

His mind shut down again, tender, pulverized senses slinking away for cover. *Poor Caro.* That was all he permitted himself, for now, all he dared allow himself.

'She told me to get out.' Imogen shook her spiky head. 'She didn't shout, just said it really softly, but without looking at me, as if she couldn't *bear* to look at me.'

He waited again, felt as if he were there, with Caro; wished, with all his might, that he had been. 'What did you do?'

'What she'd told me to do. I stormed out and slammed the door, and the key was on the outside so I turned it, locked it, and I told Mum through the door that I was going to find her sleeping pills and then I was going to swallow them *all*, because I couldn't stand any more, couldn't bear to go on living any longer, not with *you* and a mother who didn't love me or my sisters.'

Matthew saw it all then, in that moment, knew almost certainly what had happened after that, and for those few seconds at least he felt, strangely, more relief than anger. Sorrow, of course, and a brand-new kind of grief, and the most terrible pity for his wife, but a glimmer of consolation, too, because finally he did understand what had happened.

'There was no phone in there.' Imogen wept harder with each word. 'That was the whole point of the Quiet Room, wasn't it? No

412

phone, just peace and quiet. Except I'd just told Mum I was going to kill myself, hadn't I? And I didn't even *mean* it, that was the really evil part of it – I *had* felt like I wanted to die before, and I've certainly felt like it since, but not that day. That was just me being a bitch.' Self-hatred seemed almost to spill from her eyes. 'Just Imogen being a spoiled, selfish, wicked cow.'

'And you'd locked the door,' he said. 'So she couldn't get out to save you.'

The young face twisted again, tears mixed with snot, and this time she made no move to wipe it, was beyond caring.

'So she did the only thing she could do,' Matthew said. 'She went out on the balcony.' *The balcony she was so afraid of.*

'She must have been trying to climb down.' Imogen's voice sank very low, like a small, debased, living thing trying to crawl back inside her body. 'She was trying to stop me from taking pills, so she climbed over the railing.' *Tiny* voice now, little more than a whisper. 'And she fell.'

Matthew knew that she needed him to say that what she had done was not evil, that she had not meant it to happen. But he found that he could *not* say that or anything else, was again beyond words.

'And then tonight,' Imogen went on, 'I heard Susanna and Flic talking, and Susanna said Chloë had told her about things we'd done to you, and Flic got really angry with Susanna, and I knew then that it was all going to come out. What I'd done, what Flic had done. And she'd only done those things because of *me*, and I couldn't bear it, I just couldn't bear any more . . .'

'So you lit the fire.' Matthew found his voice again.

It seemed peculiarly comprehensible now. The desperate, despairing act of a depressive burdened with the worst type of guilt imaginable.

There it was. Despite everything. *Pity.* He could hardly believe he could feel that for Imogen now, yet he did. More pity than he'd ever felt for anyone.

'Why didn't you leave me in there?' she asked.

'I couldn't do that.'

'But there's nothing for me now.'

'There will be,' Matthew said.

Imogen raised her still tortured face, and met his eyes.

'What about Flic?' she asked.

# 70

They came to find Imogen a little later, and soon after that they showed Matthew into a curtained-off cubicle back in A&E, and left him.

He realized, lying back, throbbing with exhaustion and pain, that he no longer knew if it was night or day. His watch had disappeared, either during the fire or out on the Heath, or perhaps the nurse had taken it when they'd looked at his minor burns soon after his arrival, he couldn't remember. He hadn't even known he had been burned, but it seemed that just gripping the handle of the Quiet Room door and turning the key had been enough to blister them, and he hadn't noticed.

Flic's hands had to be hurting like hell.

At least, he realized, he was feeling no pity for her.

He could have asked someone the time, or got up to look at a clock, but it no longer seemed to matter, he was content – not the word, not at all – to let it go on, for now, playing its games with him. It telescoped, then expanded like elastic, then shrank back, tightened in on him, around him. One instant he was back in Aethiopia that last day with Caro; the next he was on the Heath with Imogen; then he was in their bathroom gazing, through her bitter eyes, at the pregnancy testing strip; then he was with Caro as she fought desperately to clamber down and save her child.

Unbearable.

Better, perhaps, from his selfish viewpoint, than suicide, but nevertheless, still too unendurable to contemplate.

Weariness clamped down on his mind, rendered him incapable of thought. He closed his eyes and let himself go.

*Time out.*

Susanna woke him.

'Sorry,' she said.

'It's okay.' He struggled blearily to a sitting position. 'How are you?' He checked her over. She was wearing grey tracksuit pants with an oatmeal-coloured sweatshirt top, both ill-fitting, and her dark hair was damp from washing, but other than looking pale and exhausted she appeared none the worse. 'You look fine.'

'They found me these to wear.' Her smile was rueful. 'I don't know what's happened to your bathrobe. I was taking a shower when the smoke detectors went off, and it was the first thing to hand.'

'Like it matters,' Matthew said.

'I suppose it doesn't.' Susanna sat down. 'Do you mind?'

'Yeah, I mind, just like the bathrobe.' He shook his head, remembering how she'd been during the fire. 'You were great, you know that? The way you hung in.'

'What else was I going to do?'

'You could have got out about ten times over.'

'So could you,' she reminded him.

'No,' he said.

'I suppose not,' she agreed. 'Apparently, we were all very lucky. If the smoke had been more toxic, we could have died.'

'I know,' Matthew said. 'They told me that too.'

She looked him over. 'You're still wearing your own clothes. Aren't you wet?'

'They've dried out.' For the second time that night, he thought. The memory of Kat's consoling kitchen snaked warmly, but all too briefly, into his mind.

They fell silent for a moment.

'I've talked to Imo,' Susanna said quietly.

Matthew said nothing.

'She's told me,' Susanna said, 'what she told you.'

'Right.'

'She seems to want to go on talking.'

'Does she?' His voice was flat, a little ironic.

Susanna eyed him for a moment, then went on. 'I've had a chat

415

with one of the consultants here, a woman I've worked with, and she's wangled a room upstairs for us to use for a while.' She gave a small smile. 'Professional courtesy.'

'Us?' Matthew said.

'They're keeping all the girls in.' Susanna was coping the only way she could, for now at least, with competence and calm. 'The police have been here, wanting to talk about the fire, but they've been told they'll have to wait till morning. And it'll be a while till Imo's bed's ready, which is why I think we should all go on talking now.'

'I don't know,' Matthew said, 'if I can take much more talk tonight.' He winced. 'Is it still tonight, by the way? I've lost all track of time.'

'Me, too.' Susanna's wrist was bare too. 'But it is still night.' She paused. 'I can understand your not wanting to talk any more, Matthew. But frankly, I'm afraid that if we don't let Imo go on now she's begun, she'll just clam up again.'

'Maybe,' Matthew said tautly, 'that might be best.'

'I don't think so,' Susanna said.

'You're a shrink,' he said.

'And I loved her mother,' she said.

He sighed, then abruptly remembered something that had troubled him briefly, before he'd fallen asleep. 'I hope no one's told Sylvie about any of this.'

'I've made sure of that. The same consultant has left word on her floor that no one's to go near Sylvie, at least not till morning.'

'Thank you.' He remembered something else. 'Why exactly did you call me tonight? Imogen seemed to think that Chloë had talked to you.'

Swiftly, carefully, Susanna told him about Chloë's confession, and then about her confrontation with Flic. 'I panicked rather. I heard about the forgery, saw Flic's reaction, put two and two together and made about a hundred.'

'But you do know now,' Matthew said, 'that the assault thing was bullshit.'

'Yes. I know that.' She paused again. 'What I'm still afraid of,' she said slowly, softly, 'is that there may be more for the girls to tell us.'

'More?' He gave a bitter half-laugh.

'That's why we need to let them talk,' Susanna said.

416

'Them?'

'Flic, too.'

'Christ.' He thought about her, closing the balcony doors.

'I know,' Susanna said softly.

'Is she up to it?' he forced himself to ask.

'Not by normal standards.' Susanna lowered her voice, conscious that anyone might walk by the cubicle. 'But my colleague had a word about the burns – the cuts are superficial, by the way – and apparently if she wants to join us, it shouldn't do her any harm.'

'And does she want to?'

'She didn't, of course, at first, but then I asked her if there weren't things she wanted to say to us. Things that perhaps no one had been listening to before.'

'Christ,' Matthew said again.

'What?' Susanna asked.

'You really are a shrink.'

She smiled.

'Not Chloë,' Matthew said decisively. 'I don't want her hearing any more of this than she has to. Not yet.'

'Not Chloë,' Susanna agreed.

# 71

It was an office on an upper floor, with Van Gogh prints on the walls, a vase of pinks with gypsophila, and chintz curtains at the windows.

It was, Matthew had now seen for himself, still night.

They all looked much as they felt. Displaced, wounded and drained, though whereas Imogen's eyes were dull, Flic's were guarded. Like her sister, she wore a dressing gown, her hair damp and scraped back with an elastic band. Her face was a mess of small cuts, some neatly taped. Her hands were bandaged.

'Is the pain very bad?' Susanna had asked when they'd first sat down.

'Not as bad as it was,' Flic had answered. 'They gave me something.' She paused. 'Apparently I have a high pain threshold.'

She sat apart from Imogen. Susanna had seen to it that there were enough chairs, and had arranged things so that the sisters did not have to be too close. It had been very clear to her, as soon as she'd seen them together at the hospital, that Flic was bitterly angry with Imogen for her disclosures.

'You know Imo's been fantasizing, don't you?' Flic attacked, wasting no time. 'Reaching for crosses to bear because she always feels so guilty.'

'What about Chloë?' Susanna asked benignly. 'Was she fantasizing too?'

Matthew had been sure they were all too desperately in need of rest for this encounter, and yet the instant they began, he felt their exhaustion recede, like a tide being forced out unnaturally, being kept away by the need for truth and an attempt, at the very least, to end the horrors of the night.

'I don't know about Chloë,' Flic answered. 'I don't know what she told you.'

'Yes, you do.' Susanna paused. 'Come on, Flic.'

Matthew wondered at her patience after all she'd been through.

Susanna tried another tack. 'If Imo feels it's time to talk, surely you can, too?'

'Why?' Flic asked. 'I know you said it might make me feel better, but I think what you really mean is that you hope it'll make *you* feel better.'

'I don't know,' Susanna said. 'Do you think it will?'

Something changed in Flic's eyes at that instant, Matthew thought. The hostile wariness remained, but a shimmer of something else passed through the blue – very swiftly, almost like one of those minuscule darting marine specks – and then, just as quickly, hid from sight. Defeat, perhaps, he wasn't certain – or maybe something even darker, even colder.

She looked abruptly straight at him. 'Are you sure you want to hear this?'

'Not sure at all,' Matthew answered.

'I am,' Susanna said firmly.

Flic turned to Imogen. 'And you? Are you quite sure, Imo? After all we've been through together?'

'Why not?' Imogen said dully. 'It's over now anyway.'

'I suppose it is,' Flic said.

Imogen had gone to her older sister right away – Flic told them now – and told her exactly what had happened to Caro and what she had done.

'She said that finding out about the baby had done her head in.'

Imo had been bound to tell *her*, Flic said, was incapable of keeping it from her, though she couldn't have borne it if either Chloë or their grandmother had found out.

'I never blamed her, not really, because I knew' – Flic's eyes were on Matthew as she spoke – 'that whether or not you were in the house that day, none of it would have happened if it hadn't been for you.'

'So,' Matthew said, 'my wife's death was my fault too, in your head.'

*And our child's life*, he thought, but did not say.

'Our mother's death,' Flic said, and went on.

She was the one who'd realized that the key to the Quiet Room door had to be dealt with, she who had taken it from the lock, then gone down into the garden and placed it in their mother's pocket to make it seem as if she had locked herself in before jumping to her death.

'I was sure that was what they would believe. That Mum had killed herself because of you. Because you'd made all our lives so unhappy. But I was wrong about that. No one believed that she would have done that to us.'

'They were right,' Susanna said.

'So we had to go along with the open verdict. We had no real choice, for Imo's sake. But I never forgot the truth for a moment.'

'*Your* truth,' Matthew said.

'If you choose to put it that way.'

'Invention, Flic.' Susanna was still gentle. 'You do see that, don't you? Your mother's death being Matthew's fault was something that you and Imogen invented.'

'More of a rewrite, I'd call it,' Flic said steadily. 'And all in a good cause.'

'Getting rid of me,' Matthew said.

'Of course.'

'But I didn't go away.' He worked it slowly through in his mind. 'So you invented the other things – the frauds.'

'And the assault,' Flic said.

She said it with something very like triumph, and all the while Imogen sat in silence, a sad sack, letting her sister take control, as she probably had all along.

'Tell us,' Susanna said after a few moments, 'about Isabella.'

Matthew felt a shock, as if something small and sharp and ugly was burrowing into his chest.

'What do you want me to tell you?' Flic asked. 'That I pushed her?'

He heard the words, but they wouldn't quite register. He remembered telling Jack Crocker after that first hideous police interview that he reckoned Flic might be trying to link him to Isabella's death. To her *accident*, he had said. Nothing else had ever occurred to him.

Now he stared at Susanna, then back at Flic again.

420

'I hated doing that,' she said, something in the blue eyes flickering again. 'Really. But thanks to Imo, Isabella knew that the assault hadn't actually happened.' She threw her sister a swift, contemptuous glance. 'That was why she went out – I think she was going to try to find you. And even if she hadn't, I knew it was just a matter of time, hours probably, before she told someone else – Groosi, or maybe even the police – and I couldn't let that happen.' Flic paused. 'And then old John was there, on the platform, and I realized he'd seen what had happened, so I had to try and deal with him too.'

'Dear God,' Matthew said. 'You shut him in the shelter. You hoped he'd have a heart attack and die down there in the dark.'

'I went to see him at his house, too, yesterday afternoon. I thought, maybe . . .' Flic gave a grim, suddenly painful ghost of a smile. 'I'm glad now that old John didn't die. Now that he can't make any difference.' She paused. 'Daddy was always very fond of him, wasn't he, Imo?'

But Imogen didn't answer.

# 72

*Daddy*.

Richard Walters.

The man both Sylvie and Susanna had already known, to different degrees, *not* to be the exemplary husband and father that Caro and his daughters made out. The man who, according to his mother-in-law, had neither much liked nor respected women; who had used his children, so Sylvie had once told Matthew, as his entourage.

She had known Richard was flawed, but had never dreamed how deeply or how darkly. How destructively.

'All his doing,' she said to Matthew several weeks after the fire. 'All down to him.' And then she shook her head, horribly sickened, as she was each time she contemplated the dreadful reality of what they had now learned. 'If only we had known, if only . . .'

*If only. If only.* The list could stretch forever.

They all knew more now, far more than they had ever wanted to know, about the infinitely corrupting predilections of Caro's first husband.

Caro had *never* known. Of that they were all certain.

'If she had,' Sylvie had said soon after learning the truth, 'I think she might have killed him.'

It had been a profound relief for Susanna to finally unload the truth about the cache in Imogen's bedroom. Aware of how pivotal the contents of those plastic bags had to be to understanding the teenager's problems, Susanna had taken the personal risk of

422

confessing, to Jane Ripon, the psychologist who was now part of the team evaluating Imo and Flic – the former in a secure unit in south London, her older sister in Holloway – her own breach of trust in searching the girl's bedroom.

'I thought you had to know,' Susanna said.

'Yes,' the other woman agreed. She was in her late forties, with grey curly hair and tranquil hazel eyes.

'Obviously, it was a shocking invasion of a patient's privacy.' Susanna had tensely waited for Jane Ripon to condemn her, perhaps declare her intention to report her misconduct.

'Strictly speaking, I suppose, Imogen was not your patient at that time.'

'No less morally reprehensible,' Susanna said.

'I daresay you've beaten yourself up enough for both of us since then.'

'You can't imagine,' Susanna said fervently.

'I think I probably can.'

Ripon was interested in Susanna's input, since the therapist still appeared to have at least Imogen's trust – Flic's good faith being a very different animal. They had discussed various means of trying to steer Imo to the sketches and chastity belt without Susanna having to confess to her too, since clearly that knowledge would alienate Imo forever.

Yet in the event, thankfully, Imogen had come to the subject herself.

They had been speaking of Isabella's death, and the hours preceding it.

'She caught me in my room – while I was meant to be resting, after what we'd said Matthew had done – with some stuff ... some drawings that my dad had done of me.'

The room they had been allocated for their sessions with Imogen had an institutional feel about it, yet was just comfortable enough to make it a good environment for soul-baring.

'I got in a bit of a state – I'd kept them hidden for such a long time, and I never, ever looked at them. But all the panic, the awfulness, made me remember. I told Isabella I'd forgotten I had them.'

Jane Ripon did not even glance at Susanna. 'What kind of drawings were they?'

Imogen met the psychologist's eyes. 'I suppose,' she said slowly, 'some people might call them pornographic.'

Ripon and Susanna waited, not daring to push, and Imogen described the drawings and the wearing of the chastity belt without further coaxing. There was no shame in her voice or expression as she talked, only a kind of defiant pride, yet the sense of unburdening and release was clear to them.

The teenager looked, increasingly as the weeks passed, like many of her fellow inmates. All privileges of her comfortable, cosseted home and lifestyle having been sheared away, more than an inch of blond roots had carved their way into the black, now limper hair, and the changed diet had added a touch of acne to her face and several pounds to her body. Imogen was utterly miserable, and yet she was also experiencing a measure of relief because the scheming and lies were now done with, for better or worse. She was surprised by how she felt, had anticipated with dread the return of deep depression, had at first wondered how, if the time came, she might manage to kill herself, without access to blades or pills. But the time had not yet come.

She welcomed the sessions with Susanna and Ripon. Away from Flic's influence, she found she could unload amazingly freely. After all, the fight was over. They had both lost and won. Groosi had said that Matthew would not, even when repairs were completed, be returning to Aethiopia. Nor, of course, was there any certainty of when she or Flic would be allowed to go home.

Never, perhaps, in Flic's case.

'What happened to the drawings and the belt?' Jane Ripon asked Imogen after she'd finished describing them.

'Flic told me to get rid of them. She came in just after Isabella had seen them – while I was telling Isabella that we'd lied about Matthew – and then, a bit later, she told me to dump them where no one would find them.'

'You said you told Isabella you'd forgotten you had the drawings,' Ripon said.

'I had, more or less.'

'Do you know why?'

Imogen's eyes narrowed. 'You think it's because I felt ashamed – because my own father made me pose like that.' She shook her

424

head. 'Only he didn't make me. I *wanted* to do it. So I didn't feel ashamed at all.'

'Why do you think you should have been?' Susanna asked.

'Because I liked it so much.' She smiled. 'I loved posing for him so much, I wanted to tell people about it, but Daddy told me I couldn't.' She paused. 'I suppose that's how I knew it was a bit weird, even back then, because he told me other people wouldn't understand.' She gave a grin. 'I thought at first I was going to get into a book, like Astrid, but he soon put me straight about that.'

'How did he do that?' Ripon asked.

The smile vanished. 'He didn't hit me, if that's what you mean. Daddy never, ever hit me.' Imogen's eyes grew harder. 'And he didn't really *touch* me either, if that's what you're thinking, too.'

'You said "really",' Ripon said. 'That he didn't *really* touch you.'

Imogen shrugged. 'He used to put on the chastity belt. He had to do that – I couldn't do it myself, it was too difficult.'

'How did you feel about that?' Ripon asked.

'Fine.' Imogen shrugged again. 'A bit funny at first, maybe. And then I didn't mind. I *liked* it.' She paused, gave a little sigh. 'But by the time he died, I suppose I knew a bit more, you know, which was why I hid everything, because I knew he was right, that no one else would understand. Not even Flic.' She smiled again, fleetingly. 'Flic doesn't think much of sex.'

'She didn't know about you posing for your father?' Susanna asked.

'No.' Imogen hesitated. 'Mind, when she told me to get rid of them, I did think then, for just a moment, that it was almost like she'd seen the drawings before.'

'Perhaps she had,' Ripon said.

'No.' Imogen was adamant. 'Flic knew I was paranoid about privacy, knew how I felt about snoopers. Flic's always been straight with me. If she'd known, she'd have told me.'

She was wrong about that, Ripon and Susanna had learned during their next session with Flic at Holloway.

They had been talking to her about her feelings prior to following Isabella to Hampstead tube station that Saturday, and when Jane Ripon had raised the subject of the drawings, Flic's eyes had sharpened.

425

'Did Imo tell you about those?'

Neither Ripon nor Susanna answered.

'I never thought she'd do that.' She looked surprised. 'Though I've often wondered, for her sake, if I should have told someone about them.'

'Would you like to tell us now?' Jane Ripon led her back.

'Tell you what?' Flic asked. 'If Imo's already talked about them.'

'Imo thinks you never knew they existed,' Susanna said. 'Before that last Saturday.'

Flic paused, considering. Holloway was taking its physical toll on her; like her sister, she looked, these days, a shadow of her former self; her hair was stringy, her face still scabbed from cuts, her hands still painful and scarred. Mentally, though, she seemed as acute as she had always been.

'I saw them,' she said, quite abruptly. 'Imo and our father, I mean, not the drawings – one afternoon not very long after Imo turned ten.'

The two older women waited.

'Mum was out, and I'd got a lift home from school, and I suppose I was a bit earlier than usual. That was before Imo joined me at The Grange,' she explained. 'I went up to the studio to look for Dad. I didn't call out to him – I do remember that – because I suppose I felt like surprising him. He didn't hear me coming. Neither of them did.'

She paused again, regarded Ripon and Susanna. They had both previously observed that Flic seemed to like – when she was in the mood to talk – to mull over their reactions. They seldom felt, with Flic, unlike Imogen, that it was a case of unburdening. She displayed anger more frequently than in the past, Susanna saw, yet remained, on the whole, composed, still, insofar as it was possible, a manipulator.

'Dad had left the door ajar,' she went on, 'and I could see their reflections in a mirror.' She seemed deep in memory. 'He was sketching her, and Imo –' For an instant, her self-control slipped slightly. 'Imo was naked, squatting on all fours on his couch.' There was a small frown between Flic's eyebrows. 'I say naked, but she wasn't, quite. She was wearing this *thing*.'

'The chastity belt,' Susanna said softly.

'I didn't know what it was at the time. I was only twelve.'

They were all silent for a long moment.

'You never told your mother?' Susanna asked.

'Of course not.' Flic looked at her as if the question had been stupid. 'Mum couldn't have coped with that, you know that.'

'Why did you never tell Imogen,' Jane Ripon asked, 'that you'd seen them?'

'Because I chose not to.'

'Why not?' Ripon again.

'I preferred to blot it out,' Flic said. 'To forget I'd seen them like that.'

'But you say you've wondered,' Susanna said, 'if that was right.'

'It was right for me,' Flic said.

'But not for Imogen?' Susanna asked.

Flic looked straight at her.

'You tell me,' she said. 'You're the shrink.'

'She was only twelve.'

Susanna had echoed Flic's words a few days later, during a meeting with Sylvie and Matthew at Perrin's Lane, while Chloë had been safely out of the way at school.

'I'm not suggesting' – she had chosen her words carefully – 'that any of this excuses Flic, or even begins to explain away the things she's done. But I *do* think – and Jane Ripon agrees – that it was certainly too much for her to cope with at the time.'

'How could it not be?' Sylvie had murmured, ashen-faced.

Matthew had sat silently for a few more moments, too shaken to speak. 'What about Chloë?' he asked, finally, with dread.

Susanna understood his meaning. 'We're confident she was never involved.'

'Are you sure?' He needed more, needed to *know*.

'As sure as we can be.'

'Isn't it bad enough already?' Sylvie said.

Matthew nodded, still struggling to take in the shocking new revelations. 'And neither sister ever shared that afternoon with the other?'

'Not that, no,' Susanna confirmed.

'Yet they always seemed so united, especially about me.'

'I imagine that was a much easier proposition,' Susanna said. 'Back then, though, they both seem to have gone unwittingly along with each other by pretending the posing sessions had never happened.'

'Another rewrite.' Matthew used the expression Flic had used that night in hospital when they'd talked about Caro's death.

'I think so,' Susanna agreed. 'In Imo's case, I think the fact that Richard singled her out actually made her love him even more.'

'Even though it was abuse,' Matthew said grimly.

'At a conscious level, at least, I don't think that Imo considered it abuse.' Susanna paused. 'Whereas Flic, who recognized immediately that it was, chose not to face up to the fact that the father she adored would do something so dreadfully wrong, and did her level best, instead, to blot it out.'

'Her mother,' Sylvie said, with difficulty, 'had a tendency to do that.'

'To rewrite, you mean?' Matthew said.

'Not in the same way,' Sylvie said, 'not remotely. And I'm not suggesting for one *instant* that Caro had even the smallest inkling of Richard's abuse.'

'Absolutely none,' Susanna said, swiftly, passionately.

'But she often buried her head in the sand if she could. First with Richard.' Sylvie looked at Matthew. 'Then with her daughters. Caro tried to pretend that bad things weren't happening, hoped they'd just go away.'

'Richard, you know,' Susanna said abruptly, 'was the reason Caro originally came to see me. He *made* her come.'

She had met him at a gallery opening in Camden Town, and upon learning her profession, Richard had said he thought his wife might benefit from therapy. He described Caroline as having low self-esteem, said it was foolish of her because she was very pretty and had much to be grateful for, if she could only see it.

'He was appallingly sexist and self-obsessed,' Susanna said. 'He regarded Caro as a possession. He had no real interest in her talents or feelings.'

'And you,' Matthew said, 'were afraid I might be the same kind of man.'

'Yes,' she agreed. 'I suppose I was.'

'That, you see,' Sylvie said, 'was one example of Caro's not facing up to things. She chose to see Richard's good points, preferred, I think, to blame herself rather than him for any problems they had.'

'Whereas Flic,' Susanna said, 'used her talent for revision to blame Matthew.'

'Though I guess,' he said, 'she'd say she did it for her family.'

'I think that's probably true, from her personal point-of-view,' Susanna said. 'And Jane Ripon more or less agrees with what you said, Matthew. Whenever Flic either fears or hates something or someone, or perhaps is repelled by an event – or if someone she loves seems threatened in some way – she simply *rewrites* the context or event, or expunges it altogether.'

'And yet according to you,' Sylvie said, 'she hasn't expunged the memory of what she did to Isabella, or to old John?'

'Not yet,' Susanna said.

Sylvie's swift recovery had amazed everyone. Matthew had feared that the shattering disintegration of her family might trigger another collapse, but Sylvie had drawn on her strong resources, knowing she could either sink into the depths or fight for her granddaughters. Whatever they had done (and Sylvie was not the type to shrink away from the fact that both Flic and, to a lesser extent, Imogen, were sociopaths in the making), Caro's girls needed her more than ever – though with both older sisters locked away, it was for now only Chloë whose progress Sylvie was in any position to attempt to guide.

Chloë, also damaged, of course, by all the traumas, was – pending restorations at Aethiopia – living with Kahli in her grandmother's flat. She had returned to The Grange, where her teachers reported to Sylvie that work seemed to have become a struggle, that her thoughts constantly strayed, and that she was no longer mixing as easily and naturally as she always had.

'I wish I knew what to do for her,' Sylvie said to Matthew.

'You love her,' he told her. 'You're there for her.'

'I think she misses you,' Sylvie said.

That was not the impression Chloë had given Matthew when he'd come to the flat the previous week. Even before the fire, she had been strained with him, but on the few occasions he'd seen her since then, he'd felt an invisible high, and depressingly solid, wall between them. Chloë had thanked him politely, while still in hospital, for rescuing her that night, and Matthew had assured her he didn't need thanking for that, and had tried to hug her, but she had drawn quickly away, and he had not attempted to get too close again in case he upset her.

'I miss her terribly,' he said now. 'But I don't think it's mutual. I think Chloë finds my company too difficult these days.'

'Her loyalties must be very torn,' her grandmother admitted.

'Don't misunderstand me,' Matthew said. 'I don't blame her.'

'It worries me,' Sylvie went on, 'that I'm not sure if she feels *safe* any more.'

'That's going to take time,' Matthew said.

'I hope I have enough of that to stay the course,' Sylvie said.

'You will,' Matthew told her. 'Though if any thirteen-year-old knows there are no guarantees, it's Chloë.'

He and Susanna had told Sylvie about Flic's attempt to kill them on the night of the fire, but Susanna – emotion again over-ruling professionalism, finding it almost unbearable to conceive of betraying Caro by personally accusing her child – had implored Matthew not to tell the police. Sylvie had remained silent, allowing him to decide for himself. But then, with Isabella's death and the attempt on John Pascoe's life both laid squarely at her feet, and the criminal lawyer recommended by William Standish warning Sylvie that Flic would remain in Holloway for the fore-seeable future, Matthew had agreed to let it go.

Imogen, the lawyer hoped – on a charge of arson – might possibly soon be released into her grandmother's care. Matthew remembered that Imo had begged Flic to open the doors that night, and remembered, too, what her father had done to her, and found that he didn't mind the thought of her release.

For her middle granddaughter's sake, and knowing it would have been what Caro desperately wanted, Sylvie strove stoically towards that end.

Privately, though, she dreaded it.

At the end of April, John Pascoe went to visit Flic.

There were things, he told her, over plastic cups of tea in the visitors' room, that he had not felt up to raising with her the day she'd come to his house.

'Anyway,' he said, 'you came and left so quickly.'

Flic did not answer.

He had been entirely unable to comprehend at first, John said, why she had gone off like that and left him shut up in the shelter, in the dark. Why a girl he had known and cared about for so many years might have done such an inexplicably cruel thing.

'I realize now,' he said, 'that you must have thought I'd seen what you'd done to Isabella, but I never saw anything – nothing except the poor girl falling and dying.'

Still Flic said nothing, just ran her right index finger around the rim of her plastic cup. And then she shook her head. 'You seemed so nervous around me after Isabella,' she said. 'Either looking at me strangely, *differently*, or not looking at me at all, avoiding my eyes. I was sure you must have seen.'

'I didn't,' Pascoe told her. 'I was just shocked, that was all. Who wouldn't have been after seeing something so terrible?' He thought about it. 'Maybe looking at you, right afterwards, reminded me, I don't really know.'

'I see,' Flic said, very softly.

'I would like to know one thing now,' the old man went on, 'if you don't mind, that is?' He paused, moistened his lips with his tongue, took a breath. 'Did you really mean to kill me, or just to frighten me, so I wouldn't tell anyone? Only it's been weighing on my mind rather a lot.'

'I meant to kill you,' she answered frankly. 'Not because I wanted to. Because I thought I had to.' Her face was expressionless. 'It was nothing personal, John. Nothing to do with you at all, really.' She paused. 'I'm very sorry.'

'Yes.' He nodded. 'I expect you are.'

# 73

Jasper Hughes having dealt with DS Malloy on his behalf, Matthew was entirely off the hook so far as both British justice and VKF were concerned, though it would, he felt, take years for those interviews to become distant enough memories to be recalled without actual pain.

Guilt of a different kind was, for the moment, still exacting its toll.

There was no escaping the fact that he and Caroline had plunged into wedlock without anywhere near enough consideration for her daughters. Had they never met, let alone married, both Caro and Isabella would still be alive, and Flic and Imogen would be home now, letting time heal the wounds that Richard had inflicted on them.

Kat, with whom he dined most weeks – although physical intimacy remained elusive – argued fiercely with him on the subject of his guilt. As, during their regular calls, did Ethan and Karl (both urging him to return, either to New York or Berlin). As, to his continuing surprise, did Susanna. Those girls' troubled psyches had been formed, she said, most of the emotional wreckage created, long before Matthew had come onto the scene.

'Your marriage contributed, obviously,' Susanna said, 'and Caro's death was the final straw. But the more I think about it, the more we all learn, the more I believe that *any* new husband of Caro's would have met the same sort of resistance that you did.'

He thought that was probably true.

It made him no less sad.

Imogen's lawyer had thus far failed to get her released into Sylvie's care, which at least meant that, unhappy as the situation was, life at Perrin's Lane remained comparatively tranquil.

'I've reached one decision,' Sylvie told Matthew over lunch in early May at the Villa Bianca near her flat. 'When the repairs to Aethiopia are complete, I shall sell the house and my flat and buy something nice and practical for us all.'

'Have you told the girls?' Matthew asked.

'I've told Chloë,' she answered. 'Not the other two yet.'

'Time enough for that, I guess,' he said.

He had returned to VKF and was renting a one-bedroom flat near Coram's Fields in easy walking distance from Bedford Square. He was free now, of course, to walk away, would, in time, do just that, yet the emotional and psychological entanglements of his sixteen English months were proving hard to undo, and he felt an intense need for closure.

He had made an attempt to visit Imogen, but she had refused to see him. Flic, on the other hand, had agreed to send him a visiting order, and on the Sunday prior to his lunch with Sylvie, he had gone to Holloway. Flic had sat impassively through his visit, had displayed neither aggression nor hatred, had expressed remorse for what she had put both her grandmother and youngest sister through, and for what she had done to Isabella. She had not mentioned John Pascoe, nor had she apologized to Matthew.

He believed what she had said about Sylvie and Chloë. He was not certain that he believed her words about Isabella.

'She was so cold,' he had told Kat afterwards. 'Maybe it was irrational, but I found her pretty scary.'

'I don't see that as irrational,' Kat said. 'Not after what she did.'

'The thing is,' Matthew said, 'it wasn't myself I was scared for. It was the thought of what might happen to the family if they release her.'

'Not very likely, is it?' Kat said.

'Not yet, no,' he said. 'But in time, they will.'

'That,' Kat said, 'won't be your worry.'

433

# 74

At the end of May, Sylvie invited Matthew to tea at the flat.

Susanna was there, and Chloë, spoiling Kahli with titbits and cuddles. And after tea, while the three adults discussed, cautiously, for her sake, their collective anxieties for her absent sisters, Chloë sat quietly at Sylvie's writing desk practising calligraphy.

She stood up to show her work, when it was done, first to her grandmother and then to Susanna.

'May I see?' Matthew asked.

'Okay.' She brought it over, held it out for him to see.

'It's beautiful,' he said, warmly.

She looked into his face, her blue eyes stony, and made no reply.

Susanna was out in the small kitchen, washing up, when Matthew stood up to leave.

'Stay where you are,' he told Sylvie, who was looking tired.

'I want to see you out.' She began to rise from her armchair.

'I'll see Matthew out, Groosi,' Chloë said.

Sylvie smiled, sat back down, and Matthew bent to kiss her on both cheeks.

'Be well,' he told her.

'You, too,' she said.

Kahli padded out with the two of them, into the small entrance hall.

'How's he coping,' Matthew asked Chloë, 'without the garden?'

'He misses it. He misses Flic and Imo more.'

'I know.' Matthew paused. 'I know how you must be missing them, too, honey.'

'Do you?' she asked quietly.

'I think so.' He bent to kiss her cheek.

Chloë drew away stiffly and opened the front door.

'I'll see you soon,' Matthew said.

'Goodbye,' she said.

He was part way through the doorway when he felt it – a burning, *stinging* sensation in his right side, just above his waist. He stopped dead, his hand moving reflexively to locate the source – and even before he found Chloë's long-nibbed pen, he saw her face, saw that it was filled with the most violent mixture of anger, triumph and fear.

'Dear *Christ*!' Pain and shock pitched his voice upwards.

Sylvie and Susanna came hurrying, and Kahli began to bark.

'My God,' Sylvie exclaimed, taking it in. 'Chloë, what have you *done*?'

'I'm not sorry,' she said loudly, her cheeks flushed scarlet.

'Don't pull it out,' Susanna told Matthew quickly. 'It might make it worse.'

'Why did you *do* that?' He was shaking, staring at Chloë as Susanna helped him into the small kitchen, pushed him down onto a chair, found a clean cloth. Sylvie and Chloë came in after them, and Sylvie sank onto the other chair, white-faced.

'Are you okay?' Matthew managed to ask her.

'*Me*?' She half-laughed, harshly, shook her head, watched Susanna as she crouched down, surveying the damage. 'How bad is it? Is it in deeply?'

'I hope it is,' Chloë said.

'Chloë, for the love of God,' her grandmother said.

'It's embedded a little way,' Susanna said.

'They do tell you to leave that sort of thing alone, don't they?' Sylvie said.

'They do, for longer blades, but this . . .' Susanna peered again, touched the pen gingerly.

'Get it out.' Matthew winced. 'Just pull the damned thing *out*.'

'That,' Chloë told him, visibly trembling, 'was for my mother and both my sisters and my *home*.' Her voice wobbled, seethed with rage. 'For taking them all away from me.' She began to weep,

435

tears flowing freely down her cheeks, and turned to her grand-mother. 'Maybe now you can all have *me* locked up too.'

'Chloë, for goodness—' Sylvie couldn't go on.

Susanna pulled out the pen, pressed the cloth hard against the wound. 'Can you hold it there, Matthew?'

He did so, wincing again, feeling suddenly dizzy as he saw the pen and its bloodied nib in her hand.

'I just wish I'd put it through his *heart*!' Chloë exclaimed and ran from the room, slamming the door behind her.

'My God,' Sylvie said again dazedly. 'I don't believe this.'

'I'm okay,' Matthew told her. 'Really.' He still held the cloth against his side.

'I'm going to drive you to hospital.' Susanna found a second cloth, wrapped the pen in it carefully to show to the doctors.

'I'll take a cab,' Matthew said, gritting his teeth.

'Don't be absurd,' Susanna said.

'I'm not being,' he told her. 'I want you to stay here.' His tone was calmer and very insistent. 'You can phone a cab for me.'

'Matthew . . .' Sylvie was close to tears.

'Sylvie, it's going to be okay.' He glanced at Susanna. 'I'll tell them that I fell on the pen.' He still felt weak. 'Freak accidents happen all the time.'

'But you can't . . .' Sylvie's voice was almost gone.

'Susanna, please call the cab for me.' He took a deep breath, winced again. 'And then you can give me a glass of water while we're waiting.'

'She stabbed you,' Sylvie whispered. 'I can't believe she *stabbed* you.'

'Only with a pen.' Matthew almost mustered a smile. 'It's more shock than anything, Sylvie.'

'They won't believe it was an accident,' Susanna said, reaching for the phone, checking a minicab company's card on the counter for a number, and dialling.

'I'll make them believe it,' Matthew said.

'But we can't just . . .' Sylvie looked towards the closed door.

'The rest,' Matthew said, 'is for you to decide, Sylvie.'

Susanna was giving the address to someone at the other end. She put down the receiver. 'Five minutes,' she said.

'I'll go down,' Matthew said, 'and wait outside.'

'Please don't be silly,' Susanna said.

He stood up, found that he was surprisingly steady, took the second cloth from her, the cloth that contained the slender weapon. 'Not silly,' he said. 'Not now.'

'Matthew,' Sylvie said. 'I'm so very sorry.'

'I know you are.' He tried to stoop to kiss her again, but it hurt, and he straightened up. 'I told you, I'm all right. You just sit for a while, okay?'

Susanna went ahead of him, out of the kitchen to the front door. Matthew followed. There was no sign of either Chloë or Kahli.

Susanna opened the door. 'I'll come down with you.'

'No,' he told her. 'You have to stay with Sylvie.'

Susanna nodded, for once lost for words.

'I meant what I just told her,' Matthew said. 'This is it for me. It's up to Sylvie what happens now.' He paused, needing to be clear. 'And from now on.'

'I really am sorry, Matthew,' Susanna said.

'Me, too,' he said.

# 75

Too much.

All of it.

He was ready now to leave, to head straight back to the States, to New York, to Ethan and Susan and the boys, to people who would always be there for him no matter what. Family. *His* family.

He recognized though, at the same time, that he was almost too drained to organize or make crucial decisions about his long-term future. He needed time and space to recover his judgment skills. Such as they were.

'You need normality,' Karl said on the phone.

Matthew found he couldn't quite picture normality just yet.

Trusting people. Expecting to be trusted in return.

In the meantime, in the immediate short-term, Kat was here for him. And his job in Bedford Square. Phil Bianco had sought him out, had actually apologized to him, brought him messages of support from London and Berlin, and from Laszlo King in Manhattan.

His relationship with Kat was strengthening now, but it was still new and rather tentative, had perhaps only really come into being, they realized, because of his urgent need for closeness during that most traumatic time. Yet as his situation slowly calmed, being together still felt good to them both. She was, as he had already perceived, so dissimilar, in so many ways, from Caro. Kind, too, but not nearly as soft, and far more realistic, more down-to-earth. And, of course, stronger.

'I know,' Kat said to him in mid-June, 'that you're going to have to take your time. About us – if there *is* an us. About everything. No rushing into decisions.'

No rushing.

Definitely not.

Ever again.

They decided that perhaps Kat might fly back with him on a visit to New York in a month or so, see how she liked it, how they felt together there. Matthew could have some meetings at VKF's head office and consider his options. One of which was to go freelance, or maybe even – as Karl had suggested – go into a cooperative venture with his friend and, perhaps, if she was willing, with Kat too.

He had no problems envisaging a long-term working relationship for him and Kat. But so far as their personal futures were concerned, Matthew already knew that, ultimately, Kat wanted to have children.

At least two, she had told him once. Perhaps three.

Matthew had believed, in the past, that he wanted children, too, had often pictured himself, as most men did, as a father.

Ideally, he had always felt, of daughters.

He wasn't sure about that any more.